Friday Night Flights

Susan X Meagher

Friday Night Flights

THIS TRADE PAPERBACK ORIGINAL IS PUBLISHED BY BRISK PRESS, WAPPINGERS FALLS, NY 12590.

EDITED BY: CATRIONA BENNINGTON
COVER DESIGN AND LAYOUT BY: CAROLYN NORMAN

FIRST PRINTING: FEBRUARY 2020

ISBN-13: 978-1-7343038-0-3

By Susan X Meagher

Novels

Arbor Vitae
All That Matters
Cherry Grove
The Lies That Bind
The Legacy
Doublecrossed
Smooth Sailing
How To Wrangle a Woman
Almost Heaven
The Crush
The Reunion
Inside Out
Out of Whack
Homecoming
The Right Time
Summer of Love
Chef's Special
Fame
Vacationland
Wait For Me
The Keeper's Daughter
Friday Night Flights

Short Story Collection

Girl Meets Girl

Serial Novel

I Found My Heart In San Francisco

Anthologies

Undercover Tales
Outsiders

Acknowledgments

My thanks to Millie Ireland, Catherine Lane, and Rachael Byrne for their feedback during various drafts of the book. They each had expertise in elements of the story I could only guess at, and I'm appreciative to them for sharing their thoughts and reactions.

Over the past two years, I've visited breweries and tasting rooms all over the Hudson Valley, gleaning information whenever and wherever I could find it. I'm pleased to report that my research was pure pleasure.

Dedication

To my wife, my dearest friend, and my publisher, who just happen to be the same person. My life is made better in every way by having Carrie by my side.

A child can teach an adult three things: to be happy for no reason, to always be busy with something, and to know how to demand with all his might that which he desires.

Paulo Choelho

CHAPTER ONE

Summer
Columbia County, New York

IF THE LAWS OF NATURE had been in effect, a woman would not have been significantly better looking sixteen years after you'd last seen her. But this woman was either Casey Van Dyke's doppelgänger, or adulthood had been very, very kind to her.

She stood about fifty feet away, near a small bar located in a greenhouse-style structure on what appeared to be a big farm, but was, in fact, a brewery. Two longish lines of people waited for a pair of bartenders to pull beer, but Casey wasn't in line. She stood at the end of the bar, leaning against it with an arm slightly behind her, providing a little support as she scanned the crowd, looking satisfied. A bearded guy was talking to her, and she laughed easily and often, sometimes giving him a playful elbow.

Avery Nichols settled onto a tall stool, then dropped her bag onto the table top. Actually, calling the thing a table was a stretch. It was a wooden spool that had previously been used to transport wire or cable, now serving out its second life of holding glasses for the local beer-loving crowd. As Avery shifted her gaze, she saw a bright, hopeful look on her mother's face. "Seriously?" Avery hissed, with her irritation increasing when her mom gave her an overly innocent look.

"Seriously what?" she asked, actually batting her eyes like a schoolgirl.

"I told you I wasn't interested in meeting up with Casey, Mom. I know she's your current project, but I'm not going to change my mind."

"Project? What a ridiculous thing to say. Ken," she said, snapping her fingers to catch Avery's dad's attention. "Is Casey Van Dyke my project?"

He turned and cocked his head slightly. "Project? I don't—"

"See?" her mom said, vindicated in her own mind. "Your father would know if I had a project, wouldn't he?"

"Fine. You don't have a project. But I told you I wasn't interested in reconnecting. Yet, here we are, out in the middle of nowhere on a Friday night, and blind luck has plunked Casey down right in front of us."

"They make beer here," she said, as if that was an obvious reason for driving a half hour north once they'd picked Avery up from the train station.

"You don't like beer."

"No, but you do. You love it," her mother said, beaming.

"There's a brewery right in town. My train got in at six, and we could have been there at six oh five."

"But they have food trucks here!"

Avery counted to ten, certain she wasn't going to win this argument. Her mom had run into Casey a few times over the last year, and had obviously decided that the forces of destiny were going to pull the two of them together into happily married bliss. That wasn't going to happen, but she *was* thirsty. "I'll go get in the beer line."

Avery put her hands on the table top to secure her balance on the packed dirt floor. As she pushed off, Casey looked over and started to walk their way, smiling and shaking hands with people along the short journey. Unable to look away, Avery admired her stride, seeing the same loose-limbed grace the woman had displayed in high school.

Way back before Avery had spent any time thinking about sexual orientation or gender presentation, she'd known Casey wasn't exactly like the other girls. She still wasn't, but now she clearly claimed her uniqueness, with Avery certain Casey had confidently grown into her body and her sexual orientation. If an advertiser was looking for a model to proclaim lesbian pride, she was standing right here.

"Hi, there," Casey said, leaning over slightly and speaking so she could be heard over the bluegrass music coming from outside the translucent skin of the building. She put her arm around Avery's mom and gave her a hug. "Haven't seen you in weeks, Kathy. Where've you been hiding?"

"I haven't had time to hide. My scout troop keeps me running."

Casey slowly turned toward Avery, giving her a tiny smile. "Long time no see."

"Not since graduation," Avery said, reaching out to shake her hand. Thickened calluses marked the base of each finger, with Casey's grip strong and sure. "You obviously know my mom. How about my dad?"

"I don't think I do," she said, turning to offer her hand to him. "Casey Van Dyke."

"Ken Nichols. And even though it's been a long time, I definitely remember you. Everyone around us at Senior Honors Day started to laugh when you had to run back up to the stage time after time. I recall one grumpy guy mumbling that you should give the other kids a chance."

Casey shrugged, revealing a bashful smile. "I left all of the academic honors right on that table for Avery to claim. For me, high school was only a place to play team sports until I had to get a job."

Avery hadn't taken her eyes off the woman for a second, hoping her dad continued to talk so she could gawp.

In high school, Avery hadn't even realized Casey had been in her class, at least during their first two years. But she'd come into her own as they grew older, and had created a persona that seemed not only genuine, but unique. Over a single summer, she'd shaken off her shy, almost skittish mien, to reappear as a hovering presence, barely even a member of the student body. From the first day of their junior year, she gave off the air of a woman for whom circumstances had conspired to force her to cool her heels for a bit before she was allowed to strike out on a much more interesting path.

Avery recalled her being lanky, almost skinny, kind of like a gangly puppy. Long arms and legs and unrealized physical potential. Now, as Avery looked up at her with rabid interest, Casey's chocolate brown T-shirt was filled by broad shoulders, sinewy muscle, and full, modest breasts. The kind that stood up firm and proud even without a bra. From Avery's perspective, *that* potential had been realized in spades.

Just as in high school, Casey effortlessly carried off her butch-inflected, jock style. Her khaki shorts revealed legs that had lost their knobby knees a long time ago, now lean and tan. Flip-flops were a little silly to wear at what seemed like a working farm, but the bit of straw that clung to a strap was…charming. That detail reminded Avery of the high school Casey. If she wanted to wear flip-flops, she wore flip-flops, not noticing, or even caring to notice that she was the only one. Being a high school girl who didn't mimic a larger group had taken some guts.

Avery looked up, finding dark eyes gazing at her questioningly. Her mom bumped her on the shoulder to knock her from her reverie, saying, "I haven't bragged about Avery before? Seriously?"

Casey gave her a very sweet smile, shaking her head.

"Well, she did go to on to Bard. Then all the way to Iowa to get her MFA."

"I not positive what an MFA is, but it sounds impressive," Casey said, her straight white teeth an improvement over what Avery recalled as a gap-toothed smile. She reached up to urge her nearly black hair behind an ear. It was a little past chin-length now, longer and significantly more mainstream than when she'd looked like a fledgling riot grrrl.

"I didn't actually wind up needing the masters degree," Avery said, trying to catch up with the conversation. "But I wasn't in a rush to get a job."

"Oh, she's so modest," her mom said, wrapping an arm around her and leaning over to rest her head on Avery's shoulder. "She's got a big job in New York now. And a radio show," she added, seeming like she might burst with pride.

"It's a podcast," Avery corrected, resigned to the fact that her mother would never understand the difference. "And I'm just the host. No one listens to hear me."

"I listen to some podcasts," Casey said, her level of interest so mild it was almost funny. "What's the name?"

"Um, it's one of several that *Ad Infinitum* produces. That's the magazine I work for."

"Uh-huh," Casey said, gazing at her blankly. "What's the name?"

"Oh! It's called *Short Shorts*, but you have to drill down from the *Ad Infinitum* main menu to find it."

"I think I can do that." She took out her phone, pulled up a blank note, and handed the device to Avery. "Will you write it down? I might remember *Short Shorts*, but the rest is already gone."

Avery started to type, finding herself rambling. "The podcast has a good following, especially in its category, but it's certainly not topping the charts in the app store."

"It's fascinating," her mom interjected. "I skip a lot of the stories just to listen to Avery, but if you like to listen to people read…"

Casey took a look at the screen, then shut her phone off and put it back into her pocket. "I'm still not sure what your podcast is about, but I'll try to give it a listen."

Avery squeezed her eyes shut, annoyed with herself for doing such a shitty job of convincing even one person to listen to her show. "Let me back up a little. My magazine hosts a monthly series where writers read one of their stories before a live audience. I host the program and ask a few questions. Nothing earth-shattering. That's my main job," she clarified, "running that program."

"It's a very big deal," her mom said, either lying or delusional. "Some of the most famous writers in the country go to her little parties."

Avery couldn't help but smile. "They're not parties, Mom. They're readings, held at bars big enough to accommodate a bunch of literary types who like to drink." She looked up at Casey, who was clearly just being polite. "The magazine's subscriber-based, so anything we can do to attract attention is helpful."

"Well, I'm not much of a reader, but I'm a good listener." Her gaze shifted to the table. "You people need a drink. Mind a suggestion?"

"Casey works here," Avery's mom said. "She's very important, too."

"I'm not very important, but I've been the brewmaster for almost a year now. Best job I could have ever imagined." She pointed to the lettering on her shirt, and Avery took the time to read it, trying not to focus on her breasts, which were well worth a second glance. *I'm the brewmaster. If you run out, I can make more.*

"I'll take the advice of the woman who makes the stuff," Avery's dad said. "What should we drink?"

"Our summer ale's very popular," she said, seeming very thoughtful. "But I like something with more body. How do you feel about sours? I can't take credit for this particular beer, but I'm crazy about our Triple Wild Cherry."

"Sour beer?" Avery's dad said, looking suspicious.

"It can take some getting used to," Casey admitted, "but once you develop a taste for them, sours are addictive." She held a finger up. "Hold on and I'll bring you a taste." She'd been tamped down so far, but now her personality began to shine as she talked about her work, with her smile nearly blinding. "Get ready to have your minds blown."

She disappeared into the crowd, with Avery grasping her mom's hand and holding it so tightly she began to squirm. "Will you give it a rest now? We've reconnected. Mission accomplished."

"You're not even trying," her mom said. "Where's that bubbly personality I hear when you're doing your radio show?"

She released her hand and let out a laugh. "Casey's clearly not interested in my bubbly personality, but at least she's easy on the eyes."

"I certainly think so," her mom said, as if Casey's good looks were her doing.

"Did you come right out and ask her if she's gay? I'm just trying to figure out how far you'll go in finding me a wife."

Her mother's pale blonde brows rose. "Everyone knew *that* when you girls were still in school, didn't they? Some idiots at Senior Honors Day grumbled that she should have had to take a chromosome test. Jerks," she added, scowling.

"I don't remember her ever coming to the house," her father said, gazing at Casey as she leaned over the bar.

"I'm sure she never did," Avery said. "We never hung out together."

"Wait," he said slowly. "Wasn't she the girl who punted for the football team?"

"I think she did everything you could do in sports. I remember people losing their minds over some sportsy thing, but I'm not sure that was it…"

"Sure, sure, it was in the papers for weeks," he said, showing more than his normal level of excitement. "How do you not remember that? Everyone had an opinion about whether a girl should be able to play for the local team. Some idiots started a petition to have the coach fired. They acted like she was going to upset the bedrock of civilization by kicking a ball fifty yards."

Avery shrugged. "I didn't care if we had a football team at all, so I'm sure I didn't care who was on it."

Her dad reached over and tugged on her ear. "One day I'll convert you into a sports fan so we can enjoy a game together."

Avery laughed. "That's going to be a big job, Dad. I think we should continue to girl-watch together. Let's go with our strengths."

"Get your eyes off that girl's butt," her mom said, playfully slapping her husband in the chest as he continued to stare. In her dad's defense, when Casey leaned over the bar to reach the taps it was pretty hard to resist taking a gander.

Before the family ogle-fest got out of hand, Casey returned, setting the glasses on their table. "So…" She put her hands on her hips, gazing at three tall shot glasses filled with a deep red-tinted beer.

The opaque-skinned greenhouse created a golden glow as the sun started to set. Casey held up a glass so the flattering light infused it. "See this luscious color? We blended three different brown ales together, then added tart cherries. After aging it in Cabernet wine barrels for two years, it turned into a pretty complex beer, but I'll admit it's not for everyone." She handed a glass to Avery, watching her avidly. "Give it a sniff."

Feeling like she was under a microscope, Avery stuck her nose in and inhaled, looking up sharply. "It smells like Cherry Coke."

"A little bit," Casey agreed, with her smile growing wider. "You might get some vanilla, too. Take a sip and see what you think."

Her parents weren't racing for their glasses, which wasn't surprising, given that her mom didn't like beer much at all, and her father was perfectly happy with a Budweiser.

Avery took a sip, surprised by the level of carbonation, not to mention the acid. Then she closed her eyes for a moment, and really let her senses speak to her. While it was a very unexpected taste, she could see that she might grow fond of it. Looking up, she said, "You probably hear this all of the time, but it reminds me of Sour Patch Kids—with a punch."

"It does," Casey said, grinning. "I've always loved sour candy, so I might like this more than most people would." Her expression grew thoughtful when she said, "Even though it might seem playful, this beer isn't a gimmick. They started brewing sour ales in Belgium hundreds of years ago. My predecessor was from Brussels, so he always tried to have at least one sour in the rotation."

Her mom took a tentative sip, blinked a few times, then shook her head. "I'm going to have to get used to this, Casey. I've never had anything like it, and it's going to take me a second to adjust my tastebuds." She kept her warm gaze on her and said, "I was just going to send Avery to rustle up some food for us. Will you join us for dinner?"

"Let me set you up," she said. "Pulled pork sliders?"

"Sounds great. But take Avery with you to carry everything."

"All right. Baked beans and cole slaw good for everyone?"

"Sounds great," her mom said, with her father echoing her. "We'll drink these little tasters while we guard the table. Big crowd tonight."

"Great. If you like the ale, I've got more, and if you don't, I'll switch you over to something else. I have four other beers on tap tonight, along with a cider I'm saving for special friends."

"We're easy to please. And hungry."

"Got it," she said, giving a little salute as she led the way through the crowd. They didn't have far to walk, but Casey paused to shake hands with nearly every other person they passed, adding personal greetings to many of them. Avery wasn't sure why she knew so many people by name, given a brewmaster probably spent her time inside the brewery, but the solitary girl from Hudson High had become a real social butterfly.

They exited through a propped-open door, and Avery filled her lungs with the tangy scent of barbecue coming from the charcoal grills set up next to the food truck. There were at least twenty-five people in line, patiently waiting to reach the counter and order.

In the moments it had taken to walk away from the building, some of Casey's élan had dimmed. Avery was sure she wasn't imagining it, with Casey now seeming almost businesslike. "We can go right around the back," she said, walking so quickly Avery had to race to catch her.

A middle-aged Latino was working the grill, and he called Casey over, speaking to her in Spanish for a second. She was smiling as she walked away, but the smile faded in a matter of seconds. "I'm trading Tomas some sour ale for our dinner. Wait right here."

Tomas started to fill a tray with the sliders, cole slaw, and beans, and just as Avery was about to reach for it, Casey returned. She handed the cook a generous glass, and added a kiss to his cheek. "We're set," she said, grasping the tray to head back to the greenhouse.

Avery hadn't been needed at all, feeling like the little sister foisted on a reluctant older sibling. But she did have the ability to count. "We only have three plates."

"Right. I ate hours ago, and I've got to get back to work. How did you feel about the sour? Want more?"

She felt a little silly, but Avery found herself trying to be more bubbly to get Casey to engage more. "Oh, definitely. I can already imagine how it will taste with some tangy barbecue."

"Great. I'll get you another. Full-size this time." She laughed softly. "I bet your parents will ask for water."

"My mom's willing to try new things, but my dad likes his Budweiser. He's not very experimental."

"I've got a pretty safe lager on tap. It's more complex than Budweiser, but it's in the ballpark."

"That should work."

"Great. I'll grab a pair of those and get you the challenging stuff." They stopped at the table and Casey set the plates down. "That's two no votes on the sour ale," she said, obviously seeing that the glasses were largely untouched. "Be right back with something I'm sure you'll like better." As she backed away, she added, "When I have a minute, I'll stop by with some churros."

As she walked over to the bar, she stopped to speak to more people, offering hugs and handshakes to what must have been old friends. Oddly, she gave off the vibe of a politician, able to amp up her personality in an instant. Or maybe she'd turned it down when she was alone with Avery. But that made no sense. They hadn't seen each other for sixteen years, and Avery was sure they'd barely spoken to each other even then. She was *certain* they hadn't been in the same homeroom, and couldn't recall being in any classes together, which made sense, given they were on different academic tracks. There had been little to no overlap between the kids, like her, who had been obsessed with their GPAs, and those just biding their time until they could get jobs. Casey had definitely been in the latter group. Avery didn't have a wealth of concrete memories of her, but one of them was of Casey proudly standing up at Senior Honors to identify herself. Avery could still see the grin on her face when she stood tall and said, "Casey Van Dyke. College? None."

Forcing herself to stop following Casey with her eyes, Avery said, "I don't know what happened to the shy introvert who only looked alive when she was kicking or hitting a ball, but that gawky girl is gone." She knew she was only giving her mother ammunition, but she couldn't hide the fact that she was intrigued, even though Casey clearly hadn't been. It wouldn't have done any good to try to hide her interest. Her mother could read her like the world's best clairvoyant.

It took a while to speak to everyone she knew, and a little longer to check in with a few strangers to get some feedback on the sour. It was getting late, and Casey was surprised to see the Nichols family still sitting at their table. They were either really looking forward to those churros, or Avery had developed an addiction to the tart beer, with a fresh glass now sitting next to a spent one.

If she'd had anything pressing, Casey would have just waved and kept on moving. But it was kind of fun to talk to one of the cool girls from high school, if only to show that the divide that had seemed like a canyon when they were sixteen had mostly disappeared.

As she crossed the room, still full of people who'd gotten a little louder as the night wore on, Casey slightly revised her categorization of Avery. She hadn't technically been one of the cool girls. She'd been one of the brainy ones, the ones so involved in their classes that they weren't even aware they weren't super cool. All Avery's group had cared about was getting into one of the special programs their high school reserved for smart kids, then clawing their way into the best colleges. You would have thought their lives depended on where they parked themselves for four years.

She made eye contact with Avery again, surprised to have her lock on and not let go. Kathy hadn't been kidding. Her daughter had definitely flipped at some point. But in Casey's memory, Avery was the cute straight girl who *always* had a boyfriend. She'd worked her way through the brainy guys like she was simply sampling the merchandise, never finding the perfect match.

Even though she'd had no true friends in high school, Casey had interacted with far more boys than girls, and she'd always kept her ears open when they were talking about other girls, since she was as obsessed with them as the guys were. She recalled that the smart jocks were seriously interested in Avery and a couple of her equally brainy friends. Casey smiled to herself when she thought about a guy once saying that

Avery was the kind of girl you had to work to get. She wouldn't jump into your car just because you beeped the horn.

As Casey swung by the table, she put her hand on Avery's shoulder and left it there, pleased when she leaned into the touch slightly. "Want to go get those churros?"

"Love to," she said, smiling up at Casey with a look that was almost flirty. "Be back in a minute," she said to her parents.

"We might have to wait in line for these," Casey said to Ken and Kathy. "Can you hang out for a while?"

"We're in no hurry," Ken said. He was also on his third glass, but Kathy had left her lager mostly untouched. She'd be able to drive them home.

"Great. See you in a few."

Leading the way, Casey turned right as they exited the building, refreshed by the cool air that hit her skin. "It really heats up in there when we have a full house. I need to cool off a little before I can even think about waiting in that line."

"We could go for a walk, but you'll break your neck in flip-flops."

"I know this land like the back of my hand," she said, "and I'm stone cold sober. Nothing worse than a brewmaster too drunk to talk up her beer."

"I'm up for a walk." Avery put her hand over her eyes to scan the grounds, resting it on the dark frames of her glasses. "What's out there? I can't tell if this a working farm or not."

Casey paused and turned her body, making sure it would be impossible to miss the two-story, clearly industrial building in the distance. "Um… It's a brewery?" she said, sticking her thumb over her shoulder. She didn't usually tease people she didn't know, but she found herself getting some pleasure out of poking a little fun at someone who'd once poked fun at her.

"I knew there was one somewhere around here, but I didn't know I could throw a rock and hit it."

"It's right…there," Casey said, picking up a big pebble and giving it a ride. A second later, there was a soft metallic "ping" when it hit the side of the metal sheathed building.

"How did I miss it?"

"Well, that's hard for me to know. Maybe you came in from the east? You see our grain fields from that direction."

"We came up from Hudson, so…yeah, I guess we did."

"Then maybe you're not totally oblivious," Casey said, pleased when Avery smiled at that. "Follow me and I'll show you what we're up to." She started off down the main path, pleased that even in flip-flops she still walked faster than Avery. It took just a minute to be out in the field, where the almost ripe hops climbed twenty feet into the sky.

Avery stopped and looked into the clear, dark night. "How do you hold those plants up there?"

"Trellises, but they're hidden by the fruit now. The bines are heavy, and they need support."

"Did you say bines, or vines?"

"Bines," she said, slightly distracted. She put her hand on the plant, tempted to take a taste. But she'd been out sampling already that day, and knew the ripest plant was still a day or two away from peak. Avery was gazing at her curiously, and Casey elaborated. "A vine holds on and climbs by tendrils or suckers, and a bine's stem curls around a support. Not a big deal, but it's botanically different."

"Interesting," Avery said, taking a closer look at a stem.

"They're about ready to go. We'll start harvesting by the middle of next week."

"These are…what?"

"Oh!" She laughed at herself. It wasn't odd for her to focus on details and forget that other people didn't know how to brew beer. "Hops plants. We grow almost all of our own. Actually, that's how the brewery began."

"As a farm?"

"Uh-huh. Our founders are a pair of Wall Street guys who went in together to buy a big chunk of farmland, thinking they'd eventually subdivide it for home sites." She shrugged. "You know the type of guys I'm talking about. Rich guys who have enough money to make everything they touch turn to gold."

"I certainly do," Avery said. "The same people who don't give a damn about maintaining the subways because they have a driver take them everywhere they want to go."

"Maybe," she said, not knowing a thing about subways or drivers. "So…after weekending up here for a while, they had kind of a come-to-Jesus moment and realized houses could be built anywhere. Arable, fertile land was a limited resource." She put her fingers on a hop, testing one more time that the fruit was still firmly attached. "I think it was their wives and kids who pushed them in that direction, but I don't care what their motivation was. They did the right thing."

"So…they became farmers?"

"Not exactly. Or, I guess I should say that wasn't their plan. They'd both made so much dough in the stock market that they claim they'd lost interest in chasing more." She laughed a little and added her own interpretation. "I think their wives were threatening divorce, and their kids were becoming entitled little jerks. Cutting back from their eighty-hour workweeks saved them a ton of money in alimony and child support."

"A cynical view," Avery said, smiling. "And probably the correct one. But how do people who've been on that crazy train get off? It seems addictive."

"I don't know. Both of these guys are from small towns around here. Maybe they had some good role models when they were growing up."

"Couldn't hurt, I guess. So how did they start?"

"Are you really interested?"

"Of course. I love hearing about rich people who make good choices."

"Okay," Casey said, pleased that she wasn't just talking to entertain herself. "Well, they were both still young, and had all of that stockbroker energy, so they started brewing beer, just to see if they could. Luckily, they found they had the knack for producing a good lager. I served your dad our signature beer, their first creation."

"God, I wish more of them would do that. New York would be so much nicer with fewer testosterone-poisoned multi-millionaires jacking up property values."

Casey rolled her eyes. "I don't really want those people up here, either, thank you. But my owners are pretty good guys, even though they're filthy rich, and keep tripping over ways to make more dough. When they discovered local breweries were having trouble finding good hops, they decided to jump in and fill that need. A while after that, they added grain." She put her hand on the plant again, always getting a warm feeling in her heart when she connected to one of the integral parts of her craft. "This part of the Hudson Valley used to supply hops for the entire country back in the day. The land is just perfect for it."

"Amazing," Avery said. "How long have you been in business?"

"Not long—for a brewery. They started production right about when we graduated from high school."

"And you started working for them right then?"

"It's a longer story than that. But I've been here almost thirteen years. It's gone by like that," she said, snapping her fingers. "Enough about me. I could keep talking for days, but unless you're in the business I'll bore you to death." She started to walk again, finding she talked more freely when she was moving. Threading her way along the fruit-heavy plants, she said, "So… Last time I talked to your mom, she said you were single—and looking."

Avery rolled her eyes. "She could run her own little PFLAG group. I've been single for a couple of years now, and it drives her nuts."

"Mmm. A few years can seem like a long time, can't it?"

"Oh, yeah." She sighed softly, with the sound barely reaching Casey's ear. "In my mind, my last girlfriend and I were as good as married, but it turned out that she didn't share that belief."

Casey laughed, thinking of how odd the twists and turns of life were. "You know, you would not have been near the top of my list if I'd had to guess who in our class would have wound up gay."

Avery revealed a pretty cute smile when she said, "I guess you can't tell a lesbian book by her cover."

"I guess you can't. Tell me about this almost-wife."

Avery started to walk again, with her voice taking on a reflective quality. "It's actually not a fascinating story, but it sure did have a big impact on my life." She took a breath, and continued. "Michelle and I met at Iowa. I was getting my masters, and she was in the Ph.D. program. Then we lived together in Brooklyn for a few years while she completed her dissertation. After that, she got a job at Penn."

"That's in…Philadelphia?"

"Uh-huh. I stayed in Brooklyn, since I had my current job by then. I thought we were doing the long-distance thing pretty well, but…out of the blue, she decided we needed to live together, or break up. Of course, she couldn't leave Penn, so I was supposed to quit my excellent job." Her expression was grim when she added, "She hooked up with an adjunct ten minutes after I refused to quit."

"That's like a junior professor, right?"

"Exactly. I've been vaguely trying to get back in the dating game ever since, but I haven't been motivated."

Casey stopped to give her another look, as Avery paused just a few feet away. She'd filled out in some pretty nice ways, not an unexpected development. She'd always been pretty, and popular, but she'd looked really young in high school. Now she had a sophisticated air to go with her brainy good looks. Something about dark-framed glasses on a natural blonde made her look super-smart, and her body was just about perfect. If she was single, she wanted to be. "You're not dating at all?"

"I'm not a hermit," Avery said, with her pretty smile turning a little sly. "But I haven't met anyone I like well enough to commit to. My job's really time-consuming, so I'm concentrating on that."

"Mmm. I read you on that." She started to walk again, thrilled by the scents filling her lungs. She was going to mention how the smell always gave her a buzz, but didn't really have the words to express that. Besides, most people didn't appreciate the scent of a mature plant, and she didn't like to waste her time talking about things other people weren't interested in.

"Are you single, too?" Avery asked.

"Uh-huh. I have been for…two years? Something around there."

"Was that a long-term thing?"

"Pretty long. Four years. My girlfriend was an artist, and she moved to Sedona. I didn't want to follow…"

Avery laughed a little. "We're both single because of geography."

"That's happened to me twice. My first girlfriend went to medical school at Upstate, then found a job in Utica."

"I think they brew beer around Utica, don't they?"

"Sure," she said, "but we'd broken up by then. Trying to have a long-distance relationship with someone doing a seven year residency is for…" She stopped, searching for the right term. "Is it sadists or masochists? I get my kinks mixed up," she said, laughing a little.

"Sadists inflict pain on others, masochists ask for it."

"Right. Well, I'm as far from a masochist as you can get, so I pulled the plug."

"Nothing since the artist flew the coop?"

"Nothing serious. I don't run into a lot of single lesbians around town, and I'm too lazy to travel far."

"I'm not surprised there aren't a lot of single lesbians. The gay guys got here first."

"Isn't that the truth? Gay guys found us when property was cheap enough to buy up everything with potential and improve the hell out of it. Property values are rising, but so are prices." She tried to tamp down her annoyance, but was sure she wasn't doing a good job of it. "Guess how much it cost me to have a dress shirt laundered last week?"

"Um…two fifty?"

"Yeah," she said, feeling the air leave her balloon. "It used to be a buck! A hundred and fifty percent increase in just a couple of years. It's like that with everything. I paid eighteen dollars for a pizza not long ago. Those aren't Hudson prices."

"Brooklyn's the same. A bartender demanded twenty-two dollars for a glass of wine last week when I was out with friends. I made that baby last all night long."

"But you're getting Brooklyn wages. We're not."

"Not so fast," Avery said. "I'm in publishing. We're glad to be paid at all. I've got to have a roommate just to make rent on a one-bedroom apartment."

"I live in my dad's workshop. I tricked it out to look great, but still…"

"Well, look at us," Avery said, adding a laugh. "The pride of Hudson High, just barely getting by."

"But we're happy, right?"

"I love my job," Avery said. "And my roommate is a close friend. Things could be worse."

"They sure could be. I could still be in high school," she said, very, very happy those days were gone. "Ready to get those churros?"

"I love a good churro. I buy them from a woman who sells them from a little cart in front of the Barkley Center. Two bucks each."

"Those prices haven't reached us yet. Ours are still a buck," Casey said, strangely relieved to still be getting a bargain.

⌣

As they waited in line, Avery tried to engage Casey by talking about her podcast. But it was clear Casey had never heard of any of the big-time authors Avery had bagged for *Short Shorts*. When someone hadn't heard of any of your Pulitzer Prize winners, you were barking up the wrong tree. "Um, do you come into the city often?"

"Often?" She let out a quick laugh. "Some people twisted my arm to go to Times Square to watch the ball drop about ten years ago. Once was enough."

"Seriously? You don't come into New York at all?"

"I live in New York," she said, raising an eyebrow. "I just haven't been to New York City in a long time."

"But it's just two hours away."

"And Albany's even less, but I don't go there either. Why would I?"

"I can understand skipping Albany, but there's so much to do in the city. Plays, museums, Central Park…"

Casey nodded, like she was mulling over the thought of making the trek. "I *might* like Central Park, but I'm not much for plays or museums. Unless they're outside. I went to see a Shakespeare play at Boscobel a couple of weeks ago. I couldn't tell you much about it, but it was nice sitting on the banks of the Hudson to look across at West Point while we ate our dinner."

"I've never been to Boscobel," Avery admitted. "But I always wait in line to see Shakespeare In The Park."

"I guess I'd do that, but then I'd have to drive home afterward. It's hard to stay awake that late, given that I get up so early."

"The brewmaster has to be up with the chickens?"

"She does," she said, with her smile warming up significantly. They'd finally reached the front of the line and Casey waved at the woman in the truck. "Can you hook me up with four, Esmerelda?"

"Casey," she chided, clucking her tongue. "You don't have to wait in line. Just knock on the door, like always."

The bright lights of the truck revealed Casey's pink cheeks. She must have *wanted* to stand around chatting. Maybe she was interested…

"I hate to cut in front of people when you're so busy. I feel like I should wait my turn."

"Such a silly girl," the older woman said. She handed over the sugar and cinnamon-laced sticks of fried dough and blew Casey a kiss. That was really nice to see. When the people you worked with seemed to genuinely like you, that was prime evidence you weren't an asshole.

Thinking back, she recalled that Casey had always seemed uninterested in tussling with the jerks from their school. Just then, she was hit with a memory, with a deep sense of shame covering her like a weighted blanket. Unless she'd repressed the memory, she was certain she'd never made fun of Casey's last name, or her academic performance, or her I.Q. But she was equally sure one of the girls in her clique had. Often, if her memory was correct. She just hoped Casey had been so involved in her sports that she hadn't noticed how catty and unkind high school girls could be.

A sprinkling of rain forced the bluegrass band to leave their small outdoor stage and move into the greenhouse. Once they were settled, Avery and her parents sat on some hay bales, finishing their beers while listening to the surprisingly adept musicians. The crowd, which had thinned, was very appreciative, as well as vocal, with people calling out requests and clapping loudly for particularly good banjo riffs.

There were a least ten small kids running around playing tag, and a few well-behaved dogs sniffed the ground for treats. It was actually such a wholesome scene that Avery was sure she could write a short story about it if she had the time. But she wasn't writing much these days, having found she needed not only dead silence, but lots of unstructured time to craft a decent story, neither of which she currently had.

Casey was flitting around the crowd, seeming like she ran the place. She'd obviously found her spot in the world. Not many people got to do work they loved while making a decent living—although the fact that she was in her father's workshop must have meant the living was a little shy of decent. Thankfully, she seemed not only happy, but content. That was a rare gift, and one that Avery was glad her old schoolmate had found.

The band finished up at eleven, and everyone started to say their goodbyes. Given they didn't know anyone besides Casey, Avery started to head for the exit when she felt her mom pull on the tail of her shirt. "We should wait to say goodnight."

Avery took another look, finding Casey in the corner talking very intently to a young woman. She wasn't sure Casey was trying to hook up, but it sure looked like that might have been the number one item on her agenda. "She's busy," Avery said. "We can send a note to the brewery to thank her for being so nice to us."

"Really?" Her mom guided her to the edge of the crowd. "Are you sure you don't want to wait?"

"I don't think so, Mom. Casey grew up to be a very nice-looking woman, and it'd be fantastic to have a girlfriend who could make beer, but I didn't get any vibes from her."

"Did you give her any? Maybe she's shy."

"I don't think she's shy," Avery said, taking another look as Casey leaned closer to the woman to speak into her ear. "She didn't feel any spark, either. It was just a chance to catch up."

Her mom looked so earnest. Women who had happy marriages simply couldn't understand why you weren't actively looking for one for yourself.

Avery let herself take another glance, speaking without censoring herself. "I bet she'd be a heck of a lot of fun for a night, but by tomorrow we'd probably be bored with each other."

⌒

Casey finished talking to the bartender she'd caught comping beers. A few wouldn't have bothered her, but this woman was clearly trying to jack up her tips by giving beer away, and that wasn't ever going to fly. She'd had to be more forceful than she normally was, but she truly hated to be taken advantage of, and that's just what had happened.

Looking up, she saw her buddy Ben, sitting on the bar. He was a bear of a man, about six foot three, with a full, long beard, rosy cheeks, and twinkling blue eyes. He was a gentle giant, who had very little patience with people who went out of their way to comment on his size. Casey got away with it, but only because he teased her about being gay.

Ben was in charge of distribution, and spent much of his day in the office they shared, but he loved beer, and the brewing process, nearly as much as she did. He couldn't help it that he had a head for numbers and logistics.

"Hey, you're going to break that thing," she said, walking over to poke him on the leg. "You know they'd fight a worker's comp case if you smashed your head because you were sitting up there."

"I'm agile," he said, giving her a sly smile. "Like a ninja." He jumped off, trying to land in a crouch, but he didn't quite hit his mark, and wound up having to grab onto one of the spools to avoid falling head-first onto the straw-covered ground. "Fuck! Where'd my ninja skills go?"

"How many beers did you have tonight? I saw you knock back four."

"Big man, big appetite," he said, slapping at his relatively modest belly. "But I might have had one too many for a display of my cat-like moves."

"Yeah, maybe," she said, jumping up to take the spot he'd vacated. "Where's Julie and Benji?"

"Gone home. I thought I'd help you get organized, then you can run me home."

"Thanks, buddy," she said. "I'm hoping the cleaning crew does most of the work, but I appreciate it."

"No problem. You'd do the same for me. So…" He leaned against the bar and spoke quietly. "Who's the cute blonde I saw you with?"

"Just somebody I went to high school with. Her mom's the one I like, but she's married."

"Really? I didn't know you were into older… Oh, yes I did," he said, laughing. "Is it still called an Oedipal complex if you dig older women?"

"Since I don't know what an Oedipal complex is, you'll have to ask someone who gives a fuck," she said, batting her eyes at him.

"The mom was cute too, but I've never seen you go after a married one."

"And you never will. I was joking, Ben. Kathy, that's the mom, brought her girl scout troop over for a tour a couple of months ago. We had to talk a few times to set everything up, and I found I really liked her. Not like *that*," she stressed when he waggled his eyebrows. "She's just cool."

"Well, not to be sexist or whatever, but the daughter's the one I'd go for. But she's not gay, right? I mean, she sure doesn't look it."

"Sexist?" She laughed. "How is that sexist? I think you mean ageist, but you also hit an offensive lesbian stereotype on the way to your point. Good batting average there, buddy."

"Really? The daughter's legit gay?"

"So she says, and I have no reason to doubt her. She really is cute, isn't she? When I met up with Kathy, that's the mom, I was pretty sure Avery would look good. When your mom's in her late fifties and could pass for forty, your odds of being hot are fantastic."

"Oh, yeah. Avery's like an eleven."

"An eleven? Out of ten?"

"Well, for Columbia County. After I've had five beers."

Casey laughed. "She's a nice-looking woman, but she's not an eleven. She reminded me of someone who'd model office furniture or bookkeeping software. You know?"

He laughed, nodding. "Yeah, I can see that. It's the glasses. They make women look smart. You know, when I was in Amsterdam last year a lot of the women in the red light district had glasses on. Big ones, like your friend."

"I'll make sure to mention that if I run into her again in another sixteen years."

"Sixteen years? No follow up? You looked kind of interested."

She gave him a thwap on the arm. "Like you've seen me when I'm trying to charm a woman."

"Okay, *I* was interested, but Julie won't let me go out with other women, so I have to live through you."

"Then I'm afraid I have to tell you you're not getting lucky anytime soon, pal. Avery is definitely cute, but she lives in Brooklyn, and she works for some...literary magazine? Like I know what a literary magazine is. I don't think we have much in common, other than both liking girls."

"That's not nothing, although I can't see you going to Brooklyn for any woman in the world."

"Well, I'd probably go for one or two, but not this one. She was one of the jerks who used to call me Butch Van Dyke." Her voice grew a little quiet when she added, "Or Casey Van Dope, or Dumbass Van—"

"Seriously?" Ben interrupted, his mouth having dropped open. "And you were civil to the bitch?"

"Well, she wasn't the only one. When everyone assumes you're a dyke, and your name is Van Dyke, it doesn't take a lot of imagination to—"

"No excuse. No excuse at all," he said with his voice getting so loud every member of the cleaning crew looked his way. "I hope you led her into that patch of poison oak we have out by the parking lot." He stood in front of Casey, facing her dead-on. "I had no idea you went through that kind of crap in school. How stupid were those kids? You're smart as a whip."

"You know reading's not my thing. I fell behind right away, and by junior high everyone had tossed me into the dumb kids pile. Stuff like that's like a fungus. Once it starts, it's really tough to stop."

"I got it too," he said, still gazing into her eyes, but looking a little tentative. "I was big, but not athletic at all, and that made me a target. The jocks thought I was a klutz, and the smart guys thought I was a big, dumb jock. I had to work twice as hard in math club to have anyone give me a chance."

"Kids suck, don't they?"

"A whole lot of them do. But some are nice. Benji's not a bully. I'm sure of that."

"I'm sure of it too. He's a sweetheart, just like his dad."

"I wouldn't be sweet to that woman. What's her name? Avery? I'd… well, I don't know what I'd do, but I'd do something."

"I've tried to let all of that stuff go. My life's too good to let old hurts rile me up again."

"So why'd you spend time with her if you're not interested?"

She shrugged. "I don't *specifically* remember her taunting me, so I gave her a pass. But one of her friends made it a point to torture me every time she had the chance. I'm sure Avery didn't tell her friend to knock it off, so she was spineless, if nothing else."

"I still don't see why you didn't just walk on by. You're really good at ignoring people you aren't interested in."

"Mmm, I am. Being bullied made me build up a thick skin. But I was at work, and I'm paid to be nice to our guests…" She slid off the bar and started to make sure the lines to the kegs had been cleared. "I really do like her mom, so I was trying hard to forget how Avery's little group used to piss me off."

"It's hard, isn't it," he said, giving her a very sober look.

"It is. I've gotten good at not letting people get beyond my defenses, and it's hard for me to turn that off. I found myself being pretty abrupt with her at first."

"Just at first?"

"You saw how cute she was," she said, rolling her eyes at her own lack of control. "I'm a sucker for a natural blonde with pale eyes. I couldn't tell if they were blue or kind of gray, but she looked good out there in the moonlight. I found myself really talking to her, and caring what she had to say."

"If you ask me, you should have tried to get something going with that girl you took to that play last month. Anyone who'd sit outside and swat mosquitos while watching Shakespeare clearly wanted a piece of you."

"Not my thing. After being together for a couple of hours, I realized I wasn't into her. You know I've never had sex with someone just to waste an evening."

"It's not a waste if you do it right," Ben said, chuckling.

"Like you'd know! You haven't tried to pick up a woman since you were in college."

"I did all right in college," he sniffed. "I landed Julie, didn't I?"

"You sure did," she said, slapping his shoulder, which felt like a log wrapped in flesh. "And as soon as I meet a woman like Julie, I'm going to grab her hand and race to the altar. Until then…"

"You're going to brew beer and play on the company softball team with a bunch of straight guys. As usual."

⌐

Avery's mom drove them back to the family home in Hudson, with Avery in the back seat, idly watching the dim headlamps illuminate only a portion of the road. If she'd been driving, she'd have had her brights on. Deer leapt onto the local roads with alarming frequency, and she'd witnessed many fatal encounters while growing up. Luckily, never in a car she'd been in, but you couldn't be too careful.

"Hey, Mom?"

"Hmm?"

"You never told me how you got in touch with Casey the first time."

"Oh, I heard she was working at the brewery, and I thought my troop would like to see a factory in action. Which they did," she said, looking into the rearview mirror to smile. Her mom had only been retired from the DMV for six months now, and had jumped into scouting, which had surprised and delighted Avery. There hadn't even been a troop when she'd been in school, but her mom had been a Girl Scout when she was a kid, and now that she had time she'd made it happen.

"But how'd you find her number?"

"Because of Mark." She took a look into the rearview mirror. "Her uncle? Come on Avery, you know Mark from Villa Napoli."

"That's Casey's uncle?"

"Uh-huh. Her mother's brother. Her mother and I were in school together, you know. I think she was a year ahead of me."

"Small town," Avery said. "If you grew up here, you don't have to dig far to find a connection."

"Not very far at all. So I asked Mark, and he told me she was working at Kaaterskill. I called over there and they hooked me right up. Honestly, Casey couldn't have been nicer. I think we were at the brewery for two hours. Right in the middle of the workday, too."

"She seems nice," Avery admitted. "And she's clearly attractive. But... she sure didn't seem interested in me."

"Maybe she was having a bad day. Or she was tired. She does so much over at that brewery. Besides making the stuff, she runs a program for parents of young kids."

"What?" Avery started to laugh. "She runs a day camp at a brewery?"

"For babies," she stressed. "She had to go set up for them on the day my troop was there."

"Stop!" Avery demanded. "What in the hell are you talking about? She gives babies beer?"

"No, no, she heard people complaining there wasn't much going on for infants around here. So she started a program where parents with very small kids can bring them over to the bar we were in tonight, and let the kids play while the parents have a drink or two. It's good for the community, and good for the brewery."

"How many DUIs have the police given out? That sounds nuts!"

"No, no, Casey's very careful. She only serves the lowest alcohol beer she makes, and she's the bartender. Knowing her, she keeps a very close watch on the adults."

"Who's watching the babies while the parents are passed out on the floor?" Avery asked, laughing at the image of Casey running around after a bunch of toddlers, having to climb over the bodies of their shit-faced parents.

"If anyone needs watching, Casey would be more than competent to step in, which I find utterly charming."

"You're charmed by her getting parents of babies soused?"

"They're not soused. Trust me on that. Casey started the program not to sell more beer, but because she loves kids. She told me that herself. She decided not to have a baby, but I can tell she regrets the decision."

"Damn," Avery sighed. "A single, super-attractive lesbian who wants just what I want, and she didn't give me a second look. Is that a kick in the ego, or what?"

⌒

On Sunday afternoon, Casey went out to the backyard to lie in the hammock, the most recent addition to the unending Van Dyke home improvement scheme. Her dad was a gardening maniac, fully intending to turn the acres of lawn and garden surrounding the house into something worthy of universal envy. At least it seemed like that was his goal, since he never sat down to actually enjoy it. When he was home, he was working.

Currently, he was installing a French drain on the side of the house where he'd convinced himself the rain wasn't draining properly. The landscaper he usually worked with insisted the drainage was fine, but that didn't stop him from starting the project on his own. Casey could have offered to help, but she'd stopped that years ago. Besides not wanting to be bitched at for not doing everything exactly the way he wanted, her dad genuinely seemed to prefer solitude. Leaving him alone would let him complain about how lazy she was, which apparently gave him great satisfaction. Whatever worked…

As she settled into the hammock, which rested upon a new bluestone patio off to the side of the pool, she looked up at the Japanese maple trees that ringed the stones. They'd look fantastic in the fall. Having a bright spot of red in the yard was the perfect touch.

She had a big glass of lemonade, and she could smell something good wafting from the open back door. Her mom was definitely baking, probably cookies, but biscotti was a strong possibility.

Casey put her feet up and relaxed, sure she could fall asleep if she let herself. Then her dad started making some god-awful noise with what sounded like a grinder. Sighing, she picked up her phone and started to look for a podcast. She liked anything about beer, or brewing, but there weren't all that many good-quality podcasts that focused on her favorite things. While it was sometimes fun to listen to people talk about figuring out how to home-brew, it was frustrating to hear how much bad advice there was out there.

Recalling her interaction with Avery from Friday night, she found the note she'd left and guided her browser to the page for the magazine with the unpronounceable name. Finding *Short Shorts* wasn't tough, and she pulled up the details on the most recent episode. Then the one after that. And the one after that. She'd never heard of any of the writers, which didn't surprise her. But the stories sounded so grim! She wanted something like a bedtime story, with a calm, soothing voice to help her chill. Not stories about betrayal, divorce, alcoholism, ethnic cleansing, and child soldiers. She switched over to one of her music streaming services and chose the modern country channel. They were also singing about betrayal, and divorce, and there was so much talk about beer and bars that some of the people had to be alcoholics, but at least there was some nice music to go along with it.

⌒

Two weeks after Casey had run into the Nichols', she spotted Kathy and Ken walking down Warren Street, the main business street in Hudson.

They were at the far end of the long street, closer to the river than many of the trendy restaurants, leading her to assume they were heading to her uncle's restaurant. She picked up her pace to catch up with them, and called out, "Hey, Nichols family!" when she was about a block away.

They stopped and turned, then Kathy gave her a big, exaggerated wave. "Hi there," she said. "Going our way?"

"I've just come from there. It's starting to get crowded."

"Ugh," Kathy said, rolling her eyes. "Summer people have made it almost impossible to go out to dinner without a wait."

"My uncle's not complaining," Casey said. "Business has gotten better every year."

"Ken, go put our names in," Kathy said. "I'll stay here for a minute and talk to Casey."

"All right. Good to see you again," Ken said. As he backed away, he added, "Don't get carried away, Kathy. You know how you get."

"How I get," she grumbled, showing a good-natured smile. "So? What are you up to? Big date?"

"Nope. I'm going to a meeting of the Hudson Valley Brewers Collective. We're going to... Wait for it... Sample some beers at The Tipsy Leprechaun." She thought about that for a second, adding, "Isn't that an awful name?"

"Oh, it's not so bad. I give them credit for making a go of it, given the city people wouldn't be caught dead in there."

"I guess you're right. I assume they weren't intentionally implying that Irish people drink more than most. Much of Eastern Europe has them beat by a mile." She laughed a little. "I guess The Tipsy Belarusian doesn't have the same ring."

"What's new at the brewery?"

"Not much. I had my Baby Brewers today, so that always perks me up."

Kathy gazed at her for a moment, clearly on the verge of asking a question. But she seemed visibly unsure of herself. After a second or two she said, "Do you do that to bring in business?"

"Kind of. It doesn't throw off much money, but I'm sure it draws new customers as effectively as having tastings in a bar. But if I'm going to be honest, I set it up mostly so I could play with babies. They're my favorite people."

"No possibility of having your own?"

Kathy didn't seem to be prying, but that was still a pretty personal question. Since she seemed genuinely interested, Casey went with it. "I don't have any interest in giving birth, but I'd love to be a parent. I just haven't found a woman who wants to parent with me." That sounded kind of pathetic, so she added, "It's hard to get the timing right. I was too young when I had a girlfriend who wanted to be a mom, and my last girlfriend would have had to…" She let that thought go, not wanting to get into the fact that her last lover was going through menopause when they were together. "Timing," she said, repeating herself. "It's hard to get it right."

"Mmm." She gave Casey a long look, then said, "Avery's having the same issue, I suppose, but from a different perspective. She wants to have a baby, but she's worried about doing it on her own." Her mild frown changed into a smile when she added, "That's why I'm trying to find her a wife. I want some grandkids."

"Mmm." Casey was stuck for a minute, not sure how to respond. "You don't have any other kids?"

"No," Kathy said, with her smile fading quickly. "Just Avery."

"Brooklyn's a big place, why doesn't she try some dating apps? She could probably find someone on the next block."

"That's probably true." Kathy put her hand on Casey's shoulder and gave it a squeeze. "Good luck on your quest. I'm absolutely certain you're in demand."

"Um, thanks," she said, feeling like kicking herself as she watched Kathy walk down the street. There was no way to tell a perfectly nice woman that you didn't want to even take a shot at her perfectly nice daughter because she'd been a shit, or at least shit-adjacent in high school. But it was the damn truth.

CHAPTER TWO

Two Years Later

IT WAS A BRIGHT, SUNNY Saturday in July. The kind of day Avery would have lusted for even a year ago. But today, with a bad cold, a throbbing headache, and chronic exhaustion that was an elemental part of her life, she longed for a storm. Staying inside, preferably asleep, was a need so strong she could nearly taste it. But even a brief nap probably wasn't in the cards. The baby was wide awake and full of energy, and it was Avery's job to be not only available, but friggin' cheerful.

A woman walked out of what was probably her own jewelry store and leaned against a painted wooden column. "Nice day, isn't it?"

The woman had that "Yes, I look fabulous, but I swear I don't put much effort into it," look that made Avery want to punch her in the nose. But she acted like an adult and nodded. "It certainly is."

"I might just close up," the woman said, stepping further onto the sidewalk to look up at the sky. "This is my first summer here. I thought business would be better on the weekends."

"It was twenty years ago," Avery said, realizing the woman had instantly pegged her as a native. "But the weekenders who've pushed out a lot of the old businesses spend their days drinking and eating. They don't seem to be shoppers."

"Mmm. I suppose I should stick it out, but it's tempting to go sit in the sun."

"Make sure you wear a hat if you do," she said, now so thoroughly indoctrinated into regarding the sun as a clear and imminent danger that she treated it like a threat to all.

She started to walk again, finding it odd that the shopkeeper hadn't commented on Lisbet. Most people couldn't get enough of her. But the lack of interest saved Avery from having to keep talking, which would eventually have required her to wipe her nose on her arm. Her tissues had run out blocks earlier.

As she strolled along, wishing she had the energy to walk faster, she reflected on her town. Hudson had *really* changed. Up until she'd graduated from high school, the town had been a faded, down-at-the-heels community in the upper Hudson Valley. At a hundred miles from Manhattan, it had always been too far away from the city to have a large commuter population. But it had been a big player in whaling during the Revolutionary War, standing in for New England, whose whaling ports had been effectively blockaded by the British. But whale oil did not last as a hot commodity—luckily for the whales.

At the turn of the twenty-first century, Hudson had little going for it besides good access to the river, a lot of Victorian-era homes needing serious renovation, and a train station that allowed for expensive but reliable service to Manhattan.

Avery wasn't sure who the first rural pioneers had been, but in short order Hudson had become a hot spot for New York City weekenders. The best of the row houses were snapped up, and the renovations began.

Now, as she walked along, she counted three high-quality espresso shops, one French bakery, one gluten-free bakery, and three yoga studios. When you added in the top-notch restaurants as good as anything Brooklyn had to offer, and the twee home design shops, she had to admit Hudson had become a very nice place to spend an afternoon window-shopping. But looking at windows wasn't going to pay the new shopkeepers' rent. Time would tell if anything other than restaurants and bars would be able to survive.

As she started to cross the street, a voice called out, "Avery?"

Turning, she saw Casey Van Dyke standing on the sidewalk, carrying large metallic trays, stacked three high.

"Hi, there," she said, embarrassed to be caught carrying the baby, even though that made no sense at all. "What's new?"

"Is that…" She struggled a little under the weight of her burden, managing to get a little closer. "Is that *your* baby?"

"Sure is." She knew she was blushing, but that was beyond stupid. It's not like she was a fifteen-year-old who'd gotten knocked-up because of poor impulse control.

"Are you just walking around?"

"Uh-huh. The baby loves to see the world, and the world usually loves to see her too." She turned her head and sneezed loudly. "Sorry. She was sneezing and coughing and feverish on Thursday, but perfectly fine twenty-four hours later." She patted her little sun hat. "She gave me every one of her germs, and I don't have her powers of recuperation."

"Let me run these inside," Casey said. "Don't go away!" She'd turned to keep an eye on Avery, but had only succeeded in catching the curb with her foot. Somehow, she instinctively spread her feet wide, landing on both, trays still intact. "Lucky!" Then she scampered into the side door of her uncle's restaurant.

Avery waited, speaking quietly to the sweet, fully-engaged face that gazed at her. "I'm sorry I acted like I was ashamed of you, Sweet Pea. I don't know why I get so weird when I see people I haven't run into for a while."

Movement at her side revealed Casey standing close, murmuring, "Oh, my God. I've never seen a prettier baby." She was staring so hard it looked like she was having a vision. "Is she like a couple of months old?"

"Six months tomorrow. I guess we'll celebrate her half-birthday if I can get out of bed."

Casey tore her attention from Lisbet to give Avery a long, concerned look. "You really do look awful," she said, then her eyes got big. "I mean… You don't look awful in a… You just look sick," she said, fumbling to finish her thought. "Your eyes are…"

"Droopy. Watery."

"Yeah. That's about right."

"And my nose is red and irritated."

"Um, pretty much."

"I didn't comb my hair before we left the house. That has to help."

"Hey," Casey said, with her voice lowering to a gentle, soothing tone. "I was just empathizing with you. Summer colds suck."

"Thanks," she said, now embarrassed to have made such a big deal about feeling under-the-weather. "I'm grumpy because we came up for a visit without checking to make sure my parents were going to be around. My dad's playing golf, and my mom's taking her scout troop to a swim party." She lowered her chin and rested her cheek against Lisbet's, something the baby loved. "I dreamed of two days full of naps and homemade chicken soup. Instead, I'm on full-time baby duty—as I am every minute I'm not at work."

"Is there any way I can…" Casey's attention locked onto the baby's snuggly carrier, complex enough to need a structural engineer to figure it out. Their eyes met, and Casey shrugged, clearly embarrassed. "I'd love to hold her." She blinked. "She's a girl, right?"

"Unless she tells me different, yes. Her name's Lisbet."

"Lisbet?" A big grin lit up her face. "A beautiful name for a beautiful baby."

"We're pretty fond of her," Avery said, feeling like she was getting her feet under herself again. "Want to walk us back home? Lisbet could be out all day, but I'm toast."

"My truck's right here. Let me give you a lift."

"That's yours?" she asked, gazing at the massive blue vehicle that seemed large enough for its own zip code. "Do you do the deliveries for the brewery? Man, if I ever need a grand piano moved…"

"It's big," she admitted, smiling. Then she flinched, looking like she'd been hit with a brick. "I don't have a car seat."

"It'll be fine. I wouldn't normally get into a car without one, but she's tethered to me so securely she'll be safe for a quick trip. Besides feeling like I might be developing a fever, I'm desperate to find a bathroom."

"We can go into the restaurant…"

"I'd rather go home. You can just drop me off—" She looked into Casey's eyes, so filled with longing it was impossible to ignore. "Actually, I'd love help extricating myself from this carrier. Are you up for it?"

Her expression changed to match that of a fighter pilot about to jump into the cockpit to soar over enemy territory. "I'll get you home safe and sound."

⌒

Casey acted like assassins were on every corner, waiting to take them out with a kill-shot. They only had to travel a mile, but she took the least-traveled side streets, pulling over every time she spotted another car approaching from either direction. Avery was about to wet her pants, but it was clear Casey wasn't going to be rushed.

"So…" Avery said. "You aren't giving me that 'what in the hell were you thinking' thing that everyone else has tried to hide."

"No way," she said, staring straight ahead. "If I'd found a willing woman, I'd have a house full of kids by now."

Avery flinched a little at that, certain Casey wasn't intentionally acting like a very willing baby-maker wasn't sitting right next to her, but it still stung. "Mmm. My mom mentioned you were in the market for a baby mama. No luck?"

Her cheeks colored slightly, which was a good sign. If she'd continued on blithely, she was probably a self-involved jerk. "I wouldn't say I was just looking for someone to hand over a baby, but no, I'm not dating anyone right now. I've had some promising dates, but…" She cleared her throat and quietly said, "I really am jealous."

"No nieces or nephews to spoil?"

"I've got two teenaged nephews, but they're out in Nevada. I see them once a year, and I can hardly get them to have a conversation with me."

"That will happen with Lisbet," Avery admitted. "But I'm sure I'll have her attention for quite a few years."

"Oh, you will. I have a good friend who has a kid, and he's still very much into his parents. It seems like Benji was smaller than Lisbet just a few weeks ago, but he's eight now." Another split second of eye contact. "Since Benji, Lisbet is the first baby any of my friends have had."

A little surprised at being called a friend, Avery said, "We come up every two or three weeks. Not often enough for my parents, but it's an undertaking to get Lisbet up here. I have to bring a *lot*."

"You don't live here?"

"Here?" She let out a laugh. "I've been back at work for four and a half months already. If I'd had to add a two-hour commute to my day, I'd see her so little that you'd be able to drop a different baby into this carrier and I wouldn't notice the difference." Avery dipped her head again, speaking slowly and tenderly, delighting Lisbet, who loved to be close enough to count Avery's eyelashes. No one had ever found her as fascinating as her child did. "I'm so glad no one switched you out for another baby. I'd choose you over every other munchkin in the world."

"It must be awesome to have her," Casey said, sounding like she was referring to a mystical experience. "You're going to get sick of hearing this, but I'm so jealous I'm ashamed of myself. I'd babysit every day if you lived close."

"Isn't that always the way? My dearest friends are happy to see her once every month or so, while you sound like you're thinking of how to swipe her when my back's turned. My friends clearly don't think Lisbet's birth was one of the most momentous events in world history."

"You need better friends," Casey said, her voice betraying not a shred of levity.

⌒

The carrier was just about as complex as Avery had said it was, and Casey was almost certain she'd wet her pants in the vestibule. Casey stood directly in front of her, ready to catch the baby when Avery finally unbuckled the straps and ran for the bathroom.

The baby, a warm, soft bundle of humanness, slid into Casey's hands, still entangled in her carrier. She was as quiet as a mouse, looking around curiously while Casey gently placed her in the corner of the sofa. Dropping to her knees, she squatted down so they were on the same plane, and carefully pulled the carrier from her sweaty body.

"Your mom doesn't know this yet," she said, whispering, "but you and I are going to be buddies. Do you have any other friends? Or am I your first?"

Lisbet was giving her a very curious look, really studying her. She clearly knew Casey wasn't someone in her circle, but she wasn't frightened —which was fantastic. Benji had gone through a phase where he didn't trust anyone on earth besides his mom and dad, and that had truly sucked.

A few beads of sweat slid down Lisbet's face, and Casey took a peek into the nearby diaper bag to find a clean spit-up cloth. She removed the sunhat, smiling when she saw Lisbet's white-blonde fuzz. "You've got some work to do on the dome there, little one. At this rate, you won't need a haircut for ten years." She blotted her face dry, then pulled up her T-shirt to whisk away the sweat that covered her little belly. "I guess walking around in the heat while strapped to another human isn't very cooling, huh?"

Avery appeared at her side, and Lisbet immediately swiveled her head to lock onto her, smiling when they connected. "Did you miss me?" Avery asked, speaking to her in a voice just slightly higher-pitched and more musical than her normal speaking voice.

Casey turned to say something, seeing that the front of Avery's bright blue knit top was covered in sweat. The house wasn't air conditioned, so she wouldn't be chilled, but it couldn't have been comfortable. "Do you want to go change?" she asked, trying to be diplomatic.

"I *want* to go nap," she said, turning to sneeze so loudly it hurt Casey's ears. "Sorry," she said, sniffling as she went across the room to get a tissue. "I'm feeling worse by the minute, but Lisbet has already had her afternoon nap. She's usually very active at this time of day."

"When will your parents be home?"

"Mmm… My dad didn't tee off until one, so he won't be home until dinner. Probably the same for my mom. Why?"

"Because you need to rest. Looks like you've got two options. I can sit on the floor and play with Lisbet while you sleep, or I can take her to my house to play in the pool."

"You have a pool?" she asked, acting as though Casey had said she owned the Hope Diamond.

"Uh-huh. A nice one that no one uses. My pal Benji and I spent tons of hours in the pool when he was tiny, so I know the drill."

Avery was staring at her like she was an angel sent to earth to magically fix the problems of the world.

Casey wanted to press her advantage, grab the baby and take off, but her conscience wouldn't let her. "Would you like to come, too? You could sleep in my room for a few hours, then come out and play with us."

"But..." She clearly wanted to say yes, but something was stopping her. "She's too young for sunblock. And she doesn't have a suit. The water temperature has to be really warm..."

"We keep a cover on the pool to prevent evaporation, so it's almost always too warm for me. I'm certain it's at least 85, which, if my memory's correct, is the target number, right?"

"That sounds about right. But I can't have her get sunburned, Casey. That's just not going to happen."

"Well, she's got a floppy hat that will cover her face, her ears and her neck. Does she have a long sleeved shirt?"

"Sure. A couple."

"Does she have any long pants?"

"Uh-huh. She has leggings."

"Socks?"

Avery rolled her eyes. "Yes, she has socks."

"So she'll be covered except for her hands. By two, the west end of the pool's in full shade. If I keep her back to the sun, which I will, she'll be fine."

Avery still looked a little blank, but she cocked her head slightly and said, "Why will you keep her back to the sun?"

"She doesn't have sunglasses, right?"

"No. I haven't…"

"It's okay," Casey soothed, really itching to get out of there before Avery shut down the whole plan. "I'm just letting you know that I'll be very careful with her. I'll keep the sun off her body, and her pretty eyes."

Avery opened her mouth again, but Casey interrupted before she got another word in. "I know reflection's a big issue. I'll make sure not a single ray of sun is reflected off any bare part of her." She stopped her sales pitch for a moment to gaze into Avery's eyes, which were a pretty blue-gray, just like Lisbet's. "I swear I know what I'm doing."

"But… It's a beautiful Saturday afternoon. I can't ask you to give up your day for—"

"You didn't ask. You'd be doing me a favor to let me play with her. And you," she added, although she fervently hoped to have time alone with the baby.

"You're sure?" She was right on the edge, and Casey knew how to push her over.

"We live out in the country, where's it super quiet. You can sleep for as long as you like, and when you wake up my mom will have freshly baked cookies and cheesecake to snack on."

"What the fuck?" She was staring now, clearly stunned.

"Trust me. Freshly baked lemon knots, better than anything you can buy at a bakery."

"I don't think I have a swimsuit here," she said, with a puzzled expression on her virus-ravaged face.

"Do you have shorts and a T-shirt?"

"Always," she said, finally smiling. "That's my summer uniform when I'm dressing up. I usually wear boxer shorts, but for formal occasions I have some khaki shorts." Her head tilted slightly when she added, "You'll be able to see what a post-baby body looks like. That'll cement your decision not to give birth."

Casey didn't reply. If she could have made the deal, she'd have given up a couple of fingers or a few toes to have a baby. And she fully understood how important *all* of your digits were.

Avery watched as Casey loaded the truck with all of Lisbet's gear, including the only bottle of breast milk in the fridge. Casey had insisted she didn't need another thing, but that remained to be seen. When they were out for the day in Brooklyn, she carried enough in the stroller to keep the baby alive for a week.

Lisbet was securely snuggled in her car seat, with Avery next to her in the back of the cab. Casey had been driving—carefully—for about fifteen minutes. They'd been on a county road for a while, but now they were definitely in the country. Gently rolling hills were planted nearly to the road with tall, mid-green corn, silky tassels fluttering in the wind. "My dad says the corn's not in yet, but this stuff looks ready to go," Avery said, studying it.

"Oh, this is feed corn. But we've got three farms nearby that grow sweet corn, and one had a sign out this morning saying it was in. I'm not sure it's good yet, but it's probably good enough."

"Mmm. Nothing better than fresh sweet corn. I go to the big farmer's market in Brooklyn every Saturday I'm in town. It always makes me laugh to see farms from around here selling their wares. I pay three times what my parents pay for stuff that's at least two days older."

"I'm sure there's something fantastic that keeps you in Brooklyn, but I can't imagine what that might be. I wouldn't live there if it was free, and I know it's not."

"No, it's definitely not free," Avery said, paying close attention when Casey slowed down at a stop sign and turned right. An apple orchard was on their left, the short trees groaning with fruit, all of it still bright green. She was about to comment on that when Casey turned to the right. "I didn't know there was a botanical garden up here."

"This is the Chris Van Dyke botanical garden," Casey said. "My dad's a gardening nut."

There were plants of all kinds behind the randomly spaced spruce trees that shielded the property from view. Roses, some other plants with pink flowers, then another bunch of rose bushes. Gardening clearly wasn't her thing, since Avery wasn't able to name a single other plant, but everything was pretty, covering the whole palette of greens, going from near-yellow to deep forest, along with bursts of pastels from the flowers.

"You're kidding, right?"

"Not even a little. We've got two acres in front, two in back, and two on each side of the house. Custom built. Obviously," she added, even though it wasn't obvious at all to Avery.

The sides of the lot were forested, with tall, spindly trees planted closely together, providing lots of shade. But the center of the front yard sported a deep green lawn that looked like someone had cut it by hand—with scissors. Not a single dandelion or weed had the temerity to sprout up, and if the local golfers knew about this place they'd be out there practicing their putting.

"Is gardening a passion for you, too?" Avery asked.

"No, although I'd like a garden in my own home. My dad likes to do just about everything his own way, so I stay out of it."

The house was set at a forty-five degree angle to the street, with wings on each side of a single-story ranch. The drive was gravel, which was attractively neutral against the pale gray wooden home, set off with dark gray shutters on the big windows.

"Which of the wings is yours?"

"The one on the left. I replaced the barn-style doors with ones that were insulated and had windows. It's pretty nice," she said, giving Avery a proud smile.

"The whole place is nice. It honestly looks like it should be in a magazine."

"Oh, it's definitely a passion project. My parents have been here forty years, and they've never stopped improving it."

"It's a showplace. I've never seen a home garden like this."

"If you'd like to meet the gardener, my dad's probably around the side. He's got a stand of climbing hydrangea he treats like a patient in the ICU." She parked the truck, jumped out and walked around to the passenger side to open the door for Avery.

"Your dad's a contractor, right?"

She had a cute, kind of sly grin on her face when she said, "He's the Michelangelo of Columbia County. He charges more than anyone around here, but he's still much busier than he can keep up with."

Casey took the car seat out, and started to talk to Lisbet as they crossed the ridiculously lush lawn to walk around to a spot hidden behind the right wing.

Standing in front of a tall, manmade stone wall at the edge of the lawn was a slightly taller, older, much more masculine Casey. Same slight wave to his thick hair, same strong planes to his face, same broad shoulders and long legs. But his skin tone was much darker, with a tan that made him look like a lifeguard. His muscular arms were displayed by his salmon colored tank top, and his green cargo shorts showed that his legs had been in the sun all summer.

"Hey, Dad," Casey said, making him turn around quickly.

"I didn't hear you coming," he said, flashing a smile that showed teeth that had a little bit of the gap that Casey's used to have.

"I don't think you've met my friend Avery Nichols, and I'm sure you haven't met her daughter, Lisbet."

He stuck his hand out to shake. "Are you Kathy Nichols' girl?"

"I am," Avery said. "How do you know my mom?"

"She and my wife went to school together." He slipped his hands into his pants pockets and shrugged. "You know how it is. You see people around forever, and you forget how you know them." His eyes brightened when he said, "I forgot that she used to be my go-to girl at the DMV. Only one there who knew what the hell she was doing."

"Ahh, yeah. She was good at her job."

"She left?"

"Uh-huh. She retired about two years ago. Left the minute she was able, and hasn't looked back."

"Boy, I'd love to be able to do that. I could work on my lawn every day."

"You're clearly bent on creating the Columbia County Botanical Garden right on your property. I can't imagine what else you need to do."

"That's what my wife says. But she doesn't say it with a smile like you're giving me. She thinks I'm friggin' insane."

"Who wouldn't want something so pretty?"

"My wife, for one." He gave Casey a surprisingly dismissive glance. "My daughter, for another."

"I like it just fine," Casey said, more laconic in her father's presence than she'd been before. She was leaning against that rough hewn wall, which was covered from top to bottom with a climbing plant that was just starting to reveal small white flowers. Casey was swinging the baby gently in her carrier, and her intent gaze was fixated on the plants. "I've offered to help, but…"

"She's got her own ideas," he said, like that was a fatal flaw.

"Well, your ideas are excellent, Mr. Van Dyke. I'm glad I got to see your masterpiece."

"Chris," he said, his big grin making him seem accessible and engaging. She could just see him snagging much of the home remodeling work in the county, able to charge more because of his good looks and ready smile. "Congratulations on the baby, by the way."

"Thanks. I'm very lucky to have her."

"Come inside for a minute," Casey said. "I don't think you've met my mom."

"Not many people have," Chris said, smiling when he said that, which seemed…off. Was he making fun of her for some reason? Avery generally liked to take her time making up her mind about people, but there was something about Chris that she was discomfited by.

"I don't think I've met your mom," Avery said, ignoring Chris' comment. "But I assume I've seen her around, especially if my mom knows her. Small towns and all."

"You'd have to have good timing," Casey said, leading the way to the front door, with Avery turning to awkwardly wave goodbye to Chris, who'd turned to continue working on the plant whose name Avery had already forgotten.

As they walked inside, Avery was hit by the smell of something baking. She was usually pretty good at identifying aromas, and she took an educated guess. "Is that the cheesecake you lured me over here with?"

"If today's Saturday, it's cheesecake."

"Is that a family tradition...?"

"Nah. My mom does all the baking for my uncle's restaurant. She bakes cheesecakes all day on Saturdays and doles them out as he needs them. Getting them done in one day lets her get ahead of the game."

"I had no idea she did that. I'm clearly not up-to-speed on the goings on in the Hudson Valley."

"She's been doing the baking since before I was born. I tried to convince her to split off and do some catering on her own, but she's not interested in the business side, or dealing with clients. She just likes to bake."

Avery was so distracted that she almost didn't notice the house. But with a quick glance she could see that it was the nicest family home she'd ever been to. Big rooms, oversized furniture, tall windows flooding the rooms with light. They kept walking across the stone floor, then entered a kitchen big enough to prepare a state dinner.

The woman standing in front of a stand mixer didn't look much like Casey from the back, being average height and a little doughy, but when she turned, she had Casey's smile, as well as her dark, kind eyes.

"Hey, Mom," Casey said. "We've got company. Avery Nichols and her daughter came over to hang out with me."

"Well, well, well," she said. "It's old home week for Hudson High." She took a towel and dusted off her hands. "Casey told me she ran into your mom a while ago. But she *didn't* tell me you'd gotten married."

Avery started to speak, but Casey cut in.

"Avery's on my team, Mom. The class of 2002 must have been a banner year for lesbians."

"Oh! I'm sorry for assuming..."

"I don't mind," Avery said. "Heterosexuality is the norm, so assuming it is...well, normal."

She smiled, looking even more like Casey when she did. "So you and your girlfriend decided to have a baby? That must have been…" She trailed off, not seeming very adept with small talk.

"I don't have one of those either," Avery said, watching the woman's face fall. Avery still hadn't heard her name, and now it was a little late to ask. "Um, I didn't want to run out of time, so I decided to get started. I assumed I'd have trouble getting pregnant, but I surprised the heck out of myself."

"Well, I can't say I envy you doing this on your own, but I'm sure you'll manage. Women have been doing most of the child-rearing since Adam and Eve." She turned and washed her hands properly. "Have you and Casey been friends all this time?"

Avery was stuck mute. How was she supposed to answer that?

Casey jumped in again. "We ran into each other a year or two ago, but other than that…"

"How'd you get in touch?" She took a look at the infant carrier, having not made any move to take a peek at the human inside. "Oh, I get it. Casey found out you had a baby."

"Well…"

"Good luck," she said, laughing a little. "She'll take her as often as you'll let her. I don't know why she didn't have one of her own, but…" She picked up a mixing bowl and started to load it into the dishwasher. "Casey doesn't tell me much."

"I tell you a lot," she said, not trying to press the point. "I just don't have much to say."

"Mmm." She turned back to Avery. "Are you going to swim? Casey's out there enough to get her lifeguard certification again."

Avery gave Casey a quick look. "I didn't know you'd been a lifeguard, but now I feel ever more secure."

"It's been a while, but my skills are sharp enough," she said, distractedly glancing at the counters. "Any cookies, Mom?"

"Always. I just made some lemon knots. I think they're cool by now. Check the rack."

Casey went to a tall metal rack sitting by the back door. After pulling out a tray, she looked at the cookies carefully. "You've only got about two dozen. Sure you don't mind if I take a few?"

"Go right ahead. Mark never sells many on a Saturday, since Tiramisu seems to be the date night choice. I've just never taken the time to cut the recipe down."

"These are my favorites," Casey said, taking three and handing two to Avery. "I took a whole batch of these to school once when we were supposed to bring in food, and by the time I got there I only had about five left."

Avery took a bite, and her instinct was to let out a moan. She almost stopped herself, then realized a baker wouldn't mind hearing that her cookie made a person lose control for a moment. "So good," she said. "I don't think I've ever had room for dessert when I've been to your brother's restaurant, but I'm going to have to push the bread basket away next time."

"Oh, the bread's good, too," she admitted. "I don't bake that, of course. I *could*, but I don't want the argument I'd have if I tried to get Chris to put in a brick oven."

"She's a perfectionist," Casey said, smiling at her mom. The baby had dozed off, and she started fuss a little when she woke, with Casey shooting Avery a look. "Do you need to feed her?"

"She's not due for a while. She'll let you know when she's hungry. It's the difference between mild fussiness and screaming like she's being chased by Godzilla." She leaned over and touched Lisbet's face, soothing her. "I think she's just a little disoriented. She'll be fine."

"Are you leaving the baby here…?"

Casey turned back to her mom. "Avery's got a cold, so I convinced her to a long nap while I take the baby swimming. She'll join us after she's rested up."

"Where were you when I was wrestling with the three of you kids? I could have used a babysitter back then."

"I was the one causing the trouble," Casey said. "We'll be outside."

"Thanks so much for the treat," Avery said. "It was divine."

"Is the baby old enough to have one?"

Casey gave her a puzzled look. "She's just six months, Mom. I don't think that's cookie age."

She laughed, shaking her head at her own comment. "I can never tell how old babies are."

That was kind of odd for a woman who'd had three of her own, but Avery decided some people must not sweat the small stuff. "See you later," she said, following along behind Casey.

They went out via the front door, with Casey chatting to the baby as they walked. "One of these days you're going to be able to eat one of those lemon cookies. Then you're going to know why your mom looked so happy a few minutes ago."

"How do you stay so thin?" Avery asked. "I almost walked over there and swiped another two or three, and that's after learning your mother baked those specifically for the restaurant."

"I only have one or two a day. Most days," she admitted. "I'm on my feet constantly, and that must burn a lot of calories."

They went around to the front of Casey's wing, and she put her key into a hidden slot. The doors opened wide, revealing a very cute miniature house. It was like seeing a model room at a department store, and Avery found herself kind of delighted at having it unveiled that way.

"Now this is the Brooklyn apartment I've longed for." There was a clearly demarcated bedroom, with a large bed with big, fluffy pillows propped against the wooden headboard, then a TV area, with a full-sized leather sofa and a big screen sitting atop a short bookcase that was filled with DVDs and some old textbooks. A closed door must have led to a bathroom. "What a setup," Avery added, gobsmacked.

"Here's your bed, just waiting for you to jump in. Do you want fresh air or air conditioning."

"Fresh, I think."

"Come on, then. Lie down and make sure you're comfortable. I can add pillows, a comforter, whatever you like."

Avery was wearing sandals, and she slid out of them and approached the bed. "I'm afraid if I get into this, I'll never get up again."

"Oh, sure you will. You'll have to get up to pee at some point."

"Well, that's true. Is that the bathroom over there?"

"Uh-huh. There's a shower too if you want to get in and steam some of the gunk out of your nose."

"Oh. Tissues? My nose is about to run down my face."

"Very attractive image." She produced the box, placing it on the bedside table. "I'll get Lisbet changed outside, under the pergola."

Avery blew her nose, then lay down, feeling like she was atop a cloud. "Oh, my God," she murmured, closing her eyes. "Did you pay a million dollars for this mattress?"

"Uh-huh. It seemed a little expensive, but I'm worth it."

"This is fantastic, Casey. I don't have words to express how thankful I am to you for taking over like this." She took another look around the room, finding it fit Casey perfectly—spare, and clean, with a touch of luxury. "I love your room."

"I did most of the work myself," she said, moving over to the door. "We were thinking my grandmother would use it one day." She let out a short laugh. "That's the only reason my dad let me do the renovations. But she passed away a while ago, still perfectly able to stay in her own home. She was lucky," she added quietly. "Dying in your sleep after eating a big piece of cake and drinking a glass of milk is the way to go."

"How do you…?"

"She was in her recliner, with a few chocolate crumbs on the plate, and "Murder, She Wrote" on TV. Again, not a bad way to go."

"I'm sorry she's gone," Avery said. "My grandparents are all dead now, too. It's hard," she added, able to cry at the drop of a hat that her little sweet pea would never meet the people who'd made Avery feel so very, very special as a child.

"Yeah, me too. She was pretty cantankerous, but she always had my back."

"That's a grandparent's main role. Being on their grandchild's side."

"Well, I'm going to be on Lisbet's side," she said, having settled that matter on her own. "I'm going to spoil this little pumpkin as much as you'll let me."

"I'm going to have to make an appointment to see that child, aren't I," Avery asked.

"I'll give you generous visitation rights." Casey picked Lisbet's hand up and moved it up and down in a facsimile of a wave, keeping it up until Avery peacefully closed her eyes, feeling cared for for the first time in two weeks—the last time she'd been home.

It had taken Casey a little while to wrestle Lisbet into her swim diaper, then cover every other inch of her body with fabric. The things Avery had packed must have been for a newborn, since they fit like a second skin. But Lisbet was unbelievably easy-going while Casey stretched the fabric over her chubby arms and legs, watching with those deep-blue eyes, more interested than alarmed to have a stranger dressing her. She babbled a little, sounding out vowels mostly, but she was clearly glad to go along for the ride, even though she didn't know where they were going.

Even though she'd taken the cover off the pool before she'd left the house that afternoon, Casey was certain that the eighty-five degree day had kept it toasty. But before even attempting to get in, she checked the thermometer, nodding with satisfaction when it read 87 degrees.

She was wearing some board shorts, her usual summer uniform, and she whipped off her shirt and bra to slip into a rash-guard she'd left in the sun to dry. "Sorry to flash you," she said to the baby. "But I forgot to get anything for myself, and I don't want to wake your mommy up."

Lisbet didn't pay much attention to Casey now that they were slowly entering the pool. Her dad had gone all out, having the pool contractor create a very gentle slope to enter the water. It was almost like a sandy beach, with the grippy surface the right color to imitate a Bermuda beach. She'd had a float out earlier, and she sat the baby right in the middle of it, watching her react with suspicion when a little water spilled over the edge.

She was sitting in only about an inch of liquid, and it was as warm as bathwater, but it was definitely an experience she wasn't used to.

"Do you like this, Lisbet? I sure do," she said, pushing the float out into deeper water. She used her legs to propel them now, quickly pushing the raft over to the shady side of the pool.

Casey was warm even in the shade, but she was sure the water was refreshing for Lisbet. "Next year, I'll teach you how to put your face underwater. That'll be fun, won't it?"

Her little head was swiveling around, trying to get her bearings. But she still didn't cry a single tear, too engaged to worry. This was a very secure baby. Either Avery was doing a lot of things right, or that's just how Lisbet had entered the world.

"Wanna play peek-a-boo?" Casey dunked her head, coming back up after a second. "Peek-a-boo!"

The baby's eyes had gone round, and after a couple of seconds to decide if she was frightened or not, she began to laugh. Casey kept it up, dunking herself so many times she was out of breath. But the kid kept laughing, and one thing Ben and Julie had taught her was to never stop doing something that kept a baby entertained. Of course, they weren't the ones gasping for breath right now.

The game lasted for much longer than Casey thought it would, and it only stopped because some signal went off in Lisbet's brain, and she realized she was hungry. She literally went from laughing like she was watching the funniest thing she'd ever seen to shrieking like Godzilla had just appeared. *Wow.* Avery had been right about the kid's signals.

Casey pushed Lisbet back across the pool, regretting she hadn't thought to bring ear plugs. This baby must have had a pair of extra large lungs on her, because the volume was amazing!

After wrapping her in a beach towel, Casey grabbed the bottle, which Avery had assured her didn't need to be warmed up, and went over to the hammock. It was in deep shade, and Casey was relieved to sit on it and feel a little breeze. She got Lisbet settled in the crook of her arm, and the moment the nipple entered her mouth the tears stopped. It was such a dramatic change that Casey stared at her for a moment, truly puzzled. But the baby was perfectly happy now, sucking lustily as she rushed to get the milk into her belly.

"You eat like I do when I've missed lunch."

Lisbet was an all-pro at snarfing down her late lunch, barely looking around, her wide eyes making her seem frantic. Casey had very clear memories of feeding Benji when he was an infant, and she recalled him getting distracted by the smallest noise, or from the family cat walking by. Not Lisbet. If she continued at this pace, the bottle would be gone in a minute! The last thing Casey wanted to have to do was wake Avery, but there had only been one bottle in the fridge.

Just when she thought they'd run out, Lisbet let out a sigh, then her eyes shifted from their locked-in view of the bottle to move around, seeing she was somewhere different. Her barely-visible eyebrows lifted, but she kept sucking. Less frantically, but steadily. Since she'd gulped down over half of the bottle so quickly, Casey eased the nipple from her mouth, and those tiny brows drew together, like she wasn't going to accept having her meal cut short without a fight.

She seemed small for her age, light as a feather when Casey put her up to her shoulder and began to burp her. Lisbet didn't seem to mind being soundly patted on the back, and after she let out a loud burp Casey cradled her again to let her finish.

Looking up when she heard a sound, she saw her mom exit through the kitchen door. "Well look at this," she said. "The lifeguard runs the snack bar."

"Obviously you didn't hear her start to scream when she got hungry. She's not shy when it comes to making her needs known."

Her mom reached down and ran her fingers over Lisbet's peach fuzz. "What's the connection between you two? You and Avery, I mean. You've never mentioned her." Her hand stilled, then she said, "Wait... Now I remember her. Kathy Crane's kid was one of the girls that teased you in high school."

"Yeah—"

Her mom's cheeks had flushed and her dark eyes flashed with anger. "I didn't know Kathy well, but I knew her well enough to go over to her house and give her a piece of my mind."

"I thought I was going to have to wrestle you to the ground to stop you from going. I'd never seen you so angry."

"Of course I was angry," she said, speaking loud enough for Lisbet to shift around and stare at her. "You were the toughest kid I've ever been around, and to find you in your room, crying your eyes out because of those little jerks…"

"I don't remember Avery ever saying anything specific," she insisted. "Janelle Perkins was the prime jerk—of the girls, at least. But if Avery ever told them to knock it off, she didn't do it in public. I can still see her sitting in the cafeteria, acting like she didn't even hear Janelle taunting me." She lightly touched the baby's incredibly soft foot. "Don't grow up to be a jerk, Lisbet. Your mom seems nice now, but she was kind of an asshole in high school."

"Language!"

"The baby's six months old, Mom. I promise I won't drop the 'F' bomb when she can talk."

Her mom gave the baby a careful going-over, lightly touching her head again. "She's awfully cute," she decided. "I don't usually think babies are much to look at, but this one's got a very pretty face. When she gets rid of this peach fuzz and gets some hair, she's going to be a doll. Did Avery know a guy who wanted to help her out? Or did she have to go to one of those…fertility clinics? Is that right?"

"I have no idea how Lisbet got here. Avery and I only talked to each other for a few minutes before I was trying to entice her into letting me take the baby." She looked up and smiled. "I was hoping Avery would stay home."

"Does she live in town?"

"Brooklyn. That much I know."

Her mother rolled her eyes. "What is wrong with her? It's hard enough to have a baby when you've got a husband. Doing it alone is insane." She shook her head in a very dismissive way. "Boy, that's what you get for making fun of people. They call that karma," she added, looking very satisfied.

"Nice." Casey took the spent bottle from Lisbet's mouth and started to burp her again. "You want to make Avery's life hard because she teased me?"

"I'm talking about her being gay. She teased you for it, and now she's in the same boat."

"Seriously?" Casey stared up at her. "My sexual orientation is like a curse?"

Her mom caught her by the sleeve and tugged hard. She wasn't very big, and she didn't look very strong, but all of her baking had given her an iron grip. "Listen here, young lady. I've been more than supportive of your... Of your *everything*," she stressed. "So don't give me that pout. All I meant was that the girl made fun of gay people, then she became one. That's karma."

"Really? What if she'd made fun of my .725 batting average, then became a great hitter herself. Would that be karma?"

"Why would anyone make fun of you for being a good hitter? It's not the same at all." She gently ran her hand across Casey's hair, the same way she'd just touched Lisbet. "I certainly didn't mean to hurt your feelings."

Casey pulled back and forced herself to remove the pout she knew was still apparent. "Sorry. I've still got that one sore spot, and it bugs me. Janelle and the other snots made my high school years miserable. But I learned how to ignore them, and I'm stronger for it. I should thank Avery and her gang."

"What you should do is give that baby right back without giving Avery the impression you're going to watch it routinely. It might seem like fun for an afternoon, but trust me, it gets old fast."

As Casey watched her walk back into the house, she mused, not for the first time, that her mom had fewer good things to say about parenthood than any mother she'd ever met. It was clear she tried to be connected to her kids, and her grandkids, and equally clear that it wasn't something that came naturally.

～

Avery stirred, stiff and achy. Her breasts felt like rocks, and her back hurt from lying in one place for too long. The bed seemed… She stuck her hand out, feeling much more mattress than she should have. As her eyes opened, she gasped in surprise, not recognizing a thing. It was dark, but there were windows in front of her… *Casey's place.* She took a few deep breaths, trying to get her heart to stop racing. Doing the mental calculation that now ruled every minute of every day, she realized she hadn't fed Lisbet since one o'clock, and it had to be after eight. There was no way the baby would go that long without losing her shit!

Scrambling out of the fantastic bed, she found her sandals, then tried to figure out how to get out of the room. After fumbling around, her hand landed on a lamp, and she switched it on to be able to see a normal garage door keypad by the doors. With the touch of a button, the doors opened quietly, swinging wide enough to drive a bus through.

She stopped abruptly, seeing her mother's car parked right in front of her. This was getting weirder and weirder.

Continuing to follow voices in the distance, she wound up on a patio that fronted the most beautiful pool she'd ever seen, lit with subtle, warm lights that made it seem like some kind of Shangri-La.

It wasn't easy, but she tore her attention away from the pool to find her mom, Casey's mom and dad, Casey, and Lisbet seated in a circle, all of them eating dinner.

"Am I in heaven?" she asked as she approached. "A warm, summer night. A gorgeous pool. A quiet baby. Food…"

"I thought we were going to have to leave you here all night," her mom said.

"Let me get you a plate." Casey's mom jumped to her feet and started for the house. "It's just penne with summer vegetables, but it's pretty good."

"Thank you," Avery said, too in debt at this point to refuse further favors.

"Come sit down," Chris said, getting up to pull another chair into the circle. "Your baby doesn't need a thing. But I wish you'd been here a few minutes ago. Watching Casey try to feed the baby peas and sweet potato was a kick."

"You what?" Avery tried to keep the shock from her voice, but knew she hadn't managed it. Lisbet had never had a whole piece of vegetable, and the thought of her choking...

"Mashed," her mom immediately clarified. "Casey called me when she realized Lisbet needed another bottle, so I drove over with one from the freezer. While I was at it, I brought some of the vegetables we made last night."

"Damn," Avery sighed, sitting down in a remarkably comfortable spring chair. "It really does take a village, doesn't it?"

"That's what I've been telling Chris and Marsha," her mom said, finally revealing Casey's mom's name. "I spend a good portion of every day wishing you lived closer so I could help more."

Marsha carried a bowl of penne over to Avery, adding a napkin wrapped around a fork and a spoon. "I put a little grated Parmesan on the pasta," she said. "I hope you eat cheese."

"She eats everything," her mom said. "She always has."

"I do," Avery confirmed. "I can't thank you enough, Marsha."

"Oh, it was nothing," she said breezily. "I love to cook, and having people over lets me get rid of some of the squash and tomatoes Chris grows. I'm going to have Casey take all of the excess over to the food bank on Monday. We're drowning in the things, and the season's only started."

Avery took a bite of her dinner and made very appreciative noises. "Truly delicious," she mumbled around a mouthful. "I should be feeding my baby, but you snooze you lose."

"She can wait for another couple of hours," her mom said.

"Maybe she can, but I can't. I didn't bring my pump."

"Mmm. I don't know how you girls do it," Marsha said. "Can you imagine having a kid taller or stronger than this one?" she asked, pointing a finger at Casey. "If formula slowed her down a little, all the better."

"They say breast milk can increase IQ by a few points," Casey said, not looking up from where she gently rocked Lisbet in her carrier. "Some say I could have used a boost there."

"Ridiculous," her mom said. "You're plenty smart."

"Luckily, you don't need to be a genius to do your job," Chris said. He had a perfectly pleasant expression on his face, leading you to think he was just stating a fact. But what a rude fact! "You're good at the science of beer making. You found your spot." He looked at Avery's mom and said, "My son's a CPA out in Nevada, and my other daughter's a VP at Mountain Peak in Denver. Formula didn't hurt them." He put a little extra stress on the "them," leading Avery to think he was inferring it might have hurt Casey. What in the hell was his problem with her?

Avery took another look at Casey, just able to make out her features in the gentle light. She certainly didn't look upset, but Avery would have snapped at him if he'd said anything close to that to her. Casey either had a thick skin, or she was secretly plotting his demise and needed to live at home to take advantage of every opportunity.

CHAPTER THREE

CASEY WALKED INTO HER OFFICE on Monday morning, pleased to see Ben already working away. There were a lot of benefits to working at Kaaterskill Brewery, but the biggest one was the flexible schedule. The owners were very strong believers in getting the work done when you were at your best, so they never said a word when one of the office employees wanted to come in at five a.m., or five p.m., although that had never happened to Casey's knowledge.

Julie, Ben's wife, was a social worker, now working for the school district, but when Benji had been young she'd worked at the local hospital, doing the evening shift. Since Ben was able to come in early and leave early, she could do the four to midnight shift, meaning they'd never had to pay for childcare for Benji. That also meant that Ben had been in charge of getting the kid fed, dressed, and ready for school, or day camp, depending on the time of year, which had, in Casey's opinion, made him a much better, more involved dad than most of the guys she knew.

"Hey there," she said. "Been in long?"

"About an hour," he said, checking his watch. "The baseball camp Benji's in doesn't start until ten, which is stupid, in my opinion. But he likes it because he can sleep in. Since Julie's in charge of feeding him and making sure he's got all his gear, I can get in super early."

"You could come in later, after you drop him off at camp."

"Yeah, I could," he said, stretching his big arms out in front of himself and yawning. "But then I'd still be at work when he's ready for pick-up. Sucks," he added. "Summer day camps are a huge pain in the butt. They cost a ton, and start at weird times. I guess their target audience is super rich people who don't work."

"That must be three people around here. Tops." She put her huge, stainless coffee mug on her desk and kicked off her flip-flops, then pulled her boots out from under her desk. Casey thought she kind of rocked the cargo shorts and steel-toed boots look, but she'd never gotten confirmation of that from any of her coworkers. Straight guys just did not appreciate dyke style.

As she pulled on a pair of dark green wool socks, she said, "You'll never guess who came to my pool party on Saturday afternoon."

"You had a pool party and didn't invite me? And now you're gloating over it?"

He was clearly teasing, but he did it so well it would have fooled anyone who didn't know him.

"Yeah, I think that's what I'm doing." She started to lace her fawn-colored boot. "I had a six-month-old baby all to myself for a couple of hours."

"Until the police tracked you down?"

She laughed. "I had permission, but it was a great afternoon. *Damn*, I love kids."

"I do too," he said. "So long as I'm related to them. Other than that? They're major pains in the butt. I wouldn't give you ten bucks for all of the kids in Benji's baseball camp. Bunch of little jerks."

"Yeah, well, we don't feel the same."

"I can't figure out why you like kids so much. You're crazier about them than the gymnastics coach my sister had in high school, and that guy's in prison."

"He molested your—"

"No, thank god. He liked kids younger than her. Like I said, he's in prison, but he should be dead."

"Can't argue with that," Casey said. "So…I hope we can agree that I like kids for non-perverted reasons, right?"

He smiled at her. "I leave my kid with you for long weekends, so if you're sketchy, I'm worse."

"Also debatable. But I'm not going to be able to make you understand why I like kids so much."

"Why not? You're good at explaining things. You've got a scientific mind."

"For the same reason I can't express why I don't like video games," she said. "I just don't."

"Well, that's just dumb. I gave you my number one best friend slot, and you pay me back by refusing to play Fortnite with me."

She lifted her shoulders as high as they'd go, then let them drop. "Can't explain it. Just don't like games. But seeing the world through a baby's eyes gives me a real high. They're completely innocent little sponges who aren't ever mean, or vindictive, or narrow-minded."

"Some babies are mean little cusses," he said, laughing.

"No way. They're all innocent until we screw them up." She finished with her boots, then stood and stomped on each to make sure they were comfortably laced. "I really dig being with them before they've been ruined. They're like puppies, but one day they'll be able to talk. That gives them a leg up in my book."

He gazed up at her for a minute, looking like he was on the verge of saying something. But when he hesitated she said, "Yes? I can see a question forming."

He shook his head quickly. "I…um, I don't mean this to sound rude, but does the baby-loving gene skip a generation?"

She couldn't help but laugh at the uncharacteristically timid expression on his face. "I won't tell my parents you think they hate babies."

"Not hate," he added quickly. "But neither one of them has ever shown any interest in Benji, which is kind of weird…"

She sat on the edge of his desk and said, "You're not wrong. Obviously. But the gene must have skipped two generations, since none of my grandparents were wild about kids, especially small ones."

He looked positively stunned when their eyes met. "But your grandmother loved you!"

"She sure did," Casey said, giving him a confident smile. "But she wasn't all lovey-dovey or anything. Her thing was encouraging me to be strong and courageous and self-sufficient. She had no patience for whining or crying. Heck, she wasn't much for hugging. My grandmother was a great mentor, but I don't ever remember her letting me sit on her lap."

"Huh." He gazed up at her again. "So it's a non-heritable trait?"

"Maybe." She thought for a moment, deciding whether to just brush this off. But Ben was her best friend, and she tried to be as forthcoming as she could when he asked a direct question. "I think I try to give every kid I meet a little love since I know how much they need it." She could have cried if she'd let herself, but she'd be damned if she'd cry at work—even with just Ben around. "Giving kids something I didn't get fills me up, Ben. Nothing brings me as much pleasure."

"God damn," he sighed, looking like he might cry as well. "That…"

"Nobody gets to be an adult without some bumps and bruises, right? But look at the bright side. I'm remarkably mentally healthy for a woman raised like a stray cat."

"That you are," he said, smiling up at her like he wanted to wrap her in a hug and not let her go. He shook off the feeling by picking up his mechanical pencil to start running it down a column of numbers. "Where'd you get this lucky kid, anyway."

"A woman I went to high school with. Avery Nichols. You saw her once. At Friday Night Flights."

"Avery Nichols. The name sounds familiar, but I can't place her. Does she live in town?"

"Brooklyn," she said, seeing recognition dawn in his pale eyes.

"Is that the—?"

"Yes, she's the woman who teased me in high school."

"Bullied," he corrected. "Teasing is when you make fun of someone's new shoes or a bad haircut. Bullying's when you try to destroy someone's self-image."

"Then she definitely didn't bully me, since my self-image is kind of awesome."

"Come on, Casey! What in the hell are you doing?"

"I was in Hudson, where her parents live, I ran into her on the street. She had a bad cold, and a wide-awake baby. I offered to watch the kid while Avery took a nap."

"So you're rewarding her for being a jerk in high school."

"I'm not rewarding her, Ben. And, like I told you, I don't recall Avery personally taunting me. It was her friends, one in particular, who were the idiots."

"Jerks hang around with jerks," he said, pronouncing the words like they were gospel.

"I think that's more true than not. That's why I didn't call her after we met up that night, even though she's cute as hell, and was giving me signs that she'd be up for it."

"But you spent the day watching her baby." He narrowed his eyes a bit as he said, "Isn't she the one with the mom you like?"

"I do. But not like *that*. There isn't a single female member of the Nichols family that I want to get with, okay? I'm a decent human who wanted to help out another human who was having a bad day. You may shoot me for that if you'd like."

"I don't want to shoot you," he said, with his deep voice gentling. "I just don't want you to give your time to an idiot who might hurt you again."

"I'm not fifteen any more, Ben. I don't give people the opportunity to hurt me. But if I can spend more time with a perfectly sweet baby, I'm going to grab the chance."

CHAPTER FOUR

AT TWO A.M. ON THE FOLLOWING Wednesday, Avery jerked to attention when Lisbet let out a wail. This was off-schedule for her, but those little lungs could peel the paint off the walls when she was unhappy, and Lisbet Kendall Nichols was clearly unhappy at the moment.

Avery got to her feet and peered at her daughter, realizing that her cry wasn't her usual one. She'd eaten only two hours ago, and she was reliably going for four or even more hours between meals overnight, so this wail probably didn't signal hunger.

She picked Lisbet up and tried to soothe her while checking her diaper, which was clean and dry. The baby was warm, but it had to be eighty in the room, with their ineffective fan not doing much to move the air around.

"What's the matter, sweetheart?" she murmured, with Lisbet fussing and fighting against being held. Avery put her back down and turned on the nightlight that broadcast the star-filled night sky onto the ceiling, one of their nighttime rituals. That didn't help a bit, so she removed the baby's thin cotton onesie, thinking she might be overheated.

For the next fifteen minutes she patted Lisbet while she cried, simultaneously balancing her laptop on one leg asking Doctor Internet what in the hell could be wrong. No fever. No hunger. Nothing pinching her. Then she specified Lisbet's age and had to stop herself from picking up the computer and smacking herself in the head with it. *Teething!* How had she not been better prepared? Lisbet had steadfastly refused a pacifier, so she'd never used one. Now she didn't have a nice, safe, BPA-free teething ring to soothe the child's erupting gum. Tiptoeing into the kitchen, she wet a washcloth and put it into the freezer, hoping it would quickly get cold enough to help a little.

As she walked back toward the hall she heard her friend and roommate, Freya, mutter, "Will this stop soon?"

"I'm doing my best," she said, only slightly irritated to have Freya imply that she had complete control over this.

"I've got a meeting at eight, Avery, and I have to be sharp."

"Do you want me to get you some earplugs?"

"I sleep with them in every night," she said, with an edge to her voice that Avery had never heard.

"I'm really sorry. The baby's teething, I think. She's in pain, but I'm doing my best to calm her down."

"My mother always put a little Akvavit on the gums."

"Um, I don't have any Akvavit on me," Avery said, "and I don't think I want to start giving her liquor to calm her down."

The inadequate blinds in the dining room made the space bright enough to read by, and Avery could see that Freya was wearing just a tank top and her underwear. She tossed her feet to the floor and got up in one smooth movement, then went to the chair by her futon and picked up her jeans. "Naveed is always up. I'll go sleep on her sofa."

"I might be able to calm her down soon," Avery said, even though she had no idea how to manage that. "I hate to have you out alone at this time of night."

"Fine. Then pay for an Uber for me." She'd stopped getting dressed, and now glared at Avery, another first in their seven year friendship.

"Oh…okay." She went into her room, got her phone, then pulled up the app and handed the phone over. "Go ahead and enter the address."

Grumbling to herself, Freya did, then pulled out a tote bag and started putting clothes and toiletries into it. "This can't go on," she said, pulling out her earplugs and dropping them onto the bed. "I haven't said a word up until now because I thought this was time-limited."

"I think it is…"

"My car will be here in three minutes," she said, handing the phone back. "We'll talk at work."

"I'm so sorry, Freya. Really, I am."

"So am I," she said, grabbing her purse and padding across the room in her bare feet. She took her shoes from the spot she always kept them and left the apartment, closing the door quietly.

Avery continued to stare at the door, completely befuddled by Freya's anger. She hadn't said a thing when Lisbet was shrieking every two hours when she was a newborn. Why now?"

ᴄᴄ

At four o'clock in the morning, the baby was still so upset that she wouldn't latch. These were the darks nights that tried mothers' souls, or at least it seemed that way at the moment. When a baby was so hungry she wouldn't eat, there wasn't a viable workaround. Avery was kind of glad she hadn't gone to med school, because if she'd had the ability to hook Lisbet up to an IV, she would have done it without guilt. Well, maybe just a little guilt.

ᴄᴄ

Avery shot upright when her alarm sounded, but when she put a hand down, it hit the baby. "Oh, my God!"

She lunged for her, hyperventilating until she was sure Lisbet was breathing. Then she clasped her to her chest and dropped into her rocking chair to call her mom.

"What's wrong?" she asked, sounding awake but alarmed.

"I fell asleep with Lisbet in my bed. I put her life at risk, Mom! I must've been so tired I fell asleep while nursing."

"Is she all right?" she asked, now using her usual tone of voice. Calm and unflappable.

"Yes. Yes," she sighed, relieved when the baby rooted against her, clearly ready for breakfast. "She's ready to nurse."

"You need more sleep, sweetheart. You're not able to function on so little."

"What new mom isn't tired? This was bad mostly because I think she's started teething. Why I didn't have a cold teething ring is the fridge is another item on my long list of things I've screwed up."

"Oh, right. The teething police are going to pick on you. You're *clearly* the worst mother in Brooklyn."

"I know I'm not," she sighed. "But there's so much to know."

"You're learning all of it, just like everyone does. Now feed that baby, feed yourself, and get to work."

"Oh, shit! This is a work day?"

"Is has been every other week."

"Thanks," Avery said, wishing she could crawl through the phone line for a hug. Being the one to always be the soother left her craving soothing of her own. But she had to be careful about how much she complained. Giving her mom more ammunition about how crazy it was to try to raise the baby alone in Brooklyn was an awful idea.

⌇

Avery got Lisbet dressed, then set her on the floor in the bathroom with a couple of toys while she took a lighting-fast shower. It took another fifteen minutes to get dressed, trying to look presentable for the weekly all-hands meeting.

After walking the seven blocks to the only daycare she'd been able to find that took infants, she checked her phone, seeing they were on time. The fee at this place was shockingly high, but the women who ran it were pleasant, and Lisbet never seemed to mind being dropped off. Until today. Avery had just entered the door to the infants room when Lisbet started to cry, using the same frantic wail she'd developed in the middle of the night. After talking with Ramona and Jasmine, the two main caregivers for infants, they all agreed that Lisbet was just teething. But that didn't make it any easier to leave her. Lisbet sat against a support pillow on the floor, disconsolate, while Ramona sat next to her, stroking her beet-red face.

"She'll be fine," she said, smiling at Avery. "Every baby does this sometimes. Don't worry!" She was clearly trying to be reassuring, but leaving your baby when she truly seemed to need you felt like cutting off a limb. Avery bit her lip to stop from crying right along with Lisbet, then blew her a kiss, and stepped outside the door, able to hear her cry almost as loudly as she had in the middle of the night. The daycare place was on the corner of Smith and Union, both commercial streets, but there were apartment buildings right behind it. Those residents were either very good-natured, woefully unhappy, or stone deaf.

The all-hands meeting went pretty well, and Avery was happy with the universal approval she got when she announced that Sonya Federansky was going to read at the October edition of *Short Shorts*. Avery had sealed the deal, even though Helena, her managing editor, had set the wheels in motion.

When the meeting broke up, Freya approached, looking a little sheepish. Helena always ordered in a buffet lunch after their weekly meeting, and Freya said, "Why don't we pick up some food and go sit outside."

"Love to," Avery said, relieved to see that Freya wasn't still upset. Today's lunch was from a Mexican place that was usually reliable, and they each made two tacos and added some black beans and a little saffron rice before they went out.

Their office was in an old building in Brooklyn Heights near the river, not too far from the park the city had created when Freya had just started working for *Ad Infinitum*. Avery had a number of fond memories of sitting outside in the summer, getting to know her new colleague while trying to ignore the dust, dirt and noise that came from any building project.

They sat on a bench in the full sun, soaking in the rays for the few minutes they'd have to spend. Neither of them ever set aside more than fifteen minutes for lunch, and even that was a rarity. Avery appreciated that Freya had gone out of her way to make a peace offering.

"I'm so sorry I was angry this morning." Freya took a breath. "I know none of this is your fault, Avery, and I know you're doing the best you cn."

"It's all right," Avery started to say, but Freya continued.

"But…" She pursed her lips for a second, then spit it out. "I can't get by with so little sleep. If I stay, I'll start to resent you, and I don't want that. I want our friendship to survive this."

"You're leaving?" She stared at her, totally stunned.

"I don't want to. I *don't*. I've been thinking things would be fine soon, with Lisbet sleeping through the night. But I called my sister this morning, and she says the next year can be just as bad as when Lisbet was a newborn if she has teething pain."

"No!" she gasped, wholly unprepared for that.

"I hope my sister is wrong, but she's a pediatrician…"

"I don't think I can handle another year of this," Avery said, ready to cry.

"I need my sleep," Freya continued, "and when I don't get it I snap at people." She reached out and touched Avery's arm. "I love Lisbet. Truly, I do. But I can't live with you any more."

"What… When will you leave?"

"As soon as I can. Actually, I might crash on Naveed's sofa until I find a place. I need my sleep," she said again. "It's not a wish, it's a need."

"But I can't pay your share of the rent," Avery said, trying not to cry. "With the added expenses from the baby, I'm already struggling…"

"I'll pay my share until our lease is up. If you can find someone quickly, you can renew the new lease they just sent us. If not…" She shrugged, looking upset but resolved. "I wish I could stay, but I can't."

She looked over at Freya, profoundly disappointed. "I understand. If I could have moved away last night, I would have too."

"I'm sorry," Freya said one more time. "I thought… I thought it would get easier."

Avery gazed at her for a moment, and allowed herself to say the unvarnished truth. "So did I."

⌣

Avery had gotten through the afternoon, but she'd been distracted and forgetful, two qualities that were very rare for her—at least before she'd gotten pregnant. She was a different person now. A much less focused person, and it was showing in her work.

She had a face-to-face meeting with one of the writers for their November issue scheduled for four, so she went into their conference room at three to pump, determined to have her milk stored away, with time leftover to put on a modicum of makeup and check that her hair was combed.

A hand on her shoulder woke her, making her cry out sharply. Avery looked up to see Helena, her editor-in-chief, giving her a look that showed both empathy and disappointment.

"How much sleep are you getting?" she asked gently.

"Not enough," Avery admitted. "Lisbet had a very bad night. She's started teething and I wasn't prepared…"

"I understand," she soothed. "But you can't sleep here, Avery. Is there no one who can help?"

"No one," Avery admitted, refusing to reveal that even Freya was abandoning her.

"We're going to have to work something out. I'm not sure what we can do, but we have to do something. Your editorial work is suffering, you've not brought in your usual number of new writers, and there are no new venues scheduled for *Short Shorts* for the rest of the year."

"I've admittedly been coasting for a few months. But Lisbet should be sleeping through the night soon. That will help. I *know* it will."

Helena put her hand on Avery's back and patted it gently. "When I had Cameron, I tried to get by with just Clive's help. That was a mistake," she said clearly. "It put strains on our marriage that we never recovered from. So when I remarried and we had Wyatt, we hired a night nurse. Yes, it was expensive, but it was worth every dollar." She cocked her head, with her very chic haircut showing the perfection of the style as her long bob swayed for a moment. If Helena was sincerely suggesting that Avery could afford someone to come to her house and watch the baby all night, she'd obviously forgotten the correct number of digits in her salary.

⌒

That night, Avery lay in her bed, worrying about her job. She'd been at *Ad Infinitum* since she'd gotten her MFA, and had relished each day—some more than others, of course. But she'd always acknowledged how lucky she was. AI was run by a nonprofit that had been set up by a very successful engineer who'd also been a novelist. It had always been a subscription-based magazine, now one of the very few left in America. Because they didn't have a corporate overlord, nor did they have to turn a profit, they'd always had the ability to set their own path.

Helena had hired Avery, and they were, in many ways, close. But Helena always put the magazine first, as she should have. She was a writer herself, and a good one at that, but she was an even better editor-in-chief, able to keep one eye on the budget, while fostering top-quality fiction, poetry, and long-form nonfiction, along with a bit of investigative journalism.

Every department had to pull its own weight in every way. No slacking-off, no sub-par content, no frivolous spending. Even though Avery hated to admit it, she'd been slacking-off, and had been for months. She wasn't scouting venues, she wasn't reading every publication to find new talent, and she wasn't helping out with copyediting when they were under deadline. In short, Helena had every right to call her out. But what could she do to get back to normal?

The baby started to fuss, and she got up to feed her, doing it mechanically this time, hoping she ate quickly. They were going to have to find a new roommate, or they were going to have to find a *much* cheaper apartment. But that would undoubtedly mean lucking out on a studio in a distant neighborhood. She was certain the only reason things had been as smooth as they had been so far was because daycare was on the way to her office, a mere thirty minute walk after dropping Lisbet off. If she had to move, that would change—for the worse.

CHAPTER FIVE

THE CROWD WAS BIG AND boisterous for Kaaterskill Brewery's Friday Night Flights. Since the early August evening was warm and dry, they'd set the band up outside under some hastily strung lights, which turned out to be kind of charming.

Casey stood near the entry to the Greenhouse Pub and watched the crowd, relishing being outdoors on such a perfect night. She'd have to spend a good amount of time inside later, but she was delaying that as long as possible. Outside was almost always better than inside—in August, at least.

She was about to go get a couple of tacos from the food truck when she spotted Ken Nichols carrying Lisbet through the crowd. With her excitement building, Casey threaded her way over to him, hoping she could convince him to hand the baby over for a while.

"Hi, there," she said, moving around so she could see Lisbet's face. "My God! She's like a whole new person!"

He laughed, nodding. "It's been two weeks since I've seen her, and I'm not sure I would have recognized her."

"You're not alone, are you?"

"Oh, no. Kathy's getting me a beer, and Avery's looking for a bathroom. Business as usual."

"You might not know this," she said, lowering her voice, "but I've been trained on how to attach and remove that snuggly carrier." She waggled her eyebrows, trying to look like she was telling him a very interesting secret. "Any chance I could carry her around? I'd love to introduce Lisbet to my friends."

He agreed a little faster than he probably should have. "Great! I shouldn't be dripping hot sauce on her head, and God knows I'm going to eat a few tacos. My mouth's already watering, and all I've done is smell them."

"Let's do it," Casey said, already reaching around to unclip the strap that went around his waist. The baby was wide awake, looking around curiously as Casey helped slip the straps from Ken's shoulders. "Got her," she said, holding Lisbet securely while Ken tugged the carrier away. Casey held her up in the air, letting her little legs dangle. "I love Friday Night Flights," she said, unable to suppress what she was sure was a giddy grin, "but Lisbet just took this joint from an eight to a ten." She put Lisbet to her shoulder, careful to support the back of her head, even though she thought her neck muscles were strong enough at this point. "Has she eaten?"

"She's good to go." He waved to someone, then added, "And so am I. Beer delivery."

Kathy approached and handed him a glass, with Casey noting she'd chosen a soda for herself. "Hi, there," Kathy said. "We were hoping you'd be around."

"Almost always," Casey said. "I talked Ken into handing Lisbet over, so I thought I'd take her around and introduce her to everyone. Is that cool?"

"Everyone?" Kathy laughed. "There must be two hundred people here, Casey."

"Well, just my friends. I won't be gone long."

"Take your time." She scanned the crowd, and spoke quietly. "Avery's had a rough couple of weeks. I think she could use a baby vacation." She patted Lisbet's adorable head. "Don't rush back."

"Sure? You might regret saying that…"

"Avery fed her on the ride up, so she won't need to eat for three or four hours. As you've learned, you'll know when she's hungry."

Ken's eyes widened. "It's been a while since I've been around a baby, but I sure don't remember Avery crying like this one does. It doesn't seem physically possible."

Casey held the baby in her arms and leaned her back so she could speak right into her face. "This little pumpkin has very well-developed lungs. She's a child prodigy."

"She's a human fire alarm," Ken said, reaching over to tickle under her chin.

One of the young brewery workers passed by and Casey called out to him. "Hey, Jackson, do me a favor?"

"Sure," he said, sticking his hands into his pockets as he waited for instruction.

"Look after these nice people, whose baby I just stole, and make sure they have a table and stools. There's a few extra in the third greenhouse if you can't find any. Just wheel one of the spools over to wherever they want to sit." She clapped him on the shoulder. "And go to the side door of the food truck and get them some tacos. Got it?"

"No!" Kathy said. "We can buy our own food, Casey. You don't need to spoil us like that."

Jackson acted like he hadn't heard Kathy's comment. "Got it. Tacos, table, stools."

"Three stool," she said. "There's another adult wandering around, and she probably needs one the most."

⌐

Avery had very clearly realized how much she'd needed a break, but it wasn't until she was with her parents, without her baby, that the relief began to flood through her.

As a writer, she often stopped to assess how she felt, trying, in her mind, to put words to feelings and experiences that would be lost if she didn't mark them in some way. She'd spent less time on this lifelong habit since Lisbet had been born, and she acknowledged how she'd lost some of her usual way of making a place for herself in the world.

She didn't have a single regret about how and when she'd given birth, but it was insane to act like every day was filled with joy. There were, thankfully, moments of joy that usually struck when she least expected them. But some days had just a few. It was already dinner time, and this moment was the first truly pleasurable one she'd had all day.

Lisbet hadn't slept well, and neither had Avery, mostly because of the heat. But sometime during the night Con Ed had shown up to dig a hole in the street that, when she'd checked in the morning, had to have been fifteen feet square, extending down into the earth to where only blackness revealed itself. Having jackhammers rattling your brain for a couple of hours wasn't the best way to start your day, and her nerves were still on edge. The only fun part of the experience had been when most of the lights in the neighboring apartments flicked on, windows were thrown open, and curses rained down on the workers like a summer squall. She hadn't joined in on that, of course. If her power had gone out, she'd want someone to get to the root of the problem, even if it disturbed a lot of people. But she often took pleasure in witnessing New Yorkers vent their spleens. It was probably good for the soul.

She'd had trouble getting any work done in the few hours she'd had available, since they'd had to leave for the train at ten to make sure they caught the eleven thirty. Leaving that early was kind of nuts, but her round trip ticket was *only* a hundred and thirty dollars if they went off-peak.

They'd gotten caught in a brief shower on the way to the subway, and her wet clothing had her shivering in the frosty-cold subway car all the way to Penn Station. She'd had to read the same two books to Lisbet for over two hours, since she'd tried to limit the load she had to carry. But when your baby was wide awake on a long train ride, you had to do whatever you could to entertain her. All in all, it had been a long, expensive slog. But she was home now, with people who loved both her and Lisbet. People who seemed so much calmer, and…saner. They were a little less colorful, admittedly, but sanity had its benefits when it came to protecting a small child whom you would die for without a second thought.

Avery knew that being tethered to your baby was pretty hard-wired, but having a break from Lisbet felt so damn good she knew she should have been wracked with guilt. But she wasn't. She was relishing the chance to emerge from her baby cocoon and actually look around.

"Except for the heat, I don't think I've noticed it was summer," she said when she approached her father, who was sitting alone at a table nursing a beer.

"It's been a long spring, and summer's only been in gear for a week or two. At least up here. I've been looking at the weather app on my phone every day to see the temperature in Brooklyn," he admitted. "It's been much warmer there."

"Ooo," she purred, tucking both arms around his waist and leaning into him. "You love us."

"You know I do," he said, with his cheeks coloring. He was a very connected father, and was clearly enjoying being a grandfather, but he'd never been comfortable showing much emotion.

Her mom came up behind them and wrapped them both in a quick hug. "Two of my favorite people," she said. "I wonder if we'll ever get the third back?"

Seeing her mom without the baby hit Avery like a punch. "Where's Lisbet?"

"Casey's here," her mother said. "She swooped Lisbet away the minute she saw your father carrying her."

She patted the flesh over her heart. "When will I stop overreacting every time she's out of my sight?"

"Years," her mother said. "Years and years."

"Well, I'm glad Lisbet's with someone who gets such a charge out of being with her. I assume Lisbet's already the belle of the brewery."

⌒

They ate their tacos, had a long, uninterrupted conversation, and listened to a very talented reggae group. Then, on the advice of a little boy, Avery went to the back of the greenhouse, where they'd built a fire in a pit, offering free s'mores to everyone who wanted to craft their own. She made four, gobbling down two when her father prudently only had one. She couldn't predict what would happen if a bar in Brooklyn offered not only free food, but easy access to fire, not to mention pointed metal rods, but she was certain at least one ambulance would be called. It truly wasn't that people in Brooklyn were less civilized, but if only one percent of the population were troublemakers, that meant twenty-five thousand people needed to be closely supervised, and there were only so many cops.

She'd caught brief sightings of Casey throughout the night, confirming with a thumb's up every time Casey offered the same gesture. Lisbet seemed as happy as a clam, turning her little head around to respond to all of the adulation she was receiving.

They'd been at the brewery for at least three hours, and she knew her baby vacation was nearing an end. "My breasts are ready to go," she said quietly. "Expect to hear wailing soon."

"I'll go find Casey so we can get going," her dad said. "You'll need some privacy, right?"

"Actually, I'd rather feed her here. Then she'll be sound asleep when we get home." She put her hand on her dad's and patted it. "Don't worry. I've nursed her on the subway. Whatever privacy standards I was used to are in the distant past." She looked up, able to hear the first grumbling from her very vocal baby. "Here she comes now." Looking up, she met Casey's eyes. "Good call. You got her at the early warning stage."

Casey looked a little sheepish. "She started nuzzling against me, and I don't think it was from affection."

They did the handoff, with Avery holding Lisbet up to eye-level for a moment, just to let her get her bearings. Then she draped a light blanket over her shoulder and started to adjust her clothing. Lisbet didn't like to nurse under a blanket, but she didn't actively fight it if she was hungry enough. While Avery definitely felt she had the right to nurse her whenever and wherever, sometimes it was easier to cover up. As soon as she had her in her preferred position, Avery was able to resume the conversation, but Casey was studiously looking everywhere else. That wasn't uncommon, even for women.

"Hey," Avery said. "I want to thank you for giving me a break. Even when my mom or dad is holding her, I'm still on high-alert. Not being able to see her let me stand down for a while. Much appreciated."

"We had a blast. I introduced her to at least twenty-five people. She's the belle of the brewery."

"That's exactly what I predicted she'd be," Avery said, laughing. "My six month old is the belle of the brewery, and I can't have a single beer."

"Why can't you?" Casey asked, looking at the top of her head.

"Beer is one of the many things I gave up when I was pregnant. I've been able to reintroduce a lot of things, but alcohol's strictly off the table. I miss it on a warm summer night."

"Oh, have a beer," her mom said. "One won't hurt you."

"Nice!" Avery laughed. "Should I smoke a little crack?"

"Is it the alcohol you're worried about?" Casey asked. "Or did you develop some allergy…"

"It's the alcohol," Avery said, shifting her gaze from her mom to Casey. "Have you two never heard about fetal alcohol syndrome?"

"Unless things have changed, Lisbet's not a fetus," Casey said, looking very professorial as she spoke. "A glass of our lager is four point eight percent alcohol. You weigh…what? A hundred and twenty?"

"I used to," she said, looking down at the baby. "I'm around one forty now."

"Even better. I could do the math if I had a calculator, but the amount of alcohol in your blood after one beer would be insignificant."

"So I could pump and dump?" She tried not to look as interested in the proposition as she really was. The thought of a drink to ease the stress of her week was a powerful lure.

"You wouldn't have to dump. The alcohol will dissipate significantly within two hours, and it would be undetectable within four." She smiled. "A lot of moms want to have a beer, so I've memorized the facts."

"So since she's eating now… I could feed her again at midnight?"

"It takes thirty to ninety minutes for the alcohol to reach your bloodstream, so, even though it might not look very good, the best time to have a drink is when you start nursing." She smiled, looking absolutely adorable when she revealed those white, straight teeth. "One of my chemistry teachers had a baby, and she knew the math cold."

"I'm more than willing to believe you. We've already driven Lisbet around without her car seat, why not slug some booze down?"

Casey patted her shoulder. "How about eight ounces of low alcohol beer?" She gazed at Avery with a sober expression. "The problem with drinking isn't so much the alcohol getting into the baby's blood. It's caring for a baby when you're impaired."

"I'll have plenty of supervision tonight," Avery said. "If a cup of beer hits me like a locomotive, my mom can take over."

"And I will," she said firmly.

As Casey walked away, Avery sighed. "I wish I could afford to hire her to be my au pair. My life would improve by a thousand percent."

"I'm just glad you're smiling," her mom said. "That's the first time you haven't looked stressed out all night."

"I feel like a kid on Halloween, stuffing my face with chocolate. I know I shouldn't be doing it, but I'm thrilled at the prospect of having something I love, but haven't touched in over a year."

Casey returned in a few minutes, leaning over to say, "If you don't want to get any lethal stares, we should probably go somewhere a little more private. Want to follow me?"

"I'd follow you anywhere for that beer," Avery said. "I can already taste it."

"You'd better keep an eye on her," Casey said, turning to her mom and dad. "I feel like I'm giving someone their first hit on a crack pipe."

"Let's move," Avery said, poking her in the back. "That beer's getting warm."

They walked over to the next greenhouse, devoid of plants or people. But it still smelled of earth and something green that had grown there in the recent past. There were low plywood tables set up all around the perimeter, and Casey brushed the dirt off one with her hand before they sat.

"I need to move her to the other side," Avery said, smiling when Casey's gaze flew up to the translucent roof. "You don't have to avert your eyes, you know. I've lost every shred of modesty."

"Mmm. I'm not squeamish about it or anything, but it seems like something that's between you two. I don't want to intrude."

"Can I please have that beer? I know I sound like someone who should be heading for rehab, but I've had the shittiest month I can recall, including when my long-term lover dumped me. I'm desperate for a treat. Especially one that will numb my mind a little."

Casey handed it over and Avery took her first sip. "Are you sure I'm not hurting the baby?" she asked, putting her enjoyment on hold until she vanquished her guilt.

"I'm positive. Alcohol leaves breastmilk at the same rate it leaves your bloodstream. If you stay sober, your milk will be fine."

"Then why did you say I'd get lethal stares?"

Casey laughed. "Haven't you noticed that people like to have really strong opinions without knowing the facts? There's no safe amount of alcohol for pregnant women, so people assume it's the same for nursing women, even though it's not."

"I'm convinced. Ahh, this is truly delicious," she said, closing her eyes as the caramel notes rolled around on her tongue. "Did you make it?"

"I make it all," Casey said, grinning.

"Really? I recall your saying you didn't make the sour beer I had the first time we came here."

"Oh, right. I was the assistant brewmaster when we made that. But that's the only beer we've aged that long. Most of these are fresh, so they were all made by me." She tapped Avery's leg. "Tell me about this terrible month."

She took a big sip of her beer, trying to focus on the pleasure of a well-made ale before she had to think about the past weeks. The vacation was all too short, and she tried to put the events in context. "What part do you want to hear? You've got three choices." She held up her index, middle and ring fingers sequentially. "My boss telling me to shape up or ship out, my roommate dumping me, or the fact that I'm probably going to have to move back into my parents' house to die a bitter old woman who no one can stand to be around."

"Mmm." Casey's mouth quirked up in a cute grin. "I'm going to guess that number three came about because of number two, so start there."

"Good call." She took another sip, then listened for Lisbet's usual "My hunger isn't going to kill me now" sounds. She was still snarfing away, so Avery had a minute before she had to burp her. "Lisbet's an amazingly calm baby. Honestly, if I'd had to design my first child, this little one is exactly what I would have envisioned." She tenderly patted the baby's back, fully realizing how lucky she'd been.

"No argument. I've been around more than my share, and she's the best I've seen."

"Right. But she's a human being, and she only has one way to let me know she's unhappy."

"I'm going to guess again and say that she has to cry."

"Right you are," Avery said, poking her in the shoulder. "Lisbet unexpectedly had a tooth begin to erupt in the middle of the night. My roommate, who was the soul of patience, hates to be woken up. She got up in a huff and made me pay for an Uber so she could go sleep on a friend's sofa. Freya apologized that afternoon, but she added that she was beating a hasty retreat."

"Because of one night?"

"No. She's been bothered since the beginning, but she's been thinking we were almost through with the worst of it. She called her sister, who's a pediatrician, and she told her teething might be rough, too."

"Ahh. So she's been angry, but hasn't said anything."

"Correct. She came back the next day and picked up her summer clothes, so she's clearly serious."

"What are you going to do? Can you afford the apartment alone?"

"No way. I've spent the last two weeks responding to inquiries to the Craigslist ad I put in." After taking another sip, she closed her eyes, relishing the taste once more.

"Um...no luck?"

"You'd be surprised at how few people want to share an overpriced apartment with an infant. The best offer I got was $750, plus the woman wanted the bedroom."

"Is that...bad?"

"Freya pays $1750, so I'd have to chip in an extra thousand, which I don't have. Plus, Lisbet and I would be sleeping in the open dining room. Does that sound good to you?"

"I'm beginning to see why you're considering living in your old bedroom," Casey said, looking very sober. "But how could you do your job up here?"

Trying to compose herself, Avery removed Lisbet from her breast, and shifted so she could cover herself without making Casey uncomfortable. Then she put an already drowsy baby to her shoulder and patted her firmly. Lisbet was usually a very good burper, and she let out a big one, strong enough to make Casey laugh. "That ought to do it," Avery said.

"Maybe she's got more hiding in that little body." Casey was awful at hiding her desires, so Avery turned the baby around and offered her up. "Give it a try."

"Really?" Her eyes lit up at the prospect, which was kind of hilarious.

"Sure. Let me put this thin blanket on your shoulder in case she spits up."

"I don't care," she said, reaching for her. As soon as she cradled her in her arms, Avery was able to see Lisbet from another angle. She looked so small when Casey held her, even though she'd matured so remarkably in her six months on earth. She was still a newly-hatched human who was so utterly dependent it was often absolutely terrifying.

Lisbet straightened up her back and turned her head a little. "I think she's trying to figure out who you are," Avery said. "I assume she knows she's been with you before, but it's really hard to know what she thinks, you know?"

Casey supported the baby's head in her hand and leaned her back so Lisbet could see her face. "I'm your friend, Casey," she said, speaking slowly and softly. "You're going to have lots and lots of friends, 'cause you're awesome, but I think I'm your first non-related friend. Kind of neat, huh?"

Avery didn't have the heart to tell her that Lisbet spent two days a week with five other infants who she probably considered part of her pack. But Casey was giving Lisbet such a tender look that she couldn't help but put her hand on her arm and grip it gently. "She'll be lucky to have friends like you."

Casey met Avery's eyes for a moment, looking like she was going to say something, then she turned away and focused on the baby again. "Do you want to see if you can burp a little more? I bet you can." She put her to her shoulder again and patted her firmly. Her hands were large, capable-looking, with long, tapered fingers. They were the kind of hands you'd trust with both your baby and your engine. Gentle, yet sure and strong.

"Um, I couldn't help but notice you didn't answer my question," Casey said. "If you don't want to talk about your job that's fine, but if you do…"

"I'd love to talk. Actually, I'm desperate to talk about everything that happened in the last couple of weeks." She put her hand on Lisbet and tickled the back of her neck. "But I should probably get her home. I've been trying to put her down by seven or eight, and it's already ten."

"Do you go to bed that early?"

"No," she said, laughing a little. "A woman's work is never done. Once she's down, I try to catch up on everything I didn't finish during the day. Takes hours."

"So we haven't hit your bedtime yet, right?"

"We definitely haven't hit mine."

"Then why not send her home with your parents? We can hang out for a while, then I'll run you home."

"But you don't live in Hudson. You'd have to go out of your way to take me home."

She stood, continuing to pat the baby as she started to walk. "Since you didn't say 'I don't want to,' I'm going to take that as a 'yes.' So kiss your little girl goodnight and send her on home. You're going to stay up with the big kids."

By the time Lisbet was on her way home, and they'd walked back outside to the makeshift stage, the crowd had thinned. Casey counted thirty people, all gathered around the band, who still seemed fresh and energetic.

"Want to walk around the fields? Or would you rather grab a table in the pub? I don't think I'll be able to hear you if we stay out here. The band's gotten a second wind."

"Let's go inside and sit." She put her hand on Casey's arm and squeezed it. "Don't let me drink another beer, though. I can still taste how delicious it was, but my days of drinking to get a buzz are over."

"Maybe they're just on hold. You can have a buzz when Lisbet's not nursing any more."

"That seems like a long way off, but I suppose it really isn't. I just wish there was a way to breastfeed like once a day," she said, chuckling. "I love the bond we have, and I feel like I'm doing something remarkably important when I'm giving my baby life-sustaining nutrients." She rolled her eyes. "But enough is enough! Six times a day is eating up my time, my energy, my sleep. That's what happened at work, by the way. I actually fell asleep, only to have my boss shake me awake."

"Oh, shit! I think I'd be fired on the spot if I did that, and my bosses are crazy about me."

"Mine likes me a lot," Avery admitted. "But she's got every right to be sick of my act. I chose to have a baby, and because of that choice a lot of my work just isn't getting done. My boss should pay me about half of my normal salary, because that's about how much work I'm doing."

"Jesus, Avery, don't make that offer! She'll take you up on it."

"Oh, I won't. But I've got to figure something out. I guess I have to ask my boss for ideas. She's legitimately the brains in the office."

Casey started to shake her head while Avery was still speaking. "Not a good idea. Much better to offer an option or two yourself. She'll respect you if you come up with a way to get the work done. That's all good bosses want, right? Just get the damn work done."

"But I can't do my job the way I did it before. And I can't do it at all from my childhood bedroom." She put her head in her hands and just held it for a minute, acting like it was too heavy to stay up on its own.

"What part of your job do you like the best?"

She sat up and gazed at Casey for a moment, with her sharp gaze revealing her bright mind. "Acquiring the stories for *Short Shorts*, and producing the podcast. I'm really good at both, by the way."

"Great. What part's giving you trouble?"

"Mmm." She seemed to think for another minute. "Going out and scouting new venues, which I've barely done at all since Lisbet was born. And showing up in the office—awake. Both parts are mandatory, and I'm sucking at both equally badly."

"Is there anyone in the office who could do the scouting thing?"

"Interesting idea," she said slowly. "There's an editorial assistant who's bright, and hard-working, but she's very introverted. I suppose Victoria could do it, but she'd have to push herself."

"Okay. There's one suggestion for your boss. Do a sales pitch to Victoria first, and convince her that she'd raise her standing in the office if she did the scouting."

"She really would," Avery said, looking at Casey like she'd just split the atom. "Helena's worried that she's not assertive enough to ever be able to move up. This could show both of them that Victoria has potential."

"Excellent," she said, starting to feel like they were getting somewhere. "How about going into the office? Why do you need to be there?"

"I work from home a few days a week with no trouble. But we have an editorial meeting on Wednesday that everyone goes to. I even had to go when I was on maternity leave, which I think was illegal to force me to do."

"Is anyone ever out of the office? Like at a conference or something?"

"Um, yeah. But they always call in."

"Does that work?"

"Pretty well," she admitted. "It can be annoying if they're on a cell phone, but if they can call in via video it's fine."

"Another solution," Casey said, proud of her problem-solving capabilities. "You'll figure out how to do video calls from home. All fixed," she said, slapping her hands together. "Look how easy that was. You'll live at home for a while until you figure things out, you'll work from home, and you'll have Lisbet with you every minute."

"But I'd have to go into the city to do *Short Shorts*," she said, looking up at Casey like she fully expected another solution.

"How often?"

"The first Tuesday of every month."

"Then you'll go into the city one day a month. You can even go in early and stop by the office just so they don't forget what you look like. Now we're done," she said, once again clapping her hands together and shaking them out.

"I think that might be a reasonable work-around for the short term," she said slowly. "But I truly don't want to live at home again. I've been gone for years, Casey. If we move in, I know my mom will unconsciously take over, and I can't have that. Lisbet is my responsibility, and I've got to be in charge."

"Then you'll find an apartment around here. But that's stage two," she decided, so certain of herself that Avery seemed carried away by her confidence. "Stage one is making your case with your boss and getting her to sign-off. When's your lease up?"

"Not for another two months, but Freya's willing to pay her half until the lease is up, even though she's sleeping on a friend's sofa."

"She's your real friend, right? Not just a roommate?"

"Up until now we've been good friends. Go on vacation together kind of friends. But I'm afraid our bond might be fraying…"

"Then give her the whole apartment. You move out now and pay your half. She'll be grateful for your thoughtfulness, and that might help get your friendship back in good shape." She held up her hand. "Stage one will last a few weeks to a couple of months. We've got some time to come up with stage two."

"It sounds so easy when you lay it out like that." Some of the worry lines that had creased her forehead started to ease when she smiled. "You're very good at this."

"I'm the brewmaster," she said. "Emphasis on master."

⌒

While Casey made sure everything was buttoned up for the night, Avery sat on a stool, watching the bartenders clean. A woman caught her eye, and her attention was immediately locked in. The woman clearly worked there, but Avery hadn't seen her earlier. She was pretty sexy, with a snug, vibrant pink shirt and even tighter jeans that showed off her very voluptuous body. She was probably in her forties, and had that kind of "I know who I am, and I'm not interested in your opinion," vibe that Avery didn't see nearly often enough.

The woman started to pitch in with the clean-up, but she was also directing everyone else, splitting her attention to do several things at once. Her dark hair and bronzed skin hinted that she was Latina, and when she spoke to one of the guys in rapid-fire Spanish, that confirmed Avery's guess.

Watching her, Avery had an idea for a short story, something that definitely hadn't happened since she'd gotten pregnant. Maybe even earlier than that. She was the kind of writer who needed quiet, a cleared schedule, and nothing on her mind to be able to create, so this shocked the heck out of her. But a story about a super sexy, larger-than-life Latina who ran the show in an almost all white environment really tugged at her creative instinct. She was sure she was smiling like a fool, but getting a creative zing made her whole night. Maybe her week!

Someone turned on some music, and it blared through the speakers attached to the metal hoops that gave the building its structure. The woman started to dance, and she was so free with her body that the other women started to join in. Avery almost got off her stool to get in on the action, but that would have been a little weird, since she was a complete stranger. So she just watched as they threw trash away, and wiped up the tables, swinging their hips and reveling in their bodies.

Just so she didn't forget her kernel of an idea, she surreptitiously woke her phone up and angled it so she could get a couple of photos of the woman. Because of the dim light, they wouldn't be terribly sharp, but that was fine. She just wanted to remind herself of the confident expression the woman bore. She owned the place, even though Avery was pretty sure she was just an employee. Casey was lucky if this woman was one of the brewers. She was a *dynamo*.

An hour later, Casey let her truck idle in Avery's driveway. "I hate to think of you going back to Brooklyn on Sunday," she said, staring straight ahead so she didn't have to see Avery's expression if she thought Casey was being too dramatic. "I have this image of you and Lisbet, surrounded by millions of people, none of them really caring about you."

"That's not true. Well, it's kind of true, but a few people care about us. Freya does, even though she's screwing things up for me right now. And Helena, my boss does, too. Actually, my office is kind of a second home—"

"Co-workers and bosses aren't really your friends, and they're definitely not the same as your relatives." She took a quick look at her face. "Have you been to your boss's house?"

"Well, no, but—"

"If you were sick, and couldn't take care of Lisbet, would you call your boss or a co-worker?"

"If I had too. I mean, it would be weird, but if I had no options…"

"Right. They're people you know. You need people you can *rely* on, Avery. Having a baby is a very big responsibility, and you need support. I bet you have at least ten people in Hudson you'd ask to help out if Lisbet needed them."

"Maybe not ten, but definitely some." She reached over and patted Casey's knee, making her flinch a little. "Surprisingly, I'd add you to my list."

"Yeah, it is a little surprising. I've been swinging by the restaurant six days a week ever since we graduated, but I've never even seen you in town. Kind of weird, huh?"

"Uh-huh. But what's also surprising is that I never knew how kind you were. I had an image of you as a super independent, super confident woman who was only interested in sports. I had no idea you were such a softie."

Casey nodded, tempted to say how she'd seen Avery. But this wasn't the day to tell her she'd thought she was an asshole. "Um, I'm a softie… who's also a jock. So you were half right." She clapped a hand to her knee, surprised to feel how warm her skin was. "Go get some rest. Then go make things happen at work. Will you text me after you do? I'm interested."

"I will. Put your number in my phone," she said, reaching into her pocket to pull it out.

"I'll call myself. Then I'll have yours."

"I should have been able to think of that," Avery said, chuckling. "One day my brain will function again and I'll remember all sorts of things." She reached for the door handle. "But not soon." She let out a tired laugh when she fumbled with the door to open it. "Thanks for everything," Avery added, sliding out to hit the ground with a thump when she missed the rail. "Still alive!" she said, holding her arms up like she'd scored a touchdown.

Casey watched her shuffle into the house, barely lifting her sandals from the sidewalk. The thought of Avery having to wake up in an hour or so to feed the baby made *her* tired, and she'd had eight hours of sleep the night before. She didn't recall a whole lot from the one anthropology course she'd had to take, but one thing had stuck. Humans used to raise babies collectively, and we'd lost an awful lot when we'd decided we could handle just about everything alone.

Casey was at her desk before the sun was fully up on Monday. It was a brew-day, and she had twenty things to take care of before she was lost in the process.

She looked up when Ben sauntered in, dropping two white paper bags on his desk. "Brought breakfast," he said, giving her a grin.

If she'd had any amount of heterosexuality in her, she would have married the guy. Thoughtful, patient, funny, smart, and a great dad. She could have done a lot worse, but he probably preferred a woman who actually *wanted* to have sex with him, not just someone who'd toss him a bone when he did something thoughtful.

"You're a good man," she said, standing up to peek in the bags. "I'll take whatever has cheese on it."

"Both do. I've got sausage, egg, and cheese, and bacon, egg, and cheese. Your choice."

She dug into the bag, tearing it apart. "Three?"

"I got two sausage, egg, and cheese, since I want one of each." He smiled at her. "You always pick the sausage."

"I'm predictable." She sat back down, unwrapped the sandwich, which was still pretty warm, and took a big bite. "Ooo. Delicious. Will you let me buy? I know you went out of your way for this."

"You can catch up on Friday. I've got to leave at two to take Benji to a tournament in Albany. I'll have to be in here by six to get my hours in, and no place will be open. Don't forget," he warned. "You know how I get when I miss breakfast."

"Will the tournament be the whole weekend?"

"Fraid so. Julie's coming, so we're going to make a little vacation out of it."

"Damn, Ben, August is slipping away and you haven't been over for a pool party since June."

"I know," he said, ducking his head down as he took a bite. He hated to be so unavailable, but his kid was obsessed with baseball, so he let him dictate their schedule. "Can't be helped."

"It's all right. This is the last tournament, right?"

"The very last. He starts school in two weeks."

"Ugh. Seems like he just got out."

"Agreed." They finished eating while they both continued to look at their email. Casey was in the middle of answering a request from a brewer in Massachusetts who wanted to visit and taste what they were currently working on, and she almost didn't hear Ben when he spoke.

"How's the baby?"

"Lisbet?"

"Do you have more than one?"

She laughed. "I wouldn't say I have Lisbet, but I'd like to see her more often. That might happen, actually. I think I gave Avery ammunition to convince her boss to let her work from home. That would mean that she could move up here. Cool, huh?"

"Are you interested in her? The mother, that is."

Casey wadded up the paper her sandwich came in and winged it at him. "I'm not interested in Avery's mother!"

"I meant Lisbet's mother. Are you into her? You were out wandering around with her for over an hour the other night."

"Are you checking up on me?" she asked, getting a weird feeling from him.

"Of course not. Valeria was looking for you, but I didn't want to go searching for you if you wanted to be alone."

"Huh." She stepped back to think for a moment. If she'd had time to get to know Avery, and if she planned on staying in Columbia County, things might have been different. The thought of co-parenting Lisbet was pretty awesome to even consider, but Avery was just as much a prize. When she looked at you with those big, blue eyes it was hard to keep on track. She was still the pretty, brainy girl from high school, only now she wasn't hanging out with her jerky friends...

"You still in there?" Ben asked, interrupting her fantasy.

"Yeah, I'm here. I'm..." She sighed. "I'm a sucker for a pretty face. I'd have to take it slow—for sure. But if she's as nice as she seems..." She shrugged, more confused than she normally was about a woman. "I might be able to overlook some youthful jerkiness if I could be sure she'd reformed."

"She hasn't reformed," he said flatly.

"Huh? You don't even know her, Ben. I didn't get a chance to introduce you."

"I know who she is, Casey. And I'm not sure what she was going to do with it, but I caught her smirking at Valeria and taking her picture."

"What in the fuck…?"

"Right. What in the fuck. I was behind her, just walking into the greenhouse. I saw Avery focus her phone on her, then I saw her take a couple of pictures. When I passed by, I saw this smile on her face that only made sense if she was thinking about sharing a picture of a fat woman in tight clothes with her skinny friends."

"No way! I've only spent a few hours with her, but Avery's not the type —"

"Now she's a sweetheart? You told me two weeks ago that you couldn't trust her. What's changed?"

"She seems…nice," she said, feeling an ache in her chest like something had grabbed her heart and squeezed.

"Okay. Who sits in a bar and takes a picture of a big woman shaking her ass to the music? I bet the photo's on the internet right now."

"Oh, fuck," Casey murmured. She made her hands into fists and stacked them one atop the other, then set her chin onto them. "That poor little baby. Her mom's an asshole."

CHAPTER SIX

IT TOOK A COUPLE OF WEEKS to work everything out, but Avery finally convinced Helena that she could contribute like she used to if she was allowed to work from home full-time. On a Wednesday afternoon in late August, after the last all-hands meeting she'd attend in person, Avery loaded up everything she could cram into a rolling suitcase while Freya laboriously carried her own stuff back into the apartment.

Avery was determined to handle the simple move on her own, even though her father had offered to come get her. She knew how much he despised driving in New York City, so she'd decided to put off bringing the bulk of her heavy things until they could come early on a weekend morning. For now, she'd move like her ancestors who'd come in through Ellis Island had—with what she could carry on her back.

Freya kindly carried her suitcase down the three flights of stairs, and as Avery hitched her backpack up a little higher, no doubt looking like she was running away from home, Freya placed a restraining hand on her arm.

"Wait just one minute," she said, then took a look at her phone. "Make that two minutes."

"Why—?"

"I still feel bad about the night I made you pay for a car service for me. I can't stand the thought of you trying to get up to the Smith Street platform with all of this stuff, so I'm paying for your trip to Penn Station."

"Oh, Freya, you don't have to do that," she said, delighted by the offer. "I could pay for a car service if I thought I needed one."

"It's settled," she said, stepping into the street and waving when a mid-size black sedan slowed down and stopped. Freya signaled the driver to get out to help with the luggage, and he did so, albeit reluctantly.

Freya opened the back door, quickly removed the backpack, then took Avery's hand. "I'll lower you in."

Avery smiled up at her and took both hands to support herself as she kind of fell into the backseat. Getting into a low-slung car with a baby strapped to your chest wasn't a snap!

After handing over the backpack, Freya leaned into the car and kissed Lisbet's head. "I'm going to miss both of you. I'm serious about that."

"I'll miss you, too, but I'll be back in two weeks for *Short Shorts*. Maybe we can meet for a meal beforehand."

"That will never happen," Freya said, always the pragmatist. "*Short Shorts* days are too busy. But I'll be there to help."

"Thank you." She smiled up at her. "Without you, I wouldn't have Lisbet. I'm forever in your debt."

"That's…only partially true. But I'd love to stay in your lives. When she's ready to start her Danish lessons…"

"I hope we're back in Brooklyn by then. Maybe we can live together once she's a better roommate."

"You're a very good one," Freya said, her pale blue eyes sober. "I wish I hadn't been so childish about the whole thing, but I am who I am."

"You're just fine. Truly."

"I will see you," she said, closing the door firmly.

Avery hadn't been in an Uber since she'd had the baby, and as the car smoothly accelerated toward Court Street, she realized that had been a wise choice. Having a car to yourself was a luxury she could not afford to get used to.

⌣

Avery woke with golden rays of sunlight caressing her face. She luxuriated in the sensation for a moment, then sat bolt upright. *Eight a.m!* Sliding off the bed to kneel next to Lisbet, she leaned in close to listen to her breathe. What in the hell? She'd gone to sleep at midnight, and if she'd woken up to feed the baby, she'd done so completely unconsciously.

Her breasts were filled with milk, almost rock-hard, so she must not have sleep-walked through a feeding. But Lisbet simply couldn't have slept for eight hours without being fed. She simply couldn't.

There were quiet stirrings coming from the kitchen, so she tugged on two dark T-shirts to avoid the inevitable leaks from showing, and went to investigate.

Her father was pouring himself a bowl of granola, but the coffee machine was empty. "What's going on?" she asked. "This doesn't look like your usual breakfast."

"It's not. But your mom got up twice to feed the baby, and I'm not a big enough jerk to wake her and ask for eggs." He smiled and shrugged. "It was a close call, but I decided to act like an adult."

She flipped on the switch for the coffee maker. "Ahh. That explains it. God knows I'm thankful to get some sleep, but my breasts are about to explode."

He'd been looking at her, but the moment she said that he focused carefully on his cereal. *So squeamish!*

Avery walked past him to reach the proper cabinet. "I find it hard to believe you don't know how to use the coffeemaker, but it's not too late to learn."

He shrugged again, looking less sheepish than he should have. "Your mom always does it. I'm sure I could figure it out," he insisted. "Loading the coffee machine has to be easier than repairing a washing machine."

"Face it, Dad. You're an ace appliance repair technician who can't put ground coffee into a basket." She performed the simple steps, then said, "Voila! Your coffee will be ready in fewer than five minutes."

"Thanks, honey," he said, bending slightly to wrap her in a hug. He used to be a little rougher with her, keeping up the playful way they'd interacted when she was a kid, but since she'd gotten pregnant he treated her like she was a raw egg. "I'm awfully glad to have you home."

"Aww, thanks, Dad. I haven't adjusted to the idea yet, but I'm very, very thankful that you've opened your home to us."

"It's your home, too," he said, scowling. "It always will be."

"It's *your* home," she said, returning to a long-standing disagreement. "I'm just…vacationing here until I can figure out a long-term solution."

"So headstrong," he grumbled. "Just like your mother."

"And my daughter," she said, hearing Lisbet stir. "You're surrounded by strong-willed women, but at least two thirds of us can make coffee."

⌒

Lisbet sat in the used, cut-rate infant seat Avery had bought on E-Bay, which now rested in the center of the kitchen table. Her onesie was clean, what little hair she had was lying down, and her dark blue eyes were alert as her grandmother played with her bare feet, teasing her, while Lisbet tried to figure out the game.

"Toast?" Avery asked.

"Love some. I have apple butter in the fridge. Will you get it out?"

"Happy to." She placed the spread on the table, bending to kiss her mother's cheek when she did. "I feel like a new woman. Eight hours of sleep felt like twelve."

"Well, I knew you'd argue, so I didn't tell you my plans. But when I saw those bottles of breast milk in the fridge, I made up my mind. We're going to do that for a week or two, so don't even think of complaining."

"Complain?" She laughed as she went to the toaster when the bread popped up. "I'd build a shrine to you if we were… Who does that? Catholics?"

"Probably. They're a little showy."

"Right. Well, I'm only going to argue if it's too hard for you. I know you're not used to getting up once or twice a night."

"I can manage. I'll take a nap in the afternoon."

"Super." Avery sat down and joined in the game, confusing the heck out of Lisbet, who wasn't sure who was playing with her feet, or why for that matter.

"So…" her mom said, stirring a little extra sugar into her coffee. "You're going to need a lot of things, but I know you'll fight buying duplicates."

"We can improvise until we go to Brooklyn to pick everything up. Lisbet has been sleeping in her Moses basket every time we come up. She doesn't seem to mind lying on the floor."

"You brought almost nothing with you!"

"I have a pair of jeans, a pair of shorts, underwear, and sandals for myself. Since I have two dresser-drawers full of old T-shirts, I'm set. And I brought everything that Lisbet has that's roomy, which isn't much since she's in the middle of a growth spurt. Speaking of which, I have to find her a new pediatrician."

"Really?" Her mom stared at her like she'd said something truly outrageous. "After how hard you worked to find the one you chose?"

Avery laughed. "Back then I was laboring under the delusion that every single choice I made was the difference between a perfect baby and one who'd be scarred forever." She gripped Lisbet's little foot and gave it a tug. "I've gotten slightly more realistic."

⌣

Avery sat under an umbrella on the back deck, nursing Lisbet, who seemed to like dining al fresco. The baby was fully clothed, of course, and wore a floppy hat. Avery hadn't been teasing earlier when she'd said she'd gotten more relaxed about Lisbet. But one area she wasn't going to ever be chill about was sunburn. Lisbet's skin was so fair she was afraid she'd burn from an incandescent light. While there were many, many dangerous things Avery couldn't protect her from, she'd vowed that she'd focus on the things she could control.

Her mom came out, bearing adult food.

"Now this is the way every woman should be able to parent," Avery said. "Massive help with nighttime feedings, food delivery, and plenty of emotional support. I was crazy to think I could make it on my own in Brooklyn. Just one day and I've gotten more done than I'd managed there in three."

"Once Lisbet's in kindergarten, you can think about finding your own place. Until then, we'll be a team."

"Kindergarten?" Avery stared at her. "I'm going to start looking for an apartment in Hudson this week, Mom. I need my own place."

"Avery," she said, scowling. "Don't be so hard-headed. You were a wreck in Brooklyn. Why would changing nothing but a zip code make any difference?"

"I'll be changing a heck of a lot more than a zip code. If your offer still holds, I thought I'd bring Lisbet over here after I feed her in the morning, then pick her up at the end of my work day."

"But you still wouldn't be sleeping through the night, honey. You just told me how much better you feel."

"I do. I truly do. But I can't impose on you like that. Being able to work from home is huge. I bet only ten percent of women have that option, yet the other ninety percent are doing fine. They're tired, but they're fine. We just need to work out a schedule."

"Well, I would argue more, but you're not going to find a nice apartment around here. Not one you can afford, that is. So go ahead and look. Until you find your cozy new home, I'm feeding my granddaughter during the night." She picked up half of a tuna sandwich and held it up to Avery's mouth. "I can't understand why you think you wouldn't be independent if you lived here. Take a big bite…"

Avery had notified Casey of her success in getting permission to work from home, and she'd texted her the day she'd move back to Hudson. But they hadn't communicated since. That's why it surprised her to receive a text from her on Thursday afternoon, saying she had four hours free, and wanted to see if Lisbet could come out to play.

Avery stared at the text for a long time, mired in indecision. While she wanted to pay Casey back for all of her kindnesses, letting her just take the baby, even for an hour, filled her with dread. Admittedly, there wasn't a big difference between sleeping in Casey's bed while Lisbet floated around in her pool, and letting her have unsupervised access, trusting Lisbet with her for hours seemed like a leap she wasn't ready for. She wasn't even comfortable letting her dad be entirely in charge, and he was genetically related.

She'd been working in the living room, nearly at the mental capacity she'd been able to rely on for her entire working career. It had felt so good to look at a piece of fiction and be able to spot its strengths and weaknesses with just one thorough read-through that she was nearly clicking her heels when she went outside to find her mom weeding the garden, with Lisbet safely protected by an umbrella attached to her infant chair.

"Mmm. I can't wait for those eggplant to be ready," Avery said. "A friend of mine slices them thick, scores them, then puts olive oil and salt and pepper on them. A little time on the barbecue and they're fantastic."

"You know people with a barbecue?"

"Of course not. But they have grills in the park."

"Permanent ones? With grates?"

"Uh-huh." She sat down next to the baby, pleased to find her alert and content. "You have to get on your knees to use them, since they're so low to the ground, but they work."

"Low enough so every dog that goes by can lick them or pee on them?"

"Well, now, you've taken something beautiful and ruined it forever. Happy?" Avery grasped Lisbet's foot and tickled it until she looked up at her and smiled. "Your grandmother can't look at the bright side of life, Sweet Pea."

"Your grandmother doesn't like barbecued dog pee," she said, visibly shivering. "Are you taking your afternoon coffee break? You've been at it since lunch."

"Have to keep my nose to the grindstone. We're behind because of my dragging my feet on some things. If I'm going to make Helena see what a good idea my working from home is, the only way to do that is to edit my butt off."

"How did your phone call go? Lisbet could hear your voice when you were talking. She kept staring down the hallway, like she knew you were there, but I could tell she was confused."

"It went fine, thanks." She tapped on the baby's chubby leg and added, "I'd think Lisbet's confused every minute of the day. Imagine having everything that happens be a new experience." She looked up at her mom. "Question. Would you trust Casey to take her for a few hours?"

Her mom looked up sharply. "Take her where, honey?"

"I don't know. She just texted to say she had four hours free and wanted a playdate."

"A playdate? Is that the word she used?"

"Um, I think so…" She took out her phone and looked at the message. "She asked if Lisbet could come out and play."

Her mom reached over and grasped the phone, taking a long look. "Well, I've been thinking she might secretly be interested in you, but if she is, she's working a very long con."

"You've got to read fewer detective novels," Avery said, taking her phone back. "I'm a little worried about letting Lisbet out of my control. Am I being silly?"

"Hmm." She turned and sat on her haunches, concentrating on the tiny weeds that had the nerve to poke their heads above the soil. "Is she a good driver?"

"Excellent. Beyond careful."

"We know she doesn't drink much…"

"Right. And if she does drugs, she's very, very good at hiding it."

"Good point. If she abuses drugs, she's a pro."

"Very reassuring."

"I know plenty of her family members, so we'd have leads to go on if she took off…"

"I already worked through the international kidnapping scenario. Lisbet doesn't have her passport yet, so it'd be tough to get her across the border."

"Mmm." She stood and brushed off the knees of her khaki green gardening pants. "Here's the truth, honey. Some bad things will happen to Lisbet, no matter how careful you are. Some of those bad things will happen when she's with someone else. But you've got to let go at some point, so it might be good to start now."

"What bad things happened to me?"

"Oh, god," she said, lifting her gaze to the sky as she thought. "I've got several, but the worst was when your dad left you in the car when he took you shopping. Luckily for all of us, it was early winter." She laughed briefly. "I can't begin to tell you how shook he was. Even though he knew I'd never trust him again, he had to tell me he'd done it just to let go of some of his guilt."

"He could have killed me!"

"Um, that's the point of the story, honey. It's easy to do something horribly wrong because you're tired or stressed. Casey's neither of those things, so she's probably a safer bet than you are right now."

"Oh, I forgot! I read this tip the other day, and I'm going to implement it as soon as I find a huge stuffed animal."

"Pardon?"

"It's genius," Avery said. "You buy a massive toy and put it in the passenger seat when you've got your baby in the back. Then, when you take the baby out, you put the stuffed animal in the back seat. So every time you get out of your car and see the giraffe or the panda or whatever in the front, you know your baby's in the back."

Her mom removed her gardening gloves, then headed for the back door. "I'll be back before Casey gets here. Don't let her take that baby unless she's accompanied by a huge, dirty stuffed animal."

"Dirty?"

"I'm not buying new, honey. I'm sure whatever I can find at the thrift shop will be a filthy mess, but no one's going to forget about my precious granddaughter—including me!"

An hour later, Avery and her mom stood in the driveway, waving goodbye to one brewmaster, one baby, and a giant, dirty, one-eyed teddy bear.

"I wasn't in the room when Casey said where they were going. Did she give you an itinerary?"

Avery smiled at her. "We have the same kind of phone. I got her permission to track her."

"Well, that must not have been awkward. 'Sure. You can take my baby for a drive. Just let me attach this shock collar...'"

"Don't care. I'd rather sound both suspicious and paranoid than spend the whole time worrying."

⌒

At five o'clock, Casey put the car seat carrier on her bed, making sure it was right in the middle in case Lisbet developed super-strength in the next few minutes and was able to hurl herself and the heavy thing into the air.

The baby was sound asleep, which was kind of a drag, but they'd spent about an hour playing in the grass under the shade of the tall, thin oaks and maples that hugged the yard.

She sorted through her dresser, finding her softball uniform neatly folded away. No matter where she kept her dirty laundry, her mother found it, washed it, and replaced it right where it belonged. It was sometimes annoying, but you could hardly complain about someone doing you a kindness—even if it meant she was rooting around in your room whenever she wanted.

She'd just started to cinch the web belt tight on her pants when there was a soft knock on the door. Before she could respond, it opened.

"Oh, look. The stork brought a baby."

Since Casey and Lisbet had been in the back yard, and the big greenhouse-style window over the sink had a good view of the whole area, she was sure her mom had seen them some time earlier. But they'd all developed a weird, unspoken agreement to act like they never knew who was in the house. Given that Casey always parked in the driveway, and there were security cameras there and at every entrance, all her mom had to do was look on her tablet computer to see the feed from every camera, all of which had night-vision capabilities, to know exactly what car was where. But acting like they were all kind of invisible seemed to work for them.

"Yep," Casey said. "I looked up and a great big stork was swooping in with a baby."

"What are you two up to?"

"Not much. We're going to go get a hot dog, then I'll drop her off before I go to my softball game."

"Hello, Elizabeth," her mom said, showing mild interest in the sleeping child.

"It's Lisbet."

"Lisbet? Really? That's the whole thing? What kind of name is that?"

"I have no idea, but it sounds like a variation on Elizabeth. I'll ask at some point."

"Why do you have her?"

"Because I asked if I could watch her. Avery's living with her parents now, so the baby's going to be much more available." She sat down next to the sleeping child and tenderly stroked her leg. "I'm stoked."

"You left the house before the sun rose this morning, you're playing softball tonight, and you *volunteered* to watch an infant in between."

"Exactly right," she said, gazing up at her mother with a blank expression. She usually cut the interrogations short if you didn't engage her much.

"You know, people will pay you to babysit. The least you can get out of the deal is a little spare cash."

"Thanks for the tip. I'll ask for money when I drop her off." She stood and grasped the handle of the car seat. "We're off. I don't want to be late for batting practice."

"Batting practice," her mother grumbled, her words just reaching Casey as the big doors swung open. "A woman your age still playing softball."

"See you tomorrow, Mom," she said as she flinched when she opened the back door of her truck to come face-to-face with a brown bear as big as she was, missing its right eye. The animal was a good idea, but it was going to take some getting used to.

⸺

Once Lisbet was secure in the backseat, Casey pulled out her phone and texted.

I'm going to stop for dinner, then I'll return your bundle of joy by six so I can get to my softball game. Good?

A return message appeared immediately.

Where's your game?

Ghent's rec area

Want me to meet you there? That'll give you more time to eat

Don't mind?

Not a bit. I'll be there by 6:15

Want a chili dog from Joe's?

YES! No onions, though. Lisbet doesn't like them. A chocolate malt wouldn't be refused

Casey laughed to herself, then adjusted her mirror so she could see the baby. "Your mommy's never going to lose that baby weight by eating chili dogs and malts. But don't you dare tell her I said that."

⸺

Avery parked on the street close to the neatly tended softball fields and cut across the grass. The baby had been out of her sight for barely three hours, but there was a lightness to her step that she almost felt guilty for. When you were walking alone, carrying only your wallet and keys in your pockets, you definitely felt lighter than you did when you were dragging a child in a car seat, along with a diaper bag. All of that stuff weighed on you, physically and emotionally.

Casey had parked on the other side of the park, and Avery spied her crossing the expanse of grass, all weighted down by her burdens. Avery's breasts were nearly engorged with milk, but she was truly hoping Lisbet was still asleep. Cold chili dogs kind of sucked.

She still wasn't in running shape, not that she ever had been, but she picked up the pace and met Casey in the outfield. "I'm so glad to see you," she said, reaching out to grab the white paper bag. "Oh. You and Lisbet, too," she said, laughing evilly.

"Since you're too rude to ask, I'll just tell you that Lisbet mostly slept in her car seat, in my room, but we both enjoyed ourselves."

"Ooo. She got to see her new best friend's room again," Avery said. "Did you talk about the girls or boys you have crushes on?" She reached over and touched Lisbet's head. "I'm going to try not to impose mandatory heterosexuality on her."

"Good luck with that," Casey said. "Let's get over to the bench so we can eat." She checked her watch. "I hope my digestive system works fast."

There were six grey-clad people on one side of the field, with four people in black uniforms on the other. By the time they reached Casey's people, she was smiling and clapping everyone on the back, acting like the life of the party. It took until just then for Avery to see the "Kaaterskill Brewery" logo on their backs.

"Where'd you get the baby?" a tall guy asked.

The kid who'd found a table and fetched food for her family at the brewery spoke up. She thought his name was Jackson, but she couldn't swear on it. "It's Avery's. How's it going?" he asked, waving. "Casey told me you were moving back."

"Just yesterday. I didn't know you all played softball together."

"Softball in the summer," Casey said. "Bowling or hockey in the winter."

"Hockey? Ice hockey?"

"Yup," Casey said. "Emanuel and I are the only two from this group who play. You should come watch sometime. It's exactly like the NHL, but in super slow motion."

"I've never watched the NHL in any motion, but I'm sure we'll be looking for fun once winter comes. Count us in."

"Any chance of eating?" Casey asked. "I'm about to faint."

Avery removed one dog and presented it, then fumbled in the bag for her own. The second her hand hit the warmth, Lisbet jerked, then her little eyes opened wide and she let out a wail that would have been funny if Avery hadn't been an indispensable participant in stopping the madness.

~

Since Avery didn't have anything she had to do, and she needed a break from sitting in the house, they stayed for the entire game. Actually, it was a good way to create just enough noise to keep Lisbet awake, which was her new goal, post-feeding. Keeping her up for a while might get her to sleep for longer periods at night.

The baby clearly didn't know what was going on, but the field was brightly lit, and there were occasional cheers or shouted instructions to a fielder. That was plenty of noise to prevent her from dozing.

The teams were mixed sex, but Casey was the only woman on hers. They were playing a team sponsored by the Toyota dealer in Ghent, and they had a pair of women on their team, although they only used them as pinch-runners late in the game.

Casey, on the other hand, was a starter, and a good one to boot. In her uniform, she owned some of the dyke pride she'd had as a high school kid, when she used to look like she could kick ass and take names. That was kind of cool, and Avery watched her avidly, seeing how she crisply threw the ball around when they warmed up between innings, with her cap pulled down low to protect her eyes from the lights.

She really had a gun, with Avery able to hear the snap of the ball as it hit the fielder's glove when she fired it from first to third. Since her dad was an avid Yankees fan, Avery had often been in the room when games were on. She'd never paid any attention, but she'd picked up a lot of the lingo inadvertently. Watching tonight, she had to admit she would have paid closer attention if even one of the Yankees had looked like Casey.

Avery had never felt a strong draw for butch women, but there was a chance she was changing her tune, given that she hadn't taken her eyes off Casey's butt the whole time. It looked awfully nice, even in those thick polyester uniforms.

She looked kind of nonchalant between pitches, standing near first base and smacking her hand into her glove or adjusting her hat. But just before the pitcher threw the ball, she slid into a deep crouch, with her hands low to the ground, ready to hoover up any ground ball that came near.

Casey actually didn't get the chance to show her fielding skills, merely snagging balls thrown by the second baseman or shortstop. But when it was her side's turn to bat, she showed she really knew how to play the game.

There was one out and a man on second the first time she batted, and she approached the plate like she was getting on a bus. Cool and collected. In no hurry at all. She had a cute stance, standing tall and waggling the bat a little as she waited for the first pitch. Unlike the other players, she bit right away, smacking the ball over the shortstop's head and clapping her hands together to congratulate herself when she rounded first and danced around on the base path for a moment before going back to tag up. She'd knocked in a run, and looked really pleased for a second or two. Then she snapped to attention and watched the pitcher intently until her team made two more outs, never advancing her.

The game got a little out of hand for a while, with both pitchers losing control and getting wild, but Casey was able to knock in another RBI late in the game, and her team never looked back. They won twelve to nine, and since Casey had produced four of the runs, Avery called out to her as she walked across the field at the end of the game. "Who's the star of the game? C-a-s-e-y!"

She took off her hat and bent at the waist, having to put up with some teasing from her teammates. But she seemed pretty pleased if the half-smile that never left her face was any indication.

"I did all right," she said, sitting on the bench and sticking her legs out in front of her. "I was four for five, which I can't complain about." Avery had Lisbet on her lap, and she started to fuss a little, probably having exhausted her appetite for sitting in one spot. "Mind if I hold her for a minute?"

"Be my guest."

Avery handed her over and Casey bounced her gently on her knee, being very careful to support her head, which really wasn't necessary at this point. Avery took out her phone and snapped a couple of pictures, then did a video when Casey held Lisbet over her face and spoke as though the baby was doing the talking. "I love softball, Mom. Will you buy me a uniform next time you see one in my size?"

Avery laughed when she replayed the little clip, then handed the phone to Casey. After she played it twice, showing it to Lisbet, she started to page through the gallery. "Mind if I look at your roll?"

Before Avery could consent, Casey stopped abruptly and said, "Why'd you take a picture of the woman who runs our cleaning crew?"

Avery almost swallowed her tongue. She'd completely forgotten she'd done that, and was mortified to have Casey see it. Unable to think of a foolproof fib, she went for an easy one, "No reason."

"No reason?" Her brow furrowed as she continued to look at the photo. "Don't you think it's a little odd to take a picture of someone without her knowledge?" Her gaze traveled to Avery's eyes and she added, "I do."

Avery wasn't sure why she felt so humiliated, but she could have burst into tears. She felt just like she had when her third grade teacher accused her of cheating on a spelling test. Her friend had clearly copied from her, since Hayley had been a terrible speller, but Avery didn't have the gumption to defend herself. But that had been thirty years earlier! She'd turned into a pretty well-respected member of society, yet she still couldn't figure out how to defend herself without sounding like she was lying. "I should have," she said, grasping the phone to delete both photos. "That was rude of me."

"Mmm," Casey said, looking at her the way homicide detectives sized up a suspect. "What did you do with the photo? Did you share it?"

"Share it?" she managed to get out, with her voice rising an octave. "Who would I share it with?" She blinked, trying to figure out what Casey was even getting at. "Are you asking if I put it on Facebook or Instagram?"

Casey nodded soberly.

"I don't even have personal accounts for social media. I shut them down when I got pregnant, since I didn't want to be tempted to bore everyone to death."

"You really shouldn't take photos of people when they're not aware, Avery. It's not cool. People deserve a little privacy—"

"I realize that," she said, interrupting her before she could continue the lecture. "I was wrong to take it. I admit that." She was feeling more centered now and could have thoroughly explained why she'd done it. But she didn't feel very safe with Casey at the moment, and wasn't in the mood to expound. "I was taken by the way she looked, and I wanted to capture it. For myself," she emphasized.

"All right," Casey said, shaking her head slightly as she pressed Lisbet to her shoulder while getting to her feet.

"Um, I wouldn't mind an apology from you," Avery said, starting to feel like herself again.

"Me?" Her brows rose as she stared.

"Uh-huh. It's impolite to dig into someone's phone without permission. We don't know each other well enough for that."

Her lips pursed for a second, then she nodded. "You're right. I shouldn't have done that without asking."

"Oh, you asked," Avery reminded her. "But you didn't give me time to refuse. Not cool."

"Got it. I won't do that again." She started to go down the stairs, saying, "Can you send me the video you just took? One day when Lisbet and I are on the same softball team, I want to show her what she looked like the first time she came to the ball park."

⌒

Once all of the gear was packed up and put into the back of the truck, Avery reflected on what had just transpired. The tension that had built up so quickly between them seemed to have dissipated completely, with Casey acting like everything was normal. But Avery couldn't assess if Casey had believed her or had just gotten tired of talking about it. No matter what, her taking the phone and looking through it was just weird—not seeming like something Casey would do at all.

If Avery had known her better, she would have drilled down to get to the bottom of it, but she didn't want to make a big deal of it now that Casey was acting like the issue had been put to bed. So she decided to let it go, acknowledging that making a friend always entailed some bumps and blind turns.

"I'm very thankful a superstar like you had time for Lisbet today," Avery said. "I was worried about having her out of my sight, but only because she feels like an integral part of me now. It's like temporarily losing a hand."

"I'm glad you didn't mind. I think it's good for you to have some time off, and I know it's good for me to be around such a sweet little thing. I'll take her any time you need a break."

Avery patted her back, holding on to scratch it through the thick uniform. "I don't know why you're being so generous, but I'm not going to look a gift horse in the mouth."

"I'm generally really nice," Casey said, showing a shy grin. "That's just the truth."

"Um…your basement? Chained to the radiator?"

She laughed. "Nah. My mom would hear your cries."

"Okay… Hit me."

They were next to her truck, and Casey went to the tailgate and dropped it, then sat on the edge. Avery followed suit, with Casey placing the baby's car seat next to her while Avery hopped up.

"My grandmother died a while back, and my dad's been trying to get permission to knock down her house and put up a little subdivision."

"I remember you told me about her dying. Sorry," Avery said, seeing the sadness in her eyes.

"Thanks. It's been over a year, so I'm not as sad as I was at first. My grandma was kind of a character. You'd probably seen her around."

"How would I know…"

"She and my grandfather started Villa Napoli, and she ran the place until my uncle took it over."

"No kidding? My parents didn't take me out for a nice meal until I was in high school, but I can't remember ever having a woman in charge."

"You just missed her. She retired right after I started high school. Anyway, ages ago she bought a summer place on the shore in Lake George. When she died, my uncle inherited that, and my mom got her main house. It's just outside Kinderhook."

"And…your dad's plans?"

She looked glum when she said, "I think it's a crime to knock the house down, but my mom agrees with him, and since it's hers now I guess I should keep my nose out of it."

"It's hard sometimes, isn't it," Avery said. "When you feel strongly about something, but don't have any control."

"Yeah," she said, nodding. "At this point, my dad doesn't have too much control either, which I shouldn't admit I kind of enjoy. He's wasted thousands trying to get the town and the county to approve his plans to put up four houses, but they're blocking him every way they can."

"Do you not get along with your dad?"

"Not much," she admitted. "We've always had problems, but things came to a head when I refused to work for him after high school."

"Ahh. He wanted a partner for his business."

"Partner?" She let out a hearty laugh. "He wanted me to learn masonry, since that's all he thought I was capable of. But I wasn't about to spend twenty or thirty years installing flagstone patios on the off chance he'd hand the business over to me when he was ready to step aside. He's the kind of guy who would have sold the damn thing right out from under me —after working me like an indentured servant."

She didn't look particularly upset when she delivered this awful summation of her father's character, so Avery just nodded, showing she understood they had issues.

"Now he's ready to throw in the towel, since it looks like the county is holding firm. His plan is to fix it up and flip it, but he's recently started building a big house from scratch, so he's swamped."

"How does this affect me?"

"Well, long term, it's not much of a solution. But I could ask him if he'd consider renting the house until he has time to do the renovation."

"Ooo. So this would be temporary."

"Definitely. Knowing him, he won't be able to give you a firm date, but I'd bet it would be for at least six months. Of course, if he gets distracted by another big job it could go on for quite a while. He doesn't like to start on something if he doesn't believe he'll be able to finish it."

"What kind of shape is the place in?"

"It's old. Very old. But given its age, it's in good shape. If he goes all out, I'm sure he'd be able to sell it for a good buck. But it needs a lot. New bathroom, new kitchen, upgraded plumbing and electrical. The usual."

"Sounds…like it's a little dated?"

She smiled. "It was dated ages ago. A lot of people don't like living in a place with a kitchen from the thirties. But because of that, he'd have to be reasonable with the rent. If you sweet-talked him, I bet he'd take a thousand."

"Mmm. The only places I've seen advertised around here that I'd be able to stomach cost seventeen hundred. I can afford that. *Barely*. But I'd rather not have to. A thousand would be much more up my alley."

"Want me to propose it?"

"Maybe," she said, already seeing herself in a dated, but cozy home. "How far outside of Kinderhook is it?"

"It's about twenty minutes to your parents' house. Is that too far?"

"Right on the edge," she said, thinking. "I was planning on dropping Lisbet off at my mom's every weekday morning. But I guess eighty minutes of driving isn't too bad for a whole day. Any chance I could take a look before you propose it?"

"Sure. I could take you over there now, but you wouldn't be able to see much in the dark. How about Saturday?"

"It's a date." She stuck her hand out and they shook. Casey was clearly a generous, considerate, baby-crazy woman who could also knock the cover off a softball. She was a little grabby with other people's phones, but she wasn't above apologizing when she overstepped. So far, she had all of the qualities that could make her a good friend.

⌒

Casey didn't usually eat right before bed, but she'd had visions of ice cream dancing in her head ever since she'd seen Avery gulping down that malt. Besides, some of her earliest and best softball memories were of their coaches taking the whole team to Joe's a couple of times a season, and she wanted to recapture the pleasure she got from those treats.

She had to go out of her way to reach the ice cream stand, and there was a line that had to have been fifty feet long, but she didn't mind. Half of the kids dancing around anxiously waiting to order were in their softball and baseball uniforms, so she fit right in. Of course, she was the only adult dressed that way, but she didn't care. People who made sure they never stood out in a crowd missed an awful lot of the fun in life.

While waiting, she went over the little argument she and Avery'd had earlier. If Casey had wanted to, she was confident she could have pinned her down and nibbled away at her until Avery revealed why she'd really taken the picture. She definitely knew why she'd done it, and she was embarrassed. That was for sure. But it wasn't obvious what the reason was. Of course, Ben might have been right. She might have taken it to show to her friends. But Ben had a real hot button about making fun of fat people. Having grown up as a very chubby kid, who'd turned into a pretty hefty man, he was always on the lookout for slights. But Casey didn't get the feeling that Avery spent her time showing her friends photos of large women. For one thing, she didn't have the time. But it was more than that. Avery didn't seem unkind. At all. And only a true asshole would go out of her way to make fun of someone like that.

When Casey got up to the window, she smiled at the high school kid who took her order. She was a sharp-eyed blonde, a little like Avery had looked at that age, and she seemed equally bright and pleasant.

As the young woman went to make her malt, Casey spent another minute thinking. Obviously, it was totally possible that Avery had been a little shit who'd felt superior to Casey way back when. She might have even been the ring-leader who'd egged her friends into being bullies. If that was true, it would make sense that she'd rushed home to send the photo of Valeria all around the internet, finding it hilarious that a woman of her size claimed her space in the world. But now that they'd spent some time together, Casey truly didn't think any of those things were true. She certainly wasn't going to open herself up to being too vulnerable, but until she learned different, she was going to treat Avery like any of her former classmates—with only a mild degree of skepticism. The most valuable lesson she'd learned at Hudson High was to trust everyone, but watch your back.

CHAPTER SEVEN

ON SATURDAY MORNING, AVERY WOKE at dawn, once again feeling remarkably refreshed. Three nights of uninterrupted rest hadn't fully healed her sleep-starved body, but it had improved it immeasurably. Mornings seemed like things she wanted to jump into when she'd had enough sleep, and she found herself singing softly as she went into the kitchen to turn on the coffee maker. Of all of the things she'd guessed motherhood would bring, becoming a morning person hadn't even been on her list. But she was clearly headed in that direction. It was barely six, and she was ready to hit the road, anxious about seeing her potential new home. But she and Casey had made plans to meet at nine, so she had hours to kill. Her younger self would have never believed this set of circumstances, but today's Avery went to the front door to pull in the newspaper, then happily sat at the kitchen table while she caught up on local news, waiting for the coffee to brew.

Casey jumped out of her truck at nine on the dot, and before she got to the door Avery was opening it.

"Ready?" She was dressed for the weather, with khaki shorts and a T-shirt from some band Casey had never heard of. It didn't surprise her that they had dissimilar musical tastes, but she thought they'd at least know the same groups. The baby-weight Avery wanted to lose was also on display, since the shirt was kind of slim-fit. The extra pounds all lurked around her middle, a hiding spot the roomy, square cut shirts Casey had seen her in before had masked.

"Ready and willing. Want to bring your swimsuit? It's supposed to be another scorcher, and I thought you two might enjoy a pool party."

"Oh, Casey," she said, once again looking like she wanted to say "yes," but thinking that she should refuse out of politeness. "I hate to take up so much of your day. I'm imposing enough."

She gazed at Avery in the morning light, seeing a pretty, clear-eyed woman who was not only fun to talk to, she carried an even cuter baby in her arms. "I've told you that I'm a pretty nice person," she said, letting a little smile show. "But I'm not a doormat. If I didn't want you to come over, I wouldn't offer."

"All right then," she said, grinning. "I'd love to give my mom a real day off. My being out of the house for the whole day will let her get back to her usual routine."

"You get your stuff, and I'll get the car seat out of your mom's car. Is it unlocked?"

"Always," Avery said as she started for the door. "I'll move it. Just give me a minute to get our stuff."

Casey walked over to the car, certain she didn't need help in moving a simple car seat. "Don't bother bringing swim clothes for Lisbet. I got her something."

"What?" Avery asked, turning to stare.

"Big sale at the kid's clothing shop on Warren. End-of-season stuff was super cheap."

"Casey…" Her voice reminded Casey of the tone her grandma used to use with her when she'd stayed outside until long after dinner. Mildly exasperated, but not truly annoyed.

"Go on," Casey said, waving her away. "I've got a car seat to wrestle with."

⌒

Casey drove down the tranquil, curvy road like she was expecting a speeding semi to blow around every bend. It was truly sweet to have her be so careful with Lisbet in the car, but Avery was afraid they'd never get to the house.

After twenty-five minutes, Casey slowed down even more, turning off the main road to travel down a short, dead-end street. "That's Claverack

Creek down there," she said. "Because of it, none of the streets around here go through, which means there's very little noise." She smiled. "I've been told the creek is a great place to catch frogs."

Avery held her hand up in front of the baby, testing to see how quickly she could grab a finger. She gave it her all, but Avery was able to evade her grasping hand without much difficulty. "I don't think Lisbet's going to be much of a frog-hunter in the next few months, but she might grow faster than I've been led to believe."

The last driveway on the right was long and had a nice curve to it. Nestled within the tall trees was a two story house with a stone facade that looked old. Maybe *really* old. The home was situated perfectly on a slight rise, with a well-tended lawn in the front.

"Septic field's looking good," Casey said, shattering Avery's sylvan image.

"Do you mean the lawn?"

"Uh-huh. The trees used to be much closer to the house. My dad had to pay to have about twenty of them taken down, then have a new septic system dug." She laughed a little. "My grandma never offered to pay for anything, even though she had a nice nest egg."

"It's a lovely setting," Avery said, reserving judgment on the rest of the place until they got closer. "The lawn looks like it's been there forever."

"Only about five years. It's pretty, isn't it? I love how the sun hits the porch on a summer morning. It's a great place to have breakfast."

"Breakfast outside in the sun. That's a dream I didn't realize I had, but I could get behind it quickly."

"A cold beer on a warm summer night isn't bad either." She seemed very reflective when she added, "I can't begin to guess how much beer the Gerritsens have consumed right there. You'd love the porch in the summer. Guaranteed."

"Gerritsens?"

"My mom's family. But I can see a Nichols or two enjoying a beer there as well."

"You've already moved me in," Avery teased, giving Casey's sturdy leg a swat.

"No, not really. But I'm almost certain you'd like it here. It's about as far from the craziness of Brooklyn as you can get."

Avery gave her a look. "Have you actually *been* to Brooklyn?"

"I've seen it on TV," she said, giving Avery a charming smile. "Lisbet could cry all night and no one would hear a peep."

"Or hear my screams when the Mad Killer breaks in."

"Mmm-hmm," Casey said, not commenting further. Clearly, she wasn't up on the exploits of the crazed murderer whom Avery believed lurked outside of every single-family home that wasn't closely surrounded by neighbors.

They got out, and Avery walked over to stand on the grass in front of the building after Casey offered to pull Lisbet's car seat out of the truck. Taking a minute to get a feel for the place, Avery started at the top, loving the peaked roof with two large dormers. The first floor had four windows, which flanked what looked like a Dutch door, with wrought-iron strapping to secure it in place. Whoever had built the house was really going for an old-style look. The stone was various shades of gray, and each window had beautiful cornflower blue shutters that looked like they'd actually close.

"It's awfully cute," Avery said when Casey approached. She looked down to see Lisbet blinking her eyes open. "Did your grandmother have it built?"

She smiled, looking a little smug. "An ancestor did, but not my grandmother." She tilted her head to let her gaze reach the top of the building, then slide down to the porch. "I've been tempted to do the research to find out who built it and when, but since my parents have both been dead-set on tearing it down, I've tried to put it out of my mind." She was quiet for a second before adding, "I didn't want to get more attached to it, and if I found out it was built in 1650 or something I might have chained myself to it when the bulldozers showed up."

"Sixteen fifty!" Avery stared at her. "You can't be serious."

She shook her head a little as a smile settled onto her face. "I think it's probably closer to 1800, long after the Dutch were in charge around here. If it was really old, it would have a big, open fireplace, and the second floor would have been for grain storage."

"Are you really serious? Is this stone real?"

"Real?" she asked, cocking her head.

"I thought it was that stuff you can buy that's like half an inch thick. It comes in sheets…"

"Oh, god, no," Casey said. She walked over just past the porch and slapped at the stone. "The walls are probably a foot and a half thick. But you can't see the stone from inside." Her expression turned grim. "Some of my ancestors didn't appreciate that they were living in a historic home. I assume the original beams are still there, but they and the stone have been covered by plaster walls and ceilings. I'm certain there was a fireplace, too, but it was either disassembled or covered long ago." She sighed as she looked up again, with her gaze lingering for a moment. "It's just an old house now. To uncover all of the original elements would cost a mint, if it was even possible."

"But the town wants to preserve it?"

"They do, but the house isn't landmarked or anything, so they're just slowing everything down. I'm thrilled about that, by the way. But it puts my dad in a bad spot. He can't get permission to knock down enough trees to put more houses on the property, so the only way he can make any money is to do a historic renovation, which isn't his thing." She smiled warmly. "But while he's figuring out what to do, you could live here for a pretty good deal."

"I'm intrigued," Avery said. "Want to see the house we might live in, Sweet Pea?"

"She's into it," Casey said. "We communicate without words."

"I just bet you do." Avery climbed the two steps to the porch and waited while Casey pulled a set of keys from her pocket.

"Have you ever seen a real Dutch door?"

"I have. My grade school class went to look at some Dutch houses in Kingston when we were studying New York history. I wanted my dad to switch out our door," she said, chuckling, "but he convinced me it would look stupid on our 1950s ranch."

Casey put an old-style skeleton key into the lock of the striking blue door and gave it a gentle push, with the heavy-looking thing swinging open easily. "Now remember that it needs updating. It looks like the house of a ninety-year-old woman who hated change."

Avery turned to gaze at her. "Your grandmother was ninety?"

"Sure was. My mom was a surprise. My poor grandma had two kids in high school, then she had my uncle. Just when she thought she could take a breath, she got pregnant with my mom."

"Wow. Ninety," Avery said. "I'm going to prepare myself for ancient carpet, peeling linoleum, pink appliances, and a washboard in the sink... with a pump for water."

"Not that bad," Casey promised. "In some ways," she added mysteriously.

They entered, and Avery tried to ignore the musty smell. There was no way to prevent that when a house had been empty for a while, but it wasn't nearly as bad as she'd expected. The place certainly wasn't fresh and modern, but nothing seemed broken or in need of immediate repair.

Casey went to a window and unlocked it to raise it with no problem, letting in a warm breeze. Avery stood by her, delighted to see a very deep wooden sill. "I see what you mean about how thick the walls are. This is super cool!"

"I certainly think so. When I was young, I could sit on this sill and watch the squirrels. I guess I still could," she added, plunking herself down, "but I can't sit with my feet up against the other side like I could then." She looked up at Avery. "No screens, which isn't usually a problem. My grandma closed the shutters at night, which kept most of the insects out."

"Huh." Avery looked around carefully, while trying to figure out how to ask a question that might be impolite. "Um, I understand why it would be hard to fit screens on the windows, or put in air conditioning, but the house is kind of modest for a woman whose son-in-law runs a big general contracting business, isn't it? I mean, the historic elements are gone, so your dad could have made some upgrades without hurting anything, right?"

"He sure could have," Casey said, nodding. "But my grandmother had a boatload of quirks, and one of them was to keep things just like they were until she had no choice. The house had been good enough for her parents, and their parents, and their parents, etcetera, so it was good enough for her."

"In her defense, it's not bad at all. The carpet doesn't even look worn."

"Oddly, that was the only thing she wanted replaced on a regular basis. I think my dad put this in about five years ago. He tried to talk her into getting area rugs, since the original floors are really beautiful, but she was from an era where a bare floor meant you couldn't afford a carpet."

"Hmm. And you really think I could talk your dad into renting it out for just a thousand a month?"

"Plus utilities," Casey said. "And I'm sure you could, since I already did. It took all of my negotiating skills, but he finally agreed." She turned and faced Avery. "If you want it, it's yours. But if you don't, I won't be offended." She looked a little sheepish when she added, "I'd be wounded if you thought it was a dump, but not if you just didn't think it would work for you."

"It's not a dump, Casey. At *all*. I'd be thrilled to live in a home with this kind of history. Can I see the kitchen?"

"Um, yeah, but be open-minded. It's…unique," she said, making a face.

"I've seen quite a few unique places while apartment hunting in Brooklyn. Let's see how this compares to the place I saw with a bathtub in the kitchen."

Casey stopped and gave her a very puzzled look. "*In* the kitchen?"

"Right in the kitchen. It had a piece of wood that fit over the tub, so you could use it as a table." She laughed, thinking about the dingy place, along with the nineteen hundred dollar price tag. "It was an old tenement building, with a tuberculosis window."

Casey stopped again and stared. "I need a little more info on that one."

121

"Back in the day, they thought people got sick from lack of air flow. So they put windows into interior walls. In a railroad apartment like the one I'm talking about, it added a little light to the rooms that didn't have windows. Very little," she added, amused by the look on Casey's face.

"I've just decided you might think this kitchen is ultra-modern. No tub, and no tuberculosis window."

They walked through the biggish living room to turn right into a very large kitchen. It had to be large to contain a full-sized hot water heater, along with a washer and dryer, in addition to the usual sink, refrigerator and stove, all of which looked like they were from a different era. "Well, well, well," Avery said. "This is a new one for me." She smiled at Casey, who was looking a little skittish. "You can't say it's not big. And think of the time it would save having to trudge down to the basement to do the laundry."

"That's the attitude," she said. "It's all downhill from here."

"Let's take a peek upstairs, just in case there's a coal-fired furnace in one of the bedrooms."

"Oil heat, and I'm certain it's in the basement." She gave Avery a tight smile. "Personally, I wouldn't be able to spend a lot of time down there. The dirt floor creeps me out."

"Fantastic," Avery said, rolling her eyes.

They walked upstairs together, with a few of the treads creaking under their weight. "Is that the burglar alarm?" Avery asked.

"Yup. That'll give you enough time to load your shotgun."

The ceiling of the master bedroom was on such a steep angle that Avery would have had to bend over to get to the wall, and it was cool and dim, even after the hot days they'd been having. Casey went to the window and opened it, using a wooden peg to hold the top sash up. Then she opened the shutter, revealing a very deep backyard surrounded by tall trees, allowing not even a glimpse of any neighbors.

"Now *this* is nice," Avery said. "Very cozy."

"It's usually cool up here. My dad put a new roof on just a few years ago, and he installed sheets of insulation. It helped a lot." Her expression turned grim again. "He wouldn't even try to find someone to repair the old slate roof. It probably wasn't original, but…"

Avery gave her a pat on the back. "I'm sorry he doesn't appreciate this place like you do. Or that your mom doesn't. I mean, it's her family's heritage…"

"My mom's very pragmatic. She'd been trying to get my grandma to move to our place for ten years, and I think she started to think of this house as nothing but a burden. She's just…over it, I guess."

"But you're not."

"I'm definitely not. Part of the reason I'd love to see you here is that my dad might slow down on his plans if he's making enough to cover the real estate taxes. Full disclosure," she said, smiling.

"So far, so good. I'd love to help in the battle to preserve the… What's the family name again?"

"Gerritsen. It's been anglicized to Garrison by some branches of the family, but my mom's kept it original. Want to see the smaller bedrooms? One's just right for Lisbet."

"Absolutely."

The two bedrooms in the front both had the severely sloping roof, and they were bathed in the morning light, allowing Avery to picture Lisbet waking with the dawn.

She faced Casey and said, "I've got to pee, and if the toilet flushes properly, I'm moving in."

⌒

The toilet performed up to par, and Avery seemed very excited when they got back into the truck. She rode in the back with Lisbet, as usual, and she spent much of the trip telling the baby how happy she was going to be in her new house, frequently adding that Lisbet's new best friend had been vital to the scheme. It was pretty cool to listen to Avery jabber away, clearly taking her job seriously. It was odd to admit, but Casey had never paid much attention to parents talking to their kids. It wasn't until right this minute that she realized Avery was helping the baby learn how to communicate. It was really no different from a cat teaching a kitten to groom itself, and equally necessary.

"You're awfully good with her," Casey said. "If I hadn't seen how you two interact, I would have just played with her when I had her alone. Since she can't talk, I wouldn't have thought to."

"Mmm. Yeah," she said. "I don't know if my parents talked to me a lot, but I assume they did, since I was talking and reading pretty early. But every once in a while I see a parent with a kid and can tell there's just not much of an exchange. Makes me sad."

"I have no idea when I learned to talk or read. Probably late," Casey said. "Reading, at least. I never really mastered it."

"Seriously?" Via the rearview mirror, Casey could see Avery gazing at her, looking concerned. "Do you…have a learning disability?"

"Not according to anyone who could have helped me out. Everyone believed I was either lazy or screwing around." She met Avery's gaze in the mirror. "I was behind from the beginning. I remember being in first grade and thinking I'd missed some stuff that everybody else already knew." She paused for a second, on the verge of adding more, then thought better of it. She still didn't trust Avery enough to go into any depth about her grade school days, when the teasing about her intelligence had started.

"Why didn't your teachers notice? A kid in my class who had reading problems got a decent amount of help."

"I can't say. But if anyone noticed, I sure didn't get any help." She didn't add that her father had been sure from the beginning that she was lazy, for reasons she'd never understood. If anyone had proposed giving her any intervention, she was almost certain he wouldn't have allowed it.

"That must have been hard," Avery said, sounding like she actually cared.

"Wasn't easy. College was really a bitch. Took me eight years to finish."

"Full time?"

Casey laughed at the stunned expression on her face. "Your voice broke on that one. No, Avery, not full time. After I'd worked at the brewery for a couple of years, the owners decided I had management potential. Neither of them had any education in the science of brewing, and they wanted their top people to know how to do things right."

"Wait... You can go to college to learn how to brew beer? Real college?"

"Real college," Casey said, feeling a little dissed. "SUNY Cobleskill."

"Cobleskill? I've never heard of it."

"It's in Schoharie County."

"I've never heard of *that*. It it far?"

"It's not close. Obviously. About an hour west of Albany."

"Wow. I didn't know you'd gone to college, Casey. I didn't think you were into it."

"I wasn't. And I wouldn't have considered going if they hadn't pushed me. But they proposed I work part-time for two years while I went to school full-time, so I couldn't really refuse."

"But...you said it took you eight years."

"It did. At the end of two years I'd only finished three semester's worth of work. But they knew I was trying hard, so they told me to take my time and finish at my own pace. I went back to work full time, and just took one class per term."

"Ahh. No wonder it took so long."

"Yup. Once I started taking courses in my major, a professor suggested I get evaluated for a learning disability." She looked at Avery again. "After just a little testing, I had all the help I should have had from the beginning."

"And that let you finish with less difficulty?"

"It did. I'm the proud holder of a bachelor of technology in applied fermentation, which would come in handy if I ever wanted to work for a bigger brewery." She checked the rear-view mirror to see Avery gazing at her with a warm smile.

"That's...that's really admirable. Anyone can finish college if it's easy. But sticking with it for eight years when it's not? That's something, Casey. Something big."

Casey took another peek at her, seeing Avery smiling at her with what actually might have been admiration. If she'd ever thought it was funny to laugh at people who struggled in school, she'd moved past it. Or she was a great liar. At this point, Casey would have put money on the former, but she still wasn't able to completely rule out the latter.

⟋

They arrived at the Van Dyke home at around eleven. Avery watched the doors to Casey's room swing wide, and as she started to go in, Casey said, "Why don't you get ready in here? I'll change Lisbet outside."

"Really? Why…"

"Just to give you some privacy. My bathroom's sort of small."

"Sure you don't mind?"

"Not at all. If you'll give me her hat, I've got everything else."

"You'll need swim diapers—"

"Bought some," she said, looking quite proud of herself. "I want her to come over all the time, so I stocked up."

"Again, I'm going to have to make an appointment to see her if I let you have her whenever you want to."

"I'll take her whenever you're tired or losing patience," she said, with her dark eyes gazing at Avery soberly. "If she's a normal baby, that should be five or six hours every day, right?"

"That sounds about right. I hope you don't mind the midnight to six a.m. shift."

"We'll negotiate." She lifted the car seat carrier from Avery's hand and started to talk to Lisbet when she brought it close to her face. "Let's go put our swimsuits on and dive into the deep end. Want to?"

The baby smiled coyly at her, something she'd started to do more often lately.

"I think she's ready," Avery said.

"We'll be waiting."

Avery handed over the baby's hat, then watched Casey hit a button on the side of the room to close the doors. After getting all of her things organized, Avery started to change into her suit. It took a few minutes to wrestle herself into the very unexciting two-piece, but she was glad she'd bought it. The waist-length top hid some of the loose skin on her belly, and the bottoms revealed her legs, which, except for some fat on her hips, looked pretty good.

After going into the bathroom to take a look, Avery immediately reassessed. She didn't look very good at all. The fat on her legs was much more visible than it was when she was naked. It was like the elastic pushed it down in an unflattering way. And the top didn't hide her flabby belly as well as she'd thought it would. And why did she buy a black suit? Her skin was pale to start with, and she hadn't gotten any sun at all this year, since she'd been so worried about protecting Lisbet's skin. She looked like a chubby friggin' ghost.

For the first time since she'd given birth she stared at herself frankly. Granted, it had only been six and a half months, but she'd thought she'd bounce back faster than this. If she was stuck with this lumpy body forever... She blew out a frustrated breath. If she'd wanted to keep her body in good shape, she should have spent money on a personal trainer rather than on baby furniture and co-pays at the pediatrician. You literally couldn't have it all, and when she wasn't being such an idiot, she realized that having Lisbet was worth looking a little lumpy. *Get over yourself!* she chided herself before refusing to look into the mirror for one more second.

As Avery opened the door to exit into the backyard, she stopped dead in her tracks when she saw Lisbet sitting on Casey's belly. The human raft was lying on her back, kicking gently as she did a slow lap, holding the baby's hands firmly. Lisbet looked very happy, gurgling and whipping her head around like she did when she was thrilled by a new experience.

Avery knew how to swim, and thought she was fairly competent. But she couldn't have moved down the length of the pool with the unhurried steadiness that Casey exhibited. Especially not without using her arms to provide some added power.

Lisbet looked adorable in her new suit—a bright blue onesie with a bold print covering it. But it was hard to look at Lisbet when the water was flowing around Casey's shoulders and over her perfectly-shaped breasts.

Her rash guard was very bright yellow, or maybe chartreuse was the right term. Whatever the proper name, the color looked great on her, showing off her surprisingly perky breasts, given that she likely wasn't wearing a bra. Her shorts had slipped down a little, riding low on her hips, the white background with a bright blue and green plaid demanding attention. Well, maybe it wasn't the shorts that demanded attention. Her taut belly didn't want to share the limelight with a mere pair of shorts. *Damn.* It's not like she wasn't cute enough when she was fully dressed! Her body was sick!

"You two look like a pretty pair of water nymphs," she said, speaking up so she wouldn't be able to ogle Casey a moment longer.

Casey thrust her legs down, rising up to grasp the baby and hold her above the water for a second. Then she dipped her, letting her little legs slip in for the short trip back to the faux beach. "I'm a water sign. What's Lisbet?"

"No idea. I know more about nuclear fusion than I do astrology."

"Huh," Casey said, exiting, with the baby turning to stare at the water, clearly not ready to leave. "I didn't think there was anything I'd know that you didn't."

"I don't think that comment deserves a response, so I'll compliment you on your fashion sense. When did you buy this little getup for Lisbet?"

Casey was holding the baby up to her chest, and she patted her back. "I was craving a cappuccino when I went by the restaurant yesterday. Since it's the end of the summer, the baby store I passed had a massive sale on swim clothes."

"The baby store where a little romper costs as much as a nice dinner?" Avery asked, raising an eyebrow.

"I wouldn't buy anything there at full price. But at the end of the season you can get a deal."

"Well, it's adorable, but you don't need to buy Lisbet clothes. I can afford anything she needs." She put her hand on the onesie, which was much thicker than she'd expected. "What is this made of?"

"It's kind of like a wetsuit. I thought she needed something extra since the days are getting shorter. I want to make sure she's warm enough to really enjoy it."

"Let me pay you for the suit. Besides being really cute, it's practical. Are those dinosaurs?"

"Uh-huh. I'm sure it was meant for a boy, but all of that pink stuff just annoys me."

"Ugh! Me too. I exchanged nearly all of the pink things she got for her baby shower, but it was impossible to completely avoid it. I have nothing against the color, but why do girls have to dress in it exclusively?"

"Parents must be into it, since people Lisbet's age don't have much cash on them."

The baby started to lean toward the water, with her hands out in front of her, like she was going to scoop it up. Casey immediately got back in, dipping Lisbet's legs again, and smiling when she started to kick them in a very ineffective way. "If you're looking to save a few dollars, there's a kids' resale shop in Rhinebeck that's supposed to be great. Maybe you can check them out."

"And just how do you know about shops in Rhinebeck?"

"I used to spend most of my weekends in Rhinebeck," she said, grinning slyly. "I did a lot of window shopping."

Avery was about to question her further, but Lisbet kept trying to stuff her fist into her own mouth, an early-warning sign that she was getting hungry. "You'd better let me feed her."

"You and I can have a lot of fun when you're not hungry, Lisbet," Casey said as she handed the baby over. "But your mom's got the magic potion when you are."

"Want me to go inside?"

"Of course not. Why not sit under the pergola? Those chairs are fully in the shade."

"Damn," Avery said, looking over at the large wooden structure, with a deep green vine woven through the overhead supports. "This house truly ought to be in a magazine. It's almost a shame you don't have a bigger family to make use of it."

"Good point. Why don't we make the party bigger? My friends Ben and Julie are home today." Her smile grew bigger. "Ask your parents to come over, too. We can have a barbecue."

"Oh, Casey, that's too generous! We can't impose on your family like that."

Casey shook her head slowly. "My mom's in the kitchen right now, but she won't come out on her own. Having people over isn't an imposition, since she won't acknowledge anyone's here."

"But she and your dad joined us the other night."

"Only because I'd taken you inside and you knew she was home. She never comes out when Ben's family's over."

"Is she...?"

"I don't know what her issue is, but she'd rather be alone. My dad's kind of the same. He has to be charming with clients, so he doesn't want to have to be at home."

"They don't have friends?"

"My mom has some," she said, looking thoughtful. "People she used to know from around here who've moved. She talks to two of the women a lot. For hours," she added. "Other than that, she watches TV while she plays a game on her phone."

"I'll ask my parents if they want to come take a dip. But I think they'd feel like they were imposing if they knew your parents were right inside while we were having a barbecue. I mean...they know them."

"I get that," she said, nodding. "Think about it while I call Ben. I know he'd like to meet you...and Lisbet."

"Does he know your new best friend is literally a baby?"

"He does. And so does everyone else at the brewery. They know I'm weird, so there's not much I do that surprises them."

Avery cocked her head. "It doesn't bother you that they think it's weird?"

She had a half-smile on her face that made her look particularly puzzled. "Why would it? I do what I do. If people like it, fine. If not, that's fine too."

"Now that's a healthy way of looking at the world," Avery said, patting her on the back.

"Mmm. Maybe. My belief is that what people say about you is none of your business."

"Pardon?"

"Think about it," she said, walking over to her discarded clothes to pick up her phone. "It's the damn truth."

⌇

Casey swam a few laps while Avery was getting Lisbet set up. Eventually, she got brave and walked over to the pergola, leaving a trail of drips on the bluestone. Avery found it kind of cute that she was so skittish about watching her breastfeed, but she assumed she'd get used to it. Right now she wouldn't let her eyes wander a bit lower than Avery's head, but she didn't seem uncomfortable when she sat down on another one of the comfy chairs.

"The party's getting bigger. Ben and Julie and Benji will be here in about a half hour. They're bringing beer, not that I need any more."

"Great! My dad's golfing, as usual, but my mom jumped at the chance to join us."

"Well, it is a nice pool," Casey said, teasing a little.

"Since this pergola is right in front of the kitchen, your poor mom might be getting a perfect view of my boob. Think she minds?"

"I'm sure she won't say she does," she said, smiling. "For me, that's plenty." Her gaze flicked down for a second, then she said, "It's a little hot under here. Would you rather move over where there's more air? The house blocks the breeze."

"Oh, no. We didn't have air conditioning in Brooklyn, and my parents don't have it, either, so Lisbet's acclimated to the heat. It doesn't even seem to register with her."

Casey stared at the side of her face for a few seconds. "You didn't have air conditioning in Brooklyn? You had to leave your windows open with all of that noise?"

"I had a fan," she said. "It was like old-timey days. No air conditioning, no garbage disposal, no car, no elevator. Carrying your groceries for six blocks, only to have to drag them up three flights. You could have dropped me into 1920 and I'd have felt right at home."

"Damn, Avery. I don't mind roughing it, but only when I'm camping. I need my a/c to be able to sleep."

"Lisbet's really a trouper, with very little bothering her. Not long ago, there was a big explosion that barely made her blink, and when the bank at the corner of our street was robbed, police cars roared down the street for five minutes, sirens ablaze. She looked up, but didn't cry."

"An explosion?"

"The building across from mine blew up when some unlicensed plumber was working on the gas line. Pretty dramatic," she said, making her eyebrows pop.

Casey's mouth had dropped open. "How many people were killed?"

"None. I'm not sure how, but everyone was lucky that day." She laughed, mostly at the startled look on Casey's face.

"I like the drama of tasting a beer I've been tinkering with. That's kind of enough for me." She got up and went to the lush grass that abutted the pergola and stretched out on it. "Don't mind me," she said. "I'd almost always rather be lying in the grass than sitting in a chair." She stretched out, looking so comfortable she could have been modeling for Patagonia or some other outdoorsy clothing company. "Lisbet followed me with her eyes when I moved," she said, with a delighted smile brightening her face. "She looks…interested."

"That's my goal, you know. I want to keep her interested in the world. Having her meet new people and have new experiences is a big part of that." She looked at Casey, who was still staring at the baby. "It really is a lot of work, but it's the most important work I've ever done. If I hadn't been able to work from home a few days a week, I would have missed so much."

"She would have too. It's a crime we don't pay for at least three or four months of maternity leave. How can we keep yammering about how important families are and then treat working women like crap?"

"It seems very easy to do that. Act like you care, but do nothing to help. That's politics in a nutshell."

"Ugh. Let's talk about something more interesting." Casey rolled onto her side and held her head up with a hand. She looked directly at Avery, but paused for quite a few seconds before she finally said, "Would I be prying if I asked about being pregnant?"

"I don't mind a bit. Anything in particular you want to know?"

"Everything," she said, looking very sober. "Mostly I want to know how it feels."

"Mmm." She thought for a minute. "That's a tough one, since it feels different all of the time. Sometimes minute by minute."

"Right from the beginning?"

"Oh, yeah. That's when you're just getting used to it. You're either sick or hormonal every minute, but because you've never felt like this, it's kind of freaky. I'm sure some women like their first trimester, but I couldn't wait to get to the second."

"That was easier?"

"For me it was. I guarantee you'd get a hundred different perspectives if you asked a hundred different women, but my second trimester was kind of a breeze. Even from the first, I was enmeshed with this baby," she said, stroking Lisbet's warm skin. "But by the second trimester I was in love." She closed her eyes as she tried to recreate the feelings she'd experienced. "I'd never spent much time thinking about my gender," she said, surprising herself by bringing this up. "But being pregnant made me feel one hundred percent female. It's like every bit of testosterone in my body disappeared, replaced with high-test estrogen."

"Mmm. I had a feeling it might be like that," Casey said, gazing at her intently.

"It was great. Really great. I felt like I was creating something fantastic. Something utterly unique." She smiled. "I mean, I was, but I've come back down to earth now. Every parent should feel like their child is extraordinary, but not get so involved with them that they forget other children are just as important."

"Mmm. My former sister-in-law was like that. The other way, though," she added. "She acted like the rest of the world should stop whatever they were doing to roll out the red carpet for her kids."

"Oh, I'd love to have people do that for Lisbet," Avery said, laughing a little. "I'm just realistic enough to know that won't happen. Actually," she said, thinking about this for a moment, "being in Brooklyn helped me get my perspective right. When you're in a city that big, with so many people surrounding you who will never, ever have one tenth of the things or advantages you do…" She shrugged. "If you don't feel at least a little guilty for how great you have it, you need an empathy boost."

"I'm jealous of you," Casey said softly, surprising the heck out of Avery. "I wish I would have had a baby when I was around twenty. Then I wouldn't have overthought it for all of these years."

She looked so sober, so serious. Her gaze was locked on Lisbet now, who was kind of dawdling as she ate her lunch.

"Is it too late?" Avery asked, worried that she might be prying. "Is there some reason…"

She sat up and urged her hair behind her ear. "I decided not to quite a while ago. Now I'm focusing on forming relationships with other people's kids until I can talk someone into having a baby with me."

"Ahh. Taking a shortcut isn't a bad idea." She meant that as a joke, but Casey didn't smile. "If you want to have a baby with a partner, I'm sure you can manage it. A lot of women want to give birth, but don't want to do it alone."

"If I'd gotten my wish, I'd have three or four kids by now." Her gaze met Avery's, now clearly not concerned about catching a peek. "If it was easy…" She trailed off quietly. "But it's not. Trust me on that."

Avery's mom arrived, bearing tacos from one of their favorite spots.

Casey and Lisbet were in the pool once again, with Avery sitting under the pergola, using the Van Dyke's super-fast wifi to check her mail.

"Hello everyone," her mom said when she walked over to the nearby table and put her bags down. "I brought lunch."

"We'll be out in a minute," Casey called out. "It takes me a while to kick my way down to the other end."

"Don't rush. Avery and I will get everything organized."

Avery got up to help, putting tacos on the paper plates the restaurant had included, and they both looked up when Casey emerged from the water, looking like a very athletic dyke about to hit the beach on Fire Island.

"Look at how cute she is," her mom said quietly, clucking her tongue. "Most girls don't look good in board shorts, but she sure does."

"She certainly does," Avery agreed, just then realizing her voice had dropped down to take on a sexy tone she hadn't intended it to. "I mean, yeah, she does. Must be the long legs. She's got good ones."

"More than her legs are good. Look at how she fills out that snug top. Are breasts on your wish list? I don't really know what you find attractive —"

"And you're not going to!" Avery said, racing across the patio to cut off any opportunity her mother had to say something Casey actually could hear.

⌒

After they'd eaten, Avery took the opportunity to stay under the pergola to read a book that everyone at work was talking about. She hadn't been able to dig into new fiction since Lisbet had been born, but doing so really wasn't optional. Since she was charged with finding new voices for the podcast, she had to read everything she could get her hands on. Her mother and Casey had insisted they didn't mind, and they certainly seemed to be having fun. But Lisbet was having the best time of the trio, clearly enjoying the heck out of the entire experience.

Watching how they interacted with Lisbet, Avery got a warm feeling in her chest that eventually spread throughout her body. She hadn't expected this from motherhood, but she'd found there wasn't anything she enjoyed more than having other people enjoy Lisbet. Granted, her mother had a stake in the whole endeavor, but Casey could have given the kid a glance and walked on by. When Avery considered how little interest Casey's parents had in the child, that would have been what she would have predicted. But Casey's love for kids was obviously not genetic. It came from her own tender heart.

She was idly musing over how good it felt to have a stranger delight in Lisbet's mild antics when she heard a big, booming voice call out from the driveway. "That water had better be pee-free!"

Casey waved, handed off the baby, and got out. She didn't go for the easy exit, though. She placed her hands on the coping, pushed as she tossed a foot up, then was standing and walking toward her guests while Avery was still figuring out how she'd gotten out in around a second.

A little boy ran around the corner of the house, a gleeful smile on his face. He was tall for his age, and very sturdy, with short, dark hair that stuck straight up on the top. He stopped abruptly when he spotted Avery, his smile frozen.

She stood up and walked over to him. "Hi there," she said. "I'm Casey's friend, Avery. Are you Benji?"

"Yeah," he said, looking up at her with cornflower blue eyes. The kid looked like he could be advertising just about anything marketed to rough-and-tumble young boys, with his handsome features and easy smile. "Is that your baby? Or the other lady's?"

"Mine. I'm the other lady's baby."

He narrowed his eyes slightly, then got the joke. "Casey really likes your baby. She talks about her all the time."

"She really likes you too," Avery said. She looked up as a very large copy of Benji, and an average-sized sandy-haired woman walked across the patio with Casey. The man carried a car seat, which was a little odd since Benji was clearly too large to fit into even a booster seat.

"I bet these people are your mom and dad," Avery said. "Is it weird to look so much like your dad?"

"No," he said, shaking his head firmly. "I like it."

She made eye contact with Benji's dad, and extended her hand when he got close. "It's good to meet you, Ben," she said. She wasn't great at telling how tall people were, but she was sure she'd get a crick in her neck if she had to continue looking up at Ben for long. If he'd been introduced as a former NFL player, she would have believed it immediately.

"Good to meet you, too," he said. His smile wasn't as guileless as his son's, but he also looked friendly and accessible. "My wife, Julie."

"We've been dying to meet the baby who's enchanted Casey," she said, shaking Avery's hand enthusiastically. "She's been trying to get all of the guys at the brewery to have babies, and believe me, most of them are nowhere near ready."

"I hope I'm ready," Avery said, "because Lisbet's stuck with me even if I'm not."

"She is," Casey said, giving her a surprisingly fond look. "Avery's a great mom."

"I'm trying my best, but it's a bigger job than I could have guessed. Without my parents' help, I'd have really struggled, especially in those first couple of months."

"I'm still upset I didn't run into you last winter," Casey said. "I love being around Lisbet now, but newborns really fascinate me."

"I could definitely have used the help. But better late than never."

"Definitely," Casey said.

"We brought Benji's car seat for Casey's truck," Julie said. "I went on the manufacturer's site to make sure it wasn't past its expiration date, which it wasn't."

"Oh, god," Avery sighed, trying to sound aggrieved. "If you give her a car seat, Casey might sneak the baby out of the house when I'm not looking."

"Never," she said. "Well, maybe, but I'd leave a note." She turned to Julie. "Thanks for lending it to me. I was going to buy one, but I'm sure you bought the best made. You treated this little guy like he was made out of glass."

She put her arms around Benji from behind, linked her hands together, and pushed him back and forth roughly. He could definitely take it, and seemed to like being tumbled around. He turned his head to look up at her. "Got any cookies lying around?"

"Probably. Let me go see what I can get away with stealing."

Avery watched her go into the house, and a minute later she emerged with a plate full of them. But her mom, who was clearly inside baking, given the scent of lemon, butter, and eggs that permeated the air, didn't emerge. That was clearly the accepted norm, since none of the guests commented. Avery had no idea what Marsha's deal was, but she was definitely not a social animal.

After everyone had taken a cookie break, Ben, Benji and Casey got back into the water, while Lisbet cuddled up to Avery for a nap. The pool games changed dramatically, getting rougher and louder. Casey had a Nerf football that they all tossed around, with both her and Benji acting like something dire would happen if they let the ball hit the water. Ben didn't seem to have the same drive to make the game hard, but he hung in there with them.

As mothers always did when they had a minute to chat, Julie asked all about Lisbet. Avery certainly didn't mind, but talking about the birth in detail wasn't any fun. Some women seemed to delight in recounting all of the trauma of the event, but Avery wanted to forget about the whole thing as quickly as her brain allowed. To her, it had been like having emergency surgery without anesthesia, even though she hadn't had a C-section. Getting Lisbet was worth everything involved, but she had no interest in talking about the pain that she'd been sure would never end.

"Have you been up to Baby Brewers yet?" Julie asked.

"Oh, no, not yet. My mom's watching Lisbet on weekdays, so Casey's going to have to harass her to get her to participate."

"We've already talked about it," her mom said. "Lisbet and I are going on Thursday."

"How did you get out of going last Thursday?" Julie asked, laughing softly. She reached over and covered Avery's hand with her own. "I hope I don't make it sound like Casey's off her rocker or anything."

"Off her—?"

"She didn't start Baby Brewers just so she could get her hands on more babies, even though that's what she tells people. The program was a marketing decision by Kaaterskill. Everyone up here's trying to grab a piece of the market, and they decided it would be smart to get new parents interested in the beer. Sales are up, so I think it's working."

"To be honest," Avery said, taking a look over to make sure Casey was still in the water, "her interest puzzled me at first. Casey and I were in the same class in high school, but we weren't friends. That afternoon when she saw me walking with the baby, she acted like Lisbet was the most fascinating creature on earth."

"Mmm." Julie nodded thoughtfully. "Some people strongly prefer adults, but Casey's always liked being around kids. I know she likes me, and she and Ben are best friends, but it was Benji who strengthened the friendship. She was over more than my mom when he was a newborn."

"That's…kind of funny, isn't it?" Avery said, trying not to characterize Casey's interest by using a term that might have a negative connotation.

"I suppose it can be, depending on the person. But Casey's so…" She frowned briefly. "I don't want to sound like I'm analyzing her—"

"Are you a therapist?"

"Sort of." She laughed, showing the easy, warm smile that Benji had. "I mean, I'm a social worker, and I was trained as a counselor, but I work with primary school kids now. I see problems from the kids' side, rather than the adults."

"Ahh. I didn't know what you did for a living. What were you going to say about Casey?"

"I think it's hard for her to trust fellow adults. She *can*," she emphasized, "but she has to know someone pretty well. But with kids?" She snapped her fingers. "I think she identifies with them. Or maybe she just likes their energy. She's the only person Benji can't wear out."

"I think she's a doll," Avery's mom said. "She seems very pure of heart."

"That's the absolute truth," Julie said. "She can be very self-protective, but if she trusts you, she opens up like a flower facing the sun."

⌣

In the late afternoon, most of the adults broke into the assortment of Kaaterskill products Ben had brought, while Lisbet had an early dinner. Avery was pleased that no one seemed fazed by her breast-feeding, and she didn't even try to cover up when she sensed it was a non-issue. Lisbet had eaten slowly, probably losing focus because of all of the activity, but she finally finished. Avery tugged her shirt into place before she sat Lisbet up.

"Can I burp her?" Casey asked. "I want to prime her for the belching contests Benji and I have."

"Oh, fantastic," Avery said. "I've always hoped my tiny little daughter would be able to belch." She handed the child over, watching as Casey's smile grew.

She put her up to her shoulder and gave Lisbet the strong pats she needed, laughing when the baby let out a good one. "Score!" Casey said. "I think she's going to be a champ."

She put the baby on her legs, facing her, and grasped her hands. "You're very good at holding on," she said, talking to her like she expected a response.

"She's about ready to sit up on her own," Avery said, "at least that's what the baby books say."

"Benji sat up early," Julie said, "but he didn't want to eat solid food until he was seven or eight months old."

"You should have offered him cookies," Casey said, gazing deeply into Lisbet's eyes. "Do you want to let go and see if you can stay up?"

"Give it a try, Lisbet," Avery said. "The whole world opens up to you once you don't need anyone to— She did it!" she squealed. "Did you do that because we asked you to? Or was that just kismet?"

"I don't think the kid knows what kismet is," Casey said. "At least I hope she doesn't, because I don't."

"It's like chance or fate or something like that. Look at how pleased she seems."

"She knows she did something cool." Casey looked up, but she kept one hand an inch behind Lisbet's back, and another an inch to her left. "Do you own a phone?"

"Sure. Why?"

"Aren't you supposed to take pictures of her when she does something for the first time? I mean…"

"Oops!" Avery's phone was on the table in front of her, and she grabbed it and framed a photo to show not just Lisbet, but her new friend. "Got it," she said. "Thanks for reminding me."

"I don't know what kind of parent you're going to be if you don't document everything the kid does so that all of your friends can judge her," Casey said.

"That's why I shut down all of my social media. I lurk a little to see what I'm missing out on, but Lisbet's going to appear on the internet when she puts herself on there."

"As a mom who went crazy documenting every diaper change," Julie said, rolling her eyes, "I think you're making the right choice. We backed off when Benji was still a baby, but he hates it when people in my family tease him about those old photos."

"People act like I was wearing diapers like yesterday," he grumbled.

"You're practically a man," Casey said. "But I can still pick you up and throw you in the pool."

"You can *not*," he said, indignant.

Casey handed over the baby and chased Benji all over the yard before she put on a burst of speed and caught him. He was over her shoulder in a second, then she slowed down a little, with him laughing and slapping at her back until they got to the edge of the pool. "Can too!" she said, before slipping into the water like a knife.

Ben and Julie had to get home, so Avery got up to pack up as soon as they did. Casey walked over and said, "Mind if I take over? I want to change her diaper while you're here to watch me."

"Sure. No problem. But you did fine the other day."

"I think I did, but everyone has their preferences. I want to make sure I'm meeting yours."

Avery watched her work, so competently and patiently getting Lisbet dressed again. For a moment, she let herself daydream about what it would be like to have a partner. Well, not just any partner. One like Casey. Someone who was crazy about Lisbet.

She sighed, thinking of how fantastic it would be to have someone to share not just the burden, but the worry. In six and a half months, Avery was sure she'd woken in a panic at least a hundred times, worrying about everything from whether Lisbet was breathing, to the state of her digestion, her milk consumption, and whether the bus exhaust coming in through the window would hurt her delicate little lungs. If she'd been able to give voice to some of those fears, she might have gotten right back to sleep, which would have made her work day significantly better.

Now she had her mom, and to a lesser extent, her dad close by, and they were both more than willing to listen to her and reassure her. But it just wasn't the same as it would have been with a partner. Even with her mom, she felt...indebted to her. Like her mom was doing her a favor. She didn't ever act like she minded, but she hadn't chosen to have Lisbet. A partner would have been all in from the beginning, and that would have been very, very reassuring. Especially if the woman had been a nurturer like Casey. But that would only happen when angels starting hooking up with women to raise babies, and that seemed decidedly unlikely.

⌣

Avery watched Casey put the carseat back into the family car, admiring how easily she accomplished the feat. On the day the seat had arrived, Avery had spent over an hour watching every You Tube video available, read the manual twice, and only managed to wind up sitting on the floor of the car, crying. If her father hadn't come home and figured out how to do it, she might still be there.

She was just about to slip Lisbet into the backseat when she heard a man's voice say, "Hi there."

Turning around, Avery saw Casey's dad, freshly showered, wearing an orange T-shirt and dark jeans. From the corner of her eye, she caught her mom giving him a long look. She'd always had a thing for rugged guys who performed manual labor, and Chris was the alpha king of them. The salt and pepper stubble on his chin added a little rough charm, but his warm, brown eyes really sealed the deal. He must have had to fight women, and a substantial portion of gay men, off with a stick.

"Hi, Chris," Avery said. "Thanks so much for letting Lisbet and me rent your house."

"You're doing me a favor," he said, flashing his gleaming teeth. On him, the gap between his front teeth just added to his good looks.

"We thought we'd move in next week. We want to have a few things ready before we make the trek to our new place."

"Oh, it's far from new," he said, scowling slightly. "I'll have to do some major upgrades to make a dime off the place." He scratched at the back of his head, showing off his excellent haircut. "When that will be, I have no idea. But I can guarantee you'll be able to stay for six months. Is that good enough?"

"Absolutely. Did you want me to sign a lease?"

"Not necessary," he said, waving off the idea. "I trust you, and I'm not worried about wear and tear." He took a look at Lisbet, nodding. "Don't worry about anything, including the carpet. It's all going to go."

"Fantastic. I think I have a check in my wallet." Avery tucked Lisbet onto her hip so she could reach into the car to extract her wallet from her bag. "Two months rent?"

"One's fine. I don't need a damage deposit, since it's fine with me if you rip the cabinets off the walls and pry the linoleum off the kitchen floor. Actually, that would save me time."

"Boy, I wish I could have rented this when I actually had parties. We could have easily demolished the interior for you."

Her mom held the baby while Chris watched Avery use the roof of the car to write the check, adding, "Just make the check to cash if you don't mind."

"I don't mind at all." Avery finished writing and handed it over. "First of the month?"

"A month from today's fine. Don't worry if you're a day or two late."

"Thanks so much, Chris. I'm sure we'll enjoy our new home."

"Call if you have any problems. Or let Casey know," he added. "Everything should be fine, but with a house that old you never know what's going to break next."

"Will do, and thanks." She watched him walk around to the front of the house, wondering how he'd known exactly when to come out. He'd allowed just enough time to get a check, but not enough to socialize. Yet another odd bird. Casey had a cage-full of them to contend with.

⌣

They hadn't been in the car for more than a minute when her mom said, "So what was up with all of that flirting?"

"Flirting? On whose part?"

"Yours," she said, angling her rearview mirror to grin at Avery. "You like Casey. I can tell."

"Well, she's awfully likable, and she's as interested in Lisbet as she would have been if she'd given birth to her, so…"

"You're avoiding the question. I didn't accuse you of being grateful, honey. I'm saying that you're treating her like you treated Elizabeth back when you still thought you were straight." She paused a beat, then said, "You didn't name Lisbet after her, did you?"

"My first girlfriend? No!"

"Well, say what you will, but when you were falling for Elizabeth you acted just like you were acting with Casey today."

"I'm nice to her," she insisted. "She's just about the kindest person I've ever met, and she's very easy to be around. But I don't think I'm flirting with her. At least I'm not trying to."

"Are you sure? I know you're certain she's not interested in you, but I thought that maybe…" She took a breath and spit out the rest of her thought. "You're both single, you know."

"Seriously? If that's all it took I would have been in a hundred relationships. I'll admit I like Casey a lot, but she's not my type. We have Lisbet in common, and that's about it."

"So?" She kept gazing into the mirror, her expression so intent Avery felt like she was being inspected.

"Are you really saying you don't need things in common to make a relationship work? 'Cause I'm here to tell you that you really do. If Michelle and I had only been physically attracted to each other, we wouldn't have lasted a year."

"That would have been better all around. Then you could have found someone who valued you. Michelle," she muttered, her dislike of Avery's ex much stronger than it should have been.

"We had a good run, Mom. We supported each other's careers, gave each other tons of professional feedback, had wonderful discussions about the books we'd read, the plays we saw, the articles that captured our interest…"

"That's it? That's what creates a good relationship?"

"I think so. We always blew an hour lying in bed on Sunday morning doing the crossword, and I still hold those memories very close." She searched her memory to make sure she was remembering things correctly. "It's not like that with Casey. She hasn't mentioned a single thing I'm interested in, besides Lisbet."

Her mom rolled her eyes. "You can get every single bit of that brainy stuff from your friends. For a love interest, all you need is chemistry. Then you have a baby or two and you're both hooked in for life. That's the natural order of things."

"Huh. That's very good to know. Feel free to order the hers and hers towels as soon as you get home."

CHAPTER EIGHT

LISBET HAD BEEN EATING SOLID food for over a month now, albeit just a few tablespoons per day, but that little bit of bulk in her diet filled her up enough that she was only waking up once a night. At least that's the rumor Avery had heard—since she'd been conked out cold for eight hours every night that week.

They'd been back in Hudson for ten days, and she felt as good as she had during her second trimester, when she had energy, and optimism, and was sure she'd sail through the rest of her pregnancy. That had been a little over-optimistic, but she'd done just fine. And now that they'd adjusted to the quiet of Hudson, they were ready to move to an even quieter spot.

Avery wasn't even sure exactly where her new house was. In her mind, it was just south of Stockport, but the town didn't claim her address. So she would use the Stottville address the post office believed was correct. She didn't much care who claimed her, since all she needed from a governmental body was electrical service. She had well water, a septic field, and oil heat, all new experiences for her. This was living far off the grid in her opinion, although her father assured her she was mistaken.

Her dad was going to take her to Brooklyn at the crack of dawn the next morning, but she wanted to clear out her childhood bedroom that afternoon when he got home from playing golf. She had a feeling they'd be too tired to finish up the next day, so every little bit they could get done now would help.

Her dad's truck was small, a little Japanese number that he'd had for at least fifteen years. But he knew it like the back of his hand, and he'd insisted it was plenty big for her bedroom furniture, at this point the only things she had to move.

Two of their neighbors came over to help, and while the guys were arguing about the proper way to place everything she spent a minute double-checking the closet.

Out of nowhere, she felt a tightness in her chest, then realized she was about to cry. It was still unreasonably hot, and Lisbet, cranky from all of the tumult, began to wail.

Avery resettled her, holding her the way she'd liked when she was tiny and her tummy was upset, kind of like a running back with a squirming football. Her little legs kicked in frustration, but her crying settled down to a grumpy "I'm pissed off but I don't know why" kind of cry.

Avery certainly wasn't pissed off, but she could hardly stop herself from bawling right along with the baby. Her parents had allowed her to take her bed, her dresser, and her desk, all of which had populated the room since she could remember. Now the space was just an empty square, painted a pale lilac, with marks and scuffs on the walls from years of use.

She wasn't usually very sentimental, but her natural level of sentiment had grown since she'd given birth. Actually, she was more emotional about everything. But being upset about leaving puzzled her, since today certainly wasn't the first time she'd done it. Since she'd gone to college, she'd never returned for more than holidays. But this felt like more of a break than that original departure had been. One she wasn't entirely ready to make. She and Lisbet were going to be completely on their own, and that filled her with anxiety. While she craved independence, the time they'd been in Hudson had been healing in so many ways. Having her mother get up with the baby in the middle of the night, having lunch delivered to her while she worked, and enjoying a homemade dinner every evening was something she certainly wouldn't get any longer. And even though she'd gotten used to being alone while living in Brooklyn, this felt different, more permanent. Maybe even irrevocable.

A noise from behind made her turn to see her mom, giving her a sad smile. "I never thought you'd really leave… You know?" Her chin was quivering, and Avery felt like her heart had been pierced.

"I do know," she said, losing the battle to stanch her tears. "I haven't even had my little sweet pea for a year and I can't bear to think of her leaving me one day."

"It's pretty awful." Her mom sighed deeply and wiped her eyes with her hands. "But you've always been the most independent girl I know. You'll be fine," she said, putting an arm around her and hugging her tight.

"Thanks," Avery said, touched that her mom would try to cheer her up when she was sad too. "The house isn't perfect, but I think we'll be good there. I just have to buy some furniture for the living and dining rooms, and get a car." She let out a laugh. "That's kind of a big list, isn't it."

"Too big for someone as thrifty as you are. I want you to take my car for a while. Just until you can find a nice used one."

"Oh, mom, I can't do that!" she said, staring at her. "You need your car."

"I know I do, honey. But I don't need it every minute. Just until you buy one," she insisted. "The car seat's in it, so it's ready to go."

"But—"

"Avery," she soothed, "can you imagine how worried I'll be if you have to call a cab to leave the house? Come on now, give in for a change."

She pondered the offer for a minute, then nodded. "All right. I'd be worried every second if I knew I couldn't get Lisbet to the hospital quickly." She let out a sigh. "Everyone tells you about all of the annoyances of parenting, but no one talks about how you worry. It's constant."

"And it never stops," her mom said, giving her another very welcome hug.

⌒

It took a while to get everything roughly where it belonged, then a little longer to move a few pieces to their optimal spots. When she had everything where she wanted, Avery looked around her new house.

Now that her bed was centered on the wall facing the windows, she was very happy with the room. She'd made up the bed with pale blue sheets and the quilt she'd been given by her paternal great-grandmother when she was small. It was carefully handcrafted, with tiny dark blue stitches that she recalled staring at when she'd take a nap. It was intended for a child, with little sailboats on some of the panels, a girl wearing a sunhat, yellow ducks, and white tulips on the four corners, their stems still bright green all these years later. She had no idea what style of quilt it was, but it hardly mattered. She'd treasure it and use it even if it had been worth thousands of dollars to a collector.

In the corner, she'd placed her dresser on an angle. Her desk rested in the other corner, with the wooden chair tucked into the well. All of her clothing, which consisted of almost nothing, was in the closet, and her bathroom was stocked with all of her and Lisbet's personal care products— with Lisbet having significantly more than she did.

Back in her Brooklyn days, she'd had to wear a little makeup when she met with authors and club owners, but she'd left all of it in her old apartment, along with all of her dressy clothing. She'd probably pack that up tomorrow, but she was tempted to dump it all. The Columbia County Avery was going to be make-up free.

Across the hall, Lisbet's room was also perfectly outfitted, but Avery was still vaguely wrestling with her decision to have the baby sleep in her own room.

Best practices were to have your child in your room, but not in your bed, for the first year. But Avery thought that moving the baby into her own space when she was old enough to really know what was going on would be a pain in the butt. Since she had a very good monitoring system that she'd gotten at her baby shower, she thought she'd be able to hear the slightest noise Lisbet made, even from across the hall. But actively going against best practices made her feel like she was being reckless.

Standing there in the hallway, she patted Lisbet's back while she spoke to her. "If I thought you'd be safer lying right next to me I wouldn't hesitate," she murmured. "But I think this will work out better in the long run. What do you say?"

Lisbet rested her head against Avery's shoulder and let out a heavy sigh.

"That's how I feel, too," she said, feeling like they were actually conversing. "There's never a perfect answer, is there. Let's take a peek in here. I think you'll like it."

The Moses basket was where the crib would be when it arrived, with a view of the window, but far enough away that a draft wouldn't chill the baby. The changing table would sit by the crib, and the rocker would be in the corner with a reading lamp next to it. On the floor, all of the baby's books would be lined up. They'd read every one already, and Avery assumed they'd go through each one four or five more times before she needed to buy more complex tales.

"What do you think, babydoll? You've never slept more than five feet from me, you know. Are you up for it?"

Lisbet had little to say, so Avery took that as a nonverbal "Yes." "All right. That's settled. Now all we need is…everything."

Unless she and Lisbet were both in bed, there would be no place else in the house to hang out. No living room furniture. No dining room furniture. She'd fill the drawers with her kitchen utensils tomorrow, and she had some pots and pans and plates and glasses, but truly only enough for two, since she'd never fed anyone but Freya, and even those occasions had been pretty infrequent.

She went down to the kitchen, and was standing there looking out the big window when she felt her father's arm drape around her shoulder. "Why don't you come home tonight. I'll happily sleep in the den. You and your mom can share the bed."

"It's all right, Dad," she said, turning to give him a hug. "I know it's stark, but I'll fill it up."

"Not tonight you won't. I don't think I'll be able to sleep thinking of you roaming around in this big, old place. No screens on the windows, no curtains…"

"No one can see in from the street, but I promise I'll buy some. They'll help with drafts, which I'm sure we'll have. These beautiful old windows are very cool, but they're single pane."

"Sure you won't come home? Just for a night?"

Avery leaned her head on his shoulder, reassured by his mere presence. "I don't think so. That's just delaying my need to get acclimated. It'll be odd to be out here alone, but we'll adjust. I know we will."

"Maybe your mom should stay here tonight. I know she'd feel better."

"I'm fine," Avery insisted. "Now you two go home and enjoy the peace and quiet. Mom can relish a full night's sleep after a week of being my night nurse."

"All right," he said, sighing heavily. As he left the kitchen, he said, "You were a lot easier to handle when I could pick you up and make you do what I wanted."

"That didn't last long, did it?" she asked, seeing his small smile begin to grow.

"Not long at all."

⁓

It was only six o'clock on a hot, humid Saturday night in Columbia County. The sun would be up for at least another two hours, giving Avery time to go to the store and stock up on some staples. But she didn't have any cookware, so she couldn't even make a bowl of pasta. Why had she been so hard-headed? They should have had dinner at home, then come up here to sleep.

Lisbet was sitting on the floor in the living room, working on her crawling instincts. She didn't have it down yet, but Avery was sure she was going to eventually be a crawler. Right now she was going backwards, but that was progress. Last week she'd rolled across the entire living room. It had taken her a while, and she seemed a little dizzy when she was finished, but clearly proud of herself for winding up on the other side of the room. The baby was as stubborn as she was, and that wasn't truly a compliment.

"I think we've got to go to the store to get a sandwich from the deli, babydoll," she said. "Your mommy hasn't thought this all through, and she was too headstrong to let your grandparents take over. Par for the course, huh?"

Her phone rang and she went over to the counter to pick it up. "Hi, Casey," she said, smiling when she saw the picture of her grinning at Lisbet when she'd sat unaided for the first time.

"How's it going? I swung by your house after I made my dessert delivery. Your mom said you've flown the coop."

"I have, but I was a little premature. We don't have any food or cookware."

"We'll have to fix that, won't we," she said, her tone of voice playful. "What sounds good. I'm just a couple of blocks from the restaurant."

"Oh, I couldn't impose on you like that. Really. I'll be able to find something at the store."

"Chicken, fish, or veal. Pick one."

Avery smiled at her perseverance. "Um, it's too hot for a big meal. I was just going to have a sandwich… I'm just trying to think of how to get some boiled carrots or peas—"

"Meatball or chicken parm."

"Seriously?"

"I'm always serious about food."

"I guess I could manage part of a chicken parm sandwich…"

"I can manage all of it that you don't. Lisbet needs carrots?"

"Or peas. Or sweet potato. That's all she's had so far, except for baby cereal."

"Got it. I'll be there in about forty-five minutes. I know the address," she said, laughing a little as she hung up.

Avery walked over to the baby and sat down next to her. "Your buddy's coming over for dinner, Sweet Pea. I'm not sure what you're going to get, but I'm certain it's going to be a lot better than what I've planned for."

She held up one of Lisbet's blocks and put it in front of her, then topped it with another, waiting for the baby to knock them over, her new favorite activity. "You probably don't realize this yet, but I don't have this all figured out. If a lot of people weren't willing to bail us out, we'd be screwed."

The sun was just setting when Casey walked up the sidewalk to the house. She was about to knock when Avery walked over to peer out at her from the open half-door. "Hi," she said, beaming a smile that was kind of impossible not to return. "I've got no furniture, a fact I should have mentioned. How do you feel about sitting on the front steps."

"I've done that a couple of hundred times. Do you have—"

"No," Avery said, laughing a little. "If you're not looking for baby things, I don't have it."

"I was hoping you'd have something to sweep the steps off with. But if you don't mind getting the seat of your pants dirty…"

Avery opened the bottom door and walked out with Lisbet sitting on her hip, drooling. Avery flicked the drool off with her finger, and went to the top step to sit. "You know," she said, sounding like she about to spill a yarn. "When I was young, I was close to obsessive about cleanliness. That eased up as I got older, and having Lisbet has let me pretty much forget about it. For myself," she added. "I'm careful about keeping her clean and dry. We're homing in on seven months and she still hasn't had a bit of diaper rash."

Casey sat next to her and started to pull items out of the bag. "You and I are going to like our dinner, but Lisbet's either going to have to try something new, or she's going to have to stick to breast milk." She took out a small container and shook it. "How do you think she'll react to summer squash. That was the only thing close to baby food they had on the menu tonight." She let out a soft laugh. "I didn't think you wanted to give garlic-laden broccoli rabe a try, and roasted white potatoes seemed a little vitamin-poor."

"Good instincts," Avery said. "I'm trying to get her to try different foods, but my main goal is to get as many nutrients into her as I can."

"Sounds like a good goal."

"Well, I know I'll give in sooner than I'd like, but while she's totally under my control I want her to learn to like vegetables." She laughed. "I'm sure it won't be long before she's eating chicken fingers and macaroni and cheese for every meal."

"What's up with that? Benji eats regular food now, but the only thing on the kid's menu at a lot of places is chicken fingers or really awful pizza. Are we trying to make sure kids don't like real food?"

"Got me. I don't think I'll be able to fight Big Chicken Fingers when the time comes, since I truly don't want to be that mom who acts like every preservative is going to kill the kid, but I'm sure I won't like it."

"I give you credit for trying to be pragmatic. My sister-in-law was the mom who supervised every bite that went into her kids' mouths, and now my nephews pretty much live on pizza and tacos. I'm not sure if that's all they like, or if they're just doing it to drive her nuts." She laughed a little. "It works, by the way. She lectures them constantly, and they ignore her just as often."

"How old are the kids?"

"Seventeen and twenty. She and my brother have been divorced forever, so I don't get to see her when I visit. Not complaining!" She pulled out a napkin she'd used to wrap up some real silverware. "You should have seen the look I got from my uncle when I was poking around in his kitchen, taking whatever I wanted. If they hadn't been so swamped he would have thrown something at me."

"Casey! I didn't want you to make a fuss."

"Where else was I going to get a vegetable that wasn't a French fry? Besides, I love their chicken parm. Feel free to dig in while I mash this squash."

"I've been to Villa Napoli many times, but I've never noticed sandwiches on the menu," Avery said as she started to unwrap the gargantuan sandwich.

"They aren't. But Hernando, one of the cooks, likes me. The Casey Special is a whole loaf of Italian bread cut in half, layered with breaded chicken cutlets, tomato sauce, and provolone, then stuck under the broiler until it bubbles. I swing by and pick one up whenever I need to eat something filling."

"Looks great," Avery said, eyeing it carefully. She took a big bite, with Lisbet watching her curiously. "Divine," she said, mumbling around a mouthful. "I usually order the linguini with white clam sauce, but I might ask for the Casey Special next time."

"I'm ready," Casey said, looking at the mashed up squash. "How do we do this?"

"Well, it helps to sit her up in a good infant seat, but I left the janky one I bought at my mom's. I guess I'll see if Lisbet will let me use my fingers, since I also left her soft utensils."

"Was that a good idea?"

"She's going to be there as much as she's going to be here, so..."

"Right, right," she said. "I forgot that important detail." She took a bite of her half of the sandwich. It was always better when she ate it hot, but even a lukewarm Casey Special was pretty darned good. "Tasty, huh?"

"Very." Lisbet was still staring at her, and Avery laughed when she noticed. "She's not usually wild about eating solid food, but she's licking her chops tonight."

"It's the smell of tomato sauce. She can just tell she's going to love it one day soon."

"You're probably right," Avery said, giving her a wry smile. "Okay, baby girl. Let's see what you think of squash." She took a pea-sized bit and held it to Lisbet's lips. Tentatively, she accepted it and began to smack her mostly toothless gums together. She didn't look wild about it, but she also didn't spit it out. "So far, so good." Avery took another bit and held it next to her sandwich. "If I was in an experimental mood, I'd dip it into the tomato sauce right now. But I only like to add one food at a time so I can see how she reacts."

"She looks happy enough."

"It's the other end that sometimes doesn't react well. Her intestines have to like the food, too."

"Mmm. Very appetizing dinner conversation." She put the image out of her mind and occupied herself by taking another big bite.

The sun had dipped behind the hills, but it was still plenty light out. Sitting there, Casey let her mind wander to the many happy days she'd spent with her grandmother, often sitting right on this porch. She had been an ace card-player, and she'd taught Casey how to play gin at a pretty tender age. Sitting outside in the evening, drinking lemonade, while playing cards for hours was one of her favorite memories.

"You seem contemplative tonight," Avery said.

"Mmm. Just thinking. You know what I don't know?"

"I can't guess."

"I don't know how you decided to have Lisbet. Or how… If that's something you talk about."

"Oh, I don't mind revealing how ridiculously impulsive I was about the most important decision of my life," she said, laughing as she shook her head. "My mom has just stopped lecturing me about it."

"Um…details?"

"Well, I've always been certain I wanted to have kids. I would have had one with Michelle, but we lived a hundred miles away from one another, and I knew I wouldn't be able to count on her for much practical support."

"Right, right," Casey said, recalling Avery's ex worked in Philadelphia.

"I'd been looking for a woman who wanted to co-parent, but not having much luck."

"I hear you on that score."

"Right," she said, reaching into the container to give Lisbet another tiny bite. "I was on vacation, in Copenhagen, which is where my friend Freya is from."

"Your roommate."

"Exactly. Her sister's a lesbian, also, for what it's worth. She's a pediatrician, and her office was in a building with a fertility clinic. We were sitting around on like the second night I was there, and Marit suggested I meet her for lunch so we could talk to a friend of hers who worked at the clinic."

"Um…why?"

"I was also surprised," Avery said, nodding. "But Freya had obviously told her I was thinking about the process. Marit made it sound like it was no big deal to get information, so I went, and we had a nice lunch. I found out I could buy sperm for much less than I'd have to pay in New York, and

157

we worked out that I was at peak fertility right then." She shrugged, looking a little puzzled by her choices. "They assured me I had less than a ten percent chance of getting pregnant, so it didn't seem like a huge decision." She started to laugh. "But it sure was!"

"Wow," Casey whispered. "You got pregnant on a vacation dare."

"I kind of did," she agreed. "But it was clearly meant to be, since everything aligned perfectly."

"Damn, Avery, a woman I know from college spent like six months trying to pick the perfect donor. She had a husband, and she really wanted the baby to look as much like him as possible, but still…"

"I just asked for donors who would allow the child to contact them in the future. There were only a handful of them, and I weeded out anyone who had autoimmune diseases, cancer, or heart disease in their immediate family. That left two guys, and I flipped a coin. A krone," she added. "I kept it, of course."

"Was he a blond too?"

"Uh-huh. Blue eyes." She smiled. "My mom accuses me of trying to clone myself, but I truly did flip a coin. The other guy had dark hair and darker skin, and I probably should have picked him just so Lisbet wasn't consigned to a life of constant sunblock application."

"You couldn't have picked a better donor, since Lisbet's perfection itself," she said, reaching over to tickle the babbling baby's foot. "What's her full name?"

"Lisbet Kendall. I'd always thought I'd name a daughter Elizabeth, since some of my favorite writers share that name, but given her donor's Danish, I went with the Danish equivalent." She laughed. "My mom thinks I named her after my first girlfriend, which is kind of weird. Why would I name my baby after the first woman who broke my heart?"

Casey gave her a playful look, hoping Avery could take a joke. "Well, when you have a baby because of a dare when you're on vacation…"

"Okay, my mom was justified in thinking I'd lost my senses. But I love the name, and I like that it's both very common and very uncommon."

"There's a guy at work who named his daughter Soffya. With two f's and a y. I think he and his girlfriend had the same idea as you did in trying to be unique, but the kid's going to hate having to spell it like six times whenever she meets someone new."

"I haven't had much trouble with Lisbet, but a few people have spelled it with a 'z.' I can live with that."

Casey leaned back and looked at her for a second. "You know, you're awfully calm about…everything. I don't think I would be if I was a new mom."

She smiled and batted her eyes. "Count your blessings you didn't run into me right after Lisbet was born. I was a worried mess for a couple of months." She stopped, with her eyes narrowing briefly. "I stayed with my parents during my measly six weeks of maternity leave, but once I returned to Brooklyn I quickly got over myself. I had to gut it up and get on with life, which I think was the best thing for me."

"Do you miss it? Brooklyn, that is."

"Not yet. I'm sure I will when I have a craving for a good curry or something else I can't easily get here. But the Hudson Valley's more diverse than it was when we were kids. I'll be able to stick it out for a few years."

Casey stared at her. "Just a few years?"

"Oh, yeah. I'm going back as soon as I can manage it. I've already got applications in for pre-K. If Lisbet gets into a place I can afford, we'll go back when she's three."

"That's awfully soon," Casey said. "Won't you have all of the same problems that made you leave?"

"No," she said, clearly having through this through. "I don't think so. Pre-K will be much less expensive than daycare. And if I have more time I might be able to find a roommate. Maybe another single mom."

"Mmm," Casey said, nodding. "If you really want to go back, I have a feeling you'll make it work." She watched Lisbet chew on her mother's finger, reminding herself to enjoy the baby as much as she could while she was still young—and in the same county.

They spent a half hour sitting on the porch, watching fireflies come to life. Avery didn't know as much about them as Casey did, but they seemed to enjoy them equally well.

"When I was a kid, the trees came much closer to the house," Casey said. "I'd go running after the lightning bugs and would almost always trip over a root or run right into a trunk. Toughened me up," she said, laughing a little.

"Your grandmother must have been chasing you the whole time!"

"Oh, no, not at all. She didn't believe in babying kids. I can still hear her sitting on the porch, kind of distractedly yelling, 'Rub it off' when I'd hurt myself. I learned not to cry for attention."

"Ooo. But a little girl needs attention."

"Yeah, but not too much. I think it's a mistake to make a kid feel like every little bump and bruise is a major event." A very sober look settled onto her face. "I'd want my kid to be physically resilient, but I wouldn't try to toughen them up emotionally. That never works."

"Um…personal experience?" Avery asked tentatively.

"Kind of. My grandmother thought I was a baby for being afraid of the basement. She made fun of me for that instead of reassuring me. That…wasn't great," she added. "I was lucky that I was pretty tough in general. My sister was kind of a wimp, and even as a kid I could tell my grandmother wasn't crazy about her."

"Casey! Your grandmother didn't like your sister?"

"She *was* a wimp," she said, clearly teasing. "I was riding my bike over here when I was in first grade, and my sister was afraid to go with me, even though she was in sixth. W.I.M.P.," she added, still smiling.

"Toughen up," Avery whispered, leaning over to speak into Lisbet's ear. "The Van Dykes don't put up with any nonsense."

"I'll admit the Van Dykes are bad," Casey said, "but the Gerritsens are worse."

Casey picked up all of the trash from their meal, and tucked it back into the bag she'd brought everything in. "I'd leave this here, but I bet you don't have a trash can."

"All true. It's hard to pry money out of my hands, but I'm not cheap enough to have to run out to the bin every time I have to throw something away."

"I'll take this stuff with me. Are you good? Need anything?"

"Um…would you think I was a wimp if I asked you to look around to make sure no one's hiding under the bed?"

"Under the bed? Really?" She gazed into Avery's eyes, seeing she was a little embarrassed to have asked.

"Uh-huh," she said, nodding soberly. "Mad killers sneak into houses in broad daylight, then hide under the bed until everyone's asleep. Common knowledge," she said, with just a hint of a smile showing.

"I'm game. Do you want to stay out here while I look? Or might a different, but no less murderous person snatch you right off the porch while I'm gone?"

"Thanks! I never considered there'd be two!"

"Come inside with me," Casey said, purposefully soothing her voice. "While you make sure your doors are locked, I'll check both upstairs and down."

"You'll check downstairs? Even though you're afraid of the basement?"

"I think I'm less afraid of the basement than you are of the Mad Killer. Besides, my grandma would be proud of me if I gutted it up."

"Thank you," Avery said, looking up at her like she was just a little older than Lisbet.

"I'm on the job," Casey said, heading upstairs. As she walked, she called out loudly, "If anyone's up there, I'm going to find you and kick your ass, so you might just as well jump right out the window."

"I don't mind being teased, so long as you humor me," Avery called up.

"Good, since I don't think I can stop teasing."

There were no monsters hiding under the bed, but the house was so empty Casey felt like she was leaving Avery and Lisbet in a place that still didn't have an occupancy permit. "Um, you're going to tell me I'm nuts," she said, after having checked every inch of the house, "but we could switch houses until you get some furniture. All I do is sleep in my room, but you've got a whole thing going on with feeding the baby and working…"

"You are nuts," Avery said. "But in the kindest way possible." She took Casey by the arm and guided her to the door. "We're going right to bed, secure in the knowledge that the Mad Killer isn't here—tonight, at least. We'll be fine." She slipped her arms around Casey's waist and hugged her, surprising her a little. They hadn't really hugged, and she'd gotten the impression Avery wasn't into being physically affectionate. But the hug was sweet, and conveyed a lot of emotion, which touched Casey deeply. "Thank you so much for arranging all of this. I think we'll be very happy here."

"I just hooked you up with a good opportunity," she said, feeling the loss when Avery let her go. "And I made some points with my dad in the process. It was driving him crazy to continue to pay the property tax bill while not having any income from the place."

"You and your dad are very generous people." With a very gentle push, she directed Casey to the door.

She stood right in the threshold, and grasped the frame. "Who else is going to Brooklyn with you and your dad tomorrow?"

"No one. All I have to pick up is Lisbet's crib, her dresser, and a rocker."

"That can't be all you have. What about clothes?"

"I have some…"

"What about the stuff from your kitchen?"

"Well," she said, looking pensive. "I've got some dishes and some utensils. A few pots and pans. A rice cooker. A French press. Oh. Books," she added, rolling her eyes. "I've got way too many books, and Lisbet has quite a few of her own…"

"That all won't fit in your dad's truck. We'll take mine. I'll pick you up at six, then we'll swing by your parents' house. Unless you think you need his truck, too."

"But…" Her pale brown brows were as high as they got.

"As my grandmother would say, don't be stupid," she said, turning to walk down the stairs, thinking of how many nights she'd walked down the old sidewalk on her way home. Having Avery there was honoring the old place by holding off the bulldozers for a few months at the very least. Casey was sure her grandmother would like that, and honoring the woman who'd always made her feel like she mattered was as important as anything in her life.

When Casey arrived at the house early the next morning, both of the Nichols girls were ready to rock. They drove over to the family home, and Avery handed the baby over to Kathy. Ken and Avery got into the truck, and Casey saw that Lisbet was on the verge of tears as Kathy held her little hand up to wave goodbye.

"Just made it," Avery said, laughing a little from the back seat. "I hate to leave Mom with a crying baby, but she'll only be upset for a minute."

"Your mom?" Ken asked.

"I meant—"

"That was a joke, honey." He turned around slightly and gave Avery's leg a pat. "I think today will be fun. Since I'm not driving, that is."

"Have you driven to Brooklyn before?" Casey asked.

"Twice," he said. "My blood pressure's finally back down to normal. Just took twelve years," he added quietly.

"I've never even been to Brooklyn, much less driven there."

"And you call me a wimp," Avery said, giving Casey a friendly scratch on the shoulder.

Ken appointed himself the DJ, and he did the job pretty well. His musical tastes were a little more "trucks, women, beer and broken hearts" than Casey's, but she liked good ole boy country well enough.

He really came through when they hit the Bronx, handing her enough gum from the stash she kept in one of the cup holders to chew her way through her nerves. She'd never driven into the city at all, and doing it for the first time in a big truck right when the city was waking up wasn't anything close to fun.

She'd been driving a large truck for a long time, and usually kind of owned the road. But in the Bronx, where almost all of the traffic was eighteen-wheelers going to or from the huge distribution centers that Avery told her were located all around, she felt like she was on a tricycle. The whole experience reminded her of a post-apocalyptic movie, where the social order had completely broken down. A hundred thousand cops couldn't have kept an eye on all of the speeders, dangerous lane-changers, and tailgaters. There must have been ten or twenty people killed every day, yet Avery and her father spoke idly about nothing in particular, neither one acting like they should be praying for their lives!

Her GPS calmly instructed her through Manhattan, which was better, but then they crossed a bridge and things got real. Bike messengers completely ignored their own safety and all traffic laws, pedestrians crossed the street whenever they damn well wanted, acting like they couldn't even see the cars bearing down on them, and every van in town was double-parked on the narrow streets. When you added in the pot holes, which were friggin' constant, Casey was sure her own blood pressure had picked up every point that Ken had lost.

Actually, since it was now eight thirty, and the delivery trucks that had been in the Bronx were now trying to squeeze down streets clearly laid out a hundred years before cars even existed, Ken seemed a little frazzled too. He was normally pretty chatty, but he'd shut up completely. From then on, the only voice that wasn't singing through the speakers was the navigation instructions, an annoyance that was almost constant. If Casey never heard "recalculating" again, it would be too soon.

Avery was quiet too, but she didn't seem afraid. Casey had learned Avery's sense of direction was terrible, so she'd stopped relying on her, making that annoying GPS voice mandatory.

Finally, she pulled up to Avery's building, blocking the fire hydrant. She wasn't going to stay long, but she had to calm down before she could bear to think of wedging her huge truck into a parking spot meant for a dirt bike.

Ken finally spoke, and there was a touch of reverence in his voice when he said, "Better you than me."

"I don't drink and drive," Casey said, hearing how high and tight her voice was, "but if someone handed me a beer, I'd chug it."

"Thank god, I'm not driving," he said, finally letting out a laugh. "After we get everything loaded, I'm going to run down to the bar we passed a couple of blocks ago."

"I think I left a beer or two in my fridge," Avery said.

"You're not going to have it for long," he said as he threw the door open and stood on the sidewalk for a minute, getting his sea-legs. Casey wasn't going to say a thing if he had to have a pop before they hit the road again. If she could have, she would have joined him.

⌒

Loading a crib, a changing table, and a rocker into a truck should not have been much trouble. Casey had helped friends move entire bedroom suites with a hell of a lot less hassle. But carrying everything down three flights of stairs, then loading it all into the bed of the truck, now illegally double-parked in front of the building, was a pain in the butt. Avery had gone up to pack her kitchen things while Casey waited in the truck, and she'd already convinced a passing cop to keep his hand off his ticket book. With this many illegal parking jobs, it was possible the entire city budget came from parking fines. What a friggin' mess!

Eventually, Avery walked up to the passenger window and leaned on the sill. "I've got all of my kitchen stuff in the boxes you brought from work." She cocked her head and gazed at Casey with what looked like awe. "How did I think I was going to move without boxes?"

"Not to put too fine a point on it, but this operation was half-assed from the beginning. Lisbet's furniture alone wouldn't have fit into your dad's truck. What were you two thinking?"

"Umm…we weren't?" she said, looking pretty cute when she made fun of herself. Avery reached further in, grasped Casey's hand, and squeezed it tightly. "I can't tell you how thankful I am for this. This goes way beyond the call of duty."

"It's been fun," she lied outrageously. Her hands were still shaking, but she thought she'd be able to convince herself to drive home. "So just the kitchen stuff's left?"

"Unless you want to carry my books down." She held up a hand. "I'm happy to leave them. Freya said she didn't mind."

"Do you want them?" Casey asked.

Avery nodded almost imperceptibly.

"We've got enough boxes, I think. Let's give it a try." She got out of the truck, letting Avery slide in to hopefully charm the next parking enforcement person from slapping an undoubtedly expensive ticket on her windshield. "See you in a few."

Casey started to trudge up the stairs, afraid she'd have heat stroke by the time they got the boxes of books down. It didn't seem possible, but Brooklyn had to be ten degrees hotter than the Hudson Valley. Why in the hell did so many people want to live in such a shithole?

‿

They'd stopped for a calorie-laden, nutrient-deficient, fast-food lunch, so they didn't reach the house until two thirty. Avery was ready for a nap, and she hadn't carried a single thing down the stairs. She would have, and she was fairly certain she could have, but neither her dad nor Casey would hear of it. Her dad still treated her as gently as he had when she'd been pregnant, but Casey didn't seem to consider her frail. It felt more like she was just certain she was stronger, which she clearly was.

After Casey parked by the kitchen door on the side of the house, they all got out. Avery noted her dad looked a little shaky. His job was technically manual labor, but it didn't require a lot of heavy lifting. Most appliances now were made up mostly of modules, and he spent his days removing ones with a burned out part and replacing them with a shiny new one. She was certain he didn't ever have to carry anything up or down three flights of stairs, and just as certain he was glad for that.

He stood behind the truck, hands on his hips, looking up at the bed like it was five feet high.

Casey walked around and put a hand on his shoulder. "Do you think we can find a delivery service that'll bring us a six pack?"

"I'll go," Avery said. "Where's the closest place? I haven't driven around here yet, so I don't know the hot spots."

"Mmm." Casey looked at her thoughtfully. "There's no place very close. You'll have to go over to Route 9."

A car pulled up, and Avery turned to see her mom, along with Lisbet and two of their neighbors. As the men got out of the car, Casey walked over and took Lisbet from her car seat. "I've got the most important cog in the machinery," she said, tucking her onto her hip.

Avery's dad walked over to the other side of the car, accepting the six pack of Budweiser. "I knew I'd made the best decision of my life in marrying you," he said, pulling a beer from the plastic holder and nearly shotgunning it. He was going to be a stiff, sore puppy in the morning, but she knew he wouldn't have had it any other way. He'd gotten more protective ever since she'd been pregnant, and she'd come to appreciate the change. It was like he was acknowledging that her job was kind of tough at times, too, even though it didn't require feats of strength. He was a darned good dad, and if he had any sense at all, he'd let Jeff and Dave do the majority of the work, while he and Casey served as supervisors. It was time for them to punch out.

CHAPTER NINE

EARLY SEPTEMBER WAS ALMOST ALWAYS warm in Brooklyn, at least in Avery's experience. But this year amped the warmth up quite a bit. Summer was still hanging on tenaciously, warning autumn to keep its distance.

Kids were back in school, still carrying a lot of their summer energy, not seeming to mind having a little more structure to their days. At least that's how they seemed as they raced out of PS 25 in Bed-Stuy. It was just two thirty, and Avery had tons of time to kill until she had to be at tonight's location to set up for *Short Shorts*, her first since the move. She should have gone to the office, but Helena hadn't specifically asked her to come, so she'd decided to soak up some Brooklyn magic while she had the chance.

She'd only been away for a little more than two weeks, but it seemed much longer. Everything appeared to be a little brighter, a little louder, a little dirtier. But it was her kind of seedy, and she loved it.

If she could only ignore the fact that she'd have to get to the bar soon to monopolize the bathroom to pump, she could have convinced herself that she was once again footloose and fancy free, with no obligations other than a demanding job. The sun was shining, and the birds might have been singing if she could have heard them over the shouts of the kids. A group of moms were waiting patiently by a railing, and they seemed to have formed a clique, talking quietly while they scanned the crowd for their little ones.

She was feeling really buoyant when she stepped off the curb, only to be nearly crushed when a delivery van whipped around a double-parked car and caught her tote bag, ripping it off her arm and flinging it into a shallow puddle, with some of the water splashing against her shins. The waiting women all made sympathetic noises about how no one paid attention anymore, but her heart was banging so hard in her chest she could barely make out the words. Her life hadn't flashed in front of her eyes, but she was immediately overwhelmed by images of Lisbet being raised by her grandparents.

There was no place to sit, but she compelled her shaky legs to guide her over to a bike rack, then leaned against it, trying to catch her breath. The images kept assailing her, and she found herself simply letting them come, hoping that acknowledging them would allow them to pass.

If this had been her last day on earth, it would only take weeks for Lisbet to basically forget her. Her grandparents would become her parents, leaving no trace of the bonds so deeply etched into Avery's brain she was certain they would always remain.

Her hands were shaking so hard she could barely get a grasp on the dripping wet canvas bag, which she'd been able to retrieve. She was going to believe there was nothing but water in that puddle, since that was the only way to thrive in a big city. You had to shake off the bumps and bruises and move on without a second thought. But as she got herself together and started to walk toward Franklin Avenue, she didn't think she'd be able to do that this time.

The truth settled on her like a scratchy blanket on a hot day, stifling her. She was no longer footloose and fancy free, and those days were not simply on hold. They were over. Raising a child wasn't *a* priority—it was *the* priority.

By the time she got to the bar, she was over the fright, but the thought remained that she was no longer living her own life.

Avery found a barstool in the otherwise empty room and sat down until she could shake off some of the disturbing feelings. It was pretty odd that it had taken her all of these months to realize that having Lisbet had destroyed her old life, but it was an unassailable truth. Things would never again be what they had been. She was living a new life now, one that was so inextricably entwined with Lisbet that she couldn't afford to be so cavalier about her choices.

Tonight, after she finished up, she was going to have to take an Uber to Penn Station, something she never would have done before. But walking around alone, at night, in a neighborhood she didn't know well wasn't an option any more. The expense would be hard to swallow, but she had to get home to her baby intact. Now she just had to worry about being murdered by the Uber driver, a threat she'd never considered until this second. *Great. Just great.*

Casey left work around three, watching the brewery get smaller in her rearview mirror. Actually, this was one of her favorite views of the place. The plant looked like a simple farm from this part of the long driveway, and she loved that rural vibe.

It took about twenty minutes to get to Kathy and Ken's, and she paused for a moment before she parked. A car she didn't recognize was in the drive, and she didn't want to interrupt if Kathy had a friend over. Then she had second thoughts, deciding Kathy might have a better visit if she didn't have to keep an eagle eye on Lisbet.

She parked and walked up to the door, knocking gently just in case Lisbet was asleep. When she got no answer, she walked around to the side of the house, spotting the pair near the vegetable garden Kathy was tending.

"Any tomatoes left?" Casey asked.

Kathy looked up and smiled. "I was hoping you'd come by today. I meant to get your cell phone number from Avery so I could text you with an invite, but I forgot, and I didn't want to bother her when she was at work. She gets very tense about her radio show."

"You're proud of her, aren't you?" Casey asked, seeing the pleasure in her eyes.

"Of Avery? God, yes. If Lisbet makes her as proud as I am of my girl, she'll be a very lucky woman."

"I think Avery's the lucky one." She squatted down and lifted the light blanket that covered the baby's car seat, seeing that she was sound asleep.

"She's got parents who love her a ton, and a baby who couldn't be sweeter if she tried."

"We've all been lucky. We get along well, and we're healthy. That's plenty to keep me happy."

"That would be enough for me, too," Casey said. "I'm not sure that's true for Avery, though. I think she needs more than that."

Kathy rolled her eyes as she sat back on her heels. She was wearing bright orange Crocs, and they were caked with mud. "I know that was true before, but I'm hoping she eventually realizes that you can't have everything." She smiled at Casey. "She's always gotten what she's wanted, mostly through hard work. But some things just aren't possible." She put her hands on the soil and pushed herself to her feet. "I love my daughter more than I have words to express, but I also really like her. Having her around more has let me acknowledge how much I've missed her. And now that Lisbet's here…"

"I miss Lisbet when I haven't seen her for a couple of days," Casey said. "And we're basically strangers."

"That's not even close to the truth." She extended a hand and pulled Casey to her feet, showing some hidden strength. "I'd never insist that a stranger join us for dinner. I've got a couple of heirloom tomatoes still warm from the sun, and I'm going to make BLTs, my favorite sandwich. Are you in?"

"Let me text my mom and tell her I won't be home. Can I help you put your gardening things away?"

"Either that or take the baby inside. Your choice."

"Ha! You think you can trick me. But I'll surprise you by rinsing off your tools. See you in a minute."

⸎

Given Avery's bedroom had been cleared out, Kathy had obviously been forced to improvise. She was using an end table to change diapers, and she now had only the Moses basket to use as a crib.

"This room looks very, very big," Casey said as she poked her head in. "How did everything fit before?"

"It was a tight squeeze." Lisbet only weighed about eighteen pounds, but she looked bigger while lying on the small end table, kicking her little legs wildly as Kathy tried to get her changed. "It's going to get a little more crowded when I buy a crib—which I'm going to do very soon."

"Avery doesn't want one here?"

"She's the cheapest girl in town," Kathy said, laughing. "But Lisbet's at the point of not being able to extend her legs in that little basket, and I'm not going to put her on the floor."

Some framed pieces were still on the wall, and Casey took the time to check them out. "The University of Iowa," she said. "Avery told me she got a master's degree from there, but she never said how she wound up in Iowa. Do you have family there or something?"

"Hmm? Oh, no," Kathy said. "According to Avery, Iowa has one of the best schools for aspiring writers." She pointed to a framed article that hung by the window. "That was her goal, you know. To write full time. When her book was published, we thought she was well on her way."

Casey felt her mouth drop open. "She wrote a book?"

"Sure did," Kathy said, clearly proud. "It was reviewed in the *New York Review of Books*, and I'm told that's a very big thing."

Moving closer, Casey read the article carefully. "Wow. Whoever wrote this really thought she had promise. He said so like three times." She looked at Kathy. "Why didn't she stick with it?"

"Money." She let out a soft sigh. "*Ad Infinitum* offered her a full time job while she was still working on finishing the book. But even though it got great reviews, she only sold a few thousand copies. Avery tells me that's the norm, by the way. Especially for a book of short stories. She couldn't afford to quit her job at that point, and the job keeps her so busy she hasn't had time to write another book."

"But she likes her job, right? She says she does."

"Oh, yes. I'm sure she likes it. But if she could manage it, she'd write. At least I think she would. It's hard to tell sometimes." She smiled warmly. "My girl doesn't always tell you everything that's on her mind."

"She certainly doesn't boast. She's never mentioned that she wrote a book."

"In her world, everyone's written a book. She doesn't seem to think it's unique." Her smile grew. "But I do. She's the first one in either of our families to graduate from college, and she's a published author. I couldn't be more proud of her." She'd finished up with Lisbet, and now leaned over to speak right into her face. "Your mommy's the smartest person I've ever known, Lisbet. You're going to have to work to keep up with her."

She picked the baby up and handed her to Casey. "I'm not sure where she got it from, but Avery's always been driven. Whatever she does, she does well."

"Including having a perfect baby," Casey said, smiling down at the child. "Your mommy's off in the big city right now, slaying some dragons." She looked at Kathy, who was putting her diaper changing accessories into a tote bag. "Do you know what she really does at her job? It sounds pretty…vague to me."

"I think I do," she said, wrinkling her nose just the way Avery did. "But sometimes I'm not so sure. Since she's been home, she's been editing pieces for the magazine. Even I can understand that. But today? I'm not really sure how the radio show's done. Isn't it kind of odd to have a show in a bar?"

"Search me. I'm very familiar with bars, but I've never been to one where people read stories."

"Everything's a little different in Brooklyn," Kathy said, and Casey didn't have any reason to disagree.

⌒

By six o'clock, at least half of the staff from *Ad Infinitum* had arrived at the bar. Avery was immensely grateful they'd shown up to help, and she started assigning them little tasks, freeing her to supervise. Helena arrived a short time later, looking cool and professional as always. She was only about ten years older than Avery, but she'd always seemed much more mature. Or maybe worldly was more precise.

Helena seemed to know everyone who was anyone in publishing, and she used her influence to hook new writers up with agents, help them nail down book deals, and generally try to get promising talent recognized in any way she could. She'd tried to convince Avery to continue to write, but she honestly felt like she'd done her best work on her short story collection, and the two years of work she'd put into creating it had barely returned enough to cover a few months of her living expenses. Gone were the days when a writer could sell a piece or two a year and make ends meet, and Avery was too practical to hold onto dreams that didn't seem likely to pan out.

She'd only been in Brooklyn for six hours, but being surrounded by her work family gave Avery a boost that soothed her soul. It was a thrill to be around people who spoke the same language, were all interested in roughly the same things, and were similarly dedicated to promoting good writing. When you shared a passion, friendships followed.

She was walking over to an engineer who was adjusting sound levels when she heard her name. Turning, she smiled and waved at Freya who was walking in with Rebecca, an assistant in the promotions department. It had been a while since she'd seen the woman, since she worked on another floor, and Avery did a double-take, certain that Rebecca had either gained weight in a very specific spot, or was pregnant. She wasn't showing much, but her clingy jersey dress showed just enough of a bump to make Avery take notice.

"Surprise," Rebecca said, patting her belly after giving Avery a hug. "If you come back, we can take turns walking our kids to school."

"That's fantastic!" Avery gushed. "When are you due?"

"Early March." She put her hands on Avery's arms and spoke slowly. "I need you to tell me how easy it was to give birth. Lie if you need to, but you have to convince me."

"Piece of cake," Avery said. She let out a laugh. "Ask Freya. She was with me until my mom and dad got to the hospital. We just watched TV and laughed, right?"

"Sure," she said, smiling. She pulled Avery in for a hug. "It was such an ordinary day I hardly remember it."

"Henry must be thrilled," Avery said.

"Oh, he is, but he's as worried as he is excited. He's just in the second year of his residency, so he's got four more to go. Our timing wasn't great, but…" She shrugged. "I was switching birth control pills and… Bam!"

"You've got my number. If you have any questions, just text me. And I'll have lots of clothes for you. I'm going out of my way to buy unisex styles when I can, so they should work for a boy or a girl."

"I'll take you up on that. Henry doesn't earn much, and god knows I don't either. We might have to take in a roommate."

"No one wants to live with a baby they didn't give birth to," Freya said, revealing a slightly guilty smile. "At least that's what I'm told."

By seven fifteen, the three writers who were going to read were nervously pacing around the jury-rigged backstage Avery's interns had constructed with only a black drape and a staple gun. She didn't tend to get nervous at readings, mostly because she always crafted at least fifteen questions for the little chat she conducted, and they never had time for more than three or four. Being prepared had always been her antidote to anxiety.

She'd edited each of tonight's pieces, cutting one down by almost a thousand words, the other two with less severe shearing. It wasn't that any of them were truly too long, but they had to fit into the format, which only allowed twenty minutes for each story. Michael Stefanic, the writer whom she'd had to cut so harshly, was still a little testy about the edits. But he'd agreed in the end, wanting the publicity from the podcast more than he'd wanted to protect his precious words. He was off in the corner, smoking, even though it was clearly against the law. She was about to go and banish him to the sidewalk, but she wasn't in the mood to get into an argument. Besides, she had to find a private spot to pump before it was time to take the stage. She waved to Freya, who'd already helped solve a few logistical problems. "I need to find a quiet spot for about twenty minutes. Can you help?"

"I've already found a place," she said, smiling with accomplishment. "It's not pretty, or very clean, but it's private. You don't mind using the employee toilet in the kitchen, do you?"

"Mind?" It took her a moment to wonder who wouldn't mind. "If that's the only option, I will thank you sincerely and go get my pump."

"The only other option is a park down the street. I really tried," she added. "The world just isn't very accommodating for working mothers."

Casey cleaned the kitchen after dinner, while Kathy sat at the table, giving Lisbet a bottle.

"I like to watch her eat," Casey said, turning to smile at the scene. "I've never seen anyone who likes food as much as she does." The baby's eyes were wide open, and her little hands shook and twitched as she tried to gulp the milk down as quickly as possible. "She always looks kind of frantic, like she's afraid someone will take the bottle away before she drains it."

"I don't remember Avery being like this," Kathy said, looking down at the baby fondly. "But I was so tired back then that I've probably forgotten ninety percent of what happened."

"I think Avery's tired too, but she sure doesn't complain."

"No, she's not much of a complainer. She's as hard-headed as they come, though. Living on her own when she could stay here for free? The kid's insane." She let out a laugh. "I've got a lot of nerve talking about her, since I'm almost as bad, but a mother has the right to give her kid a hard time."

"She's really lucky to have you," Casey said. "We talked about her work a little, and I got the impression she needed quiet to get anything done."

"She always has. When she was in first grade, she'd be in her room, doing her homework with Ken's big headphones on. No music playing, mind you. Just the headphones. I'm still amazed she was able to work in that noisy apartment of hers."

"That's in the past," Casey said. "The only noises she'll hear now are from wildlife. Her new neighborhood's quieter than mine, and we have twice the acreage."

"I didn't look around much on Saturday. Is it really that rustic?" Kathy stared at her, looking a little jumpy. "She's never lived outside of a city, you know. There aren't bears up there, are there?"

"Bears?" Casey laughed. "I don't think so, but it's well past suburbia. I guarantee she'll see more deer than people."

"Well, she's definitely not a fan of rural life, but maybe she'll change her mind if it's quiet." She smiled up at Casey. "Either that or she'll move back here, which I would truly love."

⌒

Casey stepped outside to go home after they'd managed to keep Lisbet awake until eight, with Kathy hoping she'd sleep through the night if she stayed up later. It really tugged at Casey's heartstrings to watch the child settle down in her basket and smack her little Cupid's-bow lips together like she was very, very satisfied to be horizontal. But she looked so small and helpless lying on the floor of the mostly empty room that Casey would have slept right next to her if given the chance. She didn't want Ken and Kathy to realize how quirky she was, or she would have suggested the idea. But they didn't know her well enough to realize she was a little odd, but entirely harmless.

Ken walked her out, and stopped by the car in the driveway. "Did you see Kathy's new wheels?"

"This is Kathy's?"

"Uh-huh. Went out this morning and bought it without saying a word." He laughed. "Last time she bought a car I slowed her down by at least a week, doing all kinds of research and trying to get a better deal. I guess she wasn't in the mood for more of that."

"I didn't know you could buy a car and take it right home."

"I didn't either. But she told them she'd take it then or not at all, so they hustled to prep it. Knowing her, she got them to throw in the new car seat. She's very persuasive," he added, his smile showing he found that an attractive trait.

"Did you know she was even interested in buying a car?"

"I had no idea. But once Avery decided to move out, I should have guessed. Actually, I'm surprised she didn't buy the new one for her, but since Avery's just as stubborn, that might have been a long standoff."

"Mmm. Yeah, Avery's pretty independent. Do you think she'll accept Kathy's old one?"

"I think so. She clearly has to have one, and according to the dealer the old car was only worth a few thousand dollars. I don't think her pride will get in the way—this time." He laughed, looking a tiny bit like Avery when he did. "But you never know."

Only by begging her Uber driver to rush did Avery get to the twelve oh eight train. She hadn't voluntarily been up that late in months, but she was still buzzing from the evening, which had gone exceedingly well.

She'd picked the stories because they'd had a common theme, but she hadn't been sure they'd work well together, given the authors' varied styles. But Stefanic's harsh, almost brutal imagery had been a nice counterpoint to Greenfield's pastoral setting. And Ahmad's stories were always colorful and sensual, a calming, soothing antidote to whatever craziness was going on in the world.

Talking to such talented writers, as well as the super-literary groupies who tended to follow *Short Shorts* wherever it roamed, always gave her a high. But getting an immersion back into the world of carefully chosen words after spending most of her days with a beautiful little creature who could only babble had been rejuvenating.

Avery had no idea why words had grabbed her attention at such an early age, and had never waned as the dominant force in her life, but it was a fact she couldn't ignore. While she could hardly have been more grateful for her parents' and Casey's help in getting her relocated, she craved the creative chaos of her adopted home. She had no idea how she'd get back there, but it called to her like the mountains or the sea called to other people. The problem was that everyone understood why a person was drawn to the mountains. Far fewer could comprehend wanting to live in a place where a delivery truck nearly crushed you, while the bystanders just nodded like it had been the most expected thing in the world.

⸻

It was almost two a.m when Avery parked on the street in front of her parents' house, registering a strange car in the drive, but too tired to think about it much. She entered the house quietly, then tiptoed down the hall to see that Lisbet was sleeping soundly, with one little arm tossed above her head.

Heading back to the living room, Avery removed her clothing as she walked. A quick trip to the bathroom only slowed her down slightly. She took a T-shirt from her bag and tugged it over her head, then dropped to the sofa and pulled the sheet her mom had set out up to her chin. Being horizontal had never felt so good.

She was sure she'd been asleep when Lisbet's car-alarm cry went off, and as she stumbled to her feet she saw that the clock on the VCR read two fifteen. *Fantastic.*

⸻

Getting up and out wasn't an easy task. Avery was so tired she ached, but she dutifully fed Lisbet and drove to her new home at eight a.m.

The new place was stark, but that was kind of a benefit. Not having a place to lounge would force her to sit at her desk, where she always worked more efficiently. Just to avoid having to go back downstairs, she carried the sandwich her mom had made with her, peeking into the plastic grocery bag to find a sleeve of vanilla wafers, her favorite cookie. She was smiling with contentment as she sat down and booted up her computer. She didn't have internet yet, and thought she might not get it at all. Her phone could serve as a hotspot to download files without a problem, and doing it that way would prevent her from goofing around much. She didn't have much patience for poking around the web at slow speed, and doing the hotspot guaranteed a tortoise's pace.

She walked over to sit on the wide window sill as her computer came to life. It was a sunny, warm day, and all she could see was the vivid green of the leaves that decorated every tree. Her ruminations of the night before seemed kind of silly now. The constant noise of Brooklyn did nothing but raise your blood pressure. If she still had any after nearly being mowed down by a truck, that is. She shivered, realizing it had only taken two weeks to have the calluses that had formed around her nerves start to thin.

Avery popped the last of her cookies into her mouth, determined to finish editing a five thousand word piece that had to come in at thirty-five hundred. Helena was very patient with pieces that needed every word to convey their truth. But this one, while good, was bloated. Avery was certain it would be a stronger piece when it lost the fat, and equally certain the writer wouldn't agree. The excitement she'd heard in the guy's voice when she'd called to tell him they'd accepted the piece would definitely be absent after he'd read her suggestions. But the sooner this young writer learned to pare things down, the better he'd be.

She could edit on her computer when she needed to, but she much preferred looking at the words in print. The sheets she'd printed off were now marred with red ink, looking a little like a crime scene.

She looked at the clock on her computer, then lifted her head to stare out the open window. She'd known it was afternoon, but had no idea the sun was more than halfway to the horizon. Racing to transcribe and send off the edits, she took her plastic bag and ran down the stairs. It had been an excellent day. She'd pumped and stored six packets of milk, gotten a difficult edit done, and hadn't even been tempted to lie down and nap. Best of all, the only noise she'd heard was a lawn mover, and even that hadn't been especially loud. Wouldn't it be funny to find she was really a country mouse?

When Avery pulled up to the house, she wasn't surprised to see Casey's truck. Slightly...unhappy, but not surprised. It wasn't that she didn't appreciate everything Casey had done for her and Lisbet. But she'd been looking forward to spending the evening with her baby—alone. Now she'd have to be social, something she just wasn't in the mood to be. While she could be an extrovert, it always took her a day or two to recover from having to be really out there. And *Short Shorts* always stretched her affability to its limits.

As she went into the house, some of her grouchiness disappeared the moment Casey walked toward her, holding the baby like a little prize. "Look who's home," she said in a soft, sing-song tone. "Your favorite person in the whole world."

"What's going on?" Avery asked, forcing herself to refrain from saying, *Why are you here?*

"Your mom called to say she needed to run some errands. She thought it would be easier to leave Lisbet at home, so I came over after I dropped the desserts off at the restaurant." She stopped, giving Avery a concerned look. "That's okay, right? I don't want to butt into your time with Lisbet."

"It's fine," she said, angry with herself for being so territorial, not to mention ungrateful. "Boy, just looking at her is making my breasts leak. Mind if I feed her?"

"She's due. She's been doing that thing where she roots against anyone who's holding her."

Avery took her and cuddled the baby for a few moments, smiling when she started to babble excitedly, clearly glad to see her. "How did my mom get out to do errands? I have her car."

"You don't have the one she bought yesterday."

Avery stared at her, watching Casey's expression slide into a playful smile. "Apparently she showed up at the dealer, bought the one she wanted, and forced them to give it to her before they'd prepped it fully. That's why she had to go back today."

Avery rolled her eyes. "I was so tired last night that the fact there was a different car in the driveway didn't register. Obviously, I was just as groggy this morning." She shook her head, trying to absorb everything. "I don't know why I'm surprised. My mom's too generous for her own good."

"No arguments there. But I think she might have used this as an excuse. She told me she'd been wanting a new car for a year or two, but couldn't justify the expense. Now she can."

"Well, I should complain, but I really do need a car. I'm going to drown in the expense of getting my house furnished."

"Hey! Check out what I brought." Casey went into the kitchen and emerged with a high chair, the very high-end model that investment bankers dragged from their cars when they were returning to their Brooklyn brownstones from their weekend places in the Hamptons.

"Did you say brought, or bought. Because if you said bought…"

"No way," Casey said, holding her hands up. "Julie's parents are kind of rich, and they showered Benji with all of the baby stuff normal people realize they don't really need."

"But…they must want it if they still have it."

Casey smiled. "Julie's always wanted to have a second, but she hasn't been able to talk Ben into it. Maybe seeing Lisbet will convince him he needs a daughter, too."

"Not sure it works that way, but I'll gladly use this until they need it." Avery looked the chair over, nodding with satisfaction. "I definitely don't need anything this fancy, but it's fantastic." She let out a laugh. "I wish Ben and Julie had given birth to twins, since I'd love one this nice for my house."

"Do you need one?"

"No, I'm set. I bought mine at a second-hand shop in Brooklyn. It probably doesn't meet all of the current safety standards, but my dad checked it out and says it's sturdy enough."

"Kids are so expensive," Casey agreed. "I think Julie would have liked twins, but Ben's good with one."

"How can I thank them? Should I write them a note or send a nice bottle of wine or something?"

"Wine?" Casey laughed. "Ben's not a wine guy. But they'd appreciate a note."

"I'll do it after we have dinner." She sniffed, trying to detect the scent of anything coming from the kitchen. "I know what Lisbet's having, but how about us?"

"I was going to go home, but I can cook…"

"Let me take you out. It's the least I can do for all you do for us."

"What about your parents?"

"My mom can take my dad out for dinner when they get home. She's clearly got money burning a hole in her pocket."

They went to Avery's favorite spot, the local drive-in ice cream stand where Casey had stopped the night Avery went to watch her play softball. Avery had never been able to figure out how Joe's managed to make good burgers, dog, and even tacos, given they couldn't have had much room in the kitchen. Late on summer evenings, there could be thirty people in line for their homemade ice cream, which really was worth the wait. But they managed to have a good crowd for lunch and dinner, too. In her opinion, having made a lifelong quest to find the best, their chili cheeseburgers were the ne plus ultra.

It was still warm enough to sit outside, even though the sun was just about to set. Lisbet was in her car seat carrier, which Casey had set on the picnic tabletop. She kept teasing the baby by holding a French fry above her head, saying, "One of these days, you're going to know the joy of junk food, Lisbet. I bet you can't wait."

"She's still just got the one tooth. I think she's pretty happy with the status quo."

"She sure seems happy," Casey agreed. She dipped a fry into a mound of ketchup and popped it into her mouth. "How about you? I couldn't help but notice you didn't look overjoyed at seeing me tonight."

"Ooo." Avery reached over and grasped Casey's arm, holding it for a second. "Am I really that transparent? Or are you just really good at reading people?"

"Mmm…both?"

"I'm sorry if I didn't look happy. I'd planned on grabbing Lisbet and going home. I wasn't in the mood to be social with you or anyone else." She sighed, closing her eyes. "I was up until well after two, and I worked nonstop today. I didn't think I had it in me to be conversational, but now that we're out and I'm chowing down on my favorite high-calorie meal, my mood has improved."

"A good cheeseburger can do that," Casey agreed. "My mom's on another one of her diets, so we've been getting a lot of vegetables. She thinks meat's the culprit for the weight that's crept up on her." She let out a laugh. "No matter what the diet is, it always allows for generous servings of cookies."

"Tell her to try breastfeeding. I'm not sure how much I've lost, but the shorts I bought after I had the baby are almost too big to stay up."

"I think it's a little late for that for my mom, but she'd do it if she could. I think she looks great, but her self-image is pretty bad."

Avery wiped the chili from her hand and reached over to pat Lisbet's leg. "I'm going to try to keep my little Sweet Pea from getting into that 'I'm only worthwhile if I'm thin' thing we drop on girls, but I assume society will counteract all of my positive messages."

"It can do that." Casey looked at Avery for a moment, then said, "Girls have to be thin, straight, tall, but not too tall, and smart, but not too smart. Sometimes I wish Lisbet had been a boy. The world's easier for them."

Avery shrugged. "In some ways. But I'm glad she's a girl. I think I'll have a better chance of understanding her as she grows up." She met Casey's gaze and smiled. "I've never understood boys."

"Even when you were dating them? You always had a boyfriend in high school."

"Not always…" She smiled, remembering a detail that she hesitated just a moment before revealing. "I had my first encounter with a penis right in this parking lot. That's a fact I'm not going to share with Lisbet, by the way." She look a look around, seeing only families. "The old owners didn't care if you parked your car over in the corner and sat in it for hours. I think the new folks keep a closer eye on kids."

"Well, well, well," Casey said. "I've never been fond of sex in cars, but I guess you do what works."

"We didn't have sex-sex. I was actually shocked at the fact that he whipped it out. I took a look, but I wasn't going to do any more than that."

Casey laughed. "I knew guys who liked you. I was always impressed that they didn't think you were a slam-dunk."

"Um…you mean that they had to work to get me to have sex? Because I didn't—"

"No!" She laughed harder. "They had to work to have you pay any attention to them at all. You had to be convinced."

Smiling, Avery nodded. "I guess that's true, but that was probably because I wouldn't admit to myself that I was a lesbian." She took a fry and nibbled on it, slowing herself down so they'd get cold and make her not want as many of them. "So you sat around with guys discussing girls? Kind of cool."

"Nah. This was senior year, when I was on the football team. There was a lot of standing around and waiting during practice and I eavesdropped a lot." Her smile grew wider. "The smart guys really liked you, and the less smart guys were always trying to understand what your appeal was. They liked the girls they didn't have to work for better than you."

"Interesting. I had a steady boyfriend senior year. And no, I didn't understand them even when I spent a lot of time with them. By the time I stopped dating guys, which was during my senior year at Bard, I was at my nadir."

"Na—what?"

"Low point. I'd broken up with the guy I'd been seeing, certain I had no idea what men liked, wanted, or feared. That hasn't changed."

"Mmm. I work with almost all guys, and as near as I can tell they want to hang out with other guys. Even the most sensitive of them seems to prefer sitting around after work having a beer, delaying going home as long as possible." She held up her hands. "I don't get that. Why get married and have kids if you'd rather hang with your buddies?"

"Got me. When I had a girlfriend, I wanted to be with her more than anything. There wouldn't have been anything they'd offer after work that would have made me want to delay going home."

"Me too. I love the guys I work with, but if I had a girlfriend…" She tugged on Lisbet's tiny bootie-clad foot. "A girlfriend who was an adult, that is, I'd race out of work at three on the dot."

Hesitating for a second, Avery had to force herself back on track to reply. Sometimes when Casey referred to how tough it was to find a partner who wanted a baby, she felt at best invisible, at worst outright rejected. But she was certain Casey wasn't trying to be rude, so she tried, largely unsuccessfully, to convince herself that she was simply oblivious. "That will be a lucky woman," Avery managed to say. "I hope you find a fertile young thing who's ready to pop out a whole litter of babies for you."

"One or two's plenty. I'd forgotten how much work they were." She touched the baby again with her usual tender care. "But I'm really glad you had this one."

⌒

They'd driven separate cars, and were both heading to their respective homes when Casey's phone rang. She had it in its usual hands-free holder, and she instructed it to answer. "What's up?" she said, seeing the call was from Avery.

"Did you see that playground we just passed?"

"Uh-huh. It's new. Why?"

"Lisbet's never been on a swing. Want to be our safety net?"

"Sure," she said, smiling to herself as she pulled over to turn around. "Meet you there in two minutes." She was pretty sure Lisbet was too small, but what the heck?

The playground was on a small parcel of land the town had recently developed, creating a decent-sized playground with all of the features that were supposed to create a safe play space. Personally, Casey thought a big cardboard box and an imagination were enough for little kids, along with balls, bats, and trees to climb when they got older. But she acknowledged that almost no one thought having a free-range kid like she'd been was a good idea any more.

Avery got out of her car, leaving the door open while she took a look around. "Everything looks perfect, doesn't it? The infant swing doesn't even look like it's covered with bacteria, even though I'm sure it is."

"Top notch," Casey said. "But isn't Lisbet a little small to be in one of these?" She sized up the bright yellow swing, clearly made for a small child, but maybe not as small as this particular child.

"They say they're safe for babies over six months." She met Casey's eyes and smiled. "I loved swings when I was little. Am I pushing her?"

"Maybe. But we can give it a try." When those big blue eyes blinked up at her, Casey wasn't able to refuse.

Avery got Lisbet out and Casey sat on one of the full-sized swings. "Let's see if the likes the concept." She wrapped her arms around the chains and held her hands out. "I'll stay slow and low."

Avery handed the baby over, with Casey just then realizing she'd probably wanted to share this first-time experience herself. But Avery got out her phone and started to focus it.

"I want to try to get a good video."

"Ready to rock, Lisbet?" Casey asked, keeping her feet on the ground as she rocked back and forth very gently.

Avery was in front of them, talking excitedly to the baby, and Casey could feel Lisbet pushing, like she was trying to get to her mom. "I think she likes it. We can do a little more."

She was holding her facing Avery, so she couldn't see her face. But when Casey took her feet off the ground and increased the arc, Lisbet wasn't urging her to do more. "Is she smiling?"

"A little. I think she liked it better when you were traveling less."

"Then we'll slow down." She went back to the way they'd been doing it, and Avery put her phone away. Lisbet seemed perfectly content now, babbling and making the silly noises that always entertained Casey.

Avery got on the swing next to theirs and started using it adult-style. "I haven't been on a swing in years," she said, with a big smile. "It's very freeing."

"Oh, yeah. I had one in a tree right where your septic field is. A nice one."

"Really? Why not have one at your house?"

"Because my dad didn't want me to screw up one of his precious trees," she said, thinking of how long she'd begged for permission to put one up. "I just mentioned it to my grandma, and we were on our way to the hardware store."

"You…made it yourself?"

"Uh-huh. I wasn't a little kid," she said, thinking back. "I think I was already in second grade."

"Second grade!" Avery stared at her like she'd said something utterly ridiculous.

"Yeah. That's plenty old enough to drill holes in a board and knot the rope so it doesn't slip through. The only hard part was getting the rope lengths even. I was up and down that tree twenty times," she added, laughing at the memory of her bruised and scraped knees.

"No ladder?"

"My grandma wasn't a fireman," Casey said, laughing a little. "The branch I chose was twenty-five feet high. At least."

"Wow," she said, with the breeze making her golden hair trail behind her as she pumped her legs. "I've always admired your determination. You're not the kind of person to let any obstacle stop you."

"I'm not?"

"Of course not! No one who came out with a bang like you did in high school is going to let her goals slip by. You wanted a swing, and you got one."

"That wasn't a big deal. Any kid could cut some rope."

"Don't be ridiculous. If I'd asked for a swing and my parents had refused, I'd ask again in a few months. It wouldn't have occurred to me to find a tree and do it myself."

"Really?"

"Really," Avery insisted. "It was that drive of yours that I was in awe of in high school."

Even though she was having a blast swinging, Casey had to stop so she could see Avery's face clearly. "You were in awe of me," she said, after stopping, getting up carefully, and standing in front of her, admiring how free and childlike she seemed pumping away on the swing.

"Definitely."

"That's...not believable," Casey said, just stopping herself from calling Avery a liar.

"I was! Up through junior year, I knew who you were, but I don't think I'd ever really paid attention—other than putting you in the jock category."

"That was a whole category?"

"Sure. Most people were into one thing. Primarily, at least. Like the science nerds, and the debate nerds, and the word nerds. That was my nerd-dom, in case you hadn't noticed. I put you in the jock category, and since I wasn't interested in sports, I never saw you play volleyball or basketball or any of the other stuff you did. I also don't think we ever had a class together, so you weren't on my radar. Then you showed up for senior year, and bam! I noticed you big time. *Big* time," she emphasized.

"I was different," she said, gazing at Avery with a sober expression, still able to feel the pain that had caused her to change. "I had a different attitude."

"You definitely had a different look..."

"I did, but that's not what I mean. I decided I wasn't going to play the game any more."

"Mmm. I'm not really following—"

She was sure Avery knew what she meant, but she wasn't afraid to spell it out. "People had been taunting me for being gay since I started junior high, which was long before I had any real idea of what being gay meant. The only thing I was dead certain of was that it was the worst thing you could be accused of."

Casey had been trying to hide the pain that thinking of those days could still summon, but she must have done a pretty poor job of it. In a second, Avery skidded to a stop, then got up to approach her and put a hand on her shoulder. "I didn't know that," she said softly. "If you were as confused by the whole thing as I was…"

"You were confused?"

"Oh, yeah. I didn't know what any of that meant either. I'm certain I was in high school before I realized 'faggot' meant a guy who had sex with guys. I thought it was a slur the boys in my class used for everyone."

"Mmm," Casey said. "I'm pretty sure the gay boys didn't feel that way, but yeah, I'm sure a lot of kids aren't even sure *why* they make fun of other kids. They just pile on."

"I assume you identified as gay by high school, right?" She smiled, the remarkably attractive expression reminding Casey of all of the times she'd seen Avery walking down the hallway with her boyfriend of the month, wishing like hell she could hold that hand one day, while being absolutely sure that would never happen.

"Sure did." She nodded briskly. "I'd had crushes on girls for a long time, but I'd never done anything with anyone."

"Really?"

Avery put her hand on Casey's back and guided her over to a bench. When they sat down, Lisbet cuddled up to her body, sighing as she settled down. "Yeah," Casey said. "One day during the summer after junior year, I was in my uncle's kitchen, making up hundreds of orders of caprese salad, when it hit me. I was gay, and that wasn't going to change."

"That's a big day in every queer kid's life," Avery said, empathy filling her eyes.

"I'm sure it is. So…" She tried to put herself back there to recall exactly how the thought had come to her. "Right there, I decided to stop caring how people labeled me."

"You just…decided?"

"Uh-huh," she said, hearing her voice come out low and firm. "I decided to own it." She smiled, thinking back to her quest, which took up every spare minute. "We had a computer in the living room, and I stayed up every night after my parents went to bed, reading everything I could about lesbians. I embraced that shit," she said, chuckling. "I cut my hair super short, then dyed the sides to make it obvious things had changed. I spent the last weeks of summer vacation forcing myself to believe that I no longer gave a fuck, and when school started I was ready."

"So brave," Avery murmured. "You were the talk of the entire school, you know. For weeks and weeks. No one knew how to treat you."

"That's because I turned the tables on the little shits. No one could insult me if I refused to be insulted."

"Riiight," Avery said, nodding. "I remember being in the cafeteria one day when someone called you a dyke as you walked by their table. You stopped on a dime, turned around, and put your hands on the table, getting really close." She started to laugh. "It was that little jerk Aaron Adams, and he looked like he was about to wet his pants."

"I don't remember that one, since that kind of thing happened all the friggin' time…"

"No, it didn't," Avery said, sitting up straight and gazing at Casey. "Maybe before, but not when we were seniors."

"Really?" she asked, suddenly unsure of the progression of events. "You think it slowed down?"

"No, it stopped," Avery said, clearly certain. "It might have stopped that day! You glared at Aaron so hard that everyone else in the cafeteria shut up. I swear you could have heard a pin drop. Then you said something like, 'I am *definitely* a dyke. Got any more news flashes?' Or something like that. From then on, when people talked about you, they whispered."

She shrugged. "I'd been a victim for a long time. It took a while to make it clear I was over it."

"Not long, Casey. I'm certain of that. One of my friends was apoplectic about you that first week of school. I remember her going on and on about how you weren't even ashamed of yourself. But she was at the table with me that day, and I'm sure she never said another thing to you. She still bitched about you, and anyone else who didn't kiss her ass, but she only did it off campus." She let out a laugh. "You might not have realized how much bigger and stronger you were than a lot of the boys and most of the girls, but once people saw that you were angry, they shut *up*." Her smile grew until Casey could see her teeth. "That was *so* cool. If I hadn't been so deep in the closet, I would have begged you to let me be your friend."

"I had plenty of slots open," she said coldly, unable to even look at Avery. "When I left my house in the morning, I put my headphones on and listened to my iPod until whatever teacher I had for first period made me take them off. I tried to convince myself I was the only person in that whole school, and I got pretty damn good at it."

"Damn," she sighed. "If Lisbet has a tough time in school, I'm taking her out and teaching her at home. No one should have to feel like they have to create a barrier around herself to feel safe."

"That wouldn't have helped me," Casey said. "As school got better, home got worse."

"Because of the way you looked?"

"That…but I think it was more because of how I acted. I wouldn't take any shit from my parents, which was a pretty dramatic change, since my normal way was to just go along. But that year I stuck to my guns and made them adjust." She reached down and checked Lisbet's skin to make sure it wasn't chilled, then rested her hand on her head and stroked her fuzzy blonde hair. "I almost wound up living in your house to finish the year. My grandma was going to take me in, but my mom really didn't want her to. I stayed at home just to make sure they didn't have a falling out over it." She shook her head slowly. "Tough year."

"Figuring out how to be an adult is tough for everyone, I think," Avery said, putting her hand on Lisbet's leg and patting it gently. "I'm still not entirely comfortable doing that. I felt like a jerk for moving out, since I know my mom really wanted me to stay."

Casey turned and gazed into her eyes for a few long seconds. "You have to decide whose life you're living. It's guaranteed that you can't make everyone happy, so you might as well make sure you're doing the right thing for yourself. And your baby."

"Words to live by. I think I'll have you take over Lisbet's self-esteem training."

"Wish I could, but she's got to do it for herself."

"How long did you keep your hair cut that way? What was that even called?"

"Not sure. I just played around with it until I was satisfied. My mom *hated* it," she stressed. "That was the thing that pushed her buttons. I started out with it about two inches long all over, but then I clipped the sides and back until you could see my scalp."

"You clipped it yourself?"

"Uh-huh," she said, laughing at the amazed look on Avery's face. "I knew what I wanted, so I got a set of clippers and started cutting. I'll admit it's harder to cut your own hair than it looks, though," she added. "That's how I wound up with the back so short."

"God, I still hesitate to have more than an inch cut off. I don't think I've ever gotten it into my head that it'll grow back."

"Go crazy," Casey said. "It was fun to play with my hair to get a look that matched how I felt inside, even though when I dyed it it almost killed my mom. I think I started off with purple, but I changed it a couple of times."

"It looked cool," Avery said. "Super cool, actually."

"It was." She took a band from her wrist and gathered her hair up, putting the band around it to make a pony tail. Then she rubbed her hand across the back of her head, where it was clipped very short. "It kept me so cool I decided to keep it."

"Oh, wow," Avery said. "It looks like the fur on a plush animal, dark and fuzzy." She shut her mouth, then tentatively said, "I meant that as a compliment."

"That's how I took it. My first girlfriend used to call me Fuzzy Wuzzy."

Avery laughed. "That's awfully cute. You know, I've seen a few women with one side shaved, but I like your way better. It really suits you."

"Thanks. When Lisbet's a little older I'll take her to the barber with me. We can match."

"Fine by me. I've already decided I'm going to let her express herself however she wants. And if she wants to mimic her best friend, I'll pay for both of your haircuts."

Casey stood up and grasped Lisbet to her chest. "I think you'd better get this little Fuzzy Wuzzy to bed."

"I'll be right behind her. I got about five hours of sleep last night, and that's not enough for me to think clearly."

"I'll put her into her seat." Casey got her settled, then kissed her fingertips and pressed them to the baby's head. As she stood, Avery was right there, closer than normal. She looked like she might be looking for a hug, but Casey didn't feel comfortable giving her one. She had a lot to think over before she got even an inch closer to truly trusting Avery, but tonight it seemed like a possibility, which would have made seventeen-year-old Casey pretty darned happy.

CHAPTER TEN

THE NEXT DAY DURING LUNCH, Casey ran over to the Greenhouse Pub and fired up the propane heat lamps. It was around sixty-five outside, but with the dark, overcast skies, the greenhouse wouldn't soak up much warmth. The kids who came to Baby Brewers were usually dressed properly, but she didn't want to have anyone get chilled. One of her guys brought over a soda keg of cider, and she hooked it up to the tap, and checked out the room one more time. The floor was just sheets of plywood on bare dirt, but they'd covered it with straw at the beginning of the season for insulation and to avoid having anyone slip. That wasn't an ideal surface for babies, but it wasn't too bad. Everyone had learned their kids were going to get dirty, and they seemed perfectly fine with that, so long as they got a beer or two in exchange for the grime.

⌐

Casey usually worked from seven to three, when her assistant Glen took over to shut the plant down for the day.

When she'd first started as the assistant brewmaster, she'd copied the habits of her boss, routinely putting in ten or eleven hour days. Since she'd been switched to salaried status when she'd been promoted, she'd wound up making less than she had when she was hourly. Given she was working harder, and had a lot more stress, that wasn't going to work. Without asking for permission, she started to cut back. Over time, she realized the owners seemed to prefer talking to her than her boss, who was kind of a pain in the ass, so she kept nipping away at her hours until she was working just forty a week. Since then, she only worked overtime when it was truly necessary, and she'd never gotten any blowback from the change.

At three, she spoke to Glen to make sure he understood exactly what had to be done to finish off the day, then she stopped by her office to say goodbye to Ben. He was just standing up to grab his briefcase. "Taking off?"

"Sure am. Do you have Diapered Drunks today?"

"Still hilarious," she said, backhanding him in the gut. "Walk me over."

They went to the side of the building that had a regular entrance, but they hadn't gotten ten feet before it began to pour. "See you tomorrow," Ben said, starting to run in the opposite direction. "You're on your own."

Casey got another ten feet when a horn honked once. She slowed down when she saw it was Kathy. By the time Kathy had gotten out of her car, the umbrella she offered to share didn't help Casey a bit. "I'm glad to see you," Casey said. "Nice day, huh?" she asked, pushing her hair from her face.

"Oh, it's glorious. I'll hold the umbrella over the door if you'll help me get the baby out." The wind started to pick up, blowing the umbrella to and fro as Casey struggled with the carrier insert. It didn't take long to see that Lisbet wasn't in a very good mood, fussing and sniffling while Casey worked.

"Is she having a bad day?"

"I think she's getting another tooth. She's been drooling like crazy, and didn't want to nap. I'm sure she's not going to be a very good playmate." She looked around at the barren parking area. "If anyone else shows up."

"People always do," Casey said, finally getting the car seat out. The wind hit Lisbet's face and she scrunched it up and began to cry, really bawling by the time they reached the Pub. It took her a minute to realize she was somewhere different, but as soon as she did she lifted her head and let those dark blue eyes scan the whole place. Then Casey removed her from the car seat and walked around with her, explaining how the taps dispensed nature's greatest alchemy—beer.

"Don't listen to her, Lisbet," Kathy said, fighting to get the umbrella to collapse. "She's got an agenda."

There was a knock on the doorframe, and a woman hesitantly opened the door and peeked in. "Is this the baby place?"

"It certainly is," Casey said, rushing over to greet her third guest. No matter the weather, people always showed.

⌒

When she'd set up the program, Casey had purposefully made three-year-olds the upper age limit, not wanting to have bigger kids knocking over the littler ones. She'd assumed that most of the kids would be close to the upper number, figuring it was tougher for parents to keep toddlers occupied. But that hadn't been accurate. It was the parents of infants who'd been going stir-crazy and really needed some adult interaction.

Today, Lisbet was right in the middle of the age range, with three kids younger and three older. The older ones had a better idea of how to play with each other, and they'd settled into the big space behind the bar, sharing the toys their parents had brought. The babies were in the front, by the bar, where it was a little warmer.

One dad, one mom, and Kathy sat at the bar, chatting like they'd just emerged from a month-long silent retreat. The kids, two of whom were just two and three months old, stayed in their car seats, which rested on the bar. Only Lisbet and a little boy named Colvin did anything close to play. They each sat on a blanket, surrounded by the pillows their adults had put down to support them, babbling at each other while shaking toys in the air. It really didn't seem like they were interacting much, but every once in a while their eyes would meet and one or the other would scream. Even though she was used to it by now, they still sounded more like monkeys than babies to Casey. Not that she minded. Everyone was having fun, and socializing helped each parent from going mad. The Baby Brewers had a very modest goal, but she was confident they consistently surpassed it.

⌒

Avery stood at the top of the stairs and called down when she heard a sharp rap on the frame of her door. "I'm coming, but it's open."

Her mom popped in, holding a very curious baby. Her gaze moved all across the empty rooms, then hit the stairs as Avery was coming down. When their eyes met, she started to giggle.

"There's my baby girl," Avery said, sticking her arms out and making her hands into pincers. "I can't wait to get my hands on her."

She kissed her mother on the cheek as she enveloped Lisbet into a hug. "Did you girls have fun?"

"I certainly did, and Lisbet didn't complain." She started to walk through the living room, then poked her head into the kitchen. "You can't live like this," she said, her expression grim.

"I'll get things. There's no rush."

"Avery! You don't have anywhere to sit, and you don't have a table of any kind. No place to put a TV…"

"Well, I'm not going to have a TV at all, so you can let that go. And Lisbet has her high chair, so she's set. I'll get some furniture soon."

"When?"

"I've been checking out Craigslist and eBay. I just haven't had a lot of spare time."

"Well, if you don't have something by the end of the weekend, your father and I are going to load up his truck with our stuff."

"And what will you sit on?"

"I'll buy new things." She scowled as she walked into the dining room, equally bare as the other spaces. "Speaking of which, I've got a crib on hold at the resale shop. I'm going to pick it up as soon as your father gets home." She put her hand up to forestall any complaint, and when she spoke again she sounded weary. "Why were you in such a hurry to get into this place?"

"I like it," she said. "It's a great space for working, and being away from Lisbet lets me concentrate better."

"Well, you're going to be concentrating on my living room furniture if you don't get your act in gear." She kissed both her and Lisbet on the tops of their heads and walked out, grumbling to herself as she made her way to her new car.

"Your grandma's mad at us," Avery said quietly. "Do you think it would have helped if she'd seen us sitting on the porch steps to eat our dinner? Bet not!"

CHAPTER ELEVEN

ON SATURDAY MORNING, AVERY WOKE from a deep sleep to Lisbet's crying. On her feet and crossing the hallway in just a few seconds, she heard a difference in the cry. It didn't seem like her "I'm starving" wail, and it was hours before she was due for a meal.

"What's wrong, Sweet Pea?" She picked her up and checked for all of the usual problems, but other than a soggy diaper, there wasn't anything obviously wrong with her.

"Hold on a minute," she said. Placing the shrieking child back in her crib, Avery raced to the bathroom. She'd gotten her first postpartum period the night before, and it was a doozy. "I know you're upset, sweetheart, but I'll be upset if I bleed on the floor," she called out.

She'd only been gone for two minutes, but when she turned on the nightlight the baby's face had turned as red as a beet, and she was thrashing around inconsolably.

Avery's only option was to hold and try to soothe the baby, but nothing worked. Lisbet willingly took her breast, but spit the nipple out in just seconds, crying even harder.

"Oh, baby, I wish you could tell me what's wrong," she murmured. Lisbet was warm, but Avery was pretty sure that was from crying. Her onesie had been washed several times with the same soap, her diaper was the same kind she always wore, and she hadn't added any new food to her diet. She was just furious about something, and didn't have the words to tell Avery what that was.

⌒

At seven, the baby still hadn't cried herself out. Avery's cramps had gotten worse, much worse than they'd been before she'd been pregnant. She'd spent an hour on the internet reading about other peoples' babies who'd had similar episodes, and, as usual, there were fifty different reasons for the unexpected tears, with each person rock solid their solution to the problem was the perfect one.

Having not slept well herself, Avery was just about at the end of her rope. When your baby cried for no reason it began to get under your skin, especially when you were feeling crappy and hormonal to start with.

Lisbet was two hours past her usual breakfast, and she'd fought against even taking a bite of cereal or her favorite vegetables. Worried about her getting dehydrated, Avery tried to get her to take a little water, but she'd hated it, letting it run down her face as her wailing got even louder. Trying anything she could think of, Avery took off her onesie and her diaper, then covered a portion of the bed with a sheet of plastic and the softest towel she owned, thinking there might be something in her clothing or diaper that was irritating her. But even as she did it she knew it was a waste of time. Lisbet was woefully unhappy, not just mildly discomforted, and Avery's only option at that point was to take her to an Urgent Care center. But that just seemed like it would make matters worse. With no fever, no rash, and no other signs of illness, what would they do? What *could* they do?

Around ten o'clock Lisbet finally fell asleep, but she was fitful. She was still on Avery's bed, a place she'd never been while asleep. But Avery reasoned it was all right if she watched her closely. No one in America paid more attention to the "babies should sleep alone in their cribs" motto than she did, but this was a special exception.

Her phone buzzed on the nightstand, and that tiny noise made Lisbet gasp and stare at her for half of a second, then start crying again.

"Want to go look at furniture?" Casey texted. "I've got a lead."

Avery stared at Casey's text for a few seconds. Her timing was usually impeccable, but today Avery wanted to throw the phone against the wall until it broke into a thousand pieces.

"Bad day. I'll text you if things change for the better."

As irritated as she was, Avery had to admit that Casey was her favorite kind of texter. She didn't need to sign off or have the last word. If Avery said she'd call later, Casey dropped it. That alone gave her bonus points as a friend.

"Okay, sweetheart, we're going to go down our checklist one more time. Are you hungry? Yes. Will you eat? No. Are you thirsty? You have to be. Will you drink? No." As she watched her shriek, Avery's stomach began to ache. The stress of having Lisbet cry so hard and so long for no reason made her feel like she might vomit. For just a second, she let her mind wander to whether she'd still hear the baby if she put her in the basement or on the porch. The neighbors would definitely hear her on the porch, but the basement might work. Not for long... Just long enough for Avery to take a long, hot shower—

She didn't physically slap herself, but she did the mental equivalent. For the first time since she'd given birth, Avery knew she wasn't in the right mental space to be alone with her baby. Instead of beating herself up over that, she picked up her phone and texted Casey.

Close to a melt-down

If you could put some earplugs in and keep an eye on L for a while...

It took fewer than five seconds for Casey to write back.

Six minutes

Relief washed over Avery like a gentle wave. Casey would be there soon. Avery knew she could set her watch by the estimate. She went downstairs to unlock the door, then went back upstairs to plug in her breast pump and get it set up. She'd just started to pump when Casey knocked at the door. Hoping she'd try the knob, Avery listened carefully, able to feel the air change as the door opened. "Avery?"

"Upstairs."

She heard Casey's tread, and spoke loudly to drown out the baby. "I'm pumping, so avert your eyes if you don't want to see something gross."

Casey stopped right in the doorway. "How long has she been crying?"

"Since four. Pretty much nonstop. She won't eat, and I have no idea why." She had a little more to add, but her tears choked her words. "I'm out of patience."

Casey really had to speak loudly to be heard over the wailing. "It's a beautiful day, and I bet Lisbet hasn't explored much around here. I'll take her for a walk. How's that?"

"Sounds great, but I can't imagine it will work."

"Can I…" She cleared her throat. "Do you mind if I come in and pick her up?"

"I was considering putting her in the basement, so…"

Clearly going out of her way not to catch a peek, Casey entered the room and scooped Lisbet up. "She's warm."

"Just from crying. She gets flushed and sweaty when she's upset like this. That's why I took her diaper off." She took a breath, feeling a little better just having someone to talk to. "I'll have fresh milk ready in ten or fifteen minutes…"

"Poor baby," Casey sighed, quickly exiting the room. Avery heard her start to walk in the hallway, soothing Lisbet as best she could. "Are you sure she doesn't have a fever?"

"There's a thermometer in the bathroom medicine cabinet. Do you know how to use it?"

"Um…do you put it under her tongue?"

"Other end," Avery said, almost smiling when she imagined the look on Casey's face. "Her doctor told me to use a rectal thermometer until she was a little older. It's more accurate."

"Ooo. That's…"

"Want me to do it? I really don't think she has a fever, but if you're worried…"

"On second thought, who am I to doubt a mother's judgment?" She poked her head into the room. "I'll do it if you think it's important, but that seems…icky."

"Welcome to my world. All icky, all the time."

"Let us get out of your hair. Do you have any milk in the fridge?"

"Freezer. Do you know how to warm it?"

"I do. I'm going to put her in her snuggly thing for our walk, okay?"

"Did you bring earplugs?"

"Didn't have time. You sounded desperate."

"Hey, Casey?"

She stuck her head in the room again, still not letting her gaze land on Avery.

"Thanks a million. I'm so happy to have a friend I knew would race over here."

"We'll be gone for at least an hour. Enough time for you to take a nap," she ordered. "I'd close your curtains, but you don't have any."

"I took down the old blinds, but haven't gotten around to buying curtains. They rank at about number twenty on my long list of things I need." She took in a calming breath. "Sleep is a solid number one."

⌒

At two o'clock, Avery woke with a start, disoriented, then panicked when her eyes landed on the towel-covered plastic on her bed. For a split second, she thought she'd fallen asleep with Lisbet next to her. Then she remembered that Casey had her, and her heart rate slowed down again. It took a minute to get her bearings, but eventually she allowed herself the delicious sensation of lying in bed, not worrying about a thing.

She heard a shuffling sound, so she got up and started to go downstairs. Lisbet was sitting on the floor, playing with Casey, and both of them seemed delighted.

"Oh, sure, soothe my baby when I couldn't make any headway for *hours*. I'll see myself out."

Casey turned to give her a sweet smile, clearly not minding being teased. "We missed you," she said. "Lisbet especially."

Avery finished descending the stairs, then squatted down next to Lisbet, getting a smile and a giggle. "What magic did you work on this baby?"

"Absolutely none. I took some milk out of the freezer, warmed it up, and she drank it like it was the best thing she'd ever had. Then I put her in her snuggly carrier, and by the time we were at the street, she was quiet. Hasn't cried since."

"You little baby-monster," Avery chided, tickling Lisbet's leg. "You almost drove me to sticking you in the basement so I could have a minute's peace." She looked up at Casey. "She calmed down when you fed her?"

"Uh-huh. Right away. She was famished."

"But she wouldn't eat when I tried to nurse her."

"Is anything different? Did you eat anything weird? When we have a problem with a batch of beer we eliminate anything that's new or different to isolate the problem."

"Nothing," Avery said. "I mean, I took some ibuprofen before I went to bed last night, but my doctor assures me that very little of it passes into breast milk."

"That's not something you take all the time, right?"

"Mmm, no. I took it for days after I gave birth, but that might be the only time."

"Well, that might be it. Maybe it made your breast milk taste funny."

Avery stared at her for a minute. "Will you look something up for me?"

"Sure. What."

"Look up if getting your period makes your milk taste different. I got mine yesterday for the first time since I gave birth." She pulled Lisbet over to her by tugging on her legs playfully. The baby normally liked to have Avery scoot her around that way, and she giggled as she moved. "Want a snack, sweetheart?"

It wasn't her usual schedule, but Lisbet usually didn't mind nursing for a few minutes just about any time. Avery pulled her shirt up, then teased the baby with her nipple. She latched on immediately, but as soon as she got a little she spit the nipple out and made a face. "Don't bother looking it up," Avery said, slapping herself on the head. "It's the taste. If she likes the packs in the freezer, but won't take it when it's fresh, we have our answer."

"I've got confirmation," Casey said. She met Avery's gaze, looking a little sheepish. "It says most babies don't notice the difference, but some do. I think Lisbet has a very well-developed sense of taste."

"Now what do I do? I'm having the period from hell, and my baby's on strike against the only plant that makes her favorite food."

"How much do you have in the freezer?"

"Mmm. About six packs. I've got more than that at my mom's, though."

"Looks like you're going to have to use your supply, and hope it goes back to normal after your period's over."

"Fantastic," Avery grumbled.

"Well, she seems happy now, and you look a lot better. I think we can hit the road."

"Road? What road are we hitting?"

"My mom told me where to find good, cheap furniture. You're going to have at least a sofa and a kitchen table before this day is over." She stood, then bent over and picked Lisbet up. "Maybe we can go by and get the rest of your favorite food while we're at it, Lisbet. I know where the Fort Knox of breastmilk is, and one of your other favorite people is the head guard."

⌒

Lisbet rode in peaceful silence in the high-end car seat Casey had borrowed, seeming exactly like the happy, calm child she'd been the day before. Avery stroked her leg, saying, "I scared myself this afternoon. Having the instinct, even briefly, of putting her somewhere that I couldn't hear her shook me."

"I'm glad you called. Really glad." Casey looked in the rearview mirror to meet Avery's eyes. "I want you to promise that you'll call next time it happens. It doesn't matter if it's the middle of the night. Really," she stressed.

"I will. I would have called my mom, but she was out with her scout troop and I didn't want to worry her when she was stuck somewhere."

"I'm not worried. At all. You did the right thing, even though I'm going to bet you didn't want to call."

"I *truly* didn't want to call. But my instinct to protect Lisbet kicked in. Even when it's me I have to protect her from, the instinct is still there." She shivered at the thought, but put words to it anyway. "I used to be so judgmental about people who shake their babies. I mean, obviously it's horribly wrong, but if you didn't have a good grip on your emotions, you could easily get to the point where you absolutely lost it. Having a baby cry and cry and cry can push you past the edge."

"Maybe she cried because she's sick of living in an empty house," Casey said, with Avery able to see the teasing glint in her eyes when she glanced at the mirror.

"Yeah, that's probably it. Or maybe she misses Brooklyn like hell and is super bummed that we're still here."

"I know that wasn't it! There isn't a baby in the world who'd prefer Brooklyn over the Hudson Valley. That place was designed to shake a baby's nerves."

"I swear Carroll Gardens is a quiet neighborhood. Damn, compared to the apartment I had before the one you saw, it was like a tomb." She laughed a little. "I can't imagine how much you would have hated the previous place."

"I hated the place I saw." She smiled. "Well, I hated it mostly because it was on the third floor, but still…"

"I know. Your delicate ears can't put up with city noise."

"I didn't think to ask at the time, but why didn't we move your bed? Not that we had much room in the trunk."

"I decided to give it to Freya to show her I hold no hard feelings. It was one of those mattresses they deliver to your apartment in a stunningly small box. It was comfortable enough, but having my old box spring is so much better. When I'm at my parents', I'll use the sofa. It's fine."

Casey didn't reply, but Avery could see her shaking her head, looking adorably puzzled at the thought of having the UPS guy dump a box of mattress in the lobby.

Casey stood in front of a used sofa, certain she hated it, and equally certain that Avery should buy it. "I'll agree it's ass ugly, but it's big enough for two adults, it doesn't smell bad, and I think it might be indestructible. For a hundred bucks, you can't go wrong."

"I've never even seen a sofa like this. It looks like it should be in one of those hotels in the Poconos. The ones with the heart-shaped hot tubs."

Casey scratched her head, having trouble even describing the sofa. It was vaguely oval, with a footstool that tucked into the curve in the center. Was there such a thing as a kidney-bean shaped sofa? She ran her hand over the fabric, which was so nubby it might have snagged a silk shirt. But she was sure it would hold up to anything Lisbet threw at it—literally. "I think it's the right choice. It's super firm, so you and Lisbet could nap on it together when she's a little older."

"The fabric will chafe her skin!"

"Then put a throw over it." She pulled Avery away from the clerk, who was lurking around like a vulture. "It's cheap and smells fine. I think it's the best we're going to get. If we take the kitchen table and chairs, too, I bet we can get her to knock fifty bucks off."

Avery rolled her eyes. "If you can get everything for fifty bucks less, I'm sold. But if that thing spontaneously combusts, I'm coming after you!"

⸜

The polyester pod, as it had been dubbed, was situated under the window in the living room, with the table and chairs happily resting in the kitchen. The place still looked like a transient hotel, but they'd made progress. Casey sat down on a chair, scowling when it creaked under her weight. She got up, turned the chair over, and inspected it by yanking hard on the legs. "These rungs are a little loose. I'll tighten them up for you."

"Is there a lever you turn?"

Casey gazed at her for a second. For a woman whose dad was an appliance repairman, she hadn't picked up one practical trait. "Um, no. I'll take them apart, sand out the joints, and glue them back together. Tightening up our dining rooms chairs was one of the first projects I ever took on."

"Were you still in diapers?" Avery asked, laughing.

"Nope. And I didn't get paid, now that I think of it, but I was proud of myself for doing it right. Those babies are still solid all these years later."

"If it's easy, just tell me how. I'm pretty handy."

"Do you have a dead blow hammer?"

"Um, no."

"Clamps to hold the chair together while the glue dries?"

"Do I look like a woman who has clamps?"

Casey stopped herself from saying something inappropriate. A nursing mother probably wouldn't think nipple clamps were funny, anyway. "No, you do not. I've got all the stuff, so I'll do it. Won't take long." She started for the door. "I'll run by my house and get the tools. Want me to pick up dinner?"

"Um… How do I refuse out of politeness, but accept out of hunger?"

Casey smiled at her. "I'll bring dinner. What's your favorite kind of food?"

"Mmm. Thai, Japanese, Mexican, Italian, Chinese. I like Korean a lot, but I'd be surprised to find it around here."

"I'll let you know when a good Korean spot opens up. Until then, stay hungry and think Italian. I'll be back in an hour."

At eight o'clock, Avery was pleasantly full, the remnants of her linguini with clams still bringing a smile to her face. Her Windsor chairs were decorated with enough clamps to prevent them from ever wobbling once the glue set, and sitting on the weird sofa wasn't half bad. Since the sofa was curved, her and Casey's feet were much closer together than their bodies were, but that made conversing quite comfortable. She pointed at Casey's Doc Marten's, saying, "Are those from high school?"

"Much newer. I still dress like I did then, but I replace things as they wear out."

Not for the first time, Avery took a quick glance at Casey's whole look. It was pretty much early twenty-first century lesbian gear. A blue tank top covered by a blue and green flannel shirt, stiff, dark jeans, and her big boots. She even wore a braided leather cuff on one wrist, and a smooth leather one on the other, something that Avery currently saw on young guys in Brooklyn. Her hair was down, and Avery marveled at how lucky Casey was to be gifted with such perfect locks. There was just a little wave to the dark, glossy strands. It always looked good, so she probably didn't even have to spend time trying to get it to behave.

Any way you sliced it, she was a young lesbian's dream. Tall, strong, and determined, but very, very gentle. The problem, and it was definitely a problem, was that in all of their time together Avery had never gotten even a hint that Casey spent any time looking at her in the same very fond way she was currently devoting to Casey. Which was just a little hurtful. It was hard to feel attractive when your breasts leaked, you were carrying around extra weight, and your body was a long way from looking like it had only two years earlier. But to have a single lesbian who desperately wanted to be parenting a child sitting right next to you and you while treating you like a sister? That was a real slap in the face.

CHAPTER TWELVE

ON SUNDAY MORNING, AFTER A late breakfast with her mom, Casey took a football and headed for the portion of the yard out behind the pool. She didn't play around with her kicking very often, but hockey season was starting soon, and she wanted to develop a little stamina in her legs.

They had a lot of land, most of it covered by thin trees. They were tall, over sixty feet, and planted close together. Actually, she guessed they hadn't technically been planted at all. They were probably the result of blown-in seeds after this land had been reclaimed for housing. There was still farming in the area, a good amount of it, but nothing like there had been in the nineteenth century when her father's family had settled in Columbia County. And the seventeenth century Gerritsens wouldn't recognize a single thing.

Her work-out plan was, admittedly, odd, but she loved to kick. Having no one to kick to, and having a strong leg, she would have spent her whole time chasing after the ball if she went to an open field. So she kicked into the trees, not getting a lot of distance, but liking to watch the ball careen around before landing not too far away.

Squaring her shoulders, she took two steps, then dropped the ball with both hands as she thrust her right leg forward, feeling the thump on the top of her foot. A smile settled onto her face when she felt the stretch in her hamstring. When she was kicking well, it felt like her foot hit the ball the moment she dropped it.

A tree about twenty feet away shivered when the ball hit it, then dropped straight down. She ran to catch it and give it another kick, smiling like a kid. She was committed to the hockey team, but she'd join a football team in a second if anyone was looking for a thirty-six year old woman punter.

"What in the hell are you doing?"

The booming voice shattered Casey's reverie. Feeling like a scolded child, she ran to pick up her ball and walk over to the edge of the trees, where her father stood. His hands were on his hips, and his face bore a common expression. One that said, "I don't understand you at all." But he rarely expressed himself that way, usually sticking to sarcasm. "Can you take a break from destroying my landscape to help me winterize the pool?"

Ignoring the unsubtle jibe, she said, "So soon? I was thinking of using it this afternoon."

"I'm not going to pay to heat it any more, and I've got time today. Let's go." He turned to walk away, with her following behind. He paid next to nothing for heat, since he had a full array of solar panels on the roof, but arguing with him was a complete waste of her time. And one thing she truly hated was to waste her time doing something that would only frustrate her.

⌣

Several hours later, Casey lay on her bed, staring up at the ceiling, relaxing as she let her mind drift. Neither of her parents understood her fondness for doing nothing, but she'd always been a fan. She didn't need to read, or listen to music, or anything, really. It made her happy to simply rest and daydream.

Her phone rang, and she rolled over to catch it. "Hey, buddy-boy," she said when she saw that it was Ben. "What's going on?"

"Julie took Benji to a birthday party, so I've got the night free. Want to get a burger?"

"Umm, sure. But why aren't you at the party? I thought those things were full of parents."

"They usually are, but this is one of his girlfriends from school. She's having her party at one of those pottery places, and they had to wait until the store closed to get a good deal on the place."

"You didn't want to make a mug with your name on it?"

"Burger? Final offer."

"Love to. When and where?"

"Wanna head down to Dutchess? It's far, but I really like the owner of a place in Fishkill. He's on the verge of carrying our stuff, and I thought you could show off a little. Astound him with your knowledge."

"You're driving?"

"You are. You've got to be sober to have an intelligent conversation about beer, so you should only have one. As the dopey distribution guy, I can drink until I fall off my stool."

"You can have two," Casey decided. "If I have to drive to Fishkill, I don't want you snoring on the way home. I'll be by to pick you up in twenty. Wear a normal shirt."

"Yes, ma'am," he said, switching off. If she let him, he'd wear a T-shirt everywhere. That was fine most of the time, but she liked the Kaaterskill Brewery reps to look like they had a touch of class.

Ben walked down his driveway as soon as she tooted her horn. He wore a blue plaid shirt, along with a pair of dark blue chinos. When he opened the door, she wolf-whistled at him. "Look at the handsome man," she said, laying it on thick.

"You look good too. We look like we actually make beer, rather than just drink a lot of it." He buckled his seatbelt and used the buttons on the side of the seat to ease it back. "Good weekend?"

"Ehh. I'm kind of depressed," she said, not meaning it literally. "I helped my dad winterize the pool, so I've got to admit summer's over."

"Don't remind me. Benji's last tournament is next weekend. Then he's got to start working on his basketball skills. Why couldn't I have a kid who wanted to sit on his butt and play video games?" he asked, laughing a little. "I'd save a mint."

"Poor you. You'll be watching baseball, while I'm at the Octoberfest they're trying to get started in Beacon."

"You really should go to that. There's some money behind that one, and it's supposed to be big."

"Oh, I'm going. I don't want to, but I'm going. Then I'm going to the craft brewers conference in the city in October. That'll take up a whole week. Octoberfest ruins my whole month."

"Don't pout. Festivals bring in new customers. Especially when people can talk to the brewmaster."

Casey laughed. "I know that, but I hate to lose my weekends. Even if I go to something that's fun, it's still work. And I need my days off to enjoy my job. That's just my thing."

"You need your chill time. No doubt." She could see him gazing at the side of her face. "I think you're just pissed you won't be able to spend all of your free time with the zygote."

"She's a little past that. Actually, she impressed me yesterday by showing she has exquisitely sensitive tastebuds. There was a tiny change in her diet because of something minor, and the kid refused to nurse. I had to go over there when Lisbet cried so hard for so long Avery didn't trust herself to be alone with her. She was hanging on by a thread."

"Casey!" His eyes had gotten as wide as they were capable of getting. "You can't be her go-to girl every time she has a tough day. You'll be over there constantly!"

"Will not," she said, starting to get annoyed. "She's got her mom for most stuff. But she was really struggling, Ben, and she knew I could get there faster than anyone else. I was very glad she called, and if she gets into a bad place again, I want her to do the same thing."

"I'm sorry, Case, but I don't get it. I'll admit she seemed really nice when I met her, as well as cute, but you don't fully trust her, you don't want to get into her pants, and you've got nothing in common. What's the draw?"

"Lisbet," she said, confident about the strength of the connection she felt. "I mean…" She took in a breath and let the thought form in her head. "I know I'm not exactly old, and it's possible I'll meet someone tomorrow. But this might be my last shot at being involved in a baby's life. I don't want to miss this, Ben. I just don't."

"You're really serious? You're certain you're more into the baby than the baby mama?"

"One hundred percent." She let herself think back to the previous afternoon. "When I picked up that screaming baby, I was pretty sure she was sick. I mean, she was throwing an absolute fit! Avery said she'd been crying since before dawn, which just isn't like her. But I fed her, put her into the carrier that straps her close to my chest, and we started to walk. By the time we reached the street, she'd settled down, and when I reached down to wipe some of the tears from her eyes she tilted her little head up and we had… It sounds silly, but we had a real connection. She knew I was going to take care of her, and it meant so much to know she trusted me." Unexpectedly, her eyes filled with tears and she hurriedly wiped them away. "I know I'm a big dope, but that touched me."

"Aww, damn, Casey. I'll ask Julie to have another baby and give it to you. You'd be the best mom in the world."

That made her laugh, and she felt her mood lighten slightly. "Knowing Julie, she wouldn't be great at the 'give the baby away' part of that plan."

"I want you to have that bond," Ben said, appearing much more serious than normal. "I really do. And if you think this might be a once-in-a-lifetime thing, then I'm glad you're doing it."

"I am too. This is working out great for me." She let out a wry laugh. "As my dad says, I'm always looking for the easy way out, and there's no easier way to raise a baby than to have someone else give birth, house, feed, and clothe her."

On Monday afternoon, Casey dropped off the baked goods at her uncle's restaurant, then took a quick swing by Kathy's to see how Lisbet was doing. Casey wasn't sure how much milk Avery had stored, but she guessed it was getting low. While this issue clearly wasn't her responsibility, she'd thought about it at least twenty times during the day, and knew it would be on her mind that night if she didn't know the status of the supply.

It was a warm afternoon, and the front door was open, with the slanting sun streaming into the living room. She put her hand up to knock, then heard Lisbet start to babble excitedly. Casey peered inside, seeing Kathy on the floor in front of the baby, who was playing with a large assortment of kitchen bowls, measuring cups, and storage containers. The baby had a red plastic cup in her right hand, and she threw it a surprising distance while she stared at Casey.

She opened the door and said, "The kid's practically demanding that I come in," she said, laughing a little. "You know, it's a rare day I come to the door that she doesn't look happy." She got down into a squat and put her hands under Lisbet's arms to pull her to her feet. "Except for Saturday, of course. How's the milk situation?"

"Pretty good, thanks to me," Kathy said, starting to get to her feet. "Would you bring Lisbet and some of the toys into the kitchen? I'm making a tomato sauce, and I don't want it to burn."

The toys were lying on a cushiony mat Kathy normally kept in the kitchen for the baby to play on, and Casey gathered the whole thing up and carried it in one hand while she held Lisbet with the other. When they got into the room she laid everything out and the baby acted like everything was new to her. She let go of Casey's hand and started to grab the toys like Santa had just come.

Casey sat opposite her and engaged her while Kathy tended to her sauce for a minute. "I'm no chemist," she said, "but I know a thing or two about flavor."

"What did you do?"

"There were only ten packets of frozen breast milk in the freezer, so I had Avery bring over the packets she expressed this morning. Then I warmed up one of the frozen ones and added about ten percent of the fresh milk." She turned to meet Casey's gaze. "Lisbet ate it like a champ."

"Excellent!"

"Then she had twenty percent of the fresh with her next bottle, and she didn't notice the difference there either. If we can keep adding fresh to frozen, we'll have enough to ride out the storm." She bent over to pat the baby on the head. "Maybe next month she won't notice at all. But Avery's going to be diligent about keeping the frozen supply topped up, since this might be an issue for the duration."

"Babies are hard," Casey said, watching Lisbet merrily bang her toys against the table leg. "You can read everything that's written and still be caught by surprise." She laughed a little. "I should know, since I got to the end of the internet looking up what to do with a baby who's unhappy with the flavor of your breast milk."

Kathy got down on the floor again and gathered Lisbet up to hug her. "You're one lucky baby," she cooed. "You've got a whole group of people dedicated to not only keeping you healthy, but happy too."

CHAPTER THIRTEEN

BY THE FIRST WEEK OF OCTOBER, the frost had been on the pumpkins twice, but a warming trend allowed Avery to take Lisbet for an extemporaneous walk around the neighborhood after picking her up at the end of the day.

She should have put the baby in her stroller, but she liked being able to hold Lisbet to her chest, and the baby liked it too. Looking into each other's eyes while they walked around was calming for both of them.

She returned to the house as her dad pulled in, and he jumped out of his truck to walk over to them. "You're staying for dinner, right?"

"I hadn't planned—"

"Come on. I haven't seen the baby in four days. You go help your mom, and give me a minute alone with this little champ." He grasped her foot and gave it a playful tug. "You want to see your granddad, don't you, precious?"

She gurgled and shivered when he spoke directly to her, with her little arms trying to reach for him.

"If mom doesn't mind, we'll stay," she said, not really desperate to cook for herself.

"If mom doesn't mind," he scoffed. "That's a good one."

They went inside together, and she started to take off the carrier, with him lending a hand. "Kath? Is there enough food for one more? I caught Avery trying to sneak out."

"Avery's still here?" Her mom came out into the living room. "I thought you'd gone home a half hour ago."

"I thought it was a good night for a walk, and I like your neighborhood better for that. I saw a coyote by my house last week, and keep thinking one will knock me down and a whole pack of them will emerge from the woods to…" She shrugged. "Typical mother nightmares."

"Typical?" Her mom waggled her hand. "I'm not sure you'd get much agreement on that. But I've got plenty of food to go around. Your father won't get three pieces of chicken, but he can suffer with just two."

"Two's plenty. I'm going to take my pumpkin into the den. Monday Night Football's on in just a couple of hours, so we'll start with the pregame." He grasped Lisbet and put her up against his shoulder. On the way out of the kitchen, he kissed Avery on the cheek. "Any marching orders?"

"Nothing new. Just don't take your eyes off her. She's still crawling backwards, but she's faster. As usual, it makes her super happy to hold your hands and stand on her own."

"I can let her walk?"

"Anything you like will be fine. God knows she'll tell you if she doesn't like it. Yet another opinionated Nichols woman."

"Just the way I like them," he said, happily heading to his den, with Lisbet looking over his shoulder with a slightly concerned look in her big blue eyes. She was still very social, and still very amenable to other people holding her, but Avery had noticed she was starting to get picky. She just hoped the baby didn't shy away from her grandparents. That would destroy them—especially her dad.

She went back into the kitchen and poked around at the vegetables. "Are you going to roast these?"

"I was going to mash the potatoes, but I suppose I could roast everything. Do you prefer that?"

"Mmm. You can get by with less oil or butter, so, yes. I've only got five more pounds to lose, and I'd love to do it by the end of the year."

"I think you had those jeans before you got pregnant, didn't you?"

"Uh-huh. They were a little large then, and a little tight now." She slapped at her thigh. "I worry that my legs will never go back to how they were, though. The weight has settled right here on the sides."

"You look fantastic, sweetheart. I saw Janelle Perkins with her mom the other day. I'm not sure how old her little boy is, but I think he might be three." She lowered her voice, like one of Avery's old classmates might be lurking in the corner to hear her gossip. "The poor girl's fifty pounds heavier than she was in high school. Either she's gained weight recently or she kept every ounce of baby weight."

"Janelle? Are you sure? What's she doing around here?"

"Living here. Didn't I tell you? She left her job after she had the baby, then her husband got into some kind of trouble." Now she was truly whispering. "The FBI was involved."

"Janelle Perkin's husband had the Feds on him and you didn't mention that?"

"I think they're divorced. Or divorcing. She's staying with her parents."

"Holy fuck! She was summa at Yale, mom. Then Harvard Law. Are you sure it's the same girl?"

"Of course I am. You should look her up, honey. I'm sure she could use a friend."

"Mmm. I'm not sure I will. She was always shitty to Casey."

"To Casey? Why would anyone be shitty to Casey?"

"I'm not sure if Janelle was just anti-gay or she also liked feeling superior to her academically."

"That's the stupidest thing I've ever heard." She turned to look at Avery for a few long seconds. "She did that kind of thing while you were friends?"

That familiar sense of shame settled on her again. "Yes. And no, I never told her to knock it off."

"Avery," she said, with the disappointed look in her eyes making Avery feel much worse than she would have if she'd gotten a lecture.

"I was spineless, for sure, but in my defense I was struggling with my sexuality. I didn't want to step up to defend Casey for being gay since I didn't want Janelle to think I might be." Her mom started to open her mouth, but Avery got in one more thought. "Yes, I'm ashamed of myself. I'm certain I'd stand up to a bully now, but..."

"It's a little late," her mom supplied.

"It certainly is. I'm very glad I've developed a backbone, but I wish I'd had one then."

Her mom went back to cooking, idly commending, "Maybe Janelle has changed, too. She seemed very pleasant."

"Maybe I'll call her. Couldn't hurt."

"That's my girl. Expect the best out of people."

"I try," Avery said. "If nothing else, I could use some baby stuff. I know what kind of things New York lawyers buy for their kids. She might have some great gear."

"I know you're teasing," her mom said, gazing at her fondly. "You've never been into all of that materialistic stuff. But I'm glad you're willing to give her a second chance."

"You don't think I lust for money? Or power? Or fame?"

"Ha! If those were your goals, you would have written one of those fantasy books for kids. Like J.K. Rowlins."

"Rowling."

"Well, whoever she is, she made a mint!"

"I think that takes a certain kind of imagination," Avery said. "One I don't have."

"Oh, how hard could it be to write for kids? Your stories have to be much harder to come up with than hers."

"It doesn't work that way, Mom. You write what you write, and your audience finds you—or doesn't. I'm sure other people have written equally good YA novels, but those writers are still working a full-time jobs somewhere. A lot of success comes from timing."

"But you're not unhappy, are you?" She was busily rubbing the chicken with a little olive oil, but she diverted just enough of her attention to carry on a conversation.

"Not even a little. I'm perfectly happy. But am I bored? Definitely."

"Oh, lord. Not this again!"

"What? When have I been bored?"

"From the time you were fifteen until you started college. I've never met a girl who had grander aspirations that you did, Avery. Where you got them, I'll never know, but you had them. I can still remember the begging you used to do to convince us to take you into the city. You would have thought they were throwing hundred dollar bills to everyone who entered the city limits."

"I don't remember going into town very often…"

"We didn't! Do you know how much it costs to pay for the train, and tickets to a show, and a meal out? We didn't have four hundred dollars to blow on a whim."

"You took me sometimes. Like when we saw *Cabaret* on my birthday. I can still sing every song from the soundtrack."

"I should hope so! You played that CD until you wore the grooves off of it."

"CD's don't have grooves, but I will admit that I was a groupie. If we'd lived closer, you couldn't have kept me at home. I would have been the kid hanging outside of the stage door, trying to get Natasha Richardson to smile at me."

"We should have known then that boys weren't really your thing."

Avery laughed. "Lots of straight girls have crushes on actors and singers. They fade over time."

"Well, yours didn't." She started to slice the potatoes into strips. "Do the same to those turnips and carrots, will you, baby?"

"Sure thing."

They were working companionably when her mom said, "So? Where's my normal helper? I'm not used to cooking dinner all on my own."

Avery grasped her arm, stopping her from working for a second. "Is it too much? I can ask Casey to give you a little breathing room."

"Don't be silly. I love having her over here. While she's playing with Lisbet I can actually get some things done." She went back to work, saying, "I know her hockey games are on Sundays…"

"She's in the city, Mom. At the convention she's been talking about."

Her mom stared at her. "That's this week? Is it October already?"

"It sure is."

"Oh, damn. You're going to have to come over at three on Thursday. I have a troop meeting, and Casey's been babysitting for me."

"Seriously? How did I miss that?"

"I'm home by the time you get here, I suppose. The troop meets at the school as soon as the bell rings, so everyone's home by five thirty."

"Damn, we really are going to have to fend for ourselves while Casey's gone." She let out a soft laugh. "I'm not sure we're up to it."

She walked over to the fridge to put the vegetables she'd cut up back inside. "Should I take Dad a beer? I don't think he got one."

"He'd like that. Lisbet must have distracted him."

Avery smiled as she took one from the shelf. "She has a way of doing that. Be right back."

She walked down the hall, hearing not the strains of a football announcer, but a country song with a very rollicking beat. She'd heard the song before, thinking it might be current. Just before she entered the room, she peeked inside to find her dad on the edge of his chair—dancing. He wasn't generally much of a dancer, but he could do a serviceable two-step, and if he'd had a couple of drinks he seemed to enjoy twirling her mother around at a wedding reception. He couldn't do that now, since he was sitting down, but he was moving as well as he could to the music, with Lisbet avidly watching him.

She was standing while holding his index fingers, clumsily trying to mimic him. She was also giggling like crazy, and shaking her little shoulders, which she could do pretty well. But when she tried to do the same with her hips, she lost it a little and he had to hold her up until she had her balance again.

Avery nearly burst out in tears, seeing how much pleasure each of them were getting from simply interacting. She was one hundred percent sure he'd been just as crazy about her when she'd been a baby, and she relished that thought, realizing this was another perk of having had a baby of her own. You were finally able to feel some semblance of how your parents felt about you.

Unwilling to embarrass her dad, she took the beer back into the kitchen, putting it back into the fridge while her mom was occupied. She still felt a little weepy, and was just dabbing at her eyes when her mom turned and gave her a puzzled expression.

"Are you okay? You seem a little down."

Avery shrugged. "I'm fine. Just thinking."

"Are you sure?" She walked over and gazed into Avery's eyes, clearly concerned. "You're not depressed, are you?"

"No," she said, laughing a little. "I'm fine. But it did hit me today how isolated I've let myself become. I've got to find some creative outlets. I'm alone all day, then I spend my nights with just the baby."

"You feel alone when you're with her?"

"Not exactly," she said, sure she wasn't explaining herself properly. "I actually like being alone a good portion of the time." She gazed out of the kitchen window, feeling a little melancholy when she stared at the garden, now covered over with straw, not a single hint of green remaining.

"What are you looking for, honey? I'm sure there are some mothers groups up here you haven't looked into."

"It's not that, Mom. I'm not just looking for someone to chat with. I want someone I can go deeper with."

"Deeper? About what?"

"Nothing in particular. I'd just like to get out of the rut. You know?"

"Not really. What you call a rut, I call a schedule."

"I'm not very fond of schedules," she said, thinking of her prior life. "When I lived in the city, I spent much of my time doing just what I'm doing now. But working to find new venues for the readings broke the monotony and gave me something to look forward to. I had to be more outgoing to forge relationships with bar and club owners." She shrugged, hating to admit her weaknesses. "If I'm left to my own devices, I can be hermit-like. Even though I wasn't crazy about finding venues at first, I grew to love it, and now I miss it."

"So you're lonely?"

"That's not the right word. It's more like I'm stagnating. I'm not being challenged very often. Intellectually, at least."

Her mom gazed at her for a long minute with her mouth growing a little pinched. "Oh. You're saying you haven't met anyone smart enough—"

Knowing she'd put her foot in her mouth, Avery tried to interrupt to bail herself out. "It has nothing to do with being smart, Mom. It's just that I used to interact with people who liked the same things I did."

"Such as?"

This wasn't going to go well. She couldn't say she wanted to talk about books, since her mom would gladly regale her with the plot of one of her mysteries. While Avery didn't necessarily think the literary fiction she read was superior to a good mystery, it was definitely a different genre, one that appealed to her. "All I'm saying is that you have friends and co-workers you have certain things in common with. When you don't have that connection, you miss it."

"I don't think that *is* what you're saying. I think you're saying that you're intellectually bored." She put her hand on Avery's shoulder and turned her slightly. "If I'm going to be frank, I think that's why nothing's happened between you and Casey. You think she's not smart enough to bother with."

"That's not true! At all! Casey's never shown the slightest bit of interest in me."

"What interest have you shown in her? If you ask me, she's a little shy. I can easily see her as the kind of girl who's not able to make the first move."

"I don't think that's true, Mom. She's gentle, but she's not shy. If she wanted to start something, she would have."

"And the same goes for you. If you wanted to have a relationship with her, you would have told her you're interested."

"I'm certainly not shy either, but you don't just bring that up out of the blue!"

"So you would bring it up if you thought you wouldn't be shot down?"

Avery let out a breath and told the truth. "I enjoy being with Casey. I really do. But all we ever talk about is the baby, and that's not challenging. She's a doll, but she's...not challenging," she said, repeating herself when she couldn't think of a better word.

Her mom walked over and sat down next to her. She seemed less wound-up, or maybe she'd just been frustrated earlier. Either way, whatever it had been seemed to have blown over. "You know," she said gently, "I've tried hard to not be the kind of person who tells you what to do."

"And I appreciate—"

"But I'm making an exception." She took Avery's hands and stared into her eyes. "I agree that you have to have a minimum standard for the people you date. But I think you've gotten the idea that one person can give you everything you need. That's just not true, honey, and looking for that will waste your time and continually disappoint you."

"So you want me to look for someone who I can simply tolerate?"

"Now you're being snotty. That's not what I said at all."

"I'm not trying to be snotty—"

"Well, you are, whether you're trying to or not. You need two things from a partner. You need someone who loves you exactly as you are, and you need someone who loves your baby as much as if Lisbet were her own. Demanding more than that is just being greedy." She let go of her hands and went back to the counter to pick up her knife again.

Her mom sounded a little disappointed in her when she continued. "Sometimes I think living in Brooklyn created needs in you that have made your life harder." She gave her another look, this one a little sharper than the others. "Call me an underachiever, but I'd rather have someone I could rely on when I'm struggling than some brainiac who's too busy thinking deep thoughts to come in out of the rain."

"I'm not looking for a—"

"Or, worse, someone who sneaks off with another woman when you're not watching her." Her voice gained volume when she added, "You found your intellectual equal in Michelle, then she wasted years of your time before she cheated on you. That's what prizing brains over morals will do for you."

Avery stared at the back of her mother's head for a minute, then slipped out of the kitchen, hoping to spend a few minutes with her father, who might also think she was a jerk for not chasing after Casey like she was a prize, but would never say so.

On her drive home, Avery found herself daydreaming about her first girlfriend. They'd been seniors at Bard at the time, both ostensibly straight. Elizabeth was also an English major, and they'd shared a class or two, but had never struck up a friendship. But one night, they wound up sitting by a fire pit in the backyard of a house that a group of their classmates had rented. It had been a small party, and everyone else had gone inside when the temperature dropped. But the fire was still burning hot, and they were engaged in a similarly heated discussion about the death of post-modernism and what had replaced it. Avery couldn't even recall what her position had been, but she was certain Elizabeth had been in opposition. In retrospect, she was sure Elizabeth would have been in opposition no matter what side she'd been on. That was her way—to make you defend your ideas, even if she agreed with them.

Avery could still recall how pretty Elizabeth had looked in the flickering light of the flames, and how fiery her eyes had gotten when she'd defended a point. Avery was always trying to shoehorn her thoughts in when she was with the guys in her department, so it was thrilling to go mano-a-mano with a woman who was also a peer. They'd been pretty evenly matched—both strong-willed women who didn't give in easily.

It had gotten much colder, and Elizabeth stood up and extended her hand. Without stopping to think, Avery rose and put her own hand in Elizabeth's, ready to follow her wherever she led.

She could still recall her saying the house had gotten too crowded to finish their talk, even though neither of them had been inside for hours and had no idea how many people were still around. They got into Elizabeth's car, and when she turned to give Avery a heated look, she was sure they were going to have sex. In all of her years of making out with guys in cars, Avery had never, ever been so turned on, all without even the benefit of a kiss.

They spent the next hour making that Subaru rock, and that night still remained the best hour she'd ever spent in a car. She'd found Elizabeth incredibly attractive, even though she wasn't close to being conventionally beautiful. But a pretty face or a bulging wallet had never been what made Avery purr. It had always been a person with strong opinions who wanted to intellectually wrestle over something—anything, actually. Argument was foreplay for her, but she was *never* going to admit that to her mother.

So while Casey would have been the most attractive woman she'd ever even considered chasing, there had to be more to get her to make a move. The fact was that there was a hierarchy of reasons to tamp down her interest. One—she'd gotten no hint that Casey was interested in her. Two —she didn't want to make things uncomfortable between them, especially because of how great things were going. And three—she wasn't sure she'd be as hot for her in reality as she was from a distance. If Casey was as kind, and thoughtful, and placid in bed as she was in her everyday life—the spark couldn't turn into a fire. But Avery wouldn't tell her mom that. No mother wanted to know that her daughter partially got off on conflict, and she didn't think it was possible to properly explain to her mom, and sometimes to herself, that she was very hot for Casey's looks and personality, but possibly cool to the very things that made her such a good friend.

CHAPTER FOURTEEN

CASEY AND KATHY HAD MADE plans to take Lisbet to Brooklyn to watch Avery's *Short Shorts For The Holidays* show. They were both slightly worried about making the trip, but it seemed to mean a lot to Avery, so they'd agreed. Casey had arranged to take the day off, but she was yanked from sleep at her normal time by her father banging on her door as he called her name.

She stumbled to her feet, tugged on her robe and went to open the door. "Yeah?"

"Why aren't you dressed?"

"Taking the day off. What's wrong."

"No big deal. We got a few inches of snow overnight, and it's sleeting now. I thought you could run the snowblower before you took off."

"Is there too much snow for us to get out?"

"No, no," he said, turning to go back to the kitchen. "I just thought it would be nice to have the driveway cleared in case your mother wanted to go anywhere."

Casey stared at him as he walked down the hall. Her mother hardly ever left the house these days, and she had a real thing about driving in the snow. As she headed back to bed, she grabbed her phone and called Avery, who picked up almost immediately.

"Hi," she said. "I was just looking out the door, kicking myself for not buying a snow shovel."

"What train are you taking?" Casey asked.

"I was aiming for the 7:22." She sighed audibly. "I guess it's silly for you guys to come tonight."

"Silly? No," Casey said. "But I don't think it's smart to drive that far."

"No, it's really not. I'd be worried all day if I thought you were driving over slick highways."

"Maybe next month, huh?"

"Sure. It's not important. I'd better get going if I'm going to get Lisbet fed and dressed."

"I'm going to swing by and pick you two up. My truck will sail right down your long-ass driveway."

Avery didn't respond immediately, then said, "Do you think I'll have trouble?"

"Maybe. And maybe's good enough when it comes to safety. Get some food into that baby and I'll be by."

"Oh, Casey, I'll never be able to pay you back for all you do for us."

"I'm not looking for payback. I'm looking for access," she said, letting out a laugh. "Be ready by 6:45. See you then."

She hung up, then washed her face and combed her hair. Then she put on her weatherproof overalls, her winter boots, grabbed a down jacket, heavy mittens, and a knit cap and opened the doors to the driveway. Her boots crunched into the ice that covered the snow as she went to the real garage to fire up the snowblower, grumbling to herself about not having looked at the weather report. *That* had been dumb.

⌒

Casey bound up the stairs of the porch and knocked. In just a moment Avery opened the door and Casey felt her jaw drop.

"You look so nice," she said, then realized she shouldn't have allowed herself to sound so amazed.

"Thanks, I think," Avery said, smiling at her. "I have the *ability* to look decent. I've just been floating along on the 'I just had a baby' thing. Come on in."

Casey slipped inside, trying to retract her comment. "I just meant that I've never seen you in a dress. You look really nice."

"Thanks. Helena likes us to dress up for *Short Shorts*, even though no one in the audience does. I look out into a sea of T-shirts and denim."

"I wish I could see you in person," Casey said. "I bet you look cool up on a stage."

"It's not much of a stage, if we get one at all. This is a very low stakes production." She turned when the baby yelped out something that sounded close to a word and started to crawl—backwards—toward the front door. "Let me get her. We're ready."

Casey watched her stoop to pick Lisbet up, even though she knew she shouldn't. But a pretty woman in a dress and knee-high boots was a sight she couldn't make herself ignore. Avery complained that she needed to lose more weight, but from Casey's perspective everything was just perfect. The dress was kind of clingy, and it hugged her ass when she reached for Lisbet. Even though Casey was risking being caught ogling her, it was worth it. "Ready?" she asked, even though Avery didn't have her coat on yet.

"Almost. My coat's handing on that hook right next to you."

Casey picked it up and held it for Avery to slip into.

"I kind of like having a valet. Will you come over every morning to get us out the door?" She laughed and answered her own question. "Scratch that. You're so agreeable you'd probably be up for it."

"I'm not that agreeable." Casey grasped the baby under her arms and set her on her hip. "I'll carry her," she said. When Avery locked the door, Casey slipped her free hand around her upper arm and held on tight. "If you slip, I'll keep you upright."

"Who's keeping you upright?" she asked as they went down the stairs slowly.

"My boots. The tread's so deep I have to soak them in a tub of water after I get mud on them."

"Thanks again for this," Avery said, taking such tiny steps it was almost funny. "I called my mom and she said my dad would come get me from the train tonight, so don't you show up too. I know your tricks."

"I'll be in bed. Is your show on live?"

Avery gave her a quick look. "Have you never listened?"

"Well, never's a really long time…"

"It's not live," Avery said, rolling her eyes. "We edit it. It'll be up on Thursday."

"Got it. I'll do my best to listen this time."

"Don't worry about it. I know it's not for everyone."

"It's important to you," Casey said. "That's enough."

Avery looked up at her when they reached the truck. The tiny bits of ice that were still falling had landed on her eyelashes, making them stand out more than normal. She honestly looked pretty enough to kiss, an instinct Casey had never let herself entertain.

"You're a good person," Avery said. "A very good one."

On the first Thursday of December, two days after their freak early snowstorm, the skies opened up for an old fashioned lightening storm, also a little strange for this time of year.

Kathy had been a very loyal Baby Brewers attendee, and she and Lisbet showed up right on time that afternoon. Casey had been in the Greenhouse Pub, and she raced out with a golf umbrella when she heard the car crunch down the unpaved rock-strewn road.

"Hi there," she said, getting her big umbrella over the back door before she opened it. "This is supposed to pass in the next half hour, but you'd better come on up to the brewery. I don't feel great about being in the Greenhouse when there's lightning nearby."

"It was just a light rain when we left," Kathy said, her words barely audible with the hood of her rain slicker covering her face. She had another umbrella up, and they banged into one another repeatedly as they walked up the muddy road. "No one will mind having Lisbet around, will they?"

"Not at all. Ben's gone already, so we can have some privacy in my office."

They burst through the big door and stood there for a moment, letting the rain drip off their clothing, making a small puddle. "The weather forecasters are earning their pay these days, aren't they?" Casey asked. "Every day's a surprise." She pointed the way and said, "Let's go sit down and get sorted out." She finally took the time to look into the car seat. "Lisbet's asleep? Seriously?"

"She was awake when we left, but I couldn't get her down for a nap after lunch. I guess she's on her own schedule."

"I wish I could sleep that well." She opened the door to her office and set Lisbet's car seat down on the floor. "Whew! I'd like to see this stop soon, but the skies were awfully dark."

"Now what do we do?" Kathy asked as she slipped off her slicker. "No beer, no babies, no stir-crazy parents."

"I've got an idea," Casey said, pulling her phone from her pocket. "Have you ever really listened to one of Avery's podcasts?"

"The whole way through?" She had a guilty-looking smile on her face as she shook her head. "I'm only interested in her."

"The one she did on Tuesday's available now. Want to listen?"

"Right now?"

"Sure. Why not? I've got a Bluetooth speaker we can use."

"I guess so. But what if it's boring? I'm not good at lying and I know she'll ask what I thought."

"If it's boring, we won't admit we listened," Casey said. "Easy peasy."

At around six o'clock, Casey rolled down Avery's driveway, with Lisbet in tow. She was wide awake now, and was starting to give off her "It's dinnertime" signals, which had gotten slightly more subtle as she grew older.

It had gotten colder, and Casey hustled her across the sidewalk and up the stairs as fast as she could go.

Avery answered the door and accepted the baby. "Special delivery, huh?"

"It made sense for me to bring her home after Baby Brewers, since that saves your mom almost a half-hour of driving."

"True. But who takes the desserts to the restaurant?"

"My mom can," Casey said. "It's good for her to get out of the house once in a while. She's going to have a Vitamin D deficiency."

"But…"

"It's fine," Casey said. "I wouldn't have asked her to do it if it had been icy out, but she's generally fine driving in the rain."

Avery cuddled Lisbet while kissing her face until she wrenched it away. "I missed my baby girl." She looked up at Casey. "Did you have a decent turnout?"

"Two," she said, raising her fingers. "Your mom and Lisbet."

"Aww." Avery carried the baby into the kitchen and strapped her into her high chair. "We're having turkey meatballs and avocado, Lisbet. Your favorite things."

"Those are some of my favorite things too," Casey said. "But I don't like mine cut up into pieces the size of a pea."

"Wish I had more. I should have gone to the store today when I took my lunch break, but I got on a call and all of a sudden the day was over."

"Want me to go get something—"

"No," Avery said firmly. "You go home and eat with your family, normal people who use utensils."

"How do you know we don't shove pieces of avocado into our mouths and spit half of everything onto the floor?"

Avery laughed. "I don't, to be honest. But you have good manners when we've eaten together. I'll assume your parents do too."

"Yeah, they do. My mom's into Paleo now. Lots of lean meat and veggies. I have to get my bread and pasta fix at lunch." She started to stand up, then decided to go by the sink and wash her hands. When they were clean, she sat on the other side of Lisbet and caught whatever food was thrown her way, dropping it back onto her tray. "Um, while we were waiting out the storm, your mom and Lisbet came to my office. Since I knew your podcast dropped today, we listened to it."

"You did?" Avery asked, with her face lighting up with delight, making Casey feel like a jerk for ignoring it for so many months.

"We did. And we loved it," she said, trying to convey how sincere her compliment was. "I haven't heard a story that moved me like the one by… what was the woman's name?"

"Anwuli?"

"Yeah. The lady from Nigeria. When she was at the point of the story where she was hiding her brother from the police, I actually held my breath when she opened the door."

"It was a great story, wasn't it?" Avery said, still beaming. "It's rare to have a story like that end happily, but I was awfully glad it did. That was fiction, by the way, but it was based on an incident that happened to members of her family."

"All of the stories were good," Casey said. "But that one got to me." She patted her chest. "Right here."

"I'm so glad you got the chance to listen," Avery said. She moved in Casey's direction, looking like she might plant a kiss on her cheek. But Lisbet threw a piece of meatball at her, and she turned to playfully grasp the baby's other hand and pry a piece of avocado from it. Then she gently put it into her mouth, with Lisbet happily gumming it, not using the teeth she had, which were mostly in the front.

Avery turned to Casey again, and softly said, "I was really proud of this show, and to know that one of the pieces touched you emotionally means a lot."

Casey just smiled at her, now resolved to go back and listen to as many of the shows as they kept in the archive. Why hadn't she been doing this all along? Listening to fiction was a thousand times better than trying to read it. And listening to this particular fiction made Avery's face light up like a Christmas tree. Win/win.

CHAPTER FIFTEEN

FOR CHRISTMAS, CASEY'S WHOLE FAMILY spent four days in the mountains outside of Denver, staying with her sister and brother-in-law. Her brother and his boys also came, and even though four days with the whole gang was a little much, she always enjoyed it.

She returned home on the twenty-ninth, giving her five more glorious days of vacation to blow. On the morning after their return, she slept in, then gathered up the presents she'd gotten for Lisbet and drove over to Kathy's.

They'd had a good, deep snow in her absence, but the roads were clear. It was cold, but not too awful as she got out of her truck, carrying the sackful of presents in a red nylon bag.

Kathy opened the door while holding Lisbet in her arms. The baby shrieked with joy, then hid her face against her grandmother's neck, really burrowing. Kathy opened the storm door, and wrapped an arm around Casey, giving her a good, strong hug. "It's Santa, Lisbet! Look! Santa's come again. Twice in a week!"

The baby turned her head just enough to uncover one eye.

"Ho, ho, ho," Casey said, trying to get her voice into a lower register. "I have some presents for a very special baby."

"If that bag's full of presents, Avery will throw a fit!"

"What's she going to do? Write on me with that red pen of hers?" She let out what she hoped was an evil-sounding laugh. "I can outrun her."

"Come in and take your coat off. Have you had lunch?"

"Just had breakfast," Casey said, shrugging out of her parka. "I got home pretty late, so I stayed in bed until ten. Felt great." She held out her hands, and Kathy handed Lisbet over. "Now it feels like Christmas," she said, nuzzling her face against Lisbet's neck and shoulder. "I was with a bunch of adults on Christmas, and adults are no fun at all," she said, making her sentence into a little song.

"Did you have fun? We sure did miss you on the big day, but I've got about ten videos for you to look at. Avery treated Lisbet like she was a big movie star and we were the paparazzi."

"I don't blame her. Lisbet's cuter than any movie star I've ever seen." She slid to the floor and set Lisbet down so they faced each other. "Now you get to open your presents." Holding open the bag, she pushed one little box out, watching Lisbet decide if it was worth investigating. It was wrapped in bright green paper decorated with red polka dots, and the baby played with it for a few seconds before trying to get it into her mouth. It took forever, but with some help she finally got the paper off, revealing a plastic box. It was actually a food container that snapped closed and locked, but it was colorful, as well as safe to chew on. Having Lisbet think it was a toy was a nice side benefit.

"Now that's a great present," Kathy said. "We never have enough of those, even though the entire top tray of my dishwasher is filled with them."

"She eats a lot," Casey agreed. "Well, she eats often. The volume is still tiny, but she'll get there."

It took nearly a half hour, but Lisbet uncovered three more storage containers, a squeaky elephant, and a book made of silicone. It was only six pages long, but she could gnaw on it to her heart's content.

"That's some haul," Kathy said. "If she could, Lisbet would thank you for your generosity. But since she can't, I will." She put her hand on Casey's head and patted it like she would a doll. "You know how much I enjoy having you over here, don't you?"

"Yeah, I do," she said, looking up and smiling. "As entertaining as Lisbet is, I think you'd go nuts with just her to keep you company."

"Well, she can't keep a good conversation going, but she's still fun to be around. I'm a little worried that we're not socializing her enough, but I suppose things will improve when we can go to a playground."

"That might not be until April. We're supposed to have a long winter."

"Well, you didn't have to tell me that, but I don't have many options. I'd rather be warm, but I'll never leave New York."

Lisbet was thoroughly entertained by the book, and she busily tried to shove as much of it into her mouth as she could manage.

"I don't know that this will help much with the boredom, but I was planning on taking Lisbet for a long walk. Do you think she'd like that?"

"Not without me, she wouldn't. I'm going stir-crazy after being in the house all this time. It was bone-chillingly cold when you were gone."

"That's because I wasn't here to warm up the Hudson Valley with the heat of my personality."

Kathy patted her back as she started for the door. "I know you're teasing, but there's an awful lot of truth to that statement."

CHAPTER SIXTEEN

ON A COLD, SUNNY SUNDAY in mid-January, Casey lay on her bed, listening to a soothing, soft voice speak into her ears.

After having listened to most of Avery's podcasts, her need to consume fiction had grown stronger. Now she was plowing through the *New Yorker*'s short fiction podcast, and was sure she'd found a piece of writing that she wished she'd written herself. A desire to write had never, ever occurred to her, and she doubted it would have come up now if this story hadn't moved her so thoroughly. But it had, and she found herself attached to the story in ways she'd never experienced.

The story was really short, much shorter than the others she'd heard, but it packed a punch, saying so much in so few words that she couldn't wait to listen again. She went back to the beginning and closed her eyes, letting the reader's deliberate, musical cadence wash over her.

⌐

Avery lunged for her phone at five that night, annoyed with herself for not having turned off the ringer. But Lisbet only stirred briefly, then settled down in a matter of seconds. "Hi," she whispered, tip-toeing out of the baby's room, then closing the door behind her. "What's up?"

"Got dinner plans?"

Avery smiled, liking how direct Casey usually was. "Not good ones. Why? Are you going to offer something better than leftover fried rice?"

"God, I hope so," Casey said, laughing a little. "I'm in the mood for pasta, but it's still on my mom's forbidden list. If you're up for company, I could make pasta puttanesca or fettuccini Alfredo."

"I'm getting out the pasta pot right now," she said as she walked downstairs. "I'll take either. Cook's choice."

"Then get your mouth ready for some Alfredo sauce. I haven't made it in years, but I'm sure I can deliver."

"Literally. Come any time. I've been upstairs reading while Lisbet sleeps. I'll leave the front door unlocked."

"You've gotten pretty brave out there in the wilderness. I remember when you thought bears were going to come in through the front door and maul you while you slept."

"Bears don't have opposable thumbs, so they couldn't use a doorknob. I still think they'll come," she admitted, laughing at herself. "I'm just sure that a silly little door won't stop them, locked or not."

Casey's truck crawled up the drive while Lisbet was still sleeping. She must have been going through a growth spurt, since she was taking solid two-hour naps in the afternoon, and eating more than normal. But those long naps were pretty fantastic, letting Avery goof off, something she hadn't had time to do for a long while. She should have spent her free time making some healthy meals she could pop into the freezer, but she craved goofing-off time much more than a ready supply of quick meals.

Opening the front door when Casey's foot hit the porch, Avery held her finger to her lips. "Baby's still sleeping."

Casey gave her a smirk. "Do I usually bellow when I come in?"

"Not usually. But I didn't want you to start today." She took the bag of groceries from her and started for the kitchen. "I'm really glad you called. Even though I've been enjoying my unstructured time, I was getting antsy."

"Antsy?" Casey took off her jacket, an oatmeal-colored fleece bomber with dark leather detailing on the zipper and the slash pockets. It was a jacket a normal person would wear when it was around fifty degrees, but Casey was always, in Avery's opinion, underdressed for the weather.

"Pardon?" Avery asked, realizing she'd spaced out.

"I asked why you were antsy." She looked super butch in a fatigue-green Henley waffle-weave shirt that was partially tucked into her jeans. Most people left their shirts out, but Casey often tucked hers in right at the zipper. Maybe that was to show off her distressed leather belt with the custom Kaaterskill Brewery buckle. Whatever her reason, having her shirt tucked in a little bit pulled the fabric snug to show off the swell of her hips, which was a very good choice in Avery's opinion.

"I was just thinking that if I still lived in Brooklyn I'd go sit in a coffee shop for a couple of hours. I loved to do that back in the day. I'd alternate between reading and people-watching. It was divine."

"Mmm-hmm. So your Brooklyn plan would be to dress Lisbet up in her snowsuit, pack a bag with diapers, wet wipes, lotion, a few toys, and a book or two. Oops. Don't forget some soft food she can throw around instead of eat. Then you'd carry her, and her stroller, and her diaper bag down how many flights of stairs—?"

Avery clapped a hand over her mouth. "My fantasy only works in the past," she said, laughing. "My current situation makes sitting in cafes more of a summer pursuit. At least I hope I can do that in the summer." She thought for a minute, then had to admit, "Come to think of it, the only people I see doing that have kids old enough to entertain themselves."

"Like high school aged?" Casey asked, batting her eyes.

"Fine. Ruin my fantasy." She began to take things out of the bag. "Wine? I've never seen you drink wine."

"I don't like beer with pasta." She plucked the bottle from Avery's hand. "I don't know a lot about wine, but I thought a pinot grigio would cut through the richness of the cream sauce without overpowering it."

Avery took the bottle back and put it into the refrigerator. "Says the woman who claims not to know anything about wine."

"I didn't say *anything*, but I'm not an expert."

"I used to love wine, but I haven't had any since Lisbet was born. Luckily, I've got enough milk in the freezer to be able to pump and dump if I have to."

"We've been over this," Casey said. "Unless you get totally wrecked, you don't have to dump. But I'm glad I brought wine, if you love it."

Avery patted her back as she passed by. "I'm glad you brought you." She pulled out a chair and sat down. "I'm willing to help, but if you'd rather be in charge, I'm also willing to watch."

"I think I'll have you watch. But I might want your help with the salad."

"I'm ready when needed." She kicked another chair out and put her feet on it. "I'm not going to complain about sitting on my butt watching you cook for me. Actually, I could get used to it."

Casey smiled at her as she plucked Avery's apron from a hook she'd attached to the refrigerator. "I don't cook often, but that's mostly because my mom would rather work alone. I picked up some tricks from the cooks in my uncle's restaurant when I worked there, but my menu's pretty limited. You'd think I was really Italian."

"I thought you were."

"My mom's great-grandmother was half. What does that make me?"

"Not very. But why does your family run an Italian restaurant?"

"Because people like Italian food," Casey said, grinning at her. "My grandparents almost made it a French restaurant, since that was more popular when they opened it. I'm glad they went Italian, though. I'm wild for pasta."

"Maybe you have just enough Italian blood to make you a good cook."

"We'll just have to see." She took out a baguette and handed it over. "Even if I'm unsuccessful with the entree, I bought some good bread. Want some butter?"

"Why not? It's a little late in the day to worry about a pat of butter, right?"

"That's my motto." She went into the fridge to pull out the butter as if she lived there, then started to find everything she needed. "So," she said, filling the pot with water for the pasta. "I listened to a story today, and decided that if I had any talent, I'd write one just like it."

"Really?" Avery looked up at her, having never heard her express any interest in writing.

"Yeah. I mean, this woman's already written the story, and I could never do anything close, but it was so cool."

"What was it?"

"'Girl,' by Jamaica—"

"Kincaid," Avery finished for her. "That's a great one, isn't it?"

"You know it? Out of all of the stories in the world, you know this one?"

"Yeah," she said, grinning. "I used to do some mentoring back when I had a personal life, and that was a story I always used with young women." She broke off a piece of bread and started to butter it. "The public school by me had a big population of girls with Jamaican, Bahamian, and Haitian ties. It really resonated with them, even though they were a generation or two away from living in the Caribbean."

"It knocked me out," Casey stressed. "I listened to it three times, and when I was finished I really wanted to talk about it with someone." She turned and flashed that beautiful smile. "The list of people who I thought would be interested was really small. You were at the top."

"Fantastic. So, what caught your attention?"

"Mmm." Her eyes closed halfway as she seemed to ponder the question for a while. "I felt like that girl when I was young. It seemed like there were a million rules for how I was supposed to be, but even though I heard the rules all of the time, I always doubted I was doing them right." She'd turned away to start grating some cheese, and Avery felt that might have been purposeful. It was probably easier for her to talk about something so personal when they weren't looking at each other.

"Tell me more about that. What did you doubt?"

"Everything," she said, shrugging her shoulders. "I loved how the girl in the story was going through the list of all of the things she'd been told, then she jumps in and starts scolding herself. Like so many people have told her what to do that she's built those negative voices right in."

"Um, the way you interpret a piece is really personal, but I've read that story to be a mother giving her daughter the rules. There are just one or two places where the daughter speaks..." She got up and went to the bookcase, pulling out a binder where she kept notes from her mentoring days. A copy of the story was still in there, smudged and worn. "Check it out," she said, holding it up in front of Casey. "Where the italics are is the girl's voice. The rest is the mother."

Casey dropped what she was doing and held the binder in her hands. Her lips moved slightly as she read the words, her eyes narrowed in concentration. "I never would have known that," she said quietly. "I guess you don't get the same experience when you listen to a story." She looked up and met Avery's eyes. "I like it better when I think of the girl having all of those rules already in her head. That's what made me feel like she was telling my story."

Avery took the binder and clasped it to her chest. "That's the gift of storytelling. Every story can be read a million different ways. They don't come with manuals," she said, smiling at the sober expression on Casey's face. "If the story works for you as a self-rebuke from the girl, that's kind of fantastic," she said thoughtfully. "I'm one hundred percent certain that Jamaica Kincaid would dig the fact that you found your own meaning. Any writer would love that, as a matter of fact."

"When I get home, I'm going to write it down. I'd like to see it on paper, but I don't want those italics in it. I want it my way," she said, her grin looking a little sheepish.

Avery gently rubbed her back, so pleased for her she was about to burst. It was like watching a blind person gain sight. Now if she could only find all of Casey's teachers and give them a tongue-lashing. When you had a kid who struggled to read, it was a crime not to help her find other ways to access fiction. Our lives were incomprehensible, disorderly bits of information without stories to organize the noise into a narrative that could give our existence some meaning. Every child deserved the gift of story, even if their little brains couldn't process words in the most common way.

⌣

Casey was very glad to see that Lisbet was going to be a pasta lover. She only ate tiny bits of fettuccini, no longer than a half inch, but she clearly liked the cream, as well as the pecorino.

"That's about all I'd give her," Avery said, watching her intake carefully. "That's the richest food she's had other than breast milk, and I don't want to be cleaning it off the walls if it doesn't agree with her."

"Gross," Casey said, nodding. "Incredibly gross. But understandable." She picked up the plates and took them over to the sink.

"I'm doing the dishes. You're on baby patrol."

"Not a bad trade." She sat back down and pulled Lisbet over to her. Sitting in her high chair made their heads on the same plane, which the baby seemed to enjoy. "Do you want to try your new sippy cup again? I think you'd be into it if it was filled with beer, but your mommy thinks water's better for you."

"We'll celebrate her twenty-first birthday at the brewery," Avery said, ruffling Casey's hair as she removed the rest of the utensils from the table.

"Your mommy thinks you're going to have your first beer at twenty-one," she said, using a funny voice that usually entertained Lisbet. "Ha ha is right. I'll sneak you over there when you're about sixteen. How's that?"

"You're going to have to wait for your own kid to fill her up with beer at sixteen," Avery teased.

Casey gazed into the baby's deep blue eyes, seeing so much interest, so much intelligence, so much wonder at the world, that for the first time in a while the loss of never having a baby of her own hit her hard. Before she'd had time to censor herself, she said, "I'd have had one in a second if I wasn't pretty sure it would freak me out."

In a moment, Avery was sitting next to her, a very concerned expression on her face. "What? Why would it freak you out?"

Annoyed with herself for going down this path, she tried to slough it off. "It's hard to explain. I just know myself well, and I know it'd be hard for me."

Avery didn't give up. She stayed right there, gazing at Casey thoughtfully. "I know how much you'd love to parent," she said, her voice so gentle it was like she was physically stroking her. "Tell me why you think it would be too hard. If we talk it through you might be able to figure out a way…"

"I don't think I can." She hesitated for a moment. "Either to have a baby or explain why I don't think I can."

"No pressure, but talking might help. It always makes things more clear. At least it does for me."

"It's not a talking thing," Casey said. "It's a feeling thing."

"Okay. How do you feel."

Casey blew out a frustrated breath. "Do you mind if we put Lisbet on the floor? She's getting antsy because we're not paying attention to her."

"Sure." Avery lifted her from her highchair and put her on the living room floor. There were some toys lying there, and she scooted over to them and started grasping each one and banging it down hard. Her grip wasn't very strong, and she couldn't direct the toy very well, but she was making progress. While devoting her attention to Lisbet, and not making eye contact with Avery, Casey felt a little more freed up to talk.

"Here goes," she said. "I don't have a word for how I feel, but I know I'd hate to be pregnant. Um…I'd hate to be a mother, if I'm being honest. But I want to have a baby." She met Avery's gaze for just a second. "See what I mean? It's fucked up."

"No, it's not. It sounds like you're describing something you don't fully understand. True?"

"Pretty true. I'm glad I'm a woman," she said, certain of that fact. "I don't feel like a man, and I never have. But I don't feel a hundred percent like a woman, either."

Avery nodded slowly, not looking even mildly surprised. That was one good thing about having a friend who'd lived in Brooklyn. She'd probably seen every variation it was possible for human beings to be. "A lot of people are somewhere other than at the poles of the gender continuum. There's no spot you have to be at."

"Try that again. In English," she said, finally able to joke a little.

Avery's smile was warm and Casey relaxed a little when she reminded herself of how patient she was. "I just mean that society tries to make women one hundred percent one way, and men one hundred percent the other way. A woman's role is nurture the children, a man's is to hunt for sustenance. You know. They're opposites."

"Yeah, yeah, I get that. I guess that's what I mean, but it only really comes up when I think about having a baby." She finally met Avery's gaze head on. "It would freak me the fuck out to nurse a baby. I can't imagine my…revulsion would change if I gave birth."

"Do you find it revolting when I—"

"No! Definitely not. I think it's awesome, and I mean that in the 'fills me with awe' way. I like having breasts. I like having an adult woman do whatever she wants to them. I'm all in then. But having my body change in all of the ways it would have to in order to give birth just seems…wrong. For me," she stressed.

"I can tell you're often touched by the way Lisbet and I interact," Avery said softly. "I know you don't think motherhood's weird for other people."

"Not at all. But I want my *wife* to be the mother. I want to be the… other person who's also not the father."

Avery smiled at her, without a hint of judgement. "Last summer, we had an intern who was a trans guy. I talked with him a few times, and he told me he was three when he realized he was a boy."

"I'm not trans—"

"I'm making a different point," Avery said. "This guy identified as a man, and had for basically his whole life, right?"

"Sounds like it. Three is pretty young, and if he never changed his mind…"

"He never did. He was a guy. But some days he came to work in a woman's blouse, or wore fairly dramatic makeup."

"Like…women's makeup?"

Avery smiled at her. "What's men's makeup?"

"Um…" She let out a laugh, realizing some of her tension was leaving her body. "I don't know. So you're saying this guy wore makeup and women's clothes?"

"Once in a while. But he always had a five o'clock shadow. He spent a lot of time making sure his scruff was perfectly trimmed, so it was clearly important to him to show that he was a guy, no matter what he wore or how he ornamented himself."

"So sometimes he wanted to look like a woman—the body he was born into."

"Well, no, I think he wanted to look like himself. He didn't always want to signal that he was one hundred percent male."

"Um, you've probably guessed this, but that wouldn't fly at the brewery. At all."

"I assume he'd have trouble fitting in lots of places. Actually, I'm glad he worked in a creative field, and that he lived in a very accepting place. With all of the violence against trans people, calling attention to yourself can be awfully dangerous."

"If I was a trans guy, I'd try to pass."

"That can be dangerous too, but I think I'd do the same. But this guy wasn't looking for safe. He wanted to present the self he felt to the world." She looked very serious when she said, "I'm talking about my intern just to make the point that we're starting to look at gender without as many rules as we used to have. When you allow people to choose whatever option feels right, they sometimes choose ones that aren't common."

Casey let that sink in for a few moments. "I've never talked to anyone about this. Not in detail, at least. I'm not sure this is a gender thing, and I have no idea if anyone else feels this way, so I've pretty much tried to ignore it, which I've been able to do as long as I'm not thinking about being pregnant."

"That's my point," Avery said earnestly. "It doesn't matter if there are a million other women who feel like you do, or if it's just you. You have every right to own your feelings."

"But I feel like a woman," she insisted. "A woman who can climb a ladder with a fifty pound sack of grain on my shoulder. If I had to have the guys at work do half of the stuff I currently do because my body had changed, it would…" She looked at Avery, at a loss for how to continue. "I don't have words for how I'd feel, but I know it's not a good idea to get pregnant if I worry I wouldn't be able to tolerate it."

"You don't have to." She put her hand on Casey's knee and gave it a squeeze. "Just accept who you are and take childbirth off the menu."

"I guess I have to." She shifted to lie flat on the floor, then held herself up by her forearms so she and Lisbet were looking right at each other. "A while ago your mommy made me realize I couldn't have a baby, and I bet she didn't even realize it."

"What?" Avery asked, lying down next to her, then turning onto her side to look up at Casey. "How did I do that?"

"You told me you felt like every bit of testosterone left your body when you were pregnant."

"I didn't mean—!"

"It's okay," Casey soothed. She smiled when Lisbet backed up a foot or two to pat Avery's cheek. It was more like a tiny slap, but it was clearly meant to be affectionate. "That's pretty much what I assumed pregnancy would feel like. Having all of that estrogen flooding my system is what I wouldn't be able to tolerate. Having my hormones fluctuate when I get my period is bad enough. I hate it when I get more emotional, or feel like crying at work. *Hate* it," she stressed.

"Mmm. That's just a tiny preview of the roller coaster ride your hormones take you on when you're pregnant. It was a pain in the butt sometimes, but those hormones make you love your new baby so much you feel like you'll explode. It was awesome."

"For you," Casey said. "I want the feeling an adoptive parent gets. I'd love that, I think."

Avery put her hand on Casey's lower back and let it rest there for a moment. "Why don't we assume that your brain registers at almost a hundred percent woman, but it simply didn't choose the motherhood option from the dropdown menu."

"You think there's a dropdown menu?" The image lodged in her brain of herself as an embryo, refusing to tick the motherhood box.

"Why not? Almost everything we are and everything we're capable of comes from a hormone or a gene or something. You got the 'awesome at sports' gene. Maybe that filled up the slot that the motherhood option would have gone in."

Casey finally let out a laugh. "You didn't take a lot of biology, did you."

"The bare minimum," she admitted. "But I know enough to realize gender and identity is complex. And deeply personal." She let her hand slide up and down Casey's back for a minute, the touch strikingly intimate. "I think you're perfect, and I truly hope you get the chance to be 'an other person who's also not the father.' You'd be awesome at it."

CHAPTER SEVENTEEN

AVERY WAS KIND OF MOPING around her house on a cold, windy Saturday in January, feeling like winter might last the whole year. She would have parked Lisbet with her mom and gone into the city, but she'd taken her scout troop on a tour of a local distillery. Avery had found that a little odd, but her mom insisted the process was interesting, even though the girls wouldn't be able to sample the product.

Avery was a little behind on her work, and could have used today to catch up, but she couldn't muster the enthusiasm. She ached to do something fun, but when the shutters were banging against the house, the thought of a long walk seemed daunting, and she couldn't think of anything to do indoors that would really get her motor running.

Glumly, she thought of all of the things she could be doing if she were a single woman in Brooklyn. But she'd chosen a different path, and moaning about not being able to go to a hot new play or a museum was just stupid. You couldn't have everything wasn't just a saying, it was the absolute truth.

Her phone rang, and she got up to answer it. "It's your best friend, Lisbet," she said when she saw the screen. "Maybe Casey's going to entertain us, huh?"

"Hi there," she said. "I hope you've got something exciting planned. We're bored."

"Um, I kind of do. Since Lisbet's birthday is on Wednesday, I thought I could celebrate with her a little early."

Avery replayed the sentence in her head, noting the pronoun was "I" rather than "we."

"All right… What did you have in mind?"

"I was hoping you'd let me take her to the Children's Museum. We'd be gone for hours, which would give you a rare Saturday to yourself. What do you think?"

Ignoring her slightly hurt feelings, Avery tried to think of what she could do with a few hours to herself. Given she truly craved free time, it was stupid to refuse such a great offer. "Where is this museum? I've never heard of it."

"Poughkeepsie."

"Really? That's like an hour from here, isn't it?"

"About that. If Lisbet likes the museum we'd be gone for about five hours. You could grab a book and go to that bookstore-bar in Hudson, or one of the espresso shops."

"Now you're talking," she said, feeling her mood brighten at the prospect of carving out an afternoon very much like she used to enjoy. "I'll have her ready to go within a half hour. Swing by whenever you want."

"Great. See you both soon."

Avery hung up and bent over to pick Lisbet up and cuddle her. "Your friend wants this to be a girls day out. No mommies. Are you cool with that?"

Lisbet slapped her on the chest and laughed. She wasn't very verbal yet, but she seemed to understand when Avery was teasing her. Or she was just frequently silly. Either way was perfectly fine.

⌒

Casey knocked on the front door, waited a few moments, then tried the handle, with the heavy door gently swinging open. As she tuned her ears, she realized that Avery was speaking with someone, and it definitely wasn't Lisbet. Then Avery appeared at the top of the stairs, holding a finger up. Casey was going to go into the living room, but then she heard Lisbet say something. It wasn't words, but when Casey looked up she was sitting right at the top of the stairs, with Avery trying to herd her back into the bedroom while she continued to speak on the phone.

Casey walked upstairs, swept Lisbet into her arms and played with her for a second, whispering, "We're going to get a baby gate put onto those stairs pronto. I know your mommy's always watching you, but that's not good enough. I'll add that to your birthday present."

The baby was only half-dressed, and Casey took her into her room to finish up. From there, she could hear every word. Surprisingly, Avery sounded a little aggravated, and Casey couldn't stop herself from listening carefully.

"I have a long list of reasons why I'd prefer to avoid as many cliches as possible, Aspen. I generally find them anathema to clear, concise, original writing."

Casey rolled her eyes, quietly saying to Lisbet, "Your mommy's red pencil would be getting a workout if she read my writing. I don't even know what some of those words mean. Good thing I don't need to use them, huh?"

Avery was getting a little worked up, and her voice gained some volume. "No, I'm *not* saying all cliches are deadly. Using one where you flip the phrase slightly or finish it with some creativity can be exquisitely memorable. I read a piece just yesterday where the writer was recounting a trip to Sweden in the middle of the summer, and she said something like "at the end of the day…which I waited, and waited, and waited for, downing glass after glass of akvavit …" See what I mean? 'At the end of the day' is a cliche that's too tired to appear in a good piece, but I thought she'd tweaked it enough that it added something."

Avery listened for a minute, then jumped back in. "Right. That's exactly my point. We want to encourage our writers to stretch their imagination to encompass the world as they experience it at this moment in time, not to euphemistically harken back to language that requires neither the writer nor the reader to actively think."

She stopped again, and Casey could hear her start to pace across the room. "I'm hardly saying that. I'm not, in any way, suggesting we require nothing but neologisms before a piece merits publication. That would be absurd. What I *am* saying is that there's no room at *Ad Infinitum* for hackneyed expressions, and I'd place this 'low hanging fruit' reference squarely among them. In my note to you, I was simply pointing out that I'd like you to catch things like that, along with the other weaknesses you mentioned."

Casey got Lisbet's tights on her, and pulled down her cute little yellow sweatshirt with the baby ducks decorating the front. Then they crossed the hall and she poked her head in.

Avery waved them in, then held up a finger again, indicating she'd be finished in a minute.

She was sitting again, and she rested her hand on her desk, thrumming her fingers against it quickly. "No, Aspen, we're not teachers. If you want to simply reply with a standard rejection letter, you have that right. But the submission came from a woman who participated in one of our long-term mentoring projects for non-native speakers. Why not be a mensch and edit out the things that made you decide the piece wasn't up to our standards? That will give her feedback she might take to heart."

Casey laughed as Avery held the phone against her ear to use both hands to mimic strangling someone. "You're perfectly correct. Saying the writer might take it to heart is, in fact, a cliche. Do you know why we all use cliches in speech?" She paused for just a second, not allowing whoever this Aspen person was to respond. "Because we're trying to express quick thoughts. In speech, we're not working our language like a sculpture, whittling away everything superfluous until we have a spare, curvy, beautiful suggestion of the clunky thought we're trying to convey."

Avery rolled her eyes. "Yes. I already said that a standard rejection letter was acceptable. But make sure you sign *your* name, not mine." Her foot was now tapping, with the rubber of her soles squeaking against the wood. "I realize it's time consuming to suggest edits that will show someone why you're rejecting their work, but I guarantee your editing takes less time than her writing did."

Aspen must have said something snotty, because Avery's tone got very sharp. "Your internship might let you decide if you're called to do this kind of work, but I guarantee you'll come to hate it if one of your primary goals isn't helping other writers improve."

Aspen was allowed to speak again, then Avery shook her head. "I'd hoped you'd take the hint and be kind to this woman, but clearly that's not going to happen. Send the piece to me, and I'll make the editing suggestions." She paused just a second, then cut in again, "Yes, the point of your job *is* to make my job easier, and I'd have to say you're missing the mark."

Casey met Avery's eyes, with a smile slowly covering her face. "Yes, you can correctly assume I'm trying to help you exactly like I wished you'd done for this writer. But at this point I don't trust you to give it your best effort."

Avery nodded a few times as Aspen spoke, then replied in a calm, soft voice. "By the time the term is over, you might find that editing is the profession for you. But whether it is or not, I'm certain you'll be sick of me." She let out a surprisingly jolly laugh, then hung up, tossing her phone onto the bed. "I hate to think I was once that defensive, not to mention full of myself, but I assume I was."

"Was that a co-worker?" Casey was playing with Lisbet's feet, and she leaned over to act like she was going to take a bite from one, making her laugh. "If it was, I hope she doesn't get your name in the secret Santa drawing. Your present will suck."

Avery laughed, clearly able to take some teasing. "That was one of our many interns. Sadly, she's the one I have to work with most often. She had a lot of nerve calling me on a Saturday for something so minor, but as long as I was talking to her I decided to give her some friendly advice." She laughed again. "Maybe not so friendly, but some of the interns are major pains in the ass."

"Do you... Um, the way you talked to her was very different from the way you usually talk to me or your parents. Was that on purpose?"

"Of course." She smiled. "I code switch."

"That means nothing to me."

"Sure it does. You just don't associate the term with it. Everybody tailors their speech to their audience. I was talking to a very literary kid, who thinks she's going to be the next phenom, a female David Foster Wallace. Every conversation is like a chess match. She's always trying to find logical inconsistencies in what I say." She shrugged. "Aspen's trying to show me how smart she is by making me feel inferior. That's typical behavior for brainy kids whose whole identities revolve around being lauded for their smarts."

"I don't think I code switch much. I talk to you like I talk to my co-workers. Or my bosses, for that matter." She laughed a little. "My vocabulary isn't big enough to have extra words I save for special occasions."

Avery sometimes looked like a teacher who was talking to a student who just wasn't getting it. An expression Casey was all too familiar with. "Does it make you feel…" She shut her mouth for a second, and tried again. "How does it make you feel when I use words that aren't in your normal vocabulary? You don't ever think I'm trying to show off, do you?"

"Um…" She considered playing with her, but decided that was mean. "I don't think your vocabulary revolves around me, and if it did, I'd just feel sorry for you."

"It doesn't," she said, smiling warmly. "I just want to make sure I don't sound like a snob when I pull out words that aren't exactly in everyday usage." She stopped, wincing slightly. "I know I do that a lot."

"Not a lot. And when you do, I like it when you tell me what the weird words mean."

"Really? Oh, I'm so glad," she said, looking so sincere it was funny.

"Really. Listening to short stories lets me hear words I never use. I like trying to figure them out from the context, and when I can't, I look them up. It's fun."

"I couldn't agree more. Since I was a young girl, words have ensorcelled me."

Casey held Lisbet in her arms to walk over to Avery. Then she put her hand over Lisbet's arm to make her give her mother a tap on the head. "You're screwing with me on that one."

"Yeah, I was," she admitted, laughing hard. "I love that word, but it's far from common. It means to enchant, by the way. I just can't resist it when I have the opportunity to pull it out."

"Got it. I can't spell it, so I can't even write it down, but I can use it in a sentence. I've been ensorcelled by Lisbet Kendall Nichols, and I'm thrilled to be able to spend the afternoon with her, thanks to her very magnanimous mother." She smiled at Avery's raised eyebrow. "That was my big word of the day. I doubt there will be another."

By one o'clock in the afternoon, Avery was ensconced on a relatively uncomfortable stool in the newest of the espresso places on Warren Street. There was a good crowd, which gave the place a nice vibe, but it wasn't a good atmosphere for reading. So she went with another of her favorite Saturday afternoon pursuits—people-watching.

There were a number of small cafe tables in the center of the room, along with a shelf along the street front, where you could rest your coffee while you faced out. But since the streets were dead because of the icy wind, she turned around to face the interior of the space, hoping she didn't look like she was staring.

Most of the patrons were her age or younger, giving her the opportunity to harken back to when she'd just started out in her career.

Hudson had a decent permanent gay population, but on the weekends a lot of gay people made the trek from the city to get a taste of the country. It didn't surprise her that half of the tables were taken up by gay men, some of them obviously couples. There was only one table of women, a pair, whom she guessed were on a date. Maybe even their first since they seemed a little stiff with one another, and their laughs were frequent and forced. If she'd had to guess, this was not only their first date, it was likely their last. She didn't pick up a single "this is going great" vibe from either of them.

Idly thinking of how little she missed dating strangers, she picked up her phone to pull up the dating app she used to use. After paging through it for a while, she went to her own profile, which she'd deactivated. The thought of updating it was daunting, since she'd have to include the fact that she had a one-year-old child. That alone would scare off most women, and when she added that she was living one hundred miles north of her old haunts, she'd lose the few brave souls who'd be willing to structure their dating lives around a baby's needs. Digging deeper, she saw there were very few women who mentioned having children. That obviously didn't mean they didn't, in fact, have them. But she had to be honest and admit that she wouldn't immediately click on a profile of a woman who had a small child. Having one of your own could be arduous. How would it work to have to integrate another woman's child into *her* life? Obviously, it could be awesome with the right woman and the right child. But it could also be dreadful. What if you found a great woman who had a kid your kid didn't like? Or if the woman had a bitter ex she shared custody with? If she had to be honest, she knew she'd only seek out women with kids if she didn't match with any childless ones. But didn't that mean a lot of other women would feel the same? Yes. It definitely meant that.

Fuck.

⟶

Casey texted at two.

We've been having a blast, but Lisbet needed a nap. Mind if I wait her out and see if she wants to shut the place down at five?

Avery gazed at the message for a minute, tempted to ask Casey to bring the baby home. Then she got hold of herself and made the more generous move.

Take your time. Just text when you leave. Have fun!

Now she had anywhere from two to four hours to do exactly what she wanted. But she'd gotten out of practice on how to fill a block of time. Given her daily wish was for more sleep, she decided to go home and pamper herself. A long bath, a manicure, and a nap could fill up the afternoon quite nicely. In fact, that short, simple list was probably every mother's dream.

⟶

Some of her favorite music played from her phone, and a couple of candles rested on the rim of the tub. She was surrounded by bubbles, and warm water that nearly touched her chin.

Before Lisbet, Avery had been an avid bath-taker. She loved to soak while reading, a habit she'd gotten into when she'd been a young teenager. Today she luxuriated in the tub, and even though she'd planned on reading something fluffy, she did a little work, reading a fairly racy piece one of their interns from the previous year had submitted.

The writer, a woman named Min, had always seemed pretty buttoned-up, not to mention shy. But this piece was both sexy and sensual, something she never would have expected from the woman who appeared in the office most days in a prim sweater set and a skirt that nearly touched her knees. Avery often thought she dressed like a secretary from the fifties, so far from the other interns' style that it seemed she'd been cast into the wrong movie.

This amazing piece was not only sensual, it was skillfully written, and even came in a little light on the word count. One of this year's interns had already given it a big thumb's up, and Avery agreed wholeheartedly. She was going to pass this one around at their all-hands meeting and see if the other editors agreed. She could just see the demure smile on Min's face when she learned she was going to be published while still in college.

She dropped the pages to the floor and saw that her toes were starting to prune. If she wanted that nap, she had to get to it.

After drying off and putting on a thermal shirt and some sweats, she went into her room and flopped onto the bed. She'd made it when she'd gotten up, and didn't want to mess it up too badly, so she pulled the end of the quilt over herself, and tugged a pillow down.

Normally, she was out in seconds, but she kept thinking Casey might text any minute to say they were leaving. She shouldn't have set it up that way, but she really did want to know when they were on the way—so she could worry until they got home.

Stupid!

She kept trying different positions, but just couldn't get comfortable enough to drift off. She'd been a lifetime stomach sleeper, but had to stop that cold while pregnant. Given her breasts were still milk-producing machines, they prevented her from getting comfortable on her belly, but she'd still not truly taken to side or back sleeping. A lifetime habit was very hard to break.

Masturbation had always been a good soporific, and Min's story *had* perked her up… She rolled onto her back and slipped her hand into her roomy sweatpants. But when she touched herself she was surprised to find she wasn't wet enough to get the job done. What was up with that? Granted, she hadn't masturbated once since Lisbet had been born, but she'd assumed that was because she was so tired that she was out most nights as soon as her head hit the pillow. But now? When she had time and wouldn't be interrupted for at least an hour?

She rolled over to find a tube of lube in her bedside table, and squirted a few drops onto her fingers. That helped, but as she touched herself, she realized things didn't feel quite the same.

Avery had never been intensely curious about her body's landscape, but she had a very clear picture of how her vulva had looked prior to pregnancy. Getting up, she went to her bathroom and found her old makeup mirror. It took a little maneuvering, but she dropped her pants and angled it so she could get a good look, then nearly dropped the mirror as she let out a cry. Whose body was she looking at? Hers was pink and kind of dainty, but this one was a few shades darker, slightly swollen, and almost purple by her perineum. Touching herself clinically, she realized everything was a little larger than it used to be. Not much, but enough to feel like someone else's skin. It wasn't grotesque or anything, but it wasn't her!

Leaving the bathroom, she went back to bed, even more discomfited than she'd been before. She wasn't going to be able to find a mate, or even a sex partner, and now she wasn't even able to turn herself on? How did such a promising day turn so shitty?

⌒

The happy wanderers didn't get home until six thirty, but Casey had thoughtfully stopped by her uncle's restaurant to snare a small tray of lasagne. It hadn't been cooked yet, so Avery went upstairs to feed Lisbet and read her a story while dinner was in the oven. By seven fifteen, the baby was out like a light, and Avery walked back down the stairs to the scent of a quasi-homemade meal.

"That smells so good I was tempted to cut Lisbet's story short."

"Ooo. Is she asleep?"

"Totally." She stopped, seeing the disappointment on Casey's face. "You can always come upstairs when I'm putting her down, you know. She thinks of you as one of the clan."

"Really?" She looked utterly delighted.

"Of course. You don't have to worry about overstepping, Casey. That's never your instinct."

"Yeah, but I want to respect your time with her."

"You do. But a lot of caring for a baby is routine. Both of us would appreciate a little variety."

"Then I'll help out the next time I'm here. That'll be fun."

"Make it soon," Avery said, so happy to be able to share something that Casey clearly valued deeply. "We both dig you."

⸺

While Avery cleaned up after dinner, Casey went upstairs to check on the baby. Given the monitor was on, and they could both hear her breathing and making her cute little sleep sounds, it wasn't necessary to peek in. But Casey wanted to say goodnight alone, and this was her chance.

She kissed her fingers and placed them on Lisbet's cool forehead, gazing down at the sweet little thing lying in her crib without a pillow or a blanket or a toy. She believed Avery knew what she was doing in keeping the crib so Spartan, but this was how they treated prisoners on suicide watch. Couldn't someone figure out how to give babies some comfort while not creating a safety risk?

Casey went back downstairs, finding Avery sitting on the polyester pod. It was such a dramatic change from how the place had looked just two years earlier, when her grandmother had the rooms stuffed with not only furniture she'd accumulated over her ninety years, but photos and paintings on the walls, along with bookcases filled with ceramic figurines people had given her over the years. She hadn't been a crazy collector by any means, but compared to Avery she was an out-of-control hoarder.

The place honestly looked like the previous tenant had moved out without warning, leaving whatever she couldn't fit into her car for the bum she was divorcing. But it wasn't the lack of creature comforts that had placed the unhappy look on Avery's face. At least, Casey doubted that her thrifty friend regretted not filling the house with stuff.

"What's up?" she asked, sitting next to her.

"Just thinking." She gave Casey a thin smile. "I had time to do that today, thanks to you."

"Umm…were you thinking about things that upset you? You look like you're about to cry."

She shook her head quickly. "No, I'm not on the verge of tears. I'm just trying to be realistic." She took in a deep breath and said, "This isn't how I thought my life would turn out, but I can't avoid the facts."

"Which facts…?"

"I'm thirty-six years old, and for all intents and purposes, my sex life is over."

"Wait," Casey said, stuck on the words she'd used. "Those are three words?"

Avery stared at her for a second, then said. "Five." She held up her splayed hand and pulled in a finger as she enunciated each. "My. Sex. Life. Is. Over."

"No, no, the intensive purposes thing. You said it like it was three words instead of two. Is it?"

Avery cocked her head, clearly confused. "Two?"

"You said intensive purposes, right?"

Avery finally smiled. "That's three words. I'm referring to whatever your intent or your purpose is. Intents and purposes is the phrase." She slapped at Casey's arm. "I just confessed that my sex life was over and you fixated on the words I used? Seriously?"

"Oh, shit! I didn't mean to. I've just heard that expression kind of a lot, and I thought I knew it. But when you said it, it sounded funny…" She took a breath and grasped Avery's hand. "I shouldn't have gotten stuck on the words. But the meaning's insane, so maybe I skipped over that."

"I'm not insane, Casey. Since I got pregnant, no one even looks at me anymore. I used to get a pretty enthusiastic upvote when I cruised around town, from men and women alike. Now? Nothing."

"When do you cruise around town? There is no town here, Avery. There isn't even a post office, much less a business district."

"There is in Hudson, and Rhinebeck, and lots of other towns around here. But I'm specifically talking about Brooklyn. When I was there a couple of weeks ago I tried to flirt with a cute lesbian on the subway. Guess what she did."

"I—"

"She stood up and offered me her seat. I thought I was giving her a flirty look, but I must have looked like I was about to hit the floor."

"Maybe she wanted to sit on your lap," she said, trying to joke. But Avery didn't crack a smile. "I'm sorry I'm making light of this. Really, I am. But it's just because I can see how wrong you are, so it's hard for me to take you seriously."

"I'm *very* serious," she said soberly. "I'm usually too busy to reflect much, but I had plenty of time to do that today. Too much," she stressed. "I don't feel like the same person I was, and I clearly don't attract women any more. I've come to the conclusion that I'm not simply between girlfriends. I'm done."

"Done? What kind of nonsense is that? You're different in many, many ways, but everything you've been through has made you better."

"Not physically," she said, making a face. "You haven't seen the mess that's hidden under these sweatpants."

"I'm not even going to humor you on that. I'm sure your body's changed a little, but with your clothes on you look just like you did when we reconnected at the pub. You look great!"

"No, I don't," she said, refusing to give in. "Even when the baby's not with me, I look, and act, like someone's mom. I don't feel sexy anymore, and people pick up on that. My sex drive is *gone*, Casey. One of the things I relied on for so much pleasure in my life is gone."

"Misplaced," Casey stressed. "You might have misplaced it, but you didn't lose it. Loss is permanent, and I'm sure this isn't."

"It's been a year since I gave birth," she said solemnly. "And I didn't have any interest in sex from the time I was about six months pregnant. That means it's been a year and a quarter since I had the *slightest* interest. My sex drive should have come back by now, so I have to face the likelihood that it's permanently gone." She narrowed her eyes slightly. "The fucking internet isn't helping, by the way. If you want to depress yourself, look at the huge number of women talking about how they dread having sex once they give birth."

"No, no, no. I refuse to believe that's going to be true for you. Did you use to…" She made the least obscene gesture she could think of, holding up her hand and wiggling her fingers. "Did you like to…?"

"Of course," she said, looking a little irritated. "Frequently. But I've lost the roadmap to my own vulva. It doesn't feel like my own flesh anymore. Now it's just the part of me that Lisbet emerged from. It's kind of like the appendix. While it has a purpose, it's not vital."

Casey made a face. "That's… I don't know what to say, other than you have to give it time."

"I tried to see if I could wake it up this afternoon. I had time, I'd just read a sexy story, and I knew I wouldn't be disturbed. But there's nothing doing down there."

"Maybe you need…" She trailed off, not having any idea what Avery needed.

"I figured I might need some lubrication to help me get going, so I tried that. But my actual flesh didn't feel the same. Then I made the biggest mistake I've made all year." She shivered roughly. "I got out a mirror to take a look." She stared at Casey for a few seconds, stone-faced. "I almost threw up. It looked like I'd been in an accident."

"Oh, come on. I'm sure there have been some changes, but I bet they're minor, and I'm sure they're temporary. Where do you think second and third kids come from? Women have to get their groove back, or everyone would be an only child."

"Uh-huh. Just like Lisbet will be. Those of us who lose our sex drives stick with one baby."

Casey gave her a slap to the leg. "That's not why. There are plenty of reasons to have just one."

"Actually, that's a minor part of the problem," she said quietly. "Touching myself down there reminded me of childbirth, and I must still have a little PTSD."

"Really? It was that bad?"

"It was bad," she said solemnly. "I was in labor for fifteen hours, and they had trouble getting the epidural inserted. Only half of my body was numb, so I delivered Lisbet numb and disconnected on one side, with no pain relief at all on the other. I thought I'd lose my friggin' mind."

"I'm a little sick to my stomach just thinking about that."

"Trust me. Those women who talk about how you forget the pain the minute you see your baby are full of crap!"

Casey laughed at her outraged expression. "I always doubted that myself. I mean, I get that they're saying the pain was worth it, but that's different from saying you forget all about it. That seemed unlikely."

"Very. The people who say it's a peaceful and serene experience are flat out lying. Trust me on that. Liar, liar, pants on big, fat, fire."

"So…I get that you might have some dark memories of having that part of your body rearranged by Lisbet's exit. But those will go away. Once you reclaim your body for yourself, rather than being a baby-machine, you'll get back into the swing of things. Or maybe breast feeding slows you down. Nature might want you to concentrate on Lisbet for a while before you put another bun in the oven."

"Mmm. That might be true," she said, clearly not convinced. "But that's only the sex part." She gazed at Casey contemplatively for a full minute. "Even when Michelle and I were having problems, even when we'd largely stopped having sex, we were still affectionate with each other. That's what I miss. I desperately long to have someone hold me and stroke my back while telling me everything will be all right." She shivered, with her eyes starting to well up with tears.

"Everything *will* be all right," Casey soothed, desperate to make her feel better.

Avery shook her head, while pulling down her sleeve to dab at her eyes with the fabric. "I've been able to handle everything that being a single mother has thrown at me, and I'm damn proud of myself for that. But I wish I'd waited until I had a partner. I miss the intimacy I got from a partner more than I can express."

"You can have that again. I'm certain you will."

"You can't be certain of that. No one's going to want to step into my little family at this point. I don't regret having Lisbet when I did, but I gave up my love life to get her, and…I hadn't guessed that was the bargain I was making. I'm so sad that I'll never have anyone to rely on. Anyone to take care of me."

Casey's heart ached for her, and she was just about to remind her that she had her back. But Avery's chin started to quiver, then the tears started in earnest, making Casey freeze.

"It's hard," Avery whimpered. "I give all of my love to Lisbet, and I know she returns it in an instinctive way. But it's not the same as the love you get from someone who isn't dependent on you. I miss that so much," she said, her sobs breaking Casey's heart.

Scooting over a little, she wrapped her arm around Avery, being more assertive, and definitely more physical than she'd ever been with her. As Avery molded her body to Casey's, she leaned toward the left, like she was too sad to hold herself upright.

"This is a temporary thing," Casey said, sticking right with her as they sank lower onto the pod. "You've still got a load of hormones flowing through your body. Everything has to get sorted out again. But it will, Avery. I swear that it will."

"You're just saying that to make me feel better." she whimpered. "You don't know that."

"I do! It's nature. You're a fertile, healthy woman. You need a sex drive to want to have more children, so nature will give you a boost when you're not breast-feeding. Your body's just letting you have a little break."

"A break? Really?"

"Yes," she said, even though she was making this up on the fly. "You just got your period back like a month ago right?"

"Right…"

"That's the first step. That means your system's coming out of hibernation. Once you can get pregnant again you'll start wanting sex."

"But I didn't want it today, even though I'd just read a sexy story and felt some tingles. I think I'm broken."

"You are *not*," she insisted. "Promise."

"But even if I can have sex, I don't have anyone to have it with, and you can't fix that." She took in a deep breath, then spoke again, with her voice shaking. "Sometimes I ache for touch. For comfort."

It seemed like the most natural thing in the world. With just a shift of her hips, they were fully on their sides, with Avery the little spoon. Casey tried to show her how much she cared, how much she understood her loneliness. Gently, she touched her the way a lover would. Not a lover who was looking for sex, but one who was soothing a deep hurt.

She stroked Avery body tenderly, letting her hand glide down a leg, feeling the lean muscle. Then she touched her arm, just as thin and willowy. "You'll have a partner as soon as you're ready for one. When the time's right, you'll give off the same signals you used to send, and a woman will pick up on it and follow you around like a puppy."

Avery laughed weakly through her tears, and gripped Casey's hand, bringing it to her lips for a kiss. "That's never happened before, but I did have a decent batting average."

"That's not a surprise. I really wasn't kidding when I told you how the guys in high school were into you, and some of them were super picky. If the top jocks wanted you back then, I bet women will get whiplash when you get your groove back."

"God, I miss that," she breathed, the longing in her voice making Casey's hand start to move again.

"Any woman would be lucky to have you." She kept touching her, going a little further with each stroke. "You're such a pretty woman. And so smart. I can almost see that big brain of yours working away."

"I don't care if a woman wants my brain," she said, laughing through her tears. "I want a woman to crave my body. I can talk about ideas with a lot of people. I want someone who gets turned on when she sees me. When we kiss… When we touch."

The way those words were just bursting with sensual energy made Casey's pulse start to race. She knew she should stop. It was absolutely crazy to touch Avery like this. But a part of her thought this was exactly what Avery needed at the moment. Her self confidence had taken a beating, but she was still stunningly attractive. Casey couldn't let her think otherwise when she had such clear evidence to disprove it.

"You turn me on," she whispered, pressing into Avery's back to nuzzle against her neck.

Avery froze, and Casey almost backed out of it. But she couldn't think of a single excuse for what she'd said.

"I do?" Avery's voice was a little thin, shaking slightly.

"Just trying some dirty talk," Casey said, thinking Avery might buy it. "I thought a little of that might give your sex drive a boost."

Avery didn't respond for a few seconds, with Casey's pulse beginning to thrum. She was starting to beg the heavens to keep Avery from taking offense, or thinking she meant it—since she did, when Avery finally responded. "I used to like a little dirty talk," she said quietly. "But what you said wasn't very dirty. You must be out of practice, too."

Laughing with relief, Casey said, "Seriously. But I used to be good at it, I think."

"Let's see you try," Avery said, her voice still soft and a little tentative.

Now the spotlight was on, with Casey having to perform. Saying the things she truly felt while trying to make them sound like a fantasy scared her half to death, but she couldn't pull out now. "Um…I've put you in the 'almost a relative' category, so I don't let myself think of you in sexual terms." She molded her body closer to Avery's, letting her imagination run wild. "But every once in a while I can't stop myself, and I think of how it would be to have you naked and hungry in my bed, looking up at me with so much desire I lose my ability to focus. It's awesome," she whispered. "We really make the bed rock."

Avery pushed back against her as she let out a soft, sensual groan. Going for broke, Casey licked all around her ear, finally taking it between her teeth to gently nibble the tender skin.

"Ooo," Avery purred, sending an electric charge down Casey's body. "That's my favorite spot. You're going to wake up my sleeping sex drive with a bang if you keep that up." She pressed her ass firmly into Casey's lap, murmuring, "*Please* keep that up."

They were in it now, and Casey ignored every warning sign and alarm that rang in her head. She hoped she'd made it clear she thought of Avery as a friend, rather than a lover, but Avery had a need...a vulnerability...that she couldn't repair on her own. She needed to know she was still attractive, and Casey could easily and honestly show her that she was. This was clearly blurring the lines on their friendship, but it was definitely based on that bond. Maybe this was the true meaning of friends with benefits.

She worked on Avery's neck and ears until she was squirming around on the sofa, moaning continually. "Hold me," she murmured. "Hold me tight and kiss me just like that."

Sensation pulsed through Casey's body, urging her on. It wasn't quite like having real sex, but it was much more intimate than she'd felt the few times she'd hooked up with women she didn't care for deeply. She and Avery were bonded in a very real way, and she didn't feel tentative like she sometimes did with someone she was just starting out with. This was a woman she'd come to truly know. She trusted her now, even though it had taken months to get to this point. A smile covered her face as she continued to kiss her neck while stroking her legs. It was true. She finally trusted Avery.

"If I was your lover," she whispered, "we'd have to figure out some way I could horn in on Lisbet's territory. I hate to be shallow, but breasts make me throb." She flinched when she heard those words leave her lips. Had she lost her mind? Avery didn't need to know how she really *felt*. This was supposed to be a game!

"Ooo. You'd be disappointed," Avery said, not seeming to notice that this was a real desire that had slipped out. "Nursing bras, pads to keep them from… What am I saying? A hot woman's talking sexy to me, and I inject reality into it?"

"Give me something to work with here," Casey said, propping up the teasing vibe. "Play along."

"Okay." She took a breath. "I'd kill to have your mouth and your hands on me. My breasts are so sensitive that just breathing on them would make me wet."

Casey's mouth started to water, thinking of hovering over Avery's naked body, taking in the splendor of her full, luscious breasts. Even the thought of breathing on them made her throb.

"But I'd want more," Avery said. "I'd want you to lick them until my nipples were as hard as stones. We'd both love that," she whispered as she grasped Casey's hand, then set her foot on the sofa to raise her knee. Gently, she pressed Casey's hand against herself, with the heat of her body warming her fingers.

Casey nearly choked. She had no idea Avery would be so bold, so overtly sexual. But then she recalled that Avery *had* been a sensual animal before she'd gotten pregnant.

Casey could still recall the feeling she'd gotten from her that first night they'd reconnected at the pub. She could have taken her home, and she'd known it. Avery hadn't been blatantly flirting, but she'd had a frank, sexual, open way of looking at you that gave a big hint she was up for it. But the old hurts had made Casey close that door before she'd even been tempted to look inside. Now she was seeing all the way in, and it was hot in there! Avery might look like a cool businesswoman, but inside her beat the heart of a sexy woman who needed to let herself remember that's who she was.

Casey rubbed her face against the soft, silky blonde hair that smelled of spring and flowers and sunshine. Her hand moved slowly, teasing her through her clothing. "This space is available for pleasure. Time to wake up now," she added, patting her firmly.

"I'm wide awake," she purred. "I'm almost ready to beg you to play with my breasts, and that's the mark of a woman who's about to lose her mind."

"I wouldn't want that." She slid one arm under her neck, crossing her body to hold her by the shoulder, locking her in place. There was nothing she loved more than holding a woman just where she wanted her, then slowly driving her mad. Her other hand slithered down her body to dip into her sweats, skimming over her belly to rest between her legs. No underwear? *Nice,*" she thought, loving the slightly racy vibe of a woman who didn't need to be covered up all of the time.

Casey swallowed to get some moisture back into her mouth as she paused for a second, clearly on the road to touching Avery intimately. She smiled when the only response to the boulder that was clearly rolling down the hill was for Avery to shift her hips forward, bringing herself closer to Casey's fingers. Oddly, she found herself responding as naturally as if they were long-time lovers, acting like this was the way they always behaved. Her breath caught in her throat when her fingers brushed across the slippery skin to feel the wet heat of Avery's body. "Show me what you like," she whispered, her voice shaking from a mix of desire and fear. "Put my hand right where you need it."

In a split second, Avery's hand was atop hers, and together they moved across her sex. Casey focused on the goal—boosting Avery's self-esteem, rather than her own throbbing need. "Everything's ready for action," she whispered. "All systems are go."

"Mmm-hmm," Avery purred, her voice so sexy Casey could hardly stand it. "That feels so good I can't talk."

"You don't have to talk. Just feel me touching you while you reconnect with your body."

She didn't need guidance now, but she liked having Avery's hand on top of hers. She tried to distance herself slightly and treat Avery like she was a new sex partner. In her experience, Avery's body was just like every other woman she'd ever touched. Each was vaguely alike, yet completely unique. Her fingers were soon slipping along the tender skin, with her own vulva pulsing with sensation, wishing she had some way to satisfy herself at the same time. But she focused on Avery, who was getting more and more into it as she squirmed and moaned while Casey's fingers explored her. It only took another minute or two before she started to shift her hips, angling so Casey touched her in one particular spot. As soon as she'd hit it, Avery stilled for just a second, then shivered roughly and thrust against Casey's fingers, demanding attention.

Tightening her hold on her body, with Avery backing up against her as she let out another low moan, Casey rubbed her more firmly, keeping it up until Avery's head started to nod, her low groans rising in pitch. "That's it," she said through gritted teeth. "Just a little harder... Yes! Oh, that's so good," she moaned, shivering. Then she got very quiet, lifting her hand to hold onto Casey's arm where it held her so tightly. "That was so fucking awesome," she whispered. "I've been born again."

Casey placed a few more kisses to the back of her neck, smiling when the skin pebbled. It probably wouldn't have been hard to get her going again, but Avery's body was getting heavy, with her muscular tension disappearing.

"Do you need...?" Avery asked, her voice sounding like she was working hard to get the words out.

"I need you to sleep," Casey murmured, placing one final kiss to her pale skin. "Lie right here and let me cuddle you to sleep."

"Ooo," she whispered, yawning like Lisbet did when she couldn't stay awake for another second. "I miss cuddling." Clearly not bothered by what they'd just done, she sighed heavily and moved around until Casey was plastered to her. In seconds, her breathing changed, and in a few more seconds Casey was sure she'd fallen asleep.

It wasn't the most comfortable bed she'd ever been on, and she'd have to get up to go home at some point, but Casey turned off her brain, determined to enjoy sharing this intimacy with someone she truly cared for. But it was hard to ignore the longing she felt, wishing all of this had been their truth. She missed touch and intimacy as much as Avery did, but she could enjoy this for the brief time they had before they went back to their usual relationship: good friends, but with no added benefits.

Casey's watch vibrated on her arm, giving her the gentle nudge she needed to get her butt in gear. As she moved her arm, it brushed across something warm and pliable. Jerking upright, she blinked in the pre-dawn, seeing that she was right where she'd been at ten o'clock the night before—lying on the polyester pod with Avery.

Her mind started to race, and she moved away to stand up gingerly to have a moment to get her bearings. *What now?* Did she wake Avery? Let her sleep and sneak out of the house like a thief? Leave a note thanking her for…what? Being allowed to help wake up her sleeping sex drive? *That* wouldn't be too weird.

Having no idea which of the options was the right one, she took the easy way out. Her coat was hanging off a kitchen chair, and she slipped it on. But Avery looked so alone on that bare pod that she took a fluffy throw from the back of it and gently covered her with it. A note might have been better, but at least she was leaving with the message that she cared—at least enough to stop her from shivering.

Casey knew she wasn't going to be able to act normally until she had time to think about what had happened. But she didn't have time to indulge in that kind of thing on a Monday morning. Her crew wouldn't be in until eight, and that didn't give her long to do what she needed to do to prepare for the start of the week.

She began every Monday morning by double-checking the sanitation throughout the plant. Even though the staff did a thorough cleaning on Friday afternoon, you couldn't be too careful. She'd learned her lesson early on when they'd had to dump thousands of gallons of beer down the drain when someone had been sloppy and hadn't followed procedures. For a small brewery like hers, a mistake like that could cost them their entire profit for the month, so she'd gotten even more fanatical about everything from disinfection to general cleaning.

After she'd used her keys and punched in the code on the rolling door at the loading dock, she tossed her coat onto the little refrigerator that rested right outside her office. Then she got down to business, grabbing a seat on some stacked pallets, then switching the bottling machine to test mode to watch it work its magic for a while. Doing something she could handle without much thought was helping, and she was pretty sure her hands weren't shaking any longer.

Then she got out her testing equipment and made sure the sanitizing water they bathed the bottles in was at the right temp. She worked backwards through the brewing process, testing each component to make sure it was within specs. After checking the CO_2 levels of the bright tanks to make sure the pressure relief valves were sealed up tight, she climbed up to the top of one to take a look—even though there was nothing mechanical up there.

The brewmaster Casey had taken over for had told her a tale of a stray bird building a nest on a tank, and what a pain it had been to sanitize everything after the chicks had hatched. So even though she was sure every tank was bird-free, she still took a look once a week. She was way up on a thirty foot ladder when Ben came in through the regular door.

"Hello up there," he called out.

"Hey. Be down in a minute."

She saw him pause in front of their office, obviously noticing she hadn't gone in yet, but he didn't comment. By the time she'd finished her rounds, it was seven thirty, and she'd made tick-marks by each of the many boxes on her checklist.

As she walked into the office, she tossed her clipboard onto the desk. "How's it going?" she asked, trying to sound casual.

"Fine." He looked up at her, with his pale blue eyes seemingly able to look right through her. "What's up with you?"

"Nothing. Why?"

"Mmm. You didn't come into the office before you started your rounds, I don't see your thermos, or your mug, and there aren't any signs you had breakfast. Did you miss your alarm?" He looked at her more carefully. "Did you even comb your hair today?"

She rolled her eyes. Why did she have to be close friends with the one guy out of a hundred who looked at her hair?

"Got a late start. No biggie."

"Um…" He gave her another look. "You've never come to work in nice pants and a regular shirt. You look more like you're going to visit a client than climb around the equipment on a brew day."

She just stared at him, unable to come up with a response that made any sense at all.

"Did you hook up with someone last night?" His concerned look morphed into a smile. "Did you finally talk a woman out of her clothes?"

"No," she said, dropping into her chair so heavily the air left the cushion in a "whoosh." "Everyone had their clothes on. But I did do something with someone I think I'm going to live to regret. Maybe in the next few hours."

"Not Avery," he said, staring at her hard.

"Who else do I hang out with lately, other than people from work?"

"Oh, shit!" He looked absolutely stunned, and she was right behind him. "So? Is this good news? You don't look very happy."

"I don't know what it is." She picked up a pen and stuck it into her mouth, gnawing on the plastic cap until her teeth hurt. "Other than weird."

Her phone buzzed in her pocket and she looked at the text.

Just dropped the baby at my mom's
Have time for a coffee break?
I'm stopping for a cappuccino and I can bring you one

She gave Ben a grim look and said, "I'm going to make sure everything's set for the guys, then I'm going on a coffee break. If anything comes up, text me."

"Where are you going to be?"

"In the parking lot, I guess. Avery's bringing me a cappuccino."

"Oh, boy," he said, shaking his head. "When a woman has to look you in the eye after you have sex…"

"We didn't have sex." She stopped and corrected that. "Well, we didn't have *real* sex. Thanks for the vote of confidence, by the way," she grumbled, heading out to pace around the production floor, waiting for her call.

⌒

Avery was a nervous wreck. She'd woken as Casey closed the front door, and hadn't been able to think of another thing since that moment. She was sure her mom was puzzled when Lisbet was in her arms an hour early, but if she didn't have a minute or two with Casey alone she wasn't going to be able to get a thing done.

She'd just put her car into park when Casey came loping across the parking lot, still dressed in the nice clothes she'd worn the day before. She looked so cute it was hard to concentrate, with that oatmeal-colored jacket showing off the rich darkness of her hair, which was much more tousled than normal.

The door opened and she slid in. Avery could see her bare hand shaking when she accepted the paper cup, and she didn't think it was from the cold—even though every other person in town was wearing gloves, a down coat, and a hat.

Avery steeled her nerves and spit out the first thought she'd had that morning. "Did I guilt trip you into doing something you didn't want to do?"

"What?" Casey was looking at her like she was talking gibberish, which was a good sign.

"You heard me. I've been thinking that I might have made you feel sorry for me, and that I kind of maneuvered you into…"

"Avery," she said, her voice low and raspy. "You didn't guilt-trip me into anything." She took a long sip of her coffee, saying, "Even though it's a little cold, this really hits the spot. I didn't have time to get breakfast." She gave Avery a slow smile. "It was so cozy lying on the pod that I almost slept through my alarm."

"So…we're good?"

"I'm good," she said, with a slight smile showing. "Are you good?"

"I'm very good. My dear friend helped me realize my baby-making parts could turn back into fun parts." She turned a little in her seat so she could see Casey's expression full-on. "But I want to make sure things aren't weird between us."

"Well, it's a little weird because I now know you can nearly have an orgasm from having your ears nibbled on, but other than that…"

"Oh, god," Avery said, covering her face with her mittens. "That's not something you should have to know."

"Let's even it out," Casey said, with an impish grin revealing itself. "Backs of my knees, and sometimes across my ribs. Kissing, nibbling… Just about anything works. I'm not sure I can get hot as quickly as you did, but I'm willing to make that my new goal."

"Thank you," Avery said, grasping her free hand and squeezing it. "I was beside myself when I woke up, worried that my being so needy had screwed things up between us."

"You *were* needy," Casey said, her voice filled with tenderness. "We all get needy. And the next time it happens to me, I want to be able to talk to you about it. I doubt I'll need you to reassure me that I'm still desirable because…" She chuckled softly. "I've got a pretty good body-image. But I'm sensitive about other things. Next time one of them's bothering me, I'll want a sympathetic ear. Deal?"

"Deal," Avery said, grasping her hand again and shaking it. "Promise you'll tell me if anything else comes up? I want to make sure our relationship is solid."

"As a rock," she said, smiling once again. "Now I've got to go make sure we're making our Dark and Stormy Ale according to spec. I don't want my guys to get creative."

"Thank you again," Avery said as Casey tossed the door open.

"Thank you for the coffee. It's hard to make good beer on an empty stomach."

"I didn't bring you anything to eat! I can go get something. Really."

"Go home, Avery, and get to work. No one's going to cover those stories in red ink if you're not on the job."

"See you Wednesday? If not before."

"I'm bringing the birthday cake. If I'm not there, the party can't start."

⌒

Casey was on the production floor for the entire morning, keeping a close eye on every element. She loved brewing in the winter, when the heat they generated made the whole building warm as toast. The smells the brewing process gave off also made her feel warm and cosy on an otherwise cold, glum day. She hoped she'd recall some of these pleasant thoughts when it was July and a hundred and five in the building, but she doubted she would. A hot plant sucked. Always.

Every time she'd looked toward her office, Ben had his chair turned around, keeping an eye on her. He loved good gossip more than anyone she knew, and having to wait to hear what had happened with Avery was clearly driving him crazy. But she couldn't take another break. It didn't send a good message to her guys.

They paused at noon on the button for lunch, and she went into her office to see Ben facing the door, eyes bright. He kicked the door closed and rolled his chair close to her desk. "Details. All of them."

"Damn, man! Don't I get to eat today?"

"Did you bring anything?"

"I ran out of Avery's house and didn't stop. She brought me a coffee, but that's not going to get me through the day."

He rolled back to his desk, opened up his brown paper bag, and handed her a sandwich. "I'm keeping the pulled pork. You get the chicken."

She looked at it suspiciously, with him adding, "Julie made it. It's got avocado on it, which I know you like."

"I wouldn't normally steal from you, but I can see you're not going to let me leave." She unwrapped the sandwich and took a bite. "Good. My compliments to the chef."

"Details," he said firmly. Given he hadn't taken a bit of his other sandwich, he wasn't fooling around.

She thought as she chewed, not wanting to reveal too much about Avery, but knowing her story wouldn't make sense if she didn't give away some pretty big details. "Okay. Avery had a tough day yesterday. She was feeling down about herself, her prospects, her sex life… Everything."

"Really? I'd think she'd have her pick of women. She's cute as hell… smart…good sense of humor…calm…"

"I know, I know. But she's been single for a while, and she's convinced herself she's not going to find anyone. Her body took kind of a beating from having Lisbet—"

"I think that's true for most women," he said, making a face. "Julie felt bad about her body for two or three years after she had Benji."

"Really? You never said…"

"Really," he said solemnly. "That's the main reason I didn't want to have more kids, to be honest. Having her body change so dramatically took a toll on her that surprised the hell out of me, since I was still as attracted to her as ever. Pregnancy screws with you."

"Yeah," she said, grateful he got it. "So… We were sitting on her sofa, and I held her while she cried. We've never been close like that, but it felt like the right thing to do."

"Makes sense. Just for the record, I'd hold you if you ever cried."

"Same here," she said, laughing at the image. "But we probably shouldn't do it at work. People will talk."

"So you held her. She cried. That's not enough to make you look like you'd seen a ghost this morning."

"It wasn't. *That* started when she kind of fell to her side and I was still hanging on."

His eyes got wide as she continued. "Then I started touching her arm, and her leg, and one thing led to another…"

"You went for it?"

"I kind of did," she admitted, ignoring the fact that his mouth had fallen open. "It was super weird at first, but then I started talking dirty, and she started to like it…"

"You were talking dirty? Jesus!" He jumped to his feet and was staring at her like she was an alien life form.

"It seemed like the right thing to do," she said, feeling a little defensive. "I wanted to show her that she was desirable, and could enjoy sex again with just a little effort. And..." She held up her hands. "She did."

"God damn," he said. He dropped back to his seat, picked up a folder from her desk, and fanned himself dramatically. "This is better than the day Pete told us about that threesome he fell into."

"Pete had a threesome? I'm surprised he can get a twosome."

"Alcohol was involved," Ben said. "A lot of it from what I can tell."

"Well, I'm glad I've topped Pete in the hot stories at work competition. But if you tell the other guys..."

"Never," he said. "But I have to tell Julie. Even if I try not to, it'll come out. You know that, right?"

"I know that," she said. "You can tell Julie anything I tell you. I consider you two a single person."

"So? How'd it go when you had coffee?"

"Good. Better than I thought it would. She believes the stuff I said was made up, and is convinced I was just being a good friend."

"You weren't?"

"Oh, yeah, I was, I guess. But I meant all of the stuff I said. I'd give a lot to make love to Avery."

"Since when? You've insisted you're not into her."

"I'm not sure," she said honestly. "Things just changed kind of slowly. Once I'd convinced myself she wasn't a jerk, I started to look at her more like a pretty woman than my new friend's mom."

"Then...why don't you go for it? I got the impression she'd be up for it. No?"

"She might be." She let out a sigh. "Okay. She would be. But things are great between us now, Ben, and I don't want to screw that up."

"But you could have everything you want! A wife, a baby..."

"And my wife and my baby would be in Brooklyn. Avery's dead-set that she's going to raise Lisbet in the city, and that's not something I could ever do."

"No doubt there" he said, leaning back in his chair like the air had been taken from him. "You're still grumbling about driving down there, and that was months ago."

"Yeah. Brooklyn's only a hundred miles away, but it felt like another planet to me. A planet I don't want to explore."

"But—"

"I'm not going to do anything now," Casey said, having made up her mind in a matter of seconds. "But if she changes her mind and decides to stick around, I'd be willing to give it a try."

He smiled at her. "That's not an overwhelming endorsement."

"Well," she shrugged. "She's kind of an intellectual, and I'm kind of not."

"You're *definitely* not," he said, laughing. "You're a doer, not a dreamer."

"True. I think she's into people like her, so she'd have to stretch to be into me."

"But you're very open-minded when it comes to choosing a woman. You've been all over the map. An intellectual wouldn't be a problem for you."

"Maybe. But I've let two women go when they left the Hudson Valley. I'd rather be single forever than move to Brooklyn, Ben. I'd say I'd hate it, but hate's not a strong enough word. I'd be miserable, and the last thing Lisbet needs is a miserable…other person who's not her mother."

Ben cocked his head, looking at her with a puzzled half-smile. She could have told him about the term, but he'd had enough gossip for one day.

⌇

Avery was much less edgy when she arrived home after the chilly coffee break in the parking lot. Casey had seemed very much like herself, and that was a huge relief. But she was still thinking about it every few minutes, with the images from the night before pulling her out of her train of thought.

Casey hadn't technically done anything spectacular. Having someone slide their hand down her pants wasn't a unique experience for Avery. But she'd done it in *such a* sexy way. A way that worked amazingly well for Avery's libido.

She'd had a good number of hookups through the years, and knew that you couldn't always tell who you'd spark with. She'd been out with some women who were one hundred percent her type, and they hadn't had enough chemistry to turn a reagent strip purple. But just a few gentle touches from Casey, and her body woke up from its long, long nap.

Now she kept thinking about that touch, and the way Casey had gripped her so tightly when she'd really gotten down to business. *That* had been awesome, not to mention unexpected. She'd assumed she'd be very gentle, maybe even passive, but Casey had been anything but.

Sadly, none of that changed the fact that Casey had been putting on kind of an act. They hadn't even kissed, and Casey had refused any reciprocation. Those were not the signs of a woman who wanted to get something going with you.

After going downstairs to make herself a salad, Avery sat on the polyester pod to eat. The room was awfully glum, with nothing on the walls and no curtains on the windows. But it had seemed full of life when Casey had been there. Unwilling to linger on her thoughts, Avery patted the pod and started to walk back upstairs. She thought of the woman in Brooklyn who'd offered up her seat when Avery had flirted with her. Had that experience been more humiliating than having a friend you were into give you an orgasm while refusing even a kiss? She could flip a coin on that choice. Both of them made it abundantly clear that even though it was a huge relief that her body could respond to the right stimulation, she'd lost her allure.

Chapter Eighteen

AVERY PULLED INTO HER PARENTS' driveway on Tuesday afternoon, surprised, and a little disappointed not to see Casey's truck. They didn't have any kind of schedule, so it wasn't like Casey was breaking a promise by not being at the house, but it was always nice to see her at the end of the day.

After getting out of her car and racing for the front door, she opened it to relative silence. "Mom?"

"In the kitchen, honey."

Avery started to unwind herself from all of her winter additions; hat, scarf, and gloves. She was just about to kick off her Uggs when it registered that Lisbet's stroller hadn't been next to the front door. "Did Lisbet take herself for a walk?"

"Uh-huh. You know how independent she is." Her mom stopped what she'd been doing and walked over to give her a hug. "Your cheeks are as cold as ice! Maybe this wasn't the best day to let Casey take the baby to the library."

"The library? I thought all of their programs were for toddlers."

"Oh, they are, but Casey thought it would be nice to get her out of the house for a little bit. She drove over there, but took her stroller in case it was warm enough to go for a walk."

Avery laughed, shaking her head. "What would we do without her?" She wrapped an arm around her mom, amending, "What would I do without both of you is the better question."

"I'm related to you, but Casey sure isn't. She's just a giver."

"She is that."

"Will you stay for dinner? I'm making Casey's favorite. The girl never had meatloaf until I made it one night, and now she asks for it every time I give her an option."

"What time did she come over?"

"She was here early. They didn't brew today, so she snuck out." She turned to go back to her onion dicing. "I'm glad they like her so much, because she certainly isn't a workaholic."

"No, she certainly is not. That's intentional, you know. She said she found that her bosses respected her more when she set limits for how many hours she'd put in."

"Really? I can't see Casey doing that. She's so…flexible."

"True, but she's really good at taking care of herself. I guess the previous brewmaster worked sixty hours a week, and she didn't want to be doing the same."

"Does anyone *really* want to work sixty hours a week?"

"I think some people do, but Casey's not one of them. She promoted one of her best guys to shut down the plant at night. She goes in two hours before anyone else, and Glen, her assistant, comes in late and stays late."

"Smart girl," her mom said. "Most companies will take every hour you're willing to give."

"I think that's her point. Make it clear what you'll give and see if you can get your bosses to buy in."

There was a commotion in the living room, and Avery walked toward it to find Casey struggling to get the stroller into the house. "What was I thinking?" she asked, with her cheeks having turned pink. "Lisbet liked being in the library, but she started to cry on the walk to the truck." She made eye contact with Avery. "I think she's a cold-weather wimp, just like her mommy."

The baby was struggling against Casey's hold, and Avery grasped her and held her up in the air, smiling up at her as she kicked her little legs and gurgled. "I missed my baby girl all day long. Did my baby girl miss me?"

"She did," her mom said when she emerged from the kitchen. "She's gotten pretty dramatic when you leave in the morning. It doesn't last long, but she's so much more aware of where she is and who she's with that she's started to show her preferences."

"She's a little weepy when we leave here at the end of the day," Avery said. "And every time Casey leaves the house she stares as the door for the longest time, obviously hoping she'll race right back in."

"Aww, I didn't know she did that." Casey was beaming a smile. "Obviously, I hate to think of her being sad, but if she's going to be sad, it might as well be because she's nuts about me."

Avery gave her a poke in the belly. "You know you're her favorite. So what did you two do at the library?"

"Oh, we just hung out. They've got about a million books for little kids, so we read a couple of them. But she conked out right in the middle of one about a goose, so I carried her around while I read all of the posted notices. There's a lot of stuff going on around here in the winter. Surprised the heck out of me."

Avery started to pull Lisbet out of her snowsuit, having to put every bit of her focus on removing the suit that was in danger of being too small before winter was over. "So? What's going on around town that caught your interest?"

"There was a lot, mostly music and crafty stuff. But there's a woman who's teaching a six-week class on how to tell a story. They had twenty slots available, and the librarian told me they were filled the first day. Awesome, huh?"

"Oh, Casey," she said, thrilled at the thought of her wanting to express herself through a story. "See if there's a waiting list. Or find out if they're having another session. That would be so good for you."

"Yeah, yeah," she said, clearly having already moved on. "But I was thinking about what that meant in general. We've got so much going on around here in the summer, but even with all of the city people who spend weekends up here there's less during the other nine months of the year." Her eyes were sparkling with excitement when she said, "Why don't you talk to your boss and see if you could do a *Hudson Valley Short Shorts*. I'm sure there's a big audience of people who'd love to hear great stories."

Avery stared at her for a second. "Not only listeners, but writers. Everyone I know comes up here to get away, and a lot of established writers have moved up here permanently." She grasped Casey's hand and pulled it to her chest. "You're brilliant! We could reach a whole different audience up here, and pull in some of the writers who don't want to drive to Brooklyn to speak to fewer than fifty people."

Ideas started buzzing around in her head, and in just a few seconds she had one she knew would be great. "Most of the writers I've used in Brooklyn are in their twenties and thirties. If we did the program up here, we could intentionally skew the age range toward the other end. Wouldn't you love to hear older people tell their tales?" She started to pace, with the baby gazing at her curiously as she was carried along. "I love the concept. Really love it," she insisted, looking down at Casey who was sitting on the sofa smiling up at her. "I've done a good job of making *Short Shorts* racially and ethnically diverse, but I've ignored diversity in age. This could be my shot at fixing that." Looking down at Casey again, she said, "I don't know where I'll find the time, but I'm going to pitch the idea to Helena. Thank you," she said, bending over to place a kiss to Casey's cheek. "I've said it before, but I'll say it again. This is a brilliant idea."

⌒

Avery had decided that Lisbet's first birthday should be very low-key. Given the baby didn't know one day from the next, and had no idea what a birthday even was, she thought it was slightly mad to throw a big party. Actually, she'd been tempted to skip it completely, but her mother had put the kibosh on that. Everyone agreed not to purchase any presents, but Casey had volunteered to buy a birthday cake. She'd been very mysterious about her plans, but she'd mentioned it about six times, so Avery was sure she was doing something special.

After getting caught on a call that she'd had a tough time wrapping up, Avery raced over to her parents' house, getting a little thrill when she saw Casey's big truck parked at the curb. She knew she was acting like she had in high school, when her heart would race every time she caught sight of her current boyfriend in the hall, but she couldn't help it. There was nothing wrong with having a crush on someone, even if that crush wasn't mutual. If you didn't let it get out of hand, fantasizing about someone you found devastatingly attractive could give you a spring in your step.

Avery had two aunts, along with three first-cousins, but none of them lived close, and asking people to drive an hour to a baby's birthday party just seemed a bit over-the-top. When the weather was warm, they'd have a barbecue to get the whole clan together. So it was just the family for the party, which now definitely included Casey. That might have seemed weird to people who only considered blood relatives family, but Avery had grown up with an uncle who wasn't related in any way, and she'd cherished him. It wasn't the amount of consanguinity that mattered. It was the amount of effort the adult put into forming a relationship that Lisbet would benefit from, and no one did that better than Casey.

Avery opened the storm door, then pushed the entry door to find Lisbet cruising over to her. She'd started pulling herself up to her feet a little late, but her doctor said she was hitting her targets, so Avery had tried to stop comparing her to other anonymous babies on the internet. Surprisingly, Lisbet had gone from pulling herself up to cruising around, gently holding onto furniture for support, in less than a week. Tonight she held onto Casey's pantleg, a seriously cute instinct. Both of them were grinning at Avery, with Casey taking tiny steps as she tried to match Lisbet's pace.

"The birthday girl's been waiting for you," Casey said. "Every time a car goes down the street she stops and stares at the door for a minute."

"My precious one knows my schedule," Avery said, squatting down to plant a big, noisy kiss to Lisbet's head. "I'd swoop you up into my arms and cuddle you," she said, addressing the child, "but I'm certain you want to keep walking. Especially with such a helpful cruising partner."

"Nana baaa mamaaaa," the baby said, her little voice projecting quite well.

"I bet you're saying that it's very good to see me, aren't you," Avery asked. "Do you know it's your birthday? Just one year ago today, at just about this time, you were…" She stood up and finished her sentence very quietly, so that only Casey could hear. "Making me wish I could jump out a window."

"But then you got to hold your baby, and all of the pain just evaporated, right?"

Avery pinched her cheek firmly. "I'm very glad I didn't jump. How's that."

"Good enough."

"Where is everyone? I didn't see my dad's truck."

"I'm in here," her mom called out. "As usual. Dad ran out for some ice cream."

"I could have picked that up," Avery said. She took off her coat and her scarf and placed her boots by the front door. Lisbet grabbed onto her jeans, and they haltingly walked into the kitchen together. "Dinner smells great."

"Thanks, honey. Did you see—"

Lisbet let go and tried to walk—unaided—the two steps required to get to a big, fuzzy teddy bear that was lying on the kitchen floor, but she didn't make it. Luckily, the bear provided a cushion, and she didn't seem to mind doing a face-plant into it.

"Her birthday present?" Avery's mom finished. "She seems crazy about it."

Avery wagged her finger at Casey, who had a mildly guilty look on her face. "No presents. You agreed."

She lifted her hands in a helpless gesture. "It was the softest thing I've ever felt. One day, *years* from now, when you lift the prison regulations, she'll have something cuddly to sleep with."

"Thank you," Avery said, giving her a quick hug. "So far she's been pretty uninterested in forming an attachment with any of her toys. Maybe this one will win her heart."

"Avery had a doll she loved so much the body disintegrated on her at day care," her mom said. "She carried just the head around until she started kindergarten."

Avery laughed. "I'd still be carrying it if the other kids hadn't made fun of me."

"I warned you," her mom said, "but she insisted on taking it that first day of school. That poor little doll head stayed home from then on." Her gaze met Casey's. "She still pulled it out when she was sad or lonely, but by the time she started first grade—"

"Don't reveal what an insecure child I was," Avery said, tucking her arm around her mom to give her a rough hug.

"I've got a photo of you with that nearly hairless doll head, and I'm not sure if it's the angle or what, but you look about ten."

Lisbet was babbling away, talking to her new bear. "Be careful, sweetie. Your grandmother's vicious when she's got a camera in her hands."

⌒

The adults had salmon, green beans, and a little macaroni and cheese, with Lisbet skipping the fish. She was still eating very small amounts, but she was very fond of mac n' cheese, and green beans were also favored if Avery cut them into tiny pieces. It continued to amaze her how Lisbet had so much energy from so little food, but her doctor assured her that the baby was still getting over three quarters of her calories from breast feeding. She was down to nursing three times a day now, and showed no signs of wanting to stop. Avery was ready to move on, having been nipped one too many times, but she didn't want to rush her. As Lisbet continued to eat more solid food she'd slowly lose interest—hopefully.

"I think it's time to have our birthday cake, don't you?" Avery's mom asked, tugging on Lisbet's foot.

"I can't wait to see this cake," Avery said. "I'm not sure how you got one that doesn't have any food she's not familiar with, but…" She met Casey's gaze. "I trust you to pull it off."

She jumped to her feet and went into the living room, coming back with a big sheet of plastic and a tall cardboard box. "I made her an isolation room," she said, laughing as the rest of them stared at her. "They call this a smash cake, since the point is that the baby demolishes it, but I didn't want Kathy to have to clean the walls." She set the box down, revealing that one side had been partially cut away. "I'll just tape this plastic to the floor, and we should be good, right?"

"I suppose so," Avery said. "What do you think, Lisbet?" she asked as she removed the tray from the high chair and picked her up. "Do you want to smash a cake?"

"Want to take her clothes off?" Casey asked. "She's going to get filthy."

"Umm…really? There might be a draft."

"I don't do the laundry, so it doesn't matter to me," Casey said.

Avery laughed as her mom pulled Lisbet from her grasp and undid her lilac-colored overalls. "I had to soak these in stain remover to get the beet juice out. She won't freeze if she's in her diaper for a few minutes."

"Practical woman," Avery said, slipping Lisbet's long-sleeved T-shirt from her body. "You probably think you're getting a bath, don't you?" she asked as the baby looked around, slightly puzzled.

"You're getting a cake," Casey said after she pulled a bright blue creation from a pink box. "Your very first cake." She met Avery's eyes. "Although can you still call it a cake when it's made with bananas and dates and applesauce and oat flour?"

"No sugar?"

"None. No eggs, either. She's had every single item in this."

Avery gazed at it suspiciously. It seemed cake-like, but the weird blue color was odd. "What's the frosting?"

"A little cream cheese, which she's had, and a ton of blueberries."

"Mmm." Avery looked up at her. "All in all, it sounds pretty good. Did your mom make it?"

"Nah. I got it from that bakery on Warren. They're apparently the go-to bakery for smash cakes. My mom sent a cheesecake for the adults, by the way. She was pretty confident we wouldn't want to eat Lisbet's, if there's any left when she's done smashing it."

"Let's give it a go," Avery said.

"I've got my phone set on video mode," her dad said. "I'm ready to create a movie that will embarrass her for years to come."

"I've got mine too," her mom said, both of them kneeling on the floor in front of the box.

"How's she going to explain to her future friends that her mother stuck her in a box for her first birthday?"

"That will just be one of a hundred things she'll have to blame you for," her mom said. "The list is endless."

"Here's goes nothing," Avery said, placing the baby on the floor of the box, then watching as Casey set the cake right in front of her. She added a candle, which Lisbet ripped out the moment Casey took her hand away.

"Good thing I didn't light it," she said, laughing a little as she pulled it from Lisbet's hand.

The baby looked down at the cake, then up at the four people taking her picture. Finally deciding it was worth investigating, she slapped both hands onto it, with her eyes widening as her hands sank into the surface. It didn't dawn on her to eat it, but she loved the idea of crushing it. She began to laugh as she filled her little hands with bits of cake. Her hands were so small she couldn't get much at once, but it didn't take long for the cake to be on her chest, then her face, then in her hair. They all warned her at once when she tried to use the cake to stand, but she didn't heed the advice. Before Casey could catch her she'd done a belly flop onto it.

"Who's going to pick her up?" Casey asked as Lisbet started to cry. "I don't want the blue to stain my wheat-colored jeans."

"Stand aside," Avery grumbled. "I had to push her out of a tight spot a year ago, I guess I can pull her out of one today."

CHAPTER NINETEEN

ON THE FIRST TUESDAY OF February, a relatively warm one, Avery dropped the baby at her mom's and drove to the only espresso shop that opened early. Even though Hudson wasn't a huge town, she was sure they were big enough for a Starbucks. But there was nearly unanimous agreement from the citizens that chain stores of any kind were unwelcome, and to her knowledge the ubiquitous coffee shop hadn't even tried to secure a lease.

All of the other precious little coffee shops worked on a relaxed schedule, ones focused on visitors rather than locals. The spot she liked best opened at ten, a shockingly late hour for people actually going to work. In the store owners' defense, they would have had to open before six to catch the folks who commuted into the city, and that didn't make economic sense for the few who made the daily trek.

One spot, Caffeine High, opened at seven. They pulled a good shot, but the store didn't have the same welcoming vibe her favorite did. Every local who was willing to pay four bucks for a good cup of joe showed up early in the morning, and she found herself in line behind guys who were clearly tradesmen, with their thermal overalls, coveralls, and jeans making them look like fluffy, butterscotch-colored bears.

Today was another *Short Shorts* day, and Avery didn't technically have to be at her venue until three. But she was always a little wired up on performance days, so it made sense to use that energy to swing by the office to make sure no one forgot what she looked like.

Standing in line, she started to check her phone when someone said, "Hi, Avery."

She looked up to see Chris, Casey's dad, holding a very short cup, obviously an espresso drinker. "Hi, there," she said. "Drink up. You don't want your shot to get cold."

He smiled as he gulped it down, letting out a happy sigh. "Couldn't get my eyes open today. I had to stop for a pick-me-up."

"Still busy, huh?"

"More than ever." He crushed his cup and gave it a smooth underhand toss, turning away before it hit the trash bin from fifteen feet, clearly confident in his aim. Casey must have gotten the sports gene from him. "Hey, I'm not sure about timing, but there's a chance I might be able to start work on the house in May," he said.

"This May? Like three months from now?" Her heart started to beat faster, with thoughts of having to move so soon making her stomach turn.

"Yeah." He nodded, looking thoughtful. "I'm going to be stick-building a house in Germantown as soon as the plans are ready." His expression grew grim, making him look a little irritated. "I was supposed to have the drawings by now, but they're really screwing around with it. I figure by the time we've signed the contract it might be June or July." He pulled out his phone and checked something. "So if they're ready to go in June, I'd have a few weeks to do everything that needs to be done at your place if I started in May. If I had all of my subs lined up I might be able to get it done. You know, there's a ton of demand for starter homes around here…"

"Oh, I understand," she said, even though it sickened her to think of uprooting the baby. "Is there any way you could give me a firm date?"

"Not really. That's why I thought I'd better give you some warning. If you find something right away and want to leave quick—no hard feelings. If not, you can hope the architect gets his head out of his butt and gets the drawings for the new house over to me soon."

"So I *might* be able to stay past May?"

He gave her a very empathetic smile. It actually looked like he might have practiced it in a mirror to try to convey emotions he didn't naturally possess in abundance. "Sure. You might be able to stay for years. I make a lot more money building from scratch, so if that part of the business gets hot…" He pulled his shoulders up for a brief moment. "It's all a crap-shoot."

"Got it," she said, having to move up to give her order. "I'll start looking."

"Hey…" He tugged on her sleeve, holding her in place. "I know it might be hard for you to find a new place. So if you can guarantee you'll be out by the first of May, I'll let you have March and April for free."

"Free?" She hated to be so money focused, but two thousand dollars was huge!

"Yeah." He nodded. "Have you paid me for February?"

"No. I pay on the seventh, since you told me to just do it a month after my first—"

"Calm down," he said, chuckling. "The lady's waiting to take your order."

She was so off her stride she could hardly recall what she usually bought. After she got herself together and put in her order, she turned back to him.

"Look," he said. "I really want this to happen, so I can sweeten the deal. If you're willing to commit to leaving, you don't have to pay for February, either."

"Damn, that's tempting, but I don't know if I can find anything, Chris. It might be worth it to stick it out and hope you start on that other house."

"Let me know," he said, frowning. "Before the seventh if you want to save another thousand."

"I can't tell you how much I'd love to save the money. Three months rent would pay for my security deposit on a new place."

"Right. Well, let's hope you take me up on my offer." He started to turn, then stopped and gazed at her soberly. "Do me a favor and don't say say anything to Casey, okay?"

"Huh?" She blinked at him, then realized she'd been awfully informal with her reply.

"She's been riding me to give you a lease, but I'm not going to hold onto the house forever when I could flip it. I won't have any trouble finding someone who'll overpay for a stone house—especially if they know nothing about historic renovations." A big, wry smile covered his face, very similar to one that Casey could pull out when she was in the right mood. But Chris's had an edge to it that hers didn't, and this one didn't make Avery feel charmed in the least. "She can be a real pain in the ass when she doesn't get her way."

Avery nodded, then turned to the cashier to pay for her order. She wasn't sure who Chris was referring to, but there were few people on earth who were less of a pain in the ass than his youngest child.

Avery was in Brooklyn by ten, and she headed over to the office. She didn't really have anything to do there, and no longer had a desk to call her own, but it was too cold to wander around Brooklyn, even though she longed to.

She waved at Helena as she rushed to the bathroom the minute she got there. She normally didn't have to pump at this time of day, but Lisbet hadn't been in the mood to eat her normal amount, and Avery had been running too late to pump before she left the house, so she was a little uncomfortable. This wasn't the ideal set-up, but she didn't mind covering up and waiting in the hall if someone had to take a quick pee.

She'd just gotten the pump attached when Helena's voice floated in. "Got a minute?"

They'd known each other for years, and had few secrets. "If you don't mind watching me pump, I'm all yours."

The door opened and Helena entered. It was a little strange sharing a bathroom with your boss, while your breast was hooked up to a hand-pump, but she'd been in weirder situations. Avery noted that Helena didn't seem uncomfortable, acting exactly like she did when they were having a meeting in her office.

"I'm surprised you're still pumping," she said, as though they were talking about eating gluten.

"Usually at lunchtime, since Lisbet is down to nursing three times a day, but she wasn't very hungry this morning." She shifted her gaze to the hand pump, which she'd come to hate. "My day hasn't been great so far, but I'm sure things will turn around."

"Maybe not," Helena said, revealing a sour expression. "Casandra Daniels is under the weather and has to cancel."

"Oh, crap," Avery sighed. "I think she must have stage fright. She cancelled last time, too."

"Any ideas for substitutes?"

She went through the list of writers she knew lived close by, coming up with no promising names. An established writer wouldn't want to be thought of as a stand-in, and a newer one wouldn't be prepared. "I think we should just ask Carlos and Eugenie to slow down and take their time. I think we'll have plenty of audience participation, but just in case we don't, I'll come up with some questions to plant with people from the office."

Helena smiled. "I'd hope our audience would be able to come up with their own questions, Avery." She winked as she added, "But having planted questions is a good idea. I'm confident you know what each of our writers likes to talk about." The fondness Helena held for her was obvious in her warm smile. "You're very, very good at managing talent, you know."

"I appreciate that. Hey, as long as I have you in my office, can you spare a minute for a pitch?"

"Always." She took a look at the toilet, but quickly decided not to sit. Even for Helena, that was pushing it too far. Instead, she leaned against the wall and inclined her head. "Let me have it."

"Given that nearly every creative person leaves Brooklyn on the weekends, and half of them go to the Hudson Valley, I thought we could have a *Short Shorts* located up there."

Helena looked interested immediately, which was a very good sign. She tended to make up her mind quickly, but getting her to change it was no walk in the park. "This would be a summer thing?"

"Oh, summer would be a slam-dunk. But I was thinking of making it a year-round event. Actually, I'd like to make this a dual-purpose thing, if you're not opposed."

"Dual?"

"Uh-huh. Besides attracting new readers from the Hudson Valley, I'd like to focus on more mature writers. I think the world has had enough exposure to thirty-something New Yorkers who can't figure out how to adult."

"How to adult," Helena grumbled, hating the expression, as she hated every expression coined via a meme or a hashtag. "Agreed. If I never read another story from an older, privileged white man whining about how he's not as successful as he'd expected he'd be…"

"Well, I wasn't thinking of excluding men," Avery admitted, "but I'd like the lineups to be majority women. I'd also like to bring in writers who started later in life, or have just started, preferably people who've had real jobs. I don't know about you, but I'd rather hear from a factory worker or an electrician than another MFA who's never lifted anything heavier than a laptop."

"Get to work on it," Helena said, reaching out to squeeze her shoulder. "Let's not come down too hard on the MFAs, though. You, I, and everyone in this office is in that camp."

Avery laughed. "Not true. Freya doesn't have an MFA."

"Having an MBA from Columbia doesn't make her a woman of the people. But I get your point, and I agree with it. We need to poke our heads out of our literary bubble."

"That's exactly it," Avery said. "I want to hear from experienced adults who have punched a clock or belonged to a union."

"I'm intrigued. I have friends in Cold Spring and Croton-On-Hudson. They'll have an opinion on whether there's enough interest in the area."

"Oh, there is," Avery said. "I've already got a list of venues in my head, and if we can get this going, we could have a very successful summer." She smiled slyly. "We'll work the kinks out in the summer, then keep on rolling."

As Helena started to leave, she gave Avery another smile. "If you're working on it, it'll be great. I just wish I had two of you."

After she'd finished pumping, Avery called her co-worker Rebecca, who'd started her maternity leave. "Hi there," she said when she answered. "How would you like to have lunch hand-delivered?"

"Is this Santa Claus?" Rebecca said, chuckling. "I'm so huge I can hardly walk. Even the kitchen seems too far to reach. In other words, come soon and stay long."

"Anything you're not eating?"

She let out a wry laugh. "I gave up that battle months ago. If it's within reach, I eat it."

⌒

Rebecca really had packed on more weight than was probably wise, but Avery had nothing but empathy. She was certain she'd try to do things differently if she were to have another child, but Lisbet hadn't turned out too badly even though her mommy had eaten far too many tacos and not enough kale.

"I brought quinoa balsamic chicken bowls," Avery announced. "And sparkling water with a little lemon juice. All natural."

"Huh," Rebecca said, looking thoughtful. "The baby's going to be puzzled at having so many vitamins thrown at her, but she'll adjust." She waddled over to her sofa and sank down heavily. "You know your way around, right? Silverware by the sink."

Avery had only been at the apartment once, for a colleague's birthday party. But the place was so small, and had so few kitchen cabinets, it was easy to guess where the dishes were. "I've got it." Avery took the bowls over to the coffee table and handed Rebecca a fork and a paper towel. "Did you just say 'she?'"

"I did," she said, beaming. "I've been so invested in having a daughter, but I was embarrassed to admit that in public. Now I can act like I didn't care one way or the other."

"I convinced myself I didn't care," Avery said, "but I'm very glad Lisbet's a girl. If I have another, I think I'll care less, but I wanted at least a chance of having things in common with my first."

"That's kind of it for me, too. Having a baby's hard enough. I didn't want to have to figure out penises. I know my way around a vulva."

Avery lifted her water bottle. "To girls. And to lots of hand-me-downs. I have a couple of shopping bags worth of newborn things at home. Tell people to buy the six to nine month size if anyone asks before they buy you a gift. Then you won't have to buy a clothing for a year."

"Will do." She took a bite of her salad, moaning in pleasure. "I haven't had a good lunch in two weeks. This really hits the spot."

"Happy to help. My memories of my last month of pregnancy are still fresh. If I lived close, I'd bring you lunch every day."

"But you don't," Rebecca sighed. "At least for the moment. When I'm not moaning about how I want the baby to come, I've been spending some of my free time looking for an apartment for you."

"You have been? What do you know that I don't know?"

"Well," she said, smiling like she was about to tout a product she wanted Avery to buy. "You've said you want to move back, right?"

"Right. But I was thinking I'd come back when I found out if Lisbet got accepted to a pre-K program."

"Because of how much daycare is, right? Not because you want to be so far away."

"Well, that's mostly true," Avery said. "But it's been fantastic to have my support system in place up in the Hudson Valley. I'm happier than I thought I'd be…"

"Listen to my plan, and you might change you mind."

"I'm always willing to listen to a good pitch."

"Okay," Rebecca said, her eyes dancing with excitement. "I have to be in the office four days a week once my maternity leave is over. That means I will basically have to pay for full-time day care."

"Which is budget-busting," Avery agreed.

"Very much so. But since you've already got permission to work from home, we could share child care and have it cost absolutely nothing."

"Nothing? That's my favorite word. Tell me more!"

"Well, it would require you to be very flexible," she warned. "But I think it could work. You'd watch both kids four days a week. Then I'd watch both of them four nights a week. That would let you go out and scout locations, go to readings, and actually have a social life."

Avery stared at her for a moment, letting the details sink in. "Mmm. If that was all I had to do, I'd jump on the idea in a minute. But there's no way I'd get anything done with two babies in my apartment. I'd have to work every night."

"Probably true. But I distinctly remember your telling me that your peak alertness time was after five."

"That used to be true," Avery said. "But I've gotten into being an early-bird. I'd have to revert to my old ways…"

"Just think about it," Rebecca said, with her voice lowering into a seductive range. "Free, high-quality child care in Brooklyn. By a person you know and trust. Whose husband is training to be a pediatrician." She laughed a little. "Not that you'd benefit from that. It's not like I ever actually see this phantom doctor."

"Free child care in Brooklyn," Avery repeated, feeling like a spell had been cast over her. "That's worth…" She blinked a few times, stunned. "I could never have imagined having that."

"Well, you *can* have it, starting in just a couple of months—or as soon as I'm fit enough to take care of Lisbet. If I don't have to have a C-section, that should be May, right?"

Avery didn't want to dissuade her from the wholly incorrect belief that she'd feel fine in six or seven weeks, so she just nodded. "I had a quick chat with my landlord today, and he might need to kick me out in May."

"Kick you out? But your lease—"

"I don't have one. He's my friend's dad, and he cut me a deal on the rent. Part of the agreement is that he only has to give me two months notice. I thought that would be plenty, but…" She sighed. "Just this morning, I proposed doing *Short Shorts* in the Hudson Valley. I assumed I'd be there this summer to kick it off."

"Well, as much as I'd love to have you come back, you could just find another place to live up there, right?"

"I haven't been looking very diligently, but I take a peek every once in a while. There's only one development that's close by, and I'd have to pay close to two thousand for a two-bedroom."

"Two bedroom! Are you Bill Gates's secret daughter? You can't afford a two bedroom. No one can."

"This development only has two bedrooms. And it's literally the only place I've seen that's nice, and anywhere close to affordable. There's a real dearth of rental housing in Columbia County. I could buy a house, I suppose, but I'd probably lose money on it if I had to sell it in a couple of years."

"You could always hold on and wait for it to appreciate—"

Avery held up a hand, stopping her cold. "I *need* to be back by the time Lisbet's in preschool. I want her to grow up urban."

"That's why Henry and I have decided to stay. So?" Her smile brightened. "Let's seriously think about doing this. I think it could work for both of us, Avery."

"It's tempting. Actually very tempting. I'd lose a lot by moving, but I think I'd gain a lot too."

Rebecca took a bite of her lunch as a happy smile settled onto her face. "This is so good," she purred.

"Food rises· to the top of the list when you're too tired and uncomfortable to go anywhere or do anything, doesn't it?"

"The very top of the list." She probed at her bowl with her fork, clearly trying to get a little bit of everything in each bite. "I don't need you to decide immediately, but I'm going to have to get moving on finding someone. I'm due in two weeks, and I only get six weeks off after that."

"How well I remember," she said, thinking of how horrible her first weeks back in the office had been—and she'd had to go in much less than Rebecca was going to have to. "I'll get on it and see if there's anywhere for me to live that's close to my mom. If not, I'm coming back." She was so torn she felt like she had a thousand competing interests laid out in front of her, most of them at odds. But losing her house would make a decision imperative.

Rebecca looked like she would have clicked her heels if she could have gotten off the ground. "The good news is that the market's opened up a little in Brooklyn. I think you'll be able to get a studio close to the office for around seventeen fifty. Can you handle that?"

"Mmm. I'd rather not, but I assume I'll have to." She let out a sigh. "Only paying a thousand has let me save some money, which has been fantastic." She laughed. "Having dinner at my parents' hasn't hurt either." She extended her finger and made a circular motion in the air. "And not going out saves a ton. Add in all the cappuccinos I'm not drinking, and we're talking some cash." Her eyes opened wide. "And the alcohol! I was spending fifty bucks a week going out for drinks. That's two hundred a month in alcohol savings I've been able to sock away for Lisbet's college fund."

"Oh, I hear you. I haven't even given birth and I'm worried about paying for private high school."

"It's going to be dreadful," Avery agreed. "I can see why everyone at home thinks I'm crazy for wanting to come back, but they've never been bitten by the big-city bug." She let out a sigh. "There's no cure."

That afternoon, Casey arrived at Kathy and Ken's house a little past her norm. Ken's truck was already in the driveway, and she could smell something good wafting out of the vent in the kitchen. Chicken? Probably. Kathy made a mean roast chicken, and she tended to keep just a few dishes in heavy rotation.

After knocking perfunctorily, Casey entered, finding Ken, still in his work uniform, a pale blue twill shirt and navy blue pants, in the living room with Lisbet standing in front of him, with her little hands on his knees.

"Look at the big girl who can stand up so straight," Casey said, drawing a delighted smile and an ear-rattling shriek from Lisbet. "How's it going?"

"Everything's good," Ken said. "How was your day? Did you work late?"

"Little bit," she said, starting to take her coat off. "I'm working on a new beer, and today was our first brew. I'm not sure I'm satisfied with it, but it's still too early to tell. The alchemy of brewing," she said, rolling her eyes. "I'll go say hi to Kathy."

"I can hear you," she called out. "Don't mind me, stuck in the kitchen all alone."

Casey smiled at Ken, messed up the already messy fuzzy blonde strands on Lisbet's head, then went into the kitchen. "Are you feeling unappreciated?"

"Not really. I'm just used to you showing up earlier. Cooking's boring when I'm alone." She shot a look at the living room. "Don't tell Lisbet I find her a little dull, but the kid's got nothing to say."

"She'll start soon. At least she looks like she wants to talk."

"I'm sure she does. I can tell she's getting frustrated by not being able to communicate better." She placed green salads on the table, then added a couple of bottles of dressing. "She'd just better not say her first words in Brooklyn," she said grimly.

"Brooklyn? Why would she be in Brooklyn?"

Kathy went back to the stove to tend the potatoes she was cooking, then turned and revealed a very unhappy expression. "I tried to talk to my very frustrating child a while ago, but she didn't have much time, since she was racing across town to look at a studio apartment in Vinegar Hill, wherever the hell that is."

"Vinegar Hill?"

"I assume that's in Brooklyn, but you never know with Avery."

"But why would she be doing that now?" Casey grabbed a chair and sat down hard, with her legs feeling a little wobbly. "Why wouldn't she have even mentioned…"

Kathy walked over and put a hand on her shoulder. "I feel the same. She hasn't said a single word about this before today. I know Lisbet is her child, and she can take her wherever she wants, but I'm beginning to have some empathy for grandparents who sue for custody." She let her gaze slide to the door to the living room, where they could hear Lisbet babbling. "I don't think I can let that baby go."

CHAPTER TWENTY

A LITTLE AFTER THREE P.M. ON Wednesday, Avery heard a car coming down her driveway. She got very few visitors, and she wasn't expecting any package deliveries, so she got up from her desk and peered out the window in Lisbet's room to see what was up. Surprised to see Casey's truck, she put on her shoes and went downstairs, grabbing her coat from the hook by the door before she went out onto the porch.

Casey didn't even have her jacket zipped, even though the temperature couldn't have been more than twenty degrees. She looked up and met Avery's gaze, but she didn't smile.

"What's wrong?" Avery asked.

"We need to talk." Casey brushed right past her to enter the house, leaving Avery slightly stunned and very puzzled.

She followed her in, and stood in the entryway when Casey didn't move to enter the living room. "What's wrong?" she asked again, beginning to catastrophize.

Casey shoved her hands into the pockets of her khaki green bomber jacket and rocked back on her heels. Her eyes closed briefly, then she met Avery's eyes. "Your mom told me you're looking for apartments."

"Not…Well, technically I looked at one, but that was only because my friend—"

"You haven't mentioned a word about moving, Avery. Not a word."

She could see that Casey was upset, but that didn't make any sense. "I was going to tell you, but this just came up yesterday."

"You can't do that," she said, as if she were in charge—of everything.

Brushing past her, Avery slipped her coat off and tossed it onto the pod. Then she sat on the edge of it and considered her words carefully before responding. "I think I can, and if the circumstances are right, I'm going to. I might *need* to take this opportunity." She wasn't going to keep Chris's secret if push came to shove, but she also wasn't in the mood to stir up trouble between father and daughter if she didn't need to.

"Opportunity?" Casey walked into the room and began to pace. The room was wider than it was deep, but she covered the space in just a few long strides, before turning and going back. As she turned one more time, she spoke, like she was addressing the room rather than Avery. "There isn't an opportunity in the world that would make up for taking Lisbet away from her grandparents. None," she said, head down, feet still pacing.

"Casey," Avery said, trying to draw her attention so they could have an actual conversation, "I know you and my parents will be upset if we leave, but there are a lot of factors that go into this. I have to do what I think is right for us long term."

"For us," she grumbled, still pacing. "That's a load of crap, and you know it. Lisbet loves being with her grandmother all day. It's you who wants something different."

Avery let out a sigh, having to acknowledge the truth of that statement. "At this point in her life, you're right. But I think growing up in Brooklyn will be better for Lisbet. I think all of you know that's my goal. If we don't go now, we'll go eventually."

"How?" Casey demanded, stopping to glare. "How in the hell will she be better off around millions of strangers?"

"Um, I'd appreciate it if you'd drop the attitude, okay? I'm very willing to talk, but you're yelling at me, and I don't deserve that."

She rolled her eyes, then went into the kitchen and grabbed a chair. Turning it around so she straddled it, she rested her arms across the back and pursed her lips, obviously the only way she could stop herself from sniping. "I've dropped my attitude," she said grimly.

Even though that was an obvious lie, Avery gave it another try. "I will admit that living here has been very good for both of us. Lisbet has three people besides me who love her, and they all work hard to satisfy her every need. But as she gets older, I'll want her to be exposed to more… everything," she said, unable to pin it down much better than that.

"I don't understand," Casey said, her eyes burning with anger. "At all."

Avery was tempted to tell her it didn't matter if she understood or not, but she couldn't dismiss her concerns so easily. Casey clearly had a stake in the situation.

"I liked growing up here," Avery said. "But I want Lisbet to have more diversity—in every way. I want her to be around people of different faiths, and backgrounds, and heritages. The world is changing, and I want her to be exposed to all of it."

"You told me that you weren't in a rush," Casey snapped. "You've got years before she starts school. You're getting the best quality child care imaginable, and it's all free!"

"Listen to me," Avery said, trying hard to keep her voice level. "I have an opportunity to get free child care—"

"Which you already have."

"Please let me finish," Avery said, knowing her patience was growing thin. "I struggled when Lisbet was a newborn partially because I had to pay for child care, which was ruinously expensive. But if this works out, it won't cost me a dime."

"Great. Then you can also have this magically free child care when Lisbet's old enough to tell you what she wants. You act like her preferences don't count at all."

"Mmm. They pretty much don't," she admitted. "She's barely a toddler, Casey. She doesn't have the knowledge or the experience to know the things I know. I agree that she'd prefer for her routine to stay just as it is for many years, but that's not how the real world works. She's got to learn to adapt, and living around a wide variety of people will definitely help her along with that."

"Or she'll get lost in the shuffle and wind up sitting on a park bench, talking to pigeons," she said, still glaring. "Do you think those people I saw shuffling around with shopping carts enjoy living like that? You can look all day and you're not going to find people living outside in Columbia County."

"I'm not sure that's true, but even if it is it doesn't prove your point. I acknowledge that a lot of people with mental health issues live in big cities, but it's a leap of logic to assume the cities caused their problems." She took a breath, realizing she hadn't addressed Casey's insult. "By the way, I think I might notice if my child fails to thrive. She's not just an afterthought."

"Taking her away from her grandparents sounds exactly like the decision of a woman who's not putting her baby first. Exactly!"

Avery stood up and walked over to her, forcing Casey to meet her eyes. "You want to be honest? Fine. Let's be honest. We've been tiptoeing around this, but we may as well get it out. This isn't about Lisbet missing her grandparents. It's about you missing Lisbet. So let's just state that as a fact, and we can move on."

It was like a wall had broken, with the emotion that had been building up flowing out in a rush. Casey's eyes filled with tears in a nanosecond, and she broke eye contact to stare down at the floor as she wiped at them. "Of course I'd miss her. If you don't know how much I care for her, you've had your head up your ass."

"I know," Avery said, trying to sound soothing. She put her hand on Casey's shoulder, but it was shrugged off as she stood and backed away from the chair.

"Two things can be true at the same time. Losing her would break my heart. Fact," she said, shouting so loudly the glass in the kitchen cabinets made a tinkling noise. "And this can be a bad decision for her. Fact!"

"I understand losing her would hurt, Casey, but you can't just take your feelings about big cities and put them onto this situation while calling them facts."

"They are!"

"No, they're not. But here are the real facts I have to consider. Someone I've known for years, someone I trust, is having a baby in a week or two. She works at *Ad Infinitum*, and has to go into the office more than I do. So I'd watch her new baby, and she'd watch Lisbet in the evenings so I could get my work done. I'd essentially flip my schedule to work at night."

Casey glared at her for an uncomfortably long time. "So you'll spend your days watching some random baby, and then have someone you don't know very well watch Lisbet, right?"

"I've known Rebecca for years!"

"Then why hasn't this close friend ever been here? Why didn't she come to Lisbet's birthday party?"

"She's a work friend, but that doesn't mean she's a stranger."

"Yes, it does. If you just talk to someone at work, she's not a friend. She's an acquaintance. Lisbet will be with a virtual stranger a couple of nights every damn week."

"Four nights," Avery said quietly. "I wouldn't be able to work during the day with a newborn and a toddler, so I'd have to do all of my work at night."

"Is she going to sleep at this stranger's house?"

"It's not a boarding school, Casey. Rebecca will watch her at her nearby apartment until I'm finished with my work."

"Lisbet goes to bed at seven, and from what I've read, that might be true for another year or two. So she'll go to bed and then have to wake up to go home?"

"That's...true," Avery admitted. "But that won't be bad. She wakes up once a night anyway. Maybe waking up at ten or eleven will get her on a schedule she likes."

"Great. So you're setting her up to waking up even when she's ready to sleep through the night. That's a fantastic idea. I'm sure she'll thank you when she becomes an insomniac."

Avery closed her eyes and tried her best to summon some empathy for Casey. She was clearly very attached to Lisbet, so it only made sense that she was upset. But she didn't have any right to be this strident. None at all.

"You've got to stop," Avery said, trying to make it clear she was at the end of her rope. "This isn't a fait accompli. It's something I'm investigating, and I'd like a little room to breathe while I'm weighing my options."

Casey's eyes were like tiny smoldering fires. If this hadn't been so completely out of character, Avery might have been afraid of her. But she knew she was just upset, and didn't know how else to express it. She was acting a little like Lisbet did when she was frustrated, but the baby never pissed you off with such harsh words.

"Have you noticed how many times you've used the words 'I' or 'me'?" Casey demanded. "Why haven't I heard that Lisbet's needs are number one? Or your mom's, for that matter. You showed up on her doorstep when you needed her, but now that you've got your shit figured out you think you can just yank Lisbet away from her. That's so fucking selfish I'm at a loss for words."

"No, you're not," Avery said, now equally angry. "You've got a million of them, and they're all pissing me off." She grabbed the shoulder of Casey's jacket and pulled her along to the front door, where they stared at each other for a moment, electricity arcing between them. "Come back any time —after you calm the fuck down." She opened the door and pointed toward the yard. Casey opened her mouth, then shut it firmly, turned and stormed away, grumbling under her breath as she stomped down the walk. As Avery stood there in the cold, the engine roared to life, then she barreled down the driveway, sending gravel spraying in all directions. Avery wasn't sure how much rubber burned off her tires when she hit the street, but it was enough to leave an acrid scent that permeated the cold air for as long as she stood on the porch, stunned and confounded.

After pulling over to the side of the road to get her anger under control, Casey finally drove home, even though she craved seeing Lisbet's cheery little face. She really wanted to talk to Kathy, too, to at least empathize with her about Lisbet being taken away. But she didn't want to be the person who got into the middle of family disagreements, and knew she wouldn't be able to stop herself from doing just that if she and Kathy planted their flags on the same side.

She entered her room the usual way, through the barn-style door, and flopped down on the bed, still in her coat. She had almost everything she needed in her room, but had never put in a refrigerator. Now her throat was parched from yelling, but she didn't really want to have to make small

318

talk with her mom. But cupping her hands under the bathroom faucet was her only other option, and that wasn't very appealing.

With a grunt, she dropped her feet to the floor, stood, then straightened her hair. As she walked into the house, she noticed that the usual sweet scents that wafted from the kitchen were faint. Her mom had obviously finished her baking and was letting things cool while she washed up.

"Hi," Casey said, entering the room to walk over to the refrigerator.

"Who are you?" her mom said, with only the slightest sign of a tease to her tone. "You haven't been home for dinner in so long I don't even bother cooking for three any more."

Casey shrugged. "You don't need to cook for me tonight, either." She pulled out a bottle of water and started to chug it, not stopping until it was empty. As she put it in the recycling bin, she said, "I'm going bowling at six, so I'll grab something there."

"What's wrong?" Her mom grasped the sleeve of her jacket and kept her from taking another step.

"Nothing. I just had a hard day. I'm going to take a nap before I have to go."

"You can tell me to mind my own business, Casey, but I don't like it when you lie right to my face. You're obviously upset about something."

Sighing, she turned to face her mother. "Fine. I had an argument with someone. Now I'm going to go stew about it until I figure out what went wrong. Okay?"

"Was it Avery?" She clucked her tongue. "It had to be, since she's the only person you see anymore." She stepped in front of Casey and put her hand on her chin, tilting it left and right to get a good look at her. "I know you're crazy about that baby, but don't trick yourself into thinking Avery's the one for you, honey. She's not."

"I know that, Mom. That's not what this is about." She pulled away to go back to her room, with her mother adding one parting shot. "The first time you ran into her, you should have slapped her in the face and kept right on walking. She was a mean child, and mean children turn into mean adults."

⟳

After moping around for an hour, Casey pulled her phone out and called Kathy.

"Oh, hi, Casey," she said, sounding pretty chipper. "Dinner's almost ready."

"Ooo, darn. I should have called earlier. I just found out I have to sub for one of the owners at a big trade show in the city."

"Ugh. That sounds awful."

"Yeah. I'm not looking forward to it. I'm going to take off now so I don't have to get up before dawn to get there."

"But it's five o'clock. Won't traffic be bad in both directions?"

"Not too," she said, even though it definitely would be. "I want to get going, and my traffic app says the roads are clear." She hated to lie, but if she was going to do it, she might as well go all the way.

"Well, I hope you have fun. Will we see you tomorrow?"

"Oh, no. I won't be back until Sunday. Um…I really should go."

"Don't let me stop you, honey. We'll get by without you, but one of us might cry." She laughed. "That'll be me, but I'll try to be brave."

"I'll miss you all," she said, on the verge of tears again. "See you next week." She hung up, then texted one of the guys on her team, telling him she wasn't going to make it to bowling. This was the perfect night to go to bed at six. Nobody could hurt or annoy her if she pulled the blanket up to her chin and kept her eyes closed.

⟳

The next afternoon, after she'd picked Lisbet up from her mom's, Avery took a detour on the way home. She didn't believe Casey's story about a trip to the city, but she didn't want to express her doubts to her mom, who would never believe Casey would lie so brazenly.

Casey's street was dark as pitch, and the tasteful illumination along the driveway and at the base of a few trees and planters didn't reveal much. But there was light coming from the windows in the barn-style doors, and if

320

she strained her eyes, Avery could see Casey's truck parked in front of her room.

"Casey's hiding from us, Lisbet," she told the baby. "I think we should give her a day or two to herself, but if she doesn't come back, we're going to have to go get her."

⌇

Casey didn't come back, or call, or text, and within a day Avery lost the residual bit of anger she'd carried. She honestly couldn't imagine how she'd feel if she was in Casey's position, mostly because she never would have been interested in getting involved with a baby she wasn't related to. While she liked children in general, she wasn't fascinated enough by other people's kids to forge a close bond with one.

But Casey wasn't like her. She was kinder, for one thing, and more giving. And her love of kids was deeper and more universal than Avery's. The part that caused Avery some shame now was that she'd actively welcomed Casey in. Every step of the way.

They needed to have a long, civil discussion about this, and they needed to do it alone. Lisbet would freak out if she heard them yelling at each other, and given how they'd been on Wednesday, that was a definite possibility.

She kicked around ideas, and finally came up with one, but she needed her mom to add another day of baby-watching to her schedule. As she had with every other request, her mom agreed immediately. So on Saturday morning, Avery dropped Lisbet off with enough milk for the entire day, and drove over to Casey's, reaching her street at nine. Avery stayed in her car in the driveway and sent a text.

We need to have a long, peaceful talk, and I know the perfect place to do that
Just bring your swimsuit
Now
I'm in front of your room

The text showed it had been read, and Casey emerged a few minutes later, carrying a tote bag. She walked over to the driver's door as Avery lowered her window.

Casey wasn't smiling, but she didn't look unhappy, either. "We're not going swimming in the river, are we?"

"That idea hadn't crossed my mind. Today's swim will only be painful if you want it to be."

"Strange, but okay. Want me to drive?"

"I can. Come on. It's freezing!"

Casey walked over to the passenger side and slid into the seat. "Are you going to tell me where we're going?"

"I don't think so. I've got the whole day planned, and I'd like to surprise you."

"The whole day?" Her eyes grew wide. "We're going to talk about this for hours and hours?"

"No, you silly thing. We're going to talk, but we're also going to relax." She started the car and began to turn around.

"I guess this means we're speaking again?"

"I definitely want to speak with you, and since you came out of your room, you must want to speak to me. But I'd like to wait until we get to where we're going to talk about anything important."

"So… What? Should we stick to the weather?"

"We could, but I downloaded a book of short stories by Lorrie Moore. I'm not sure you've read her, but I can guarantee you'll like her work."

"We're going far enough to listen to a book?"

"Not the whole book, but we'll get through a few stories. We've got about a two hour drive. Feel free to close your eyes and open your ears." She paused a moment, and added, "And if you're still angry, you might want to stuff a sock in it. You've got a volume setting that surprised the hell out of me."

Casey was clearly over the worst of it, since she revealed what looked like an embarrassed smile, then leaned her seat back to close her eyes.

Casey had a long time to wonder about where they were going, but after being in the car for two hours she knew only that they were in New Jersey. The only time she'd ever been in Jersey had been to go to the shore, but she was confident they were currently nowhere near the beach. Besides, lying on the beach in February wasn't anyone's idea of a good time.

They finally pulled up in front of what looked like a modern apartment tower, and two guys raced out to open their doors and take the car away to a valet lot. Once inside the building, Avery walked up to a low counter, where smiling young people in matching golf shirts stood waiting. Before Casey could get another clue, she was signing some kind of waiver. Then they were guided to a spot where they had to leave their shoes, taking rubber wrist bands that electronically opened the tiny shoe-lockers. Moments later, they were in an elevator, going up just a few floors, standing there fully dressed, but in socks.

"Any time you want, you can tell me what in the hell we're doing…"

"If you can't figure it out when we get off this elevator, your powers of observation are pretty awful."

Just off the elevator lobby they entered a very modern, very large locker room, with quite a few naked or nearly naked women wandering around.

Avery was smiling at her when Casey finally stopped scanning the whole place.

"You've told me how much you love being in water," Avery said, "and they've got all kinds here. Super hot, hot, cool, and cold. I thought we could start out in the saunas, though, so we're nice and hot before we go outside."

"I can do that. I like being hot."

"We can pick up what they call leisure wear," Avery said. "It's a roomy shirt and shorts that look like something you'd be given in jail. But I like them better than wearing a swim suit in the heat."

"I'm not going to ask why you know what people wear in jail, but feel free to hook me up with the outfit."

⌒

There were five or six different kinds of saunas, with the temperature of each stated on a gauge attached to the outside. They'd visited a couple so far, but Casey could take as hot as they got, and she voted for the salt sauna next. 195 degrees was pretty hot, but she loved to sweat. Avery was game, and they went inside, finding there were no benches. "I guess we're supposed to lie on the floor," Casey said.

"Down we go." Avery sank to the woven mats that lined the floor. They settled themselves, with their heads on dense wooden blocks. It was pretty darned hot, but that felt great on a cold, snowy day. In minutes, Casey felt most of her lingering grouchiness leave her body as she started to sweat.

She was impressed that Avery didn't complain, but after about fifteen minutes even Casey'd had her fill. "I'm going to have to tap out."

"Oh, thank god," Avery said, laughing weakly. "Another five minutes and you'd have had to carry me out."

They got up, and Avery gripped Casey's arm for a moment. "I'd better drink up. Got a little light-headed there."

"Water, then the relaxation room," Casey said. "Although every place we've been is relaxing."

They stood at the drinking fountain, gulping down water until they were both hydrated. Then Casey led the way to the very large room filled with reclining lounge chairs lined up to face a huge stripe of tall buildings across a narrow river.

"Is that Manhattan?"

Avery gave her an indulgent smile. "Yes, I believe it is. Are you really this unaware of your surroundings?"

"My surroundings are Greene, Albany, Ulster, and Dutchess counties. This is way out of my range."

"Well, it's right in mine," Avery said, clearly waiting for Casey to decide on where to sit.

The place was like a very large first-class airline cabin, with the chairs set apart in groups of two, separated by wide aisles. Everyone seemed to want to be close to the New York view, so she headed for the opposite end, where all of the chairs were empty.

They were very close when they sat down, with their heads resting on built-in pillows. Casey pressed the buttons to recline her chair, and Avery followed until they were nearly horizontal. "Is this good?" Casey asked.

"Perfection. This is a little like being on the pod," she said. "Except the fabric doesn't feel like something you could use to scrub your tub."

"Fifty bucks," Casey said, her usual refrain when Avery complained about her sofa. "You can't find a better sofa for fifty bucks."

They were quiet for a while, listening to the tranquilizing music. The room was supposed to be for napping, and Casey was pretty sure she could be out in a matter of minutes. But Avery reached over to place her hand on Casey's leg. "I'm ready to talk if you are."

"If you can keep me awake…"

Avery smiled gently. "If you can sleep, you must not be mad at me anymore."

"I'm really not—"

"Well, I was pretty angry with you on Wednesday, but I've been thinking a lot about what you said. The parts where you weren't cursing at me, that is."

"I'm really sorry—"

"No need to apologize. You were upset, and I understand why. So let me just say this." She faced her dead on. "You were right about something big. I *am* considering the move almost exclusively for myself."

"You are?" Casey stared at her. She'd never thought she'd concede to that.

"If I'm being honest, I have to admit that." She scooted a little closer and lowered her voice further. "And that's not fair of me. I have to balance my desires with Lisbet's needs, and with my parents'." She squeezed Casey's leg, adding, "And yours of course."

"I'm not on the list," Casey said, sure that was true.

"You are," Avery stressed. "You're important to both of us. I promise that if I could stay in Hudson and be happy long term, I'd make that choice without regret. But at this point in my life I worry that I won't be satisfied. And my bigger worry is that my unhappiness will turn to bitterness, and that would filter down to Lisbet. I'm not willing to let that happen."

Casey turned to her, seeing how seriously she was taking the whole matter. "Do you really think that might happen?"

"It might." She stared out the window for a minute or two, even though all there was to see were grey skies and dull grey buildings. "I can't honestly guess at how I'll feel in a year or two, but there's a chance I'll be going stir crazy. For all of Brooklyn's faults, I've never been bored."

"Tell me what you miss," Casey said. "Be really specific."

Avery continued to stare out at the buildings like every other person in the lounge. While Casey wasn't antagonistic to architecture, she truly didn't understand why people were mesmerized by a bunch of buildings far enough away to make them look utterly lifeless. "It's hard to explain," Avery said, respectfully keeping her voice low, "but big cities excite me. They're loud, and crowded, and often really inconvenient. But you feel some weird kind of accomplishment in not just surviving, but thriving." She was quiet for a minute, then said, "People wonder how I can stand the noise, and the congestion, but that's part of the allure." She shrugged. "I love having a million things to do. I'm barely exaggerating," she said. "When you consider all five boroughs, there have to be close to a million restaurants. Dozens of plays are put on every night of the week. Fantastic orchestras. World-class opera. Stunning museums. It's all there, just waiting for you to choose."

"So... You did all that stuff? You went to the opera?"

"Um...once," she admitted. "They have a young patrons program where you can get discounted tickets. It was fun. A highlight, now that I think about it. Helena got a bunch of tickets and about ten of us went. We got all dressed up and everything."

"But you only went once in a decade."

"But if I'd fallen in love with it, I could have gone all of the time. They have rush tickets that are very affordable."

"But you didn't fall in love with it, right? If you had, you'd have gone back."

"You're not getting my point. Living in the city is all about opportunity. Just because I've never actually been to Staten Island doesn't mean I won't go."

"But if you haven't ever gone…"

"Okay. You're taking me literally, and I'm talking about something more figurative. I might only go to one event a month, but I can choose from thousands of things to pick the one that really excites me. That's just not possible in Hudson. There are things to do, of course, but the offerings are so much more limited. You'll agree with that, right?"

"I guess. But why does every city person I talk to gush about how much they love the Hudson Valley? They act like they're being held prisoner in the city, with weekend furloughs to the place they really want to be."

"Oh, they're being dramatic. We love to complain about how horrible the city is, but you don't see that many people actually pulling up stakes. Every single person I started with at work is still in the city." She pressed her lips together and added, "Except for a few who had kids and moved to the suburbs."

"Mmm," Casey said, trying not to smirk. "Well, you wouldn't have anything in common with them."

"I don't," Avery stressed. "I would never move to a suburb. They're the worst of both worlds to me. They give you none of the benefits of the city, and none of the benefits of a real, independent town. If I can't live in Brooklyn, I'll stay close to Hudson. I'm certain of that."

The atmosphere was so serene, and Casey was feeling so peaceful, that she found herself taking Avery's hand and examining it while she spoke. It was pale, and kind of delicate, the kind of hand you'd see in an illustration representing a mother's gentle touch. "Do you really think staying in Hudson could make you bitter?"

"I worry about it," Avery admitted. "I know I'll be a better mother if I'm fulfilled, both intellectually and creatively, so I'm honestly trying to do the right thing for Lisbet by making sure I'm where I need to be."

"I…" Casey cleared her throat and tried again. "I don't want you to risk that. My mom hasn't gotten what she's wanted out of life, and if she's not bitter she's damned close." She swallowed as she let herself think about her mom, adding, "It's not good for a kid to know her mother's unhappy."

"What did your mom want that she didn't get?" Avery asked, giving Casey her full attention.

"I honestly don't know. She's never been interested in opening up to me."

"Not about anything?"

"Not really. I think she's stuck, in both her job and her marriage. It's not pretty."

"Your dad's not… He's not abusive, is he?"

"Oh, no. He's…" She sighed, having given up trying to figure her father out. "He's just kind of a jerk. I'm sure he wasn't much different when she married him, so she got what she paid for. He was a very nice looking guy, who can put on the charm when he wants to. Lots of young women are overly impressed by that." She shrugged. "They're usually polite to one another, but I never sense any real love. Or any real interest in each other, for that matter."

"Do you think he…?"

"Cheats? Definitely."

"You have evidence?"

"No," she admitted, "but a good-looking man who flirts with every woman he meets would have to be very dedicated to his wife *not* to cheat. And my dad's not very dedicated to my mom."

"I'm so sorry to hear that. My parents don't make big public professions of their love, but I've never gotten the feeling from either of them that they're unhappy."

Casey smiled. "I'm pretty sure they're happy. It's a very different feeling at my house. While I think my dad loves having his nice, clean house, and dinner on the table when he comes home, I never see them laugh together. My guess is they have an unspoken bargain to keep the marriage going.

My mom gets to keep her standard of living, and my dad doesn't have to pay spousal support."

"That's it? Really?"

Casey shrugged. "They stopped sleeping in the same room over ten years ago, so it doesn't seem like sex is what's holding them together."

"Ooo. That's not good. It sounds like they've become roommates."

"Pretty much. I guess they're both kind of stuck."

"I'd rather be single," Avery said, sounding very sure of herself. "A nice house would never make up for the lack of love."

"Yeah, but you have options. My mom has no degree, no experience except for baking at home, and no work record. In a way, she's lucky my dad hasn't left her for another woman. His passion for his yard's probably what's keeping him at home."

"Your mom doesn't share that passion, right?"

"I don't think she's ever planted or picked a flower. What's the thing where you're afraid to go outside?"

"Agoraphobia?"

"Yeah, that. I don't think she's got a bad case of it, but I think she might have a little. That's why I had to start taking the desserts to my uncle's restaurant the day I got my license. She doesn't like to drive into Hudson because of the traffic—especially in the winter when the roads are slick."

"Your world can really close in on you," Avery said, sighing. "Is there some way we could help? We could take her out on the weekends if she didn't mind having Lisbet tag along."

"Would you really do that?" Casey asked, utterly charmed.

"Of course. There are plenty of things to do within an hour or two of us. What might she like?"

"Staying home and watching TV," Casey said, letting out a laugh. "I've tried, but she's not interested in going out. I think I have to let her figure this out for herself. If she wants to change, I'll support her. But she's got to want it."

Avery gave her a slap to the leg. "You're a very practical person. I like that about you. You never try to force your opinions down anyone's throat."

"Well," she said quietly, "I was doing exactly that on Wednesday. I really am sorry I was so angry." She sighed heavily. "I just felt powerless, and that can make me angry."

"You're not powerless. I promise I'll talk to you and my mom and dad before I make any decisions. We all want the same thing, Casey. We want Lisbet to have the best possible life we can give her."

Casey held her hand up and Avery slapped it. "That's the number one priority." She let that sink in for a minute, then said, "I know it sounds like I don't understand why you want to go back to Brooklyn, but I kind of do. I never would, but I think I understand what you miss." She took Avery's hand again and held it firmly. "Promise me one thing. If you go, will you let me come see Lisbet?"

"You'd come to Brooklyn?"

"Of course I would. I know you'd try to come home frequently, but you'll get busy. If I know I can see her like once a month, I'll be fine."

"That's a long drive…"

"I'd take the train down and stay over to make it worth the cost. Can I sleep on your floor?"

"If there's room," Avery said, making a face. "I'm pretty sure I'll only be able to afford a studio. But I'll happily get an air mattress for you. We might have to put it in the kitchen, but I'll figure out a way for you to spend a couple of days with Lisbet every month. You two can do something outdoorsy while I go to a matinee at the opera, or head over to Staten Island to see what's going on over there." They slapped hands again. "That's a promise."

"Um, I believe you, and if you're the only one who makes the decisions I know you'll follow through. But…what if you're not?"

"Not what?"

"Not alone. If you find a girlfriend, she might not want some stranger sleeping on the floor."

Avery smiled at her, and grasped Casey's hand to stroke it gently. "A woman who tried to interfere with Lisbet's friendships would not last long with me. My baby comes first, and any woman who wants to be with me needs to accept that. Period."

⌒

They'd stayed until they were both waterlogged, then set off for the long drive home. Avery almost took Casey up on her offer to drive, but she thought she could stay awake.

As soon as they started off, Casey took the phone and brought up the short story collection. Hearing one of Lorri Moore's tales begin to unwind perked Avery right up as she concentrated on the way Moore could caress the words into such lyrical sentences. Good writers made her heart sing, and the long drive suddenly became something she knew she'd actually enjoy.

⌒

It had been a while since Casey had assisted in waking Avery's libido up, and she hadn't tried to rouse it since. But after spending the day at the spa, she inexplicably had trouble relaxing enough to get to sleep. It took a minute to realize that images of Casey in her swimsuit were keeping her up.

While she'd always been attracted to women who were pretty much in the middle of the androgyny scale, she'd discovered that it was Casey's dyke style that made her heart race. So why was her vulva waking up again after seeing her in a surprisingly sexy swimsuit?

Casey had admitted it had been a gift from an ex, and that she'd grabbed it from her dresser because it had been the first thing she saw, but still, the suit had shown a lot of skin. A black, very snug suit with little x's of fabric up the sides had made Avery and just about every man in the rooftop pool take a long look when Casey had walked the length of the deck.

Avery experimentally let her fingers investigate, finding every part of her body had liked the look. Ignoring the question of whether she preferred Casey looking like a sporty dyke or a swimsuit model, she let her body do what it wanted, and it definitely wanted to think of Casey's breasts, the swell of her sexy hips, and the delicious curve of her firm ass. Libidos were funny things. You could tell yourself you liked one thing, but sometimes your body's menu was broader than you thought.

CHAPTER TWENTY-ONE

ON SUNDAY, CASEY GOT TO indulge in her favorite pastime, sleeping until she was damned well ready to get up. She'd snuck a look at her clock at ten, but that seemed awfully early. When eleven o'clock rolled around, she finally got up, more out of a need to use the bathroom than a desire to actually do anything.

It was another grey day, and even her insulated walls and double-paned windows couldn't completely keep out the chill. So she sought the comfort and warmth of her bed again, refusing her body's request for a warm caffeine-laced cappuccino.

Not putting in a tiny kitchen had been a mistake, but her father had explicitly forbidden her from installing one when she'd tricked out the workshop, given he didn't want his elderly, sometimes forgetful, always headstrong mother-in-law taking up residence and burning the house down.

When Casey looked at her living situation, she had to acknowledge that it was well past time to get her own place. Up until now, the plusses had strongly outweighed the minuses. The scale was starting to tilt, though. When she'd gotten home the night before, she'd noticed that some of the papers on her desk had been moved. It was bad enough that her mom insisted on doing her laundry. But being bold enough to snoop around while not even having the decency to hide it was pushing things. If Casey had anything she really wanted to keep private it would have been worse, of course, but the invasion of her privacy was still plenty annoying. She was fairly sure her mom's poking around was because she'd wanted a binder clip, or a felt-tipped marker, but it was still intrusive, and made her feel like she had no space that was purely her own.

Now that she'd yanked herself back into the awful mood she'd just shaken, she grabbed her phone and dialed Ben. "Hey, buddy," she said when he answered.

"What's up?"

"Not much. I thought you guys might like to go bowling."

"I'd love to," he said, with it taking until right that minute for her to realize there were basketballs and young boys' voices in the background. "We'll be home by four. Does that work?"

"Um...sure."

"Do you need something? You sound funny."

"I doubt that, since I sure don't feel funny. Even though Avery took me to a spa yesterday to let me soak for hours, I still feel like shit."

"That must mean she's out of the doghouse, though, right?"

"She is," Casey said, unable to stop yawning. "We both apologized, even though I'm the one who was in the wrong."

"You kind of were," Ben agreed. "You were being pretty thin-skinned for a normal person, and super thin-skinned for you. I've known you for years and have never, ever heard you yell at anyone."

"I've probably yelled less than five times in my whole life." She slid down the wall to lie on her back again. "But no one's ever made me feel that helpless." She closed her eyes for a second, then gave form to the thoughts that had been flying around in her head. "You know, you've been right all along."

"I have? That's not like me. Are you sure?" he asked, chuckling.

"You're really good at all sorts of emotional stuff. Right from the beginning you warned me to keep my distance. But I didn't, and now I'm hurting because of it."

"But you said Avery apologized. She must have felt bad to take you to a spa. They're expensive."

"She definitely did," Casey said. "She apologized a lot."

"So what's the problem? You're buddies again, and she likes you enough to try to make things right, even though you overreacted."

"That's the problem. I don't think I overreacted."

"Of course you did!"

"Nope. Given how close I've gotten to her, but mostly to Lisbet, I was one hundred percent justified in losing my shit at the thought of Lisbet being taken away without even a discussion. The problem, and it's a big one, is that I shouldn't be in this position. That's where you're right. I'm in too deep."

"Ooo. That's a tough one. How are you going to get out?"

"Well, I don't want to be all the way out. But Avery made me see that I've convinced myself I'm more important in her and Lisbet's lives than I really am. They both care for me, and I'm pretty sure Lisbet loves me, but I don't get a vote, and I never will. That sucks, but I've put myself in this position, so I can't blame Avery."

"Yeah, but she let you. If I'd been Avery, I wouldn't have let you spend so much time over there. It's…I want to say exploitative, but that might be a little strong."

"I can't blame this on Avery. I've got to get my head on straight. Lisbet is *her* child. Period. If I want to have any kind of voice, I've got to find a woman who's looking to co-parent. I need my own damn baby, and spending all of my time with Avery and Lisbet is the main thing that's stopping me from having one."

"Well, not the only thing," Ben said, with his teasing voice in play. "You're not as perfect as you think you are, buddy. Come get us for bowling at four. I know Benji will want to go, since only two basketball games in one day won't come close to wearing him out."

⌒

Avery spent several days wrestling with her conscience about whether to leave the Hudson Valley, finding herself still mired in indecision. But the rent was due, so she wrote out the check and handed it over to Casey to give to her father. It was crazy that she was *voluntarily* handing over a thousand dollars that she might have been able to save. Given she'd walked the forty minutes from her apartment to her office every single day for over ten years despite rain, snow, and hail just to save bus fare, tossing away a thousand bucks over an inability to make up her mind was epic.

It was odd, but her sticking point was that they were all too happy with things just as they were. That sounded a little crazy, but it was true. Lisbet was happy, her parents were happy, Casey was happy, and she was pretty happy too. Did it make sense to change everything on the off chance that she'd be unhappy at some undetermined point in the future? That seemed kind of wacky, but this opportunity with Rebecca might be the only time she'd be able to secure free child care. That was like being given three wishes from the magic lamp and taking a pass because it was too much trouble to give it a rub.

She watched Casey casually slip the check into her back pocket, and felt a strong temptation to ask for it back. But she couldn't, in good conscience, ask Chris to hold off due to her inability to make a decision. Now all she'd done was kick the problem to March, when she'd have to wrestle with it again—and that was only if Rebecca hadn't found a more enthusiastic day care partner by then. Adulting was hard!

On Valentine's Day morning, Avery dressed Lisbet in the heart-dappled onesie she'd gotten at her baby shower, and started to wrestle her into her snowsuit. She'd only gotten her legs in when her phone rang, so she was tempted to ignore it, but she had a special ring for people from the office, and a call at seven in the morning was rare enough to make her snap to it.

She picked Lisbet up and carried her downstairs, taking the call as she walked, "Hello?"

"Oh, good. I caught you," Helena said.

"You caught me trying to get Lisbet's snowsuit to stretch. She's growing so fast I could probably let her wear my winter coat."

"You'll have to bring her in," Helena said. "Now that she can interact, we'd have fun."

"I might be able to do that." She sat on the pod, with Lisbet looking at her curiously, clearly wondering why they weren't rushing to get ready and go. "Rebecca and I are seriously thinking of sharing child-care. I'd have to work at night, but that shouldn't be too tough to pull off."

"Mmm. That would be great for both of you, and if you really want to come home, you should, of course. But…"

Avery waited for the bomb. When Helena paused like that, she was about to lob one.

"Why don't you do that in the fall?"

"The fall? It's still winter."

"I know. But I've gotten such enthusiastic feedback about *Hudson Valley Short Shorts* that I'm ready to commit to it."

"You are?" Avery asked, feeling her mood lift.

"I am. I can pull two interns off what they're currently doing to help get you started, and you can find a few from Bard or Vassar to help out during the summer. This could be big, Avery. Even though you don't have the same population to draw from, you'll have fewer events to compete with. I think you might be able to make this bigger than *Short Shorts Brooklyn.*"

She spent just a second feeling the disappointment of having the opportunity to move taken from her, then switched to the elation of tackling something new. *Short Shorts* had been hers from the beginning, and doing a reboot, with the benefit of years of experience, was kind of a rush.

"We've got some big outdoor venues we could access," Avery said, already tingling. "If I could swing a night at Boscobel, do you think the magazine could front the money to rent it? It won't be cheap," she warned. "But it seats a few hundred people, which would be really cool."

"A few hundred?"

Helena was nothing if not pragmatic. Avery was a little skittish to even suggest a place that big, since Helena required that every project pay for itself, but she had a great deal of confidence about the project, and wasn't truly afraid of the risk.

"I'm sure I can easily find one big draw, someone well-known enough to sell three hundred tickets. With a big get, I can simply add in some lesser known writers to fill out the slate."

"Three hundred people is a big number, Avery. But if you're committed to finding a big draw, I'll approve your renting a large venue. That means you'll have to have everything set by the end of March."

"Everything? That's six weeks!"

"Well, not everything. But you'll need your main draw locked down by then, and you'll have to have the venue booked."

"Right. If I start now—like right now, I can have the info for advertising by the end of March."

"I'll let you run with it. I'm going to put Freya on finding advertisers for your new podcast."

"Podcast?"

"Of course. There's plenty of demand for two shows." She paused for a second. "You won't have time to do much work for the original *Short Shorts*, but I'd love it if you'd continue to host. Would that be stretching you too thin?"

She thought for a moment, then jumped in. "I'd love to have one day a month in the city. I'll make it work," she said, reaching up to high-five Lisbet, who was unaware there was anything to celebrate.

⌒

Casey hadn't been coming by as often ever since their fight, so Avery texted her to invite her to dinner. Inviting people to her parents' house was a little ballsy, but she'd make up for it by stopping at the grocery store on the way to her mom's. Delivering the raw materials for dinner had to trump the rudeness of inviting people without prior permission.

⌒

When Avery showed up at the house at the end of the day, a familiar warmth infused her chest when she saw Casey's big truck parked in front of the house. Even though she was still coming by every two or three days, Lisbet clearly missed her on the ones she skipped. Her mom reported that the baby would start watching the door in the late afternoon, twitching with excitement every time she heard a big engine go by. But Avery didn't relate that fact to Casey. If she wanted to be less involved, that was clearly her right, and making her feel guilty about it wasn't kind.

When she entered the house, Lisbet didn't even hear her, since she was too busy playing to notice. Casey was lying on her back, legs up in the air, with Lisbet lying on the bottoms of her stockinged feet, flying. She looked like she was about to pass out from laughing, with her arms and legs sticking straight out, her head held high, exhibiting her impressive neck muscles. Casey had a good hold on her, of course, but it was obvious Lisbet thought she was doing it all on her own.

Avery whipped her phone out of her pocket and took a movie, with neither the plane nor the pilot noticing her. After switching over to photo mode, she took a few snaps, thinking she'd make one her screen saver.

Casey finally turned her way, saying, "I'd wave, but this pilot hasn't logged many hours in the simulator."

"That's one very happy pilot," Avery said. The baby finally noticed her, squealing with delight. "I think she's so happy because she thinks she's really mastered something." She tickled under her chin, with Lisbet shutting her eyes and sneezing, just like a puppy might.

"She has. It was a very short time ago that we had to hold her head up. Now she's strong enough to fly!" She bent her knees and straightened them a few times, with Lisbet's eyes growing wide at the changing altitude, but still laughing.

"Our little girl's growing up," Avery said, already feeling wistful for her infancy, which hadn't even been gone a month.

"She sure is. Will you go into the kitchen and bring her something she really likes? A date or an orange slice or something? When I stop this, which I need to do in like two seconds, she's going to cry her head off."

"I'm on it," Avery said, racing into the kitchen before the flight simulator collapsed.

Dinner was still a ways off, and Avery stayed in the living room with her dad and Casey so that Lisbet had more things to hold onto while she "walked."

"Lisbet," she said. "Where's Fuzzy?"

The baby searched the room, seeing her teddy bear on the floor near the door.

"Go get Fuzzy," Avery said. "She wants to play with us, I think."

The kid took off, holding onto an end table, then the sofa, then a chair. She was about three feet away when she realized she didn't have any more support. She dropped to her knees, then crawled the rest of the way before plunking down on her butt, then grabbing the toy roughly and clasping it to her chest, grinning with satisfaction.

"Way to go!" Casey said. She crawled over to the baby, waited until Lisbet's hand was in the air, then high-fived her. "High fives," she said, always naming her actions. Avery watched her, thinking she was training the baby just the way you'd train a dog. But it was super cute, and might actually work.

"She's growing up too fast," her mom said, coming into the room and gazing at the baby with a melancholy expression. "She'll be walking within a week, then she'll be in school. In Brooklyn," she added, making a face.

"Um, the going to school in Brooklyn thing might still be true," Avery said. "But I have some news on that front." All eyes turned to her, with even Lisbet mirroring the others. "I can guarantee Lisbet will spend the summer right where she is."

"All summer?" her mom asked.

"All summer. Helena loves the idea of *Hudson Valley Short Shorts*, and she's assigning me a couple of interns right away. I'm going to be ridiculously busy, but we'll be here." She didn't add that she might be in a different apartment, because that would send her mom on another campaign to get them to move back into the house. One thing at a time.

Casey reached out and caught Lisbet as she fell while trying to cruise around the room still holding her bear. She was smiling, and seemed happy, but she merely said, "She'll love her first full summer here. Lots of pool parties at my place." She leaned over and kissed the top of her head. "We'll have to start shopping for a swim coverup." She looked up at Avery. "So you're happy about this?"

"Well, I feel awful about not being able to share childcare with Rebecca. She was really counting on me, and is having trouble finding anyone who wants the same setup." Her mouth widened into a big grin. "But, yeah, personally, I'm very happy about it. I'm going to get a second try at something that means a lot to me, while getting to enjoy summer here." She couldn't stop herself from adding, "I hope I get one of those invites to the pool."

"If you're happy, we're happy. High fives!" she said, gently smacking Lisbet's hand when she raised it.

Avery watched Casey when she could do so without making it obvious. She definitely seemed pleased, but not nearly as pleased as Avery had thought she'd be. Ever since their fight, she'd been a little tamped down. Avery had thought she might be imagining it, but tonight made it clear. Casey had started to pull away. No doubt about it.

Casey had taken to going out with the people from work on non-sports nights, meeting a couple of guys at one of the many bars and brewpubs in the Hudson Valley. Some of the guys swore these were professional events, checking out the competition. But she knew they were just twenty-something single guys who didn't want to stay home if there was anyplace else to go.

Tonight they were going to a place in Catskill, and she was driving, as usual. Swinging by the family dining room to check in with her parents before she left, she heard her father say, "I'm *trying* to get her out, Marsha, but she's paid me for February, so it's not going to be as easy as I thought it was."

Casey pulled out a chair and looked at her dad, who avoided her gaze. "Are you talking about Avery?"

"Uh-huh," he said, reaching for another helping of string beans. "That house I'm going to build in Germantown might be ready to go in June. If I have time to squeeze in the upgrades at your grandmother's place before I start on the new house, I can list it while all of the summer people are around to take a look." He held up a hand. "I don't want to hear your opinion, by the way. This is business."

"I realize that," she said, fighting to keep the anger from her voice. "When did you tell Avery you wanted her out?"

He shrugged. "A week ago? Maybe two? And before you get your back up, I offered the girl three free months of rent if she promised to leave by May."

She stared at him, astounded. "You offered her three thousand dollars to leave early?"

"I did," he said, looking proud of himself.

"Why didn't you talk to me about it?"

"I *said* it's business," he said, his expression turning into a glower.

"Great. What's the business end of the deal?"

"What do you mean?"

"How much work are you planning on doing?"

"As little as possible. New kitchen, new bath. I'll have to bring the wiring up to code, and there will be plumbing problems, since there always are." His brow furrowed as he thought, and she could almost see the calculations adding up in his head. "I'll have to do something to get the damn water heater and laundry out of the kitchen, but I'm sure the town won't let me knock down a wall." He mumbled, "I wouldn't complain if the place burned down…"

"Ignoring the arson angle, what's that going to cost?

He shrugged. "Doing the minimum, it'll take eight weeks, and that's if I've got all of my subs lined up."

She stared at him for a minute, trying to figure out this new info. "Why are you doing the minimum? I thought the whole point was to lure some rich weekenders into overpaying."

"Well, that was my plan, but then I had a real estate guy I trust run the comps for me. I wouldn't be able to sell it for more than two fifty or three, and that's if I refinished the wood floors and took the paint off the molding. The shell is historic, and that's worth something, but the place has been ruined by renovations. That kitchen's from the thirties, and there isn't one single original element left. I guess I could luck out and find some idiot who's willing to overpay for the exterior, but that would take a colossal dunce."

"I had no idea," Casey said, truly stunned. "I thought you were going to spend a few hundred thousand and be able to turn it around for a million."

"A million!" He laughed. "Maybe you're my dunce. No one's going to pay that kind of money for a small house with no original elements, especially when the city will give them fits if they try to add onto the footprint. The house is only two thousand square feet, you know. Rich people won't stand for less than three, preferably four."

"But the plot is huge. Wouldn't that interest some buyers? The privacy would be worth a lot…"

"Not important," he said dismissively. "You're stuck with a small house that you'll never be able to make big enough to have lots of weekend guests and parties. Having land you can't develop is the same as not having land. "

"Mmm. It would be to me," Casey said.

"Well, you're not a rich person from Manhattan, are you. Do you know the city won't even let me build a garage unless I give it a stone face? Do you have any idea how much that would cost? Ridiculous," he said, stabbing at his dinner angrily with his fork.

Her body began to tingle as she saw her future opening up for the first time in years. "What's it worth now?"

"Mmm." He thought for a minute, and she could see how much he loved stuff like this. He should have flipped houses full time, since he loved being able to turn a nasty little place into some quick cash without having a homeowner looking over his shoulder. "Exactly as it is now? Ninety-five. If I do the minimum, it'll cost me about seventy-five in labor, and probably fifteen in materials. Add ten for cost overruns, and I'm out a hundred thousand."

"What do you think you could sell it for then?"

"Two fifteen if I'm lucky. But since I'll have only invested a hundred, I'll be happy."

She looked at her mom, who was playing a game on her phone, then turned back to her dad. She knew her voice would shake if she let herself feel the excitement bubbling just under the surface, so she tried to stay cool. "How much do you want for it—as is."

He laughed, then took a bite of his chicken. "You don't have the skills to fix it up. Trust me on that. I'll admit you did a good job on the workshop, but your grandmother's place will require serious skill. There aren't many people around who could even give you advice on what to do, much less how do it."

"You're probably right. But I didn't ask you if you think it's a good idea. I asked how much you'd want."

"For you?" He smiled, clearly finding this funny. "One twenty-five."

"What's one twenty-five?" her mother asked, looking up.

Her father pointed at her with his fork. "Casey thinks she's going to take your mom's house and turn it into Gerritsen Manor."

"What?" her mom stared at her.

"I didn't say that, and I wouldn't even try. But I'd like to have my own place, and I think it would be cool to live in the house my ancestors built. Besides, I think Grandma would like me to have it."

"Oh, honey, that place should be torn down! Why do you want to move? I've always assumed you'd take over this house after we're gone."

"Um, you're not even sixty-five, Mom. You could live for another thirty years—easily. I appreciate the thought, but I've got to flap my wings at some point."

"You've waited thirty-six years to flap 'em at all," her dad said. "Sure they still work?"

"Only one way to find out. You're overcharging me, which is kind of shitty, but if your conscience doesn't bother you, have your attorney draw up the contract. I'm going to shorten your 'to do' list." Her dad was looking at her like she'd lost it, but she added one thing. "Since you haven't asked me to run to the bank for you, I assume you haven't deposited Avery's rent check for February."

He just raised an eyebrow, not responding otherwise.

"I want to give that back to her."

"Fine," he said, giving her a smirk. "Now you owe me one twenty-six."

On the first of March, Avery pulled the curtains in the living room aside to see Casey's truck pull up. It was just seven in the morning, and she'd been feeding Lisbet some mashed avocado, which was now all over her cheeks. After tossing a throw over the baby to keep her warm, she opened the door, grateful to note the wind that rushed in was only moderately cold. "Hi there," she said while Casey was still walking up the sidewalk. "What's up?"

"Why didn't you tell me my father tried to push you out of here?" She entered the house when Avery held the door open, then bent over and acted like she was going to nibble the avocado from Lisbet's face, making her laugh and try to push her away.

Following her in, Avery said, "Um…he asked me not to?" She made a face, knowing her excuse wasn't a good one. "It was the day I had to go into the city for my podcast, and I ran into him at the espresso place."

"Uh-huh," Casey said, gazing at her soberly while she took off her jacket, the army-green khaki one that made her shoulders look so broad. Then she took the baby from Avery, carried her into the kitchen, and wiped her face. She set her onto the floor, letting Lisbet grab one finger as they started to walk around the large, mostly empty rooms.

"Hey! We're eating here. I just got about three calories into her, and now the battle's lost."

"She's got energy, doesn't she?" Casey raised an eyebrow.

"Yes," Avery sighed. "She's at the low end of the weight range for her age, but she's got tons of energy. I should let her eat when she wants."

Casey squatted down and made a silly face. "Your mommy gets malts and chili dogs, but you haven't even had sugar yet. Since you're fueling your little engine with healthy stuff, you don't have the same cravings we do." She looked up at Avery with a sweet smile on her face. "We should all model Lisbet." She stood again and started to walk. "So…you met my dad having an espresso. What happened next?"

"Oh, right. He told me about getting ready to build a new house, and he thought he could renovate this place before he started on that. Eventually, he offered me three months free rent, and all I had to do was promise to be out by May. So tempting!"

Casey moved Lisbet closer, standing right in front of Avery as her warm brown eyes bore into her. "That's when you started to look at apartments in Brooklyn?"

"Uh-huh," she said, always having a tough time staying on track when Casey was this close and giving her this much undivided attention.

"So you were just trying to cover your bases?"

"I guess so. I had lunch with Rebecca, and she'd been dreaming up this child care idea, something I hadn't known she was doing. She'd found an apartment she thought I might like, and since I had the time I went over to look at it. My mistake was telling my mom, who blabbed to you."

"And I jumped all over you," Casey said. She looked like she was apologizing, but she didn't say those actual words. The expression on her face was actually better than words, anyway, since the look in her eyes was more powerful than a prepared speech.

"I can still feel your boot print on my shoulder..."

Lisbet was tired of standing still, so she pulled Casey along, taking her into the completely empty dining room. She was tall enough to look out the windows there, and she planted herself to stare at the icicles dripping fat drops of melting water onto the ground.

"I'm sorry for jumping on you, Avery. Besides all of the other reasons I owed you an apology, I didn't give you a chance to explain."

"It's all right." Avery followed them into the dining room, and gave Casey a friendly scratch across her shoulders.

"It is now," she said, turning to smile. "You've got a new landlord." She took a slip of paper from her back pocket and handed it over. "I'm going to honor the deal my dad offered you. You don't have to pay rent until May."

"What?" She stared at the check, the one she'd given Casey three weeks earlier. "You're my landlord?"

She put her hands in the pockets of her jeans and simply stood there, looking smug.

"Are you going to tell me what's going on? Or do I have to guess?"

"I'll tell you, since I don't think you'd get it very quickly and I've got to get to work."

"What are you talking about?" Avery demanded, acknowledging they were playing a game, but being very uncertain of the rules.

Casey's smile grew wide. "I bought your house from my dad. I signed the sales contract last night, and paid him off."

"Are you serious?" When Casey nodded, Avery threw her arms around her and hugged her tightly. "I'm so happy for you!"

"I am too. Really happy. Since the day I knew my mom was going to inherit this house, I've been unhappy with the plans she and my dad have come up with."

"Then why didn't you offer to buy it before?"

"I assumed he'd want a whole lot more than I had to spend, but I got him to tell me the truth about his plans." She laughed a little. "I'm glad I'd never told him I was interested in buying, since he would have jacked the price up."

"I hope you didn't pay a lot for it. The water heater in the kitchen is kind of an eyesore."

"I paid a fair price. My dad tried to nail me, but my mom put a stop to that pretty fast. I only had to pay what he truly thinks he could sell it for, which isn't a lot. If I do the work myself, I could have a nice little spot here."

"You'd fix it up and live here? Really? Your room is awfully nice."

"Oh, there are definitely plusses to living at home, but the minuses are piling up."

"So…I can stay for a while?"

"You can stay for as long as you want. I'll be able to pay the property taxes and have a little left over from your rent, so I'll put that in a separate account and use it for the building fund."

Avery clapped her on the back. "Congratulations! I certainly didn't know you had any thought of doing this, but I'm really glad to have you as a landlord. Would you like me to sign a lease?"

"No need. I'm not in a rush to make improvements, but I might start making plans. It's never too soon to make plans."

"Great. Now *I* plan on paying the rent I owe you, Casey. You didn't make an agreement with me. Your dad did, and it's a moot point now."

Casey shook her head firmly. "No dice. I paid for the place out of my savings, so I don't have a mortgage. It will cost me nothing to honor the offer my dad made you, and it'll make me happy to give you a little surplus. You just have to buy something…*anything* with the money. God knows you need a million things, and now that you'll have some security you can't use the excuse that you're just passing through any longer."

Avery grasped her arms and pulled her close. Looking into her eyes always made her feel a little off-kilter, but she forced herself to stay on track. "Did you really do this for yourself? Promise you didn't throw a whole lot of money into this house just for Lisbet and me."

"Promise," she said, unblinking. "The house means a lot to me. You two being able to stay longer is a very nice bonus. So go ahead and put those pre-school applications in, but rest assured you don't have to leave until you've got everything sorted out. Who knows? Maybe the rent in Brooklyn will be less when Lisbet's ready for pre-school."

Avery smiled at her. "I'd always guessed you were the most optimistic person in my circle, and you just cinched it."

CHAPTER TWENTY-TWO

HELENA'S WORD WAS HER BOND. Just days after she'd given Avery approval to start planning, two Brooklyn-based interns created a new channel on the inter-office communication app. Avery got a message as soon as she turned her phone on that morning, inviting her to a video chat at nine. That was a nice surprise, and after she and the enthusiastic interns spent a few minutes introducing themselves, she gave them the spiel about what she hoped they could accomplish.

They were full of ideas, reminding her of her early days with the magazine, when she'd interned the summer after her junior year at Bard, thus igniting her love of all things Brooklyn. After giving them specific marching orders, she left them to it, having far too many things to manage to keep a very close eye on them. She was determined to monitor the channel to make sure they weren't wasting their time on things she could clear up quickly, of course, but she was going to give them more autonomy than they would normally get. She just hoped she didn't regret that decision.

Starting the project would definitely be more work, but it was work she got a charge from. It also would give her an excuse to be in closer contact with people from the office, something she'd missed while spending hours a day editing in the hinterlands.

While she had every confidence Helena had assigned her the most promising interns, she couldn't trust them to find appropriate venues for the readings. Besides the fact that they didn't know the Hudson Valley, they didn't have experience in sweet-talking venue-managers into trying something different. That was her bailiwick, and it was going to be a time-consuming process.

Helena called a few days later, once again catching Avery while she was trying to get Lisbet ready to leave the house. "I found the perfect assistant for you," she said, not bothering with the usual conversational chit-chat.

"Assistant? You have the money to hire an assistant?"

"Of course not," she said, laughing a little. "But I do have the persuasive powers to talk someone great into helping you out for free."

"I like the words great and free. Where do I find this gem?"

"Right in your neck of the woods. Kinderhook is close to you, isn't it?"

"As a matter of fact, I live in metropolitan Kinderhook, as I refer to it. Give me their contact and I'll get the ball rolling."

"Sometimes even I'm astounded at my efficiency. At one o'clock this afternoon, Faith Pallone will meet you at Ginger's Luncheonette in Catskill. Lunch is on me," she added.

"You're making my lunch dates now? Not that I mind…"

"Faith suggested meeting you over lunch, so I asked her to pick the spot. Your expense account is covered in cobwebs, Avery. Feel free to dust it off and have a drink or two. You can imagine it's 1960, and you're at the Four Seasons, surrounded by editors from publishing houses too many to count."

"I'm afraid my imagination isn't that good, Helena," she said, knowing those heady days of publishing would never, ever come back.

⌐

Faith wasn't your usual intern, an earnest twenty-year-old English major. Avery wasn't certain how old she was, but she appeared to be over sixty. Since that was exactly the demographic Avery wanted to tap into, she was beaming with happiness when they sat down at the renovated diner with a surprisingly large dining room attached.

Their server wandered over immediately, asking for their drink order. When Helena had suggested they have a few drinks, she'd obviously been thinking of trendy Brooklyn restaurants, the ones with long lists of artisanal cocktails. Here the drinks were nonalcoholic, but they sounded pretty darned good. Avery observed Faith while she spoke to the server, asking detailed questions about how their lemonade was made.

Faith was very stylish, with short, snow-white hair and substantial, violet-framed glasses. She didn't wear a lot of makeup, but what she wore was subtle and very natural-looking. Avery would have immediately picked her out as a member of New York society, with her well-tailored china blue pantsuit and expensive heels. But she spoke to the server like they were co-workers, which immediately put Avery at ease. You could trust a woman who treated restaurant workers with respect.

"The lemonade sounds delicious," she said, still engaging the young woman with questions. "But I don't think it's exactly what I want. Can we have a little more time?"

"No problem," their server said. "I'll swing by in a few."

Faith turned to Avery and said, "I wanted something sweet, and I was hoping they used some cheap mix that would taste like candy. I should have known better. Ginger takes her food very seriously."

"Same for me," Avery said, "as long as someone else is cooking, that is. When I'm on my own, I take it frivolously."

"Oh, I've been in the frivolous stage myself. When my kids were small I thought it was an accomplishment to serve them something warm. I couldn't aim a bit higher than that."

"I'm lucky that my daughter's still primarily breast feeding," Avery said. "Once she's not satisfied with small bites of chicken and green beans, I'm going to be in trouble."

"Oh, Helena told me you have a baby! Tell me all about her," she said, setting her chin on her hand, looking like she was leaning in for a good story.

In a matter of minutes, Avery started to feel like she'd known Faith for years. If this hadn't been a business meeting, and if Grace had given off any lesbian vibes, Avery might have asked her out. They simply got each other.

After they'd twice asked for a little more time, Avery finally picked up the menu. "We'd better decide what we want or they're going to toss us." She scanned the listings, which were few. Luckily, she wanted every one of them. "I don't know how this place has escaped my notice, but I'm going to race over the Rip Van Winkle Bridge every week if the food is as good as it sounds."

"I think it's better," Faith said. "My older daughter's a chef in Buffalo, and she's the one who brought me here the first time. You know how people in the business all know each other."

"I don't know many chefs, but I could fill Carnegie Hall with all of the MFAs in my contacts list."

"That's my younger daughter," Faith said. "She's a sculptor who followed the creative caravan to Detroit last year, one of the few cities where an artist can still get studio space that's close to affordable." She sighed heavily. "I want both of my girls to find their own ways, but I would have preferred they'd found it nearby."

"Do you have any grandchildren?"

"Not yet." She shrugged her shoulders, looking concerned, but not overly so. "Maybe not ever. Both of the girls claim they want children, but I think they're running out of time. Brooke's married, but she's thirty-six and working sixty to seventy hours a week. Alissa's going to be thirty-four this month, which means she has a little time to spare, but she hasn't had much luck in love. Since she doesn't want to be a single parent, she's got some work to do."

"Been there. I was in Alissa's position, and just pulled the ripcord." She felt her smile grow at the mere thought of Lisbet. "Absolutely no regrets, thankfully."

Faith let out a sigh. "I suppose I should I envy you, with your youth, a good job, and a new baby." She smiled, revealing a single dimple that was pretty adorable. "But I'm in such a good place in my life I can't bring myself to crave anything I don't currently have."

"That's great to hear. I'm happy to say that my mom feels just about the same way. She's retired, has enough money coming in to let her not have to worry about paying the bills, and she's helping raise my baby— something she's been looking forward to for years. Sometimes I envy her,"

Avery admitted. "But that's mostly because she's happily married to my dad. Like Alissa, I haven't been very lucky in love."

"You want to fall in love? Leave it to me. I know more people in the Hudson Valley than you've met in your lifetime," Faith said, winking conspiratorially. "Describe your ideal man, and I'll find an acceptable facsimile."

Avery laughed. "I have an ideal woman."

"That's even better," Faith said, with her pale eyes twinkling. "I know far more women than men. I could have easily found someone for Alissa, who's also gay, but she hasn't lived in New York since she went away to college."

"Well then, you can use your skills on me. My ideal woman lives in Brooklyn, has a rambling two-bedroom apartment, and deeply craves parenting a child. Can you hook me up?"

"Rambling?" She laughed again. "Isn't that a beautiful word for an apartment? My husband and I had a near-rambling Classic Six on the Upper West Side."

Avery dramatically clutched her heart. "A Classic Six? And you call it near-rambling?"

Faith laughed. "Well, I know it's unseemly of me to say my Classic Six wasn't commodious, because it was. But I was greedy, and lusted after the Classic Seven next door. That extra bedroom would have come in very handy." She playfully dabbed at her eyes. "Boo hoo for me."

"You always judge your circumstances by what your friends have. I was insanely jealous of a friend whose studio had a little blip-out big enough for a tiny writing desk. That sounds crazy, but at least I own my jealousy."

"Oh, I'm attuned to the madness New York real estate can engender. We bought our apartment for seventy-five thousand dollars in 1985. We not only felt like we'd been robbed, we moaned about our foolishness for investing that kind of money on a silly apartment for over ten years. Finally, prices started to creep up, then they launched into a sprint that shows no sign of dying off."

"Did you sell?"

"Five years ago this month. With the proceeds, we bought a four-bedroom, three bath home in Kinderhook, on eight acres. Then we did a gut renovation. With the money we had left over, we took a cruise…to New Zealand." She rolled her eyes. "It's not a good time to be a young creative person in the city, but it certainly was in the 1980s. If you could avoid being stabbed in the street, you were golden," she added, tossing that off so cavalierly that Avery had to laugh.

Their server appeared once again, and Faith put her menu down. "We're enjoying each other's company so thoroughly that we haven't put any thought into our lunch. What do you think we should have?"

The woman pushed back her obviously-dyed black hair, revealing a full tattoo sleeve of comic superheroes. "If you don't care about calories, I'd have the chicken and waffles."

"I certainly don't care about calories," Faith said. "Avery? Do you care?"

"Not a bit. Care to split a chocolate shake?"

"I thought you'd never ask." She smiled up at the server. "Two straws, please."

⁓

Casey got ready to leave Kathy's house just before five. Her resolve to maintain some distance hadn't held, and she'd gone back to her habit of stopping by after work nearly every day. But she'd started to leave before Avery arrived, allowing herself a shaky belief that she was claiming her independence.

The front door opened, and Avery entered, all dressed up and beaming with energy. "I had the best lunch," she said, walking over to give both Casey and her mom big hugs. "I'm taking the whole gang over to Catskill for dinner first chance we get. It was to die for."

"You put on a dress to go to Catskill?" Kathy asked.

"I did. I had to meet my new assistant, and she suggested this fantastic diner. I wasn't sure how she'd dress, so I went with business attire."

Casey watched her talk, having to concentrate to avoid staring. It was still cold more often than it was warm, but people were starting to wear a little color to celebrate the first feeble signs of spring. Avery had joined the trend, looking fantastic in a simple wrap dress that showed off her newly-trim body. Breastfeeding must have done the trick, since she ate as much as Casey did, but had clearly lost all of the weight she'd gained during her pregnancy.

Her dress was navy, with small yellow polkadots covering it, along with a yellow and white silk scarf that she'd figured out how to tie artfully around her neck. Just a little eye makeup to tint her fair lashes dark, and some lip gloss made her look like a very successful professional, which, Casey had to admit, she was.

"Can you?" Avery asked, grasping Casey's arm for a quick squeeze.

"Can I what?"

"Stay for dinner? I'm bursting with information, and I'd love to talk to you about it."

Her resolve to head home early flew from her head the minute those pale eyes locked onto her. "Love to."

Because Avery was dressed so nicely, Casey did most of the baby-minding, and she sat on Lisbet's right at dinner, since that seemed like her favorite food-throwing hand.

Avery sat across the table from the baby, confusing her slightly, but she handled it well, making faces and shrieking in her direction frequently.

"So," Avery said, her eyes dancing. "My new assistant is wonderful."

"You sound like you're discussing your first crush," Kathy said.

"I'd go for Faith in a second if she wasn't happily married."

"Oh, how nice! Helena found a lesbian for you. Maybe she can introduce you to some women."

"She's not a lesbian, Mom. Sadly," she added, chuckling. "But even if she were, she wouldn't pick me. I can't see her as the type to choose youth over experience."

"How much younger are you?"

"I'm not sure, but she has a daughter my age. I got the impression she'd written for quite a few years before she met her husband, so she's probably around seventy."

"And she's going to be your assistant?"

"Uh-huh. People were talking her up when she was fresh out of Sarah Lawrence, and she'd published short stories in various literary magazines, but she put her typewriter away when she had her daughters. She hasn't written in over thirty years, but I'm going to try to coax her creative side back out. Faith might be my assistant, but she's also going to be my project," she said, smiling like that cat that ate the canary. Casey had no idea what Faith was like, but if Avery wanted to get her back into writing, she might as well dust her typewriter off.

CHAPTER TWENTY-THREE

THE BITTER END OF WINTER was Casey's least favorite time of the year. Spring seemed a long way off, fall was barely a memory, and gloomy days were more the rule than the exception. Every year she vowed to head south for a vacation, but she'd never pulled it off. And even if she'd had the drive to plan a trip this year, which she didn't, her obligations would have prevented her from having fun in the sun. The Baby Brewers might not have brought millions into the coffers of Kaaterskill Brewery, but she was very much into it, as were her loyal band of parents, all of them going stir-crazy from the long winter.

Kathy and Lisbet had attended each weekly gathering, even when it meant driving through a snowstorm. They each had their BB friends, but they didn't match up.

Kathy always sat by Josh, a stay-at-home dad whose wife worked in the city, and Mariel, a woman close to Kathy's age who watched her son's baby. Lisbet, on the other hand, loved to play with Ava, a little girl whose mom was kind of a pain in the butt. That hadn't rubbed off on Ava, though, and she and Lisbet would sit opposite each other and laugh until one of them fell over. That usually made the other one laugh harder, and then the fallen one would scramble to her feet and totter around, holding onto whatever she could grab until she inevitably fell again. It always amazed Casey at how bouncy babies were, often able to take a hard crash and shake it off without seeming to notice. Of course, other times a feather would brush by their skin and they'd lose it. You could never guess.

The group met at three and usually broke up around five, but Casey was never in a hurry to leave. She would have stayed out in the Pub and poured cider the entire night, given how much the parents loved it. When you felt you were making peoples' lives better by doing something you enjoyed, why cut the experience short?

The usual crowd was all accounted for, but they also had one newcomer, a woman who seemed deeply shy. Her baby was only slightly more outgoing, but everyone went out of their way to welcome them.

Casey felt a draft and turned to see yet another woman tentatively enter. She didn't have a kid with her, so Casey assumed she'd gotten lost. As she started to walk over to speak to her, she noticed the woman was pregnant. "Hi, there," Casey said. "Are you looking for Baby Brewers?"

"Am I allowed in?" She patted her belly, which wasn't very big. "I'm not due until June, but I'm trying to get ahead of this and find a support group before I need one."

Casey stuck her hand out. "I'm Casey, and since I started the group, I can change the rules whenever I want. From here on in, we're a group for prospective parents, and children under three. How's that?"

"It's great." The woman put her hand out and they shook. "I'm Tara. Thanks for the welcome."

Casey looked to her left to see Kathy approach. "Hi," she said, sticking her hand out. "Kathy."

"Tara's looking for support," Casey said as the women shook hands.

"I don't know anyone who's had a baby, so I need to find some people who don't look at me like I'm crazy for doing this," Tara said.

"Ooo, my daughter was the same," Kathy said. She pointed at Lisbet, who was watching her like a hawk. "That's her baby Lisbet, the one who's trying to make sure I don't run away." She put her hand on Tara's back and started to lead her over to the bar. "Let's find you a place to sit. When I was pregnant, all I wanted was a chair."

"It's not too bad yet," Tara said, "but I assume it'll get worse."

"That's parenthood in a nutshell," Kathy said. "At least that's how it seems at first."

⌒

Casey hadn't been staying for dinner at the Nichols' house unless someone specifically invited her. So Avery was a little surprised, yet pleased, to see her pull up to the house just a few seconds after her mom and Lisbet had.

It was cold out, but not brutal, so she went out without her jacket to help bring Lisbet inside. "What can I carry?" she asked.

Casey jumped out of her truck, loped over, and started to pull Lisbet's car seat from its base. "Get inside! You'll catch cold."

Laughing to herself, Avery went back in, then held the door to let them all pass. "Are you two just back from your play date?"

"We are," her mom said, starting to take her coat and gloves off. "We had a big crowd today. Seems like everyone is starting to lose their minds because of this endless winter."

Casey worked on getting Lisbet's snowsuit off, so Avery sat next to the baby and tried to distract her. It worked pretty well, and when she was finally out of her gear Avery picked her up and kissed her until she pulled away. "I'm going to kiss you and kiss you," she growled. "I can't get enough kisses from my baby girl."

"Oh, Avery," her mom said, "a girl showed up today, and her story just about broke my heart."

"Tara?" Casey said, looking puzzled. "Her story broke your heart? I got the impression she knew exactly what she was getting into."

"But she's all alone…"

"Clue me in?" Avery said. She pulled Lisbet onto her lap and started to play her favorite game, the one where Avery bounced her vigorously on her knees.

"Tara's young," her mom stressed, "pregnant, and single. She doesn't seem to have anyone she can rely on. Her parents live nearby, but they sound like awful people—"

"Oh, I don't think they're that bad," Casey interrupted. "Well, they might be a little awful, but I got the impression they think she's making a big mistake. Sounds like they want to make it clear they're not going to support her if she gets in over her head."

"By having a baby?" Avery asked.

"Uh-huh. Her parents aren't crazy about her being gay, but her deciding to have a baby all on her own has driven them over the cliff. At least that's the impression I got."

"You two sure did learn a lot," Avery said. "You sussed out her sexual orientation, her strained relationship with her family... What else?"

"She's cute," Kathy said. "Didn't you think so, Casey?"

"Sure." She brushed that off, and continued, "I'm not saying her parents are right, but I think she's biting off an awful lot. She doesn't have a single friend who's had a baby yet, so she's really playing it by ear."

"Has she arranged for child care?"

"She doesn't think she'll need it," Kathy said. "I tried to hint it might be tough to work full-time with an infant at home, but Tara's one confident kid."

"Kid? Is she a teenager?" Avery asked.

"No, no," Casey said. "I asked. She'll be twenty-five when she has the baby."

"Mmm," Avery said. "That's a good age to have a baby, but not a great age to have much money saved."

"She's a computer programmer, or something like that," Casey said. "She must do okay, since she has her own apartment." She turned and asked, "Did you understand what she does, Kathy?"

"No idea. But whatever it is, it won't be easy to do with an infant. I think Tara's going to need some help. I just hope those stupid parents of hers come around."

CHAPTER TWENTY-FOUR

ON A DREARY SPRING MONDAY, Avery sent Casey a text.

Finished early

How does dinner in a real restaurant sound

My treat

She waited just a second for a reply.

I'd love to have dinner

Why should u pay?

Avery texted back.

It's Landlord Day

I'm buying you dinner instead of a present

As usual, Casey replied quickly.

Don't believe it, but I'll play along to get a free meal

Send me details

They met by Casey's uncle's restaurant, but not because Avery wanted to eat there. While she'd enjoyed many good meals at Villa Napoli, she wanted to talk, and knew Casey's uncle would interrupt them. You couldn't have a meal there without him dropping by two or three times, often pulling up a chair to chat if the place wasn't swamped. Actually, as outgoing and interactive as he was, it was hard to believe he was Casey's mom's brother.

It had been a while since Avery had seen Casey driving her truck, and she laughed at herself when she felt a chill the moment that blue behemoth pulled up behind her on the otherwise empty street. How had she ever convinced herself her main turn-ons were philosophical discussions? The first time a tall, broad-shouldered, dykie woman in a big truck showed up on her radar, she was like a besotted teenager again.

Casey was out of her truck before Avery even had her seatbelt off. She smiled up at her as her door was opened. "Landlord Day, huh?" Casey asked, extending her hand to help Avery get to her feet.

"Well, technically, we didn't celebrate your buying the house. So I guess this is a belated housewarming gift. But since you're my landlord…"

"Any excuse works for me," she said, smiling.

When she went over to the meter to see if they had to pay, Avery allowed herself the non-guilty pleasure of checking her out. Casey hadn't known they were going out, so she was wearing her usual work clothes. This must not have been a brewing day, since she was pretty neat and clean.

Her usual jeans were topped by a Henley shirt, one Avery didn't recall seeing before. She clearly liked not having a collar, and the khaki green color probably didn't show dirt and dust. As she often did, she'd tucked the shirt in only to show off her belt buckle, leaving the rest of it hanging out. It was a cool little affect, and when Casey returned Avery noticed the buckle was different. "Where's your Kaaterskill belt?"

She looked down, probably having forgotten what she was wearing. "Oh. A sales rep from one the places I buy yeast from gave me this." She tilted it so Avery could see.

"Brewmaster," she said aloud. "Not too cool."

"Well," she said, showing a sly smile. "I like to remind my guys I'm in charge."

"I can't imagine they ever doubt that," she said, earning a raised eyebrow from Casey. "Are you disputing my guess?"

"Nope," she said, smugly, sticking her thumbs into her front pockets. "Where are we going?"

"Have you been to the Neapolitan pizza place?"

"Just once. It was good…"

"But?"

Her smile made her look a little abashed. "It was full of city people."

Avery reached over to pat her cheek. "Well, you're with a city person tonight. Was the pizza good?"

"Excellent. But I was on a date, and it almost killed me to pay seventy dollars for two pizzas and a few beers."

"Well, I'm in the mood for a good Margherita, and I don't have a wood-fired oven. Damn the expense."

"Why'd we park down here?"

"Because I knew we'd be able to find spots close to each other. This end of the street doesn't get much business this early in the evening, and I didn't want to have to look for you."

They had about three blocks to cover, and as they walked, Avery said, "Remember what this street was like when we were kids?"

"It was like that," she said, pointing at one of the businesses remaining from their youth. The old-school barbershop looked like it hadn't been altered since the fifties, with poor signage, faded posters showing various haircut styles, and a seriously old barber sitting in one of the chairs, reading a magazine.

"Exactly. If I'd known this was going to turn into a Hipster hotspot, I might not have been in such a hurry to leave."

"But you're back. At least for the time being. You know, you might be the only person in town who grew up here, left for the city, and came back."

"I'm not the only one," Avery said, watching Casey's face for a reaction when she finished her sentence. "Janelle Perkins is back in town."

You didn't need Sherlock Holmes's observational powers to see the news didn't make her day. "Huh. Where's she living? I'll make a point to stay out of that part of town."

"Same house she grew up in. She's living with her parents, along with her three-year-old."

"Yeah, well, I never went to her house. Not surprisingly."

Avery didn't think this was the time to reveal Janelle lived just two blocks from the Nichols house. Given the expression on Casey's face, it had been a bad idea to bring her up before they got to the restaurant. Avery had wanted to slide into the subject when they had time to dig into it, but she'd kind of dropped the fact that the class bully was back in town right on her head.

Casey didn't ask a single question, and they finished their walk in silence. She held the door when they reached the restaurant, but her smile was very dim. But she put on the charm without hesitation when she approached the woman at the reception desk. "Hi there," she said, standing closer than was strictly needed, getting about the distance you'd allow for a friend. "Is there any way you can you fit us in for dinner? I know you're slammed…"

The place was completely empty, and the woman gave Casey a wry smile. "I think I can find a spot for you. Would you like to be in the back by the fire, or have a view of the street?"

"Fire," Casey said, then she turned to raise an eyebrow.

"Fire," Avery agreed. "I'm still chilly, since I'm a normal human who gets cold."

That merited a warmer smile. "I get cold too. Just not when it's nearly sixty degrees."

"Don't jinx us," the woman said. "I've finally taken my mittens out of the car and put them away for the winter."

"You're safe," Casey said as she pulled out a chair for Avery. After pushing it closer to the table, she moved to sit across from her, then looked up at the host and added, "If it gets cold enough for mittens, I'll give you twenty bucks."

"You're on." Amazingly, the woman popped her on the head with the menus, then placed them on the table. "Your server is Sarah. She'll be right by."

"Thanks," Casey said, waving as the woman turned to go back to her post.

"I didn't realize you were so friendly to strangers," Avery said, struggling for a second with her jacket. Casey reached over and tugged on the sleeve, easily sliding it off.

"Sorry I didn't introduce you," she said, looking a little sheepish. "That kid was a server at my uncle's one summer, but I couldn't remember her name."

Avery started to laugh. "Living in a small town can motivate you to make sure you don't look like hell before you leave the house, can't it?"

"Maybe you," she said, taking another look down at herself. "I might have shown up looking like a wet dog, depending on what we'd been up to today. Luckily, I was mostly in my office."

Their server approached, and after Casey grilled her on their beers, they each had a pint in front of them. Casey picked up her glass and tapped it against Avery's. "To landlords," she said, then took a sip. "Not bad. A little heavy on the coriander, but I think it'll cut through the creaminess of the ricotta cheese."

"What am I drinking? I spaced out when you were trying to make our server into a beer expert."

"You were on your phone," Casey pointed out. "And if you don't put it away, I'm taking off for your mom's. She interacts."

"Just texting her to make sure Lisbet's not upset that neither of us are over there." She picked up the device and showed that she was putting it in her purse.

"You're drinking a pale ale. I would have chosen an unfiltered one, since I think you can use a little added kick with a Margherita, but they don't have one on tap." She picked up Avery's glass and took a sip. "That's good. You'll be happy with it."

"I'm happy with just about anything. I'm still only having about one a week, so each one feels like a special occasion."

After taking a hearty sip of her own beer, Casey's expression turned sober. "Did you just run into Janelle? Or are you..." She took in a breath and tried again. "Are you hanging out again?"

"We're not going to strike up a friendship," Avery said. "But I did reach out to her when my mom told me she'd seen her at the grocery store."

Casey didn't reply verbally, but Avery could see that she had something to say. She was probably holding her tongue to see where this was going.

"She's having a tough time," Avery said. "Graduating summa from Yale and getting a law degree from Harvard is not a guarantee of success."

A dark eyebrow rose again, but Casey was really holding onto her words tonight.

Deciding to spit it all out, Avery said, "I called her, and we had coffee on Saturday. She's really fucked things up, quitting her job with a big New York firm when she had her baby, then finding out her husband had been embezzling from the corporation he worked for. He was the head of the auditing department, by the way."

Avery thought the extended sip of beer Casey took might have been an attempt to hide a smile, but she didn't comment on that.

"I called her because I was thinking of how much I've changed over the years, and I thought maybe she had, too, you know?"

Casey shook her head slowly. "Mean kid, mean adult."

Avery laughed softly at what was obviously a deeply held belief. Pithy, but deeply held. "I'm not sure that's always true, but I think it is with Janelle." She remembered a detail and started to get hot under the collar just thinking about it. "She's determined to get her old life back, you know. She swears she's not going to become a hickster."

"Hickster?"

"That's what she calls people from Brooklyn who move up here. I was incensed!"

"I'd rather be a hick than a jerk," Casey said, clearly not sharing all of Avery's sensitivities.

"We were only at coffee for an hour, but I was glad when Lisbet got sick of hanging around and started to make a fuss."

"The bad vibes were probably freaking her out," she said, clearly realizing she didn't have to be polite. "I'd ask a question or two, but I honestly don't care enough about that woman to get any satisfaction from hearing about her string of bad luck." Her expression changed slightly, and she added, "I am sorry she had a kid, though. I wish all jerks were infertile."

"I hate to wish infertility on anyone, but I can't argue with your point. If assholes didn't have kids, the world would be immeasurably improved."

Their pizzas arrived, and they each spent a minute getting their first pieces into their mouths. "So good!" Avery said. "I've never made a Neapolitan pizza, but I could learn how. You're going to have to put a brick oven in my house."

"The odds are not good," Casey said, "but my mom seriously wants one for bread, even though she says she doesn't. Maybe I'll build one for her."

The pizza got cold, as well as limp, quickly, and they didn't talk much at all while they rushed to beat the droop. But they'd eaten so quickly they each had a half pint of beer left.

"I could go for another slice," Avery said. "They need tiny little pizza pans for people who want just a few more bites."

"When I go out for pizza with the guys from work, we always order an extra for the table." She laughed a little. "Most of them are still in their twenties and believe they can eat whatever they want. They'd better cut that out or start buying bigger pants."

Avery thought of Janelle again, wondering if she'd started to stress-eat or if she'd truly never lost her pregnancy weight. Even though she was a jerk, struggling with a large weight gain wasn't anything Avery wished on her. "Uhm, I can tell you're not interested in talking about Janelle, but I had some thoughts after seeing her, and I'd like to...clear the air?"

"The air's not clear?"

"No. It's not clear at all."

She must have looked very serious, because Casey gulped down the rest of her beer, like she was prepping herself for bad news.

Avery reached over and covered her hand, holding it for a few seconds. "When you and I first ran into each other at the Greenhouse, I had brief, but very unpleasant memory of how Janelle used to tease you."

"Bully," Casey said, with her eyes narrowing. "She bullied me until I pushed her up against a locker one day and told her to knock it off or I'd beat the crap out of her."

"You did?" Avery knew her mouth had dropped open, but she was truly stunned.

"I did." Her jaw was set, eyes narrowed. But then her features softened slightly. "She didn't tell everyone?"

"She didn't tell me," Avery said. "That's something I would have remembered."

"Huh. She swore she was going to call the police," she added, with her features further softening as she actually laughed a little at that. "She acted like I'd pulled a knife on her." Her smile grew slightly, making her look satisfied with herself. "She never called me Van Dope again, though, so it would have been worth being hauled down to the station."

"I'm so sorry," Avery said, squeezing her hand before letting it go. She wanted to hold onto that strong, sure hand, to clasp it close until she was sure Casey knew how bad she felt, how ashamed of herself she was.

"I don't have any memory of you actually calling me names, you know. You're not responsible for your friends being jerks."

Avery gazed at her, sure her suspicion showed clearly in her expression. "Do you honestly believe that?"

"What? That you're not responsible for your friends?"

"Yeah. Exactly that."

She was quiet for a minute, then shook her head. "No, I don't really believe that."

"Neither do I." When Casey's gaze met hers, she said, "My grandmother used to say 'Know me, know my friends.' It took me a while to figure out what it meant, but it's often a hundred percent true."

"I think your grandmother was right." She stopped and gave Avery such a sad look that her pulse quickened. "But I wish she wasn't."

"So do I," Avery said, on the verge of tears. "I hung out with Janelle because we both had the same goals, academically at least. But I knew she was mean to you and to anyone else she felt superior to. Hanging out with a cruel person was just an inch away from being cruel myself," Avery stressed, "and I want you to know how sorry I am for having done that."

A ghost of a smile flitted across Casey's features. "What should you have done? Decked her when she was being a jerk?"

"I think there's a happy medium. I should have told her off the first time she did it, and distanced myself permanently if she did it again. But I didn't do that." She took a deep breath and told the whole truth. "I didn't draw a line with her because it didn't really affect me much."

She could see a flash of pain infuse Casey's eyes, with her own sense of shame getting heavier by the second. "That's the part I'm sorry for. For not being empathetic to you and the other kids Janelle picked on. I see now that she just had horrible self-esteem, and was trying to knock other people down so she felt like she was on a higher step than they were. But it's wrong in every way, and I was an unfeeling coward for letting her get away with it."

"Kinda harsh," Casey said, pulling the last quarter of Avery's beer over and downing it.

"Not harsh enough. Everyone has their faults, but you can't just look at the positive traits of your friends or your relatives or your public servants, for that matter. You've got to acknowledge their worst parts, and decide if you support *that* person. If someone had asked me if I'd like to hang around with a bully, I'd have thought they were crazy for even asking. But I ignored Janelle's bullying because I could slough it off, since I didn't actively participate. That's something I'm going to feel awful about for… forever," she realized.

"Jesus," Casey grumbled. "You hung out with a jerk, Avery. That's not a hanging offense."

"I'm not saying it is. But I'll never be the person who has *always* stood up to bullies. I screwed up, and I can't unscrew that flaw in my character. I can only promise myself that I'll never do it again." She gripped Casey's hand again and looked into her eyes. "I swear I'll never let things like that slide. I won't be a passive participant."

"Thank you," she said quietly. "I don't need much protecting now, but an awful lot of other people do."

"I know that. I really do know that."

"Thanks," Casey said. Her chin was tilted down, and she shifted her gaze so it met Avery's. "That night at the Pub, I would have blown you off if your mom hadn't been there. I'm very good at acting like I don't see people who've hurt me."

"I'm *so* glad my mom was there."

"I am too. I was surprised by how much I liked talking to you, but I certainly didn't trust you. *That* took me a few months. After we met up again, that is. I hung in there, just waiting for you to do something cruel." A small smile grew brighter. "I'm very glad I waited around."

"And just how long would you have waited if Lisbet hadn't been in the picture?"

"Ten…fifteen minutes. Tops," she said, playfully trying to pull the bill from Avery's hand. But she gave up very quickly, stood, and held the chair as Avery got up.

Having Lisbet was fantastic in a hundred different ways, but the fact that the baby had kept Casey in the loop might have been one of her greatest, and hopefully most enduring feats.

Chapter Twenty-Five

ON THE FIRST DAY OF APRIL, Avery reached for the doorknob of her parents' house, looking up when it opened to Casey's smiling face, which was mirrored by Lisbet's. "Your mom's making meatloaf," Casey said. "She knows I can't resist."

"I feel very welcome," Avery said. "Two friendly faces smiling at me puts a good spin on a busy day." She reached for the baby and hugged her tightly. "I love my sweet girl," she said, kissing her while she babbled, still just hitting her consonants hard, with no indication she was ready to try for actual words.

Her mom's voice rang out from the kitchen. "If there are two baby sitters out there, one of them could come in here and make a salad."

"I'll let you have a minute with Lisbet," Casey said. "I'll take kitchen duty."

"It takes a village," Avery said. "Every kid should have at least four adults keeping an eye on her."

"Only four?" Casey asked, hurrying to the kitchen to lend a hand. "I think six is about right."

⤙⤚

Casey and Kathy were in the living room with the baby, with Avery and Ken cleaning up after dinner. Casey was meeting some of the guys for a beer, and she went into the kitchen to say goodnight, finding Avery leaning against the counter, texting.

"I thought you were helping," Casey said, whipping the phone from her hand and placing it on the counter.

"She's texting with her girlfriend," Ken said, with Avery taking her dish towel and snapping it against his arm. "She's as bad as she was in junior high."

"Is she on the phone with Faith again?" Kathy called out.

"She's my assistant," Avery said. "We've got a million things to accomplish."

Kathy entered the room, lightly holding Lisbet's hand. She grabbed the phone, blocking Avery from getting it back. "She's asking if you've ever been to Egypt, honey," she said, batting her eyes ingenuously. "Is that part of your summer program?"

Avery was clearly not angry, but she did look a little embarrassed. "I like her, okay? Forgive me for making a friend."

"Oh, I think it's cute," Kathy said, wrapping her free arm around her waist. "Except for Casey, I haven't watched you form a new friendship in years. But your father's right," she teased. "You're exactly like you were in junior high. Although you were talking on the phone back then, not typing constantly."

"So? Have you been to Egypt?" Casey asked, slipping the phone from Kathy's hand to give it back to Avery. "Your buddy wants to know."

"I haven't, but if I could tag along with Faith and her friends, I'd sign up in a minute."

"Her husband's not going?" Kathy asked.

"Nope. He doesn't like to travel. Faith has developed a network of friends who either don't have partners or have ones who don't like to travel. They've been everywhere," she said, sighing. "Wouldn't it be fun to travel with a group of friends?"

"Not really," Casey said, with both Kathy and Ken agreeing. "It's a pain in the butt just to get my co-workers to decide what bar to hang out in on Monday nights." She checked her watch. "Tonight I've got to hightail it over to Rhinebeck to act like I'm sampling beer for work." She ruffled Avery's hair, then did the same to Lisbet. "See you soon. Don't text so much your fingers hurt."

Lisbet looked up at Casey with an expectant expression.

"Got to go, baby," she said, waving.

Lisbet looked like she was about to cry, with her lip sticking out for a second. She pulled her hand away from her grandmother, then squatted down like she was going to crawl. But she changed her mind and kept much of her weight on her feet, while putting her hands in front of her. While they watched this new tactic, she rocked forward, shifting more weight onto her hands. Then she spread her feet a little wider apart, then stood all on her own—no pull-up this time. She wobbled a little for a second, looking slightly drunk, still staring at Casey. Then she yelled at her, nothing decipherable, but clearly expressing her displeasure with her attempts to leave.

"Do you want to go with me?" Casey asked, starting to back up.

Avery got into the game, squatting down next to the baby. "Casey's going home, Sweet Pea." She pulled her phone out, saying, "It's movie time. Let's put one foot in front of the other, sweetheart."

"Come with me," Casey said, bending over and taking a few more steps back.

"Go slow and keep taunting her. That sounds meaner than it is," Avery added, laughing. "I'll have to find a way to edit out my voice so she doesn't think I'm a jerk when we watch this years from now."

"Come on, Lisbet," Casey said, extending her hands. "You've got this."

She stuck her little hands out, kind of robot-like, and took one step. Everyone in the room held their breath as Lisbet's eyes got big when she realized she was going solo. Then her other foot lifted and touched the ground, toe first. As her heel lightly settled onto the floor the other foot lifted, then she knocked off another three quick steps before falling headfirst into Casey's arms.

"You did it!" she yelped, fighting to stop herself from crying. "You really walked!"

"My baby girl's turning into a big girl right before my eyes," Avery said, reaching up to wipe her eyes as well. She turned the phone around, clearly showing the tears. "Lisbet, when you're a little older and you watch this, I hope you can see how crazy we all are about you. You are one well-loved baby."

Casey kissed Lisbet's cheeks, then gave her a robust hug. "I'm texting Ben to tell him I'm going to be late. I can't leave when this little slugger learned to walk just to keep me here a little longer."

That Saturday afternoon, Casey was at Avery's house, babysitting while Avery was meeting with a writer all the way down in Peekskill. She had to travel a lot to meet with the people she was rounding up for the summer, but she seemed to get a real surge of creative energy from the whole process.

Lisbet was sleeping, taking an abnormally long nap, so Casey wandered around Avery's room, looking at the piles of short stories that had been pouring in. Avery had put out a call for submissions to all sorts of places, and was about to stumble from the weight of the response. But she had two interns in the city who helped pick the ones with potential, leaving Avery and Faith a smaller pile to get through.

They already had the big name writers for June, July and August, so they were now picking the second and third stories for each program. It didn't seem like it would be that hard to pick six stories, but Avery really labored over the process. Casey's admiration for her had grown even stronger when she'd seen what care she took in making the piles into smaller categories. Looking at the titles she'd written on 3x5 cards, she smiled. "Four stars; Three stars; Promising; Close—needs mentoring; Can't Be Fixed." Knowing Avery, she was going to figure out a way to get the people from at least two of those last three groups some help. She might not get it done this year, but she'd get it done. If there was one trait she had that never faltered, it was her tenacity.

Avery came home while Lisbet was still down. She came up the stairs quietly, not even making the top step squeak the way it normally did.

"How's it going?" she asked when she entered the room and shut the door. Then she walked over to the baby monitor and listened carefully while she kicked off her shoes.

"Good," Casey said, letting her gaze linger while Avery took off her sweater. She wasn't dressed up like she sometimes was, but she still looked really good, with a pair of slim-fit khakis and a tailored navy blue blouse with a geometric pattern. No matter what she wore, her breasts strained the seams of her clothing. Casey was sure that was temporary, but she was going to miss those full breasts when Lisbet finally stopped nursing. She'd never get to touch them, but just knowing they were there was pretty nice. When Avery looked up, she switched her attention to her phone, and started to make a note. "Hey, want to give me a hand?"

"Sure." Avery walked over to Casey, who was sitting at the desk. They'd gotten a little more comfortable with each other, and it wasn't odd to have Avery stand next to her and casually drape an arm across her shoulders. Well, it might have been casual for Avery, but Casey's skin tingled where that warm flesh touched her own. "What are you doing?"

"Typing up a list for Tara," she said. "Since she doesn't have any pregnant friends, she's flying blind. I thought I could make a list of all of the stuff you used a lot in the last year."

"So you don't want the goofy stuff I got at my shower? Like the very expensive dress Lisbet grew out of by the time she was a month old?"

"Just the important stuff," Casey said, with her thumbs hovering over the keyboard. "I don't think she's having a shower, so she's got to buy everything."

"No shower? Doesn't she have friends?"

"Yeah, she said she does, but…" She shrugged. "Her friends seem clueless. I'm going to take up a collection at Baby Brewers so we can buy her something big like a stroller or a crib."

"Of course you are," Avery said, gently stroking her hair. "I would expect nothing less."

Casey could feel her cheeks coloring from the compliment. "I feel bad for her. She thinks this is going to be a no-brainer."

"I can help out, too. Rebecca from work only took about half of Lisbet's things, since she had a family shower and a work shower. Ask Ben if he'd mind my passing on the infant seat he lent us. That was a lifesaver. Oh, and the knockoff floor chair I found at the resale shop. Lisbet's chubby legs can barely fit into it now."

"Thanks," Casey said, thinking Avery was every bit as generous as she was. She was just a little quiet about it.

The next morning, Casey tried to think of reasons to get up. She had things to do later in the day, but it was just ten a.m., and her dad was making a racket outside. She had no idea what he was doing, but she could tell he was using a gas-powered machine to do it. She let herself daydream about what it would be like to have the kind of relationship where they worked together on a project, but that wasn't going to happen, and she tried to push the thought from her mind.

Her phone rang and she picked it up. "Hey buddy. What's going on?"

"Baseball tryouts for a traveling team. Ghent. Benji asked me to invite you. We'll come by and pick you up."

"Right now?"

"About twenty minutes. Why? You busy?"

"I'm free until two. I'm still in bed, though. I'd have to shower and get some breakfast."

"Seriously? You're just waking up from last night? Damn it, Casey, sometimes I'm so jealous of you it makes me crazy."

"Don't be jealous of me." She laughed. "Well, I'm pretty awesome, so it makes sense that you would be. I'll be ready in fifteen," she said, hanging up before he could call her names.

As soon as they got to the field, Benji ran off with a kid he knew from school, leaving Ben and Casey to sit in the stands and watch. "Well, this is fun," she said. "Watching from such a distance I can barely tell which one he is."

"My life," he said, sighing. "And I'm still thinking about you sleeping until after ten. That really pisses me off. I haven't slept late for nine years."

"I was only kind of dozing when you called. Tara gave me a buzz earlier than she should have, and I talked to her for a long time."

"Uh-huh," Ben said, nodding. "You know, I used to believe you wanted a girlfriend, but you've changed my mind."

"Oh, please. I want a girlfriend more than you want to sleep late."

"Not buying it, Case. It's obvious you only want access to babies, and you're too lazy to get a woman pregnant yourself."

"Um, I know you're not intimately familiar with the lesbian reproductive system, but that's—"

"I mean you should find a girl, make her fall for you, then find the right sperm donor. Put in some work, you lazy wanker."

"Wanker?"

He laughed. "Julie loves some Netflix show about a bunch of English cops. We call each other wanker all the time now."

"Well, I admit I'm lazy, but I'm ready and willing to meet a woman who wants to have a baby. I just haven't met one, so I'm enjoying what I have."

"Which is what?"

"You know exactly what I've got," she said, tired of going over the details. "I'm secure in Lisbet's life, so now I don't technically have to find a woman who wants to give birth. That should make my girlfriend search easier."

"When's the last time you swiped right?"

"Um...a while," she admitted. "I haven't been in the mood, Ben, nor have I had much time. I've been playing hockey, bowling, going out with you wankers on Mondays, and softball's about to start."

"And the rest of the time you're with Lisbet...and her mother. Now you're going to have two more women you're tied—"

"One more," Casey corrected. "Tara's having a boy."

"Great. So you're going to have two lesbians who you don't date, and two babies you're not related to. You do know that Tara's going to be calling you every second to help her out, right?"

"No way! I talk to her maybe two or three times a week."

"She's still pregnant," Ben said, enunciating each word clearly. "Look at how much help Avery gets from her mom. You're going to be Tara's mom, so you'd better clear your schedule."

"No…" she said, then stopped abruptly, with her breath catching in her throat. "Oh, fuck. She really doesn't have anyone else."

"And you've got time, and interest, and experience. I know you, Casey. You don't get pulled into something easily, but once you do—you're all in. So if you don't want to be spending all of your free time with this woman, you'd better step back and take a look."

"Um, you know, maybe I should make this easier and take a look at Tara. As a girlfriend," she said, letting the image form in her head. "She's awfully young for me, but I had a very good connection with Jennifer, and she was almost twenty years older than I was…"

"Seriously? Why haven't you given me even a hint that you were interested in Tara?"

"Um, because I've kind of been thinking of her as a younger sister. But…" She let herself think of the progression of their interactions, realizing they'd grown more intense since Tara had started calling. "Maybe she's thinking the same thing."

"Has she said anything?"

"Not specifically. But she's dropped hints about me going over there to hang out. And she was going to be in Hudson the other day and said she might swing by…"

"Uh-huh. Get your head out of your butt, Casey. If you're into this woman for more than the baby she's carrying, do something about it. But if not, you'd better pull the emergency cord. Having two pretend babies at the same time will wear you out."

"One infant and one toddler," she said, like that made it better. She sucked in a breath. "Thanks for the slap in the face. I'll figure out what I want and what I think I can have."

"Hey," Ben said, looking at her very soberly. "Don't act like there are only two women in the Hudson Valley. Pick up your damn phone and look at some profiles. I know you're a catch, but women can't find you if you're holed up in your mom's garage."

"It was my dad's workshop, but I get your point. Now let's watch some little boys act like they're ready to take the field at Yankee Stadium. Look at that little joker," she said, pointing at a cocky looking kid who wore his hat just like the Yank's left fielder did. "If that kid's got a Lamborghini waiting in the parking lot, I wouldn't be surprised."

⌒

Casey didn't even have time for lunch, since the baseball players took forever to pack up their gear and get in the car. After Ben dropped her off, she drove over to Avery's and knocked on the front door. When there was no answer, she used her key to enter, calling up, "I let myself in."

"Thanks," Avery yelled back, having to amplify her voice to be heard over the baby's screaming. "Come on up if you dare."

When Casey stepped over the baby gate, she peered into Lisbet's room to see Avery still in her sweats, with a very unhappy child on the changing table, fighting against being diapered.

"Can you try to talk some sense into my daughter while I get dressed? She thinks she's toilet-trained, but I'm sure she's not. I'd really like her not to pee all over the furniture."

"Oh, nothing would soak into the pod," Casey teased. "You could blot it right up."

"Seriously. Will you take over?" Avery asked, looking like she was about to run out of patience. "We're an hour behind schedule."

"Sure. Sure. Go get ready. You don't mind if I use force, do you?"

She was teasing, but Avery paused just a second before saying, "Do what you've gotta do."

As she left the room, Casey reached over and grabbed one of the books on the dresser and fanned the baby with it. "Your face is as red as a beet, Lisbet. And you're a sweaty little mess. Your mommy's got work to do, baby girl. Come on now and give her a break."

Big blue eyes started to follow the book, with Lisbet's crying slowing until she sucked in a couple of deep, shaky breaths. Casey dried her eyes with a tissue, then started to put a clean diaper on. But the minute she had it secured, Lisbet scrunched up her eyes and peed up a storm. "You're just looking for trouble today, aren't you."

"Now what?" Avery asked. She'd put on a nice pair of jeans and a crisply ironed blue striped blouse, and was starting to put her earrings on.

"The second I got the diaper on, she let loose."

Avery put her hand on Lisbet's forehead, then shook her head. "I think she's getting another tooth, but she's not feverish." She took a look at her phone. "I'd cancel, but I'm supposed to be at Faith's in a half hour. Since she's serving tea, I can't stand her up…"

"Get going. We'll be fine."

"But I was going to feed her," Avery sighed. "Her schedule is completely screwed up because I let her sleep so late." She looked up at Casey and smiled. "She must take after you, since she wants to stay in bed until nine on Saturday. How she knows it's Saturday is beyond me, but it's been a trend."

"Okay… How about this? We'll drive you, and you can pump in the car. I'll feed her a bottle when we get there."

"Then what? I need to spend a couple of hours with Faith. We're making our final cuts today."

"We'll come back and get you. Lisbet always loves to go for a ride, right? And I'd rather have her happy than crying, which she'll do if you leave when she's in this mood."

"You really don't mind?" She looked like she truly wanted to accept the offer, but knew she shouldn't.

"I really don't mind. Go put some shoes on and I'll get her ready."

"Ooo. You're the best." As she left the room, she added, "Bring her new dress, okay? Faith's never met her, and I don't want Lisbet to look like she lives in a dumpster."

Casey looked down at the baby, with her beet and carrot stained T-shirt, red-rimmed eyes and dripping nose. The fact that her wispy hair stuck up like she'd been rubbing a balloon over it didn't help one bit. "That's not going to be an easy task, but we'll try, huh?"

Casey was very glad Avery was in the back with the baby, since she didn't think she'd be able to avert her eyes if she was pumping right next to her. Casey had done her best to remove Avery from her collection of people she fantasized about. While she hadn't been completely successful, she still didn't want her permanently knocked out of the image-bank because of suction cups attached to her nipples. There had to have been people who got off on images of women pumping, but she was definitely not one of them.

The directions to Faith's house were pretty clear, and they were only a few minutes late when they pulled up in front of a very impressive home. "Jesus," Casey murmured, taking in the stately, two story home, perfectly situated on the property. "Does she own a bank?"

"I don't think so. In fact, I got the impression much of their money came from selling an apartment they owned in the city. A three-bedroom in Manhattan bought this house and paid for a gut renovation. Crazy, huh?"

"Timing is everything," Casey said. "And her timing was awesome."

"Oh. Oh. She's coming out," Avery said. "I don't want her to see Lisbet looking so rough."

"Go play with your friend," Casey said, finding it utterly adorable that this was the first time she'd ever seen Avery truly flustered. "I'll let Lisbet snack on her veggies, then give her a bottle. After she pees, I'll change her, put her new spring dress on, and bring her in when she's presentable. Go. Go," she urged, laughing when Avery leapt out of the car without even saying goodbye. "Your mommy's got a crush on that lady, Lisbet. And after we're all cleaned up, we're going to meet her."

⌒

Avery resisted the urge to push Faith back into her house. Instead, she tried to appear like a normal human being when she intercepted her on the steps, saying, "Our schedule was a mess today. The baby's hungry and fussy, so Casey's going to feed her, then she'll bring her in so you can meet."

"Have them come in now," Faith said. "I didn't know I'd have the pleasure of meeting your baby as well as your support team, but now that I have the chance…"

"She'll come in," Avery said. "But it's better if they stay right where they are until Casey's fed her. By the time we drag all of the paraphernalia in, Lisbet will be wild from hunger. My Sweet Pea cannot bear to miss a meal."

"Oh, but I feel like a terrible host to let a guest sit outside in a truck, Avery."

"Please don't give it another thought. Knowing how Lisbet is feeling today, it might take Casey an hour to feed and change her, and we don't have that much time to spare. We've got twenty submissions to discuss, and I need to send out acceptance letters this week. June will be here before we know it."

It took Avery a little while to get over worrying about Casey fighting with Lisbet in the backseat of the truck, but she was utterly confident of her skills. She just hoped Casey had some earplugs in the glove box in case Lisbet had another meltdown.

Once she'd cleared her mind, they got rolling, whipping through half of the pile in an hour. Out of the ten stories they'd discussed, they had three they felt were worthy of inclusion, and another one that could make it if the writer was willing to change some key elements. Given they only needed six pieces, total, Avery was feeling great about the process.

They'd been concentrating so hard they both needed a break, so Faith got up to make tea, with Avery following along down the hallway, idly looking at family photos as she moved along. They'd just reached the kitchen when Avery heard a soft knock at the door. "I think my grouchy baby's here," she said. "Want me to get it?"

"I'll come with you," Faith said. "Meeting babies is much more fun than making tea."

Faith opened the substantial black door, and Avery found herself grinning at the very attractive people who stood on the landing. Lisbet was wearing not only a curious smile, she had on her new dress, one Freya had brought back from a recent trip to France. The fabric was beautiful, a very tiny print in spring colors, decorated with a white collar. Avery planned on letting Lisbet wear the dress only when she wasn't going to be anywhere near food, which wasn't very often these days.

"Oh, my goodness," Faith said. "It's so nice to meet both of you." She extended her hand. "Faith Pallone," she said. "I've heard so many lovely things about you, Casey. Avery never stops singing your praises."

"She does the same for you," Casey said, looking a little shy. They'd been so rushed that Avery had barely noticed Casey back at the house, but seeing her from a new perspective let her realize she'd gotten dressed up.

Normally, she stopped by the house right after work, which meant she was almost always dusty and often sweaty. Her clothing usually looked like it had been clean that morning, but by the end of the day it was clear she didn't sit around an office very often.

This afternoon, she'd put on some dark jeans, and had rolled the cuffs up to show her cool brown boots, a mix of leather and suede, which were intentionally unlaced, and a hint of the grey wool socks she favored. The jeans and boots made her look like she was ready to go hunting or trapping in the wilderness, which was strangely alluring.

In keeping with her never wearing what Avery thought was a warm enough coat, her jacket was more of a shirt, a wool, black and white plaid that covered a black turtleneck.

Casey probably didn't realize this, but she looked like the lumbersexuals Avery still spotted around Williamsburg. Guys with beards, flannel shirts, and stiff-looking jeans, who carried Mac Airs in their rucksacks rather than axes. But she was certain Casey wasn't imitating anyone. She'd probably still be dressing like this in ten years, but, knowing her, she'd also rock a sexy swimsuit every once in a while, just because she was in the mood.

Somehow, she'd gotten Lisbet clean, but the greater accomplishments were that her hair was neatly combed, and she was beaming a smile. As Faith reached out to take the baby in her arms, her grin got even bigger, showing her tiny teeth, which now totaled six.

"Oh, my god, Avery. Lisbet is a carbon copy of you!"

"I don't really see it," she admitted, "But my mom agrees with you, and she has the proper perspective."

"You see the resemblance, don't you, Casey?" Faith asked.

Casey shot Avery a glance, then nodded. "It's clearer every day. But Avery's mom's just as pretty, and I think the baby takes after both of them. They all hit the lucky number in the genetics lottery."

"Come in, come in," Faith insisted. "We're standing out here like it's the middle of summer."

"We just stopped by to say hi," Casey said. "We thought we'd go for a drive until Avery's finished."

"Why don't you stay here?" Faith carried Lisbet to the back of the house, speaking to Casey as if she were an old friend. She held her hand out, pointing. "I don't mean to subvert your plans, but that path leads down to the lake. Kids love it."

"Mmm," Casey stood by the large window, gazing at the path. "Lisbet's at the age where she doesn't have the sense not to jump in. I'd be arguing with her the whole time." She gazed across the back yard, clearly assessing it. "But she'd be very happy playing on your lawn. She's gotten interested in plants lately."

"By all means," Faith said. "We were just about to have tea. I made some savory scones and a lemon pound cake. Will you join us?"

Showing a charming grin, Casey said, "We'll disturb you too much. But I'd love a piece of cake when you've finished talking."

"We'll save you a big slice," Faith said. "Now will you be warm enough? There's a chill in the air."

"I'm fine, but I'm going to change Lisbet before I let her roll around in the grass. Her party dress was a gift, and we don't want to get dirt on it before she's even had her picture taken."

"A wise woman," Faith said.

"Wise, and thoughtful, and always prepared," Avery added, hoping her smile conveyed how grateful she was.

The kitchen, which was a showplace, had a high counter that ran along two walls of windows that looked out on the yard, as well as the picturesque lake hidden behind tall fir trees. At least Avery hoped it stayed hidden. Casey had been right. The baby was at the perfect age to demand access to things far beyond her capabilities. Avery could just see her trying to walk right into the ice cold water, with Casey having to put up with the crying that would ensue when she was stopped.

She and Faith sat at the counter, sipping tea while they ate the delicious scones. "I haven't had a scone this good in months," Avery said. "I miss them."

"They're not hard to make. Would you like the recipe?"

"Sure. As long as the first instruction is 'wait until your child is in high school…'"

Faith laughed. "Oh, that's the critical bit, isn't it? My girls were only eighteen months apart, so I'd hazard a guess that I didn't have a minute to myself for the first three years of their lives. I guarantee there were no scones being made back then."

"I shiver at the thought, but I have what is probably an irrational wish to have a second baby. Not now, of course, but in a year or two. I'd always hoped for two, and I've been lulled into the likely misguided belief that two wouldn't be much harder than one."

"That's…vaguely true," Faith said, smiling indulgently. "My mother told me to not have more children than I had hands, and that turned out to be good advice. I'm glad I had two, although if I had to do it over again, I'd pick a man who wanted to be more involved with childrearing."

"Your husband wasn't…"

"Oh, Oscar's a wonderful man, and he wanted the children as much, if not more, than I did. But once the girls arrived, he acted like a father from the previous generation. My girls had a fifties childhood in many ways, even though they were born in the eighties."

"Mmm. Is that why you stopped writing?"

"Precisely. It wasn't a choice, Avery. It was a necessity."

"Oh, my. That must have been…"

"It was a difficult time. We didn't have the funds for a full-time babysitter, and I didn't want to leave the girls with someone I didn't know well. I kept thinking I'd have more time as they got older, but I found myself getting involved with their schools, and their clubs, and their sports."

"I've never even thought about having to do that," Avery said, with a chill of dread crawling up her spine. "But I'm sure I'll have to."

"I shouldn't say this," Faith whispered like she was revealing a dark secret, "but discourage your little one from playing sports. Alissa played field hockey through college, and I spent most weekends traveling across the tri-state area to watch her compete."

"Oh, god, don't even suggest that!"

"She loved it, but watching children play a sport is not on the list of things I find thrilling." She laughed slyly. "I'd never tell her that, of course, but I was very glad to pack her off to Virginia for college. If I never see another field hockey game, I will not shed a tear."

"Well, I began the day thinking I'd like to have two kids, and now I want to give the one I have away just in case she takes up a sport. Thanks for nothing, Faith!"

"Ooo, you have nothing to worry about. If you keep Casey in your life, she'll go to the matches. You can be like my Oscar, idly asking if I'd had fun shivering in the cold in the Bronx while he sat in his study, sipping tea while thinking deep thoughts." She pointed at Casey, who was holding Lisbet up to inspect a bud on a tree. "That is a patient woman," she said, with Avery able to detect the respect she already had for Casey.

"I used to think I was patient, but she has me beat. Just this afternoon I was on the verge of losing my temper when Lisbet was being a real pain. But Casey got her calmed down, and now she's back to her normal angelic self."

"Mmm-mmm," she said, shaking her head. "If I'd had Casey around when I was considering babies, I might have figured out some way to make myself into a decent lesbian." She laughed, throwing her head back and really letting a good one out. "I'd probably be awful at it, but having a supportive partner would have made me give it my all."

She continued to watch Casey, clearly fascinated by the way she cared for Lisbet. "I remember Oscar changing four or five diapers—total. He botched them so badly, probably intentionally, that I forbade him from doing another. The thought of him taking one of the girls on his own? Never," she said, shaking her head. "He's turned out to be a wonderful partner now that it's just the two of us, but I spent many a night wishing I'd picked a pediatrician or a social worker—anyone who didn't think babies were more complex than particle physics." She patted Avery on the shoulder when she went to heat more water for tea. "If I were you, I'd marry that woman."

As she walked away, Avery forced herself to look at Casey clearly. Not as Lisbet's babysitter, but as a woman. It wasn't her patience or her kindness or her ability to charm Lisbet out of a cranky mood that made her so damned appealing. Well, it was partially those things, but only because they were a few of the elements that made her such a wonderful person.

Her patience and kindness weren't limited to babies, since she was just as giving with not only Avery, but nearly everyone she encountered. Casey was a fantastic person in nearly every way.

She could feel a trickle of sweat start to roll down her back, and knew her face had become flushed. She'd been fully cognizant that she'd had a crush on Casey for months, but she'd convinced herself she was solely interested in her body. Now she had to admit that noticing that big, blue truck parked by the house perked up her whole day, and she had to acknowledge that she'd started to leave her house earlier and earlier, just to be with her for a little longer.

Her head was spinning by the time Faith sat down with hot cups of tea. "Avery?" she said softly. "Are you all right?"

"How…how do you make it with someone you don't have much in common with?" she blurted out, unable to make her mouth behave.

Faith gave her a sly smile and put a hand on her back, leaning close to speak conspiratorially. "Even though Oscar wasn't the partner I needed when the girls were small, one of the things that makes our relationship good now is how different we are."

"Really?" Avery cocked her head. "But doesn't...isn't one of the things that brings you together your shared love of...whatever?"

"It can be, but it can also make you feel like you're looking in a mirror. Goodness knows I have a healthy self-image, but I'm not interested in being with someone like me. I want someone who lets me see a different world."

"But I've always thought I'd wind up with someone like me. My long-term girlfriend and I agreed on nearly everything. And it made things so... easy," she said softly.

"But you're not together now, Avery. That must mean at least one of you didn't think things were so easy."

"We'd..." She swallowed nervously, having talked about this with very few people. But Faith was such a good listener that she felt safe with her. "We'd lost the spark. For the last couple of years we were together we were more roommates than lovers. I still loved her, and I think she was still in love with me, but when someone new arrived on the scene, she went for the person who brought that spark back to life."

"An all-too-common event. Of course, that could have happened in any situation. But for me, part of sexual attraction is the new, the unexplored, the parts you don't, and probably can't understand."

"Really? You like not understanding your partner well?"

"I do. There's definitely some risk, or maybe even fear involved in choosing someone unlike yourself. You truly can't know what's in their brain." Her smile grew when she said, "I know as much about physics as Oscar knows about infants, or writing, for that matter. But I love hearing him talk about his work, and he's interested in how I spend my days. That's all you need, Avery. Someone who's interested in what interests you. Someone who never dismisses your passion. I suppose it would be nice if they shared it, but that's simply not a requirement. So long as they find *you* fascinating, and you feel the same about them, you're set." She patted her back firmly. "If you and Casey have that, lock that woman down, as the kids say."

"I'm very fond of her," she insisted, "but I've always been attracted to feisty people. You know that type. If you say it's a nice day, they talk about the storm that's heading your way." She swallowed. "That's always been the thing that creates sparks for me."

"And Casey doesn't feel strongly about things?"

Avery started to shake her head, then she stopped. "She feels very strongly about Lisbet, and maybe me. I thought we were going to have to move to Brooklyn, and she got so upset I didn't recognize her…"

"Mmm. A woman who'd fight to keep you close?" One of her thin, gray eyebrows rose. "You might be more attracted to someone who likes to argue about the weather, but I'd rather have someone who'd only waste her energy fighting for the important things—like me."

"I…" She found her attention pulled to the back yard, where she watched Casey lying on what had to be cold stones, holding Lisbet up so she could fly, with both of them laughing their heads off.

Faith touched her again, and she turned to look at her. "I'm certainly not telling you who you should be attracted to, but if you don't want to lose Casey, don't ever let my Alissa meet her. She's desperate for exactly what you have right there."

⌒

On the way home, Avery idly played with Lisbet's hair, smoothing it down as she thought. She'd been a very poor conversationalist, but that was because she hadn't been able to get her brain to accept the revelation she'd had with Faith.

She and Casey had tentatively renewed their connection over two and a half years earlier, and had been in constant contact for ten months. That was more than enough time to build a baby from scratch. If they were meant for each other, why had neither of them taken a step?

When she thought of the night Casey had given her pity sex, Avery kept coming back to some of the details which were permanently etched in her brain. Casey had told her in very clear terms that Avery turned her on. She'd even said that any woman would be lucky to have her. While she'd claimed she was just talking dirty, Avery wasn't sure about that. Casey wasn't much of a bullshitter, so there was a very good chance she'd been telling the truth. But if she *had* been turned on, why hadn't she tried to go further?

Taking a peek at Casey in the rearview mirror, Avery was sure she knew the answer. The ball had been in her court, not Casey's. She could have, she *should* have turned around and kissed the hell out of her. The evening would have gone from pity sex to awesomeness if she hadn't been so... She wasn't even sure how to characterize her mental state that night, but she had not been confident enough to make a blatant pass.

So the ball might still be in her court, even though it had lost some of its bounce from sitting out in the cold all winter. The question was, what to do now?

As always, she tried to reason things out. She didn't often give into her instincts, but it was a strong one that dreamed about putting Lisbet to bed, closing her door, then pulling Casey into her room to make love to her until dawn. But giving in to that instinct scared the shit out of her. The urge to leave Hudson had been very strong just a couple of months earlier, and she would never play with Casey's heart if she wasn't certain she would be able to stay right where she was.

Since she was engaging in every form of fantasy, she let herself imagine Casey moving to Brooklyn with them, but that thought only lasted for a moment. Casey wouldn't be happy there. That was the kicker. Asking someone to follow you when you knew they'd be miserable wasn't a loving act, and she never wanted to be less than loving with Casey. While she was a very strong, very independent woman, her soul was gentle, almost fragile.

Avery had spaced out, not noticing Lisbet had dropped the toy she'd been gnawing on until she made a funny noise, like she was really saying something in another language.

Casey looked in the mirror, meeting Avery's eyes. "Was it just me, or did that gibberish sound a little more like a word?"

"It did," Avery said. "I was just thinking that." She took her seatbelt off to lean over and get the toy, with Lisbet grabbing it and biting down hard. "She's clearly teething. I hope it's not another long night."

"I don't have anything going on. We'll tag-team her."

"I could make dinner…"

"Can you?" She smiled into the mirror. "I've cooked for you, but you've never cooked for me."

"I can definitely cook. Lisbet's into elbow macaroni, peas, bits of chicken, and beets these days. She'll accept a bite of a turkey meatball, but it's not her favorite. How's that for a meal?" Before Casey could respond, she amended the offer. "I'm in the mood for spaghetti. What do you think?"

"Perfect. Need anything from the store?"

"I don't think so. I froze some sauce a while ago, and it's pretty good, if I do say so myself."

"I don't doubt that for a minute," Casey said, giving her a fond smile. "I can't see you cooking if you weren't going to do it right."

She continued to sneak glances at Casey while thinking about their possible future. If the first summer of *Hudson Valley Short Shorts* went well, Helena would definitely want to keep it going. With an interesting new project, and near-total control, Avery's job was fun again. As fun as it had been when she'd first started *Short Shorts*. But Helena couldn't afford to keep it going if they didn't sell tickets.

Since Helena had been hinting around about how the original *Short Shorts* had been coasting for the last few months, Avery knew she'd have to go back to Brooklyn to really manage it if she wasn't needed full-time in the Hudson Valley. Then what? That would be a real kick in the teeth to decide to stay, only to *have* to leave.

Her stomach hurt from mulling these unanswerable questions over, but she thought she'd be able to make some decisions by the end of the summer. Then she'd know if HVSS would continue to get funding, and she'd have spent a whole year back home. That was plenty of time to know if she could make a commitment—a permanent one—to Casey as well as to the Hudson Valley. She idly played with Lisbet while watching the back of Casey's head, which she found nearly as interesting as her face. Either she was really falling for her, or she'd lost her friggin' mind.

⌒

They had to eat in shifts, since Lisbet had once again turned into a little monster once they'd gotten home. It truly didn't happen often, and Avery was very aware of how lucky she was to have such a low-stress baby. But sometimes it took every bit of her patience to stay calm when Lisbet was losing her shit.

Casey had eaten first, then she'd taken over to allow Avery to gulp down some lukewarm spaghetti. Now Casey was upstairs, and Avery could hear her soft, rhythmic footsteps pacing back and forth across Lisbet's floor. The crying had nearly stopped, with only an occasional burst of emotion from the baby. Avery wasn't sure where the soft music she heard came from, but after she'd cleaned the kitchen and washed the dishes, she went up to investigate.

Only one dim light was on, and as Avery peeked into the room she saw Casey holding the baby against her shoulder, the way Lisbet had liked to be held when she was tiny. Casey wasn't exactly dancing, but she was definitely moving rhythmically to put the baby to sleep. Lisbet's eyes were closed, and she looked a little limp, but she'd had a burst of tears just a few minutes earlier, so she might not have been fully out.

Casey caught sight of Avery and put a finger to her lips.

Quietly, Avery entered the room to check, putting her hand on Casey's back to hold her still. But Casey kept moving, giving Avery a playful grin. "Can't stop," she whispered. "You've got to go with us."

Smiling at her, Avery settled her arm around Casey's waist and let her lead. It was one of the most intimate moments they'd ever shared, which was odd, given they'd kind of had sex. But working to put your baby to sleep with a woman who cared for her as much as Casey did touched her heart so deeply she was afraid she'd burst into tears.

Casey was strong enough to hold Lisbet close with one arm, and she slid the other around Avery, creating a little cocoon. They were all wrapped around each other, with Lisbet sighing deeply as she cuddled harder against Casey, with Avery gently scratching her back.

The music from Casey's phone was a surprising mix of soft, soothing, symphonic pieces. Avery had recognized a bit of Bach, and now a Brahms lullaby was softly playing. Avery had never heard Casey play classical music, but knowing her, she'd downloaded it for its baby-soothing properties. That's just the thoughtful kind of thing she'd do.

As they moved about the room, Avery felt as peaceful as she could ever recall being. Or maybe the better word was contented. She could do this all night long, basking in the peace of holding her daughter and the woman she was truly and deeply fascinated by.

CHAPTER TWENTY-SIX

AVERY WAS SO BUSY ONCE they were deep into April that she literally didn't have time to stop and smell the flowers. But when she looked out the window of her bedroom one morning, she realized the trees were so leafed out they were beginning to block the view of the houses in the distance.

She didn't have time to consider her view for long. It was just six thirty, but Lisbet was already stirring. She was waking earlier, and going to bed a little later, now not ready to relax until almost eight. When Avery went into the room, Lisbet was lying on her belly, kicking her feet up into the air one at a time. The first time Avery had seen her flipped over she'd nearly fainted, but a frantic call to the pediatrician had assured her that since Lisbet could easily roll over, and roll back, and that her neck and shoulder muscles were strong, the risk of SIDS from lying on her stomach was greatly reduced. Given that Avery had always been a stomach-sleeper herself, it made some sense that the baby liked it that way too.

She was just about to pick her up when she heard a noise in the driveway. Casey's big truck was cruising down the drive, and Avery took her phone from the pocket of her robe and called her. "What's up?" she asked.

"I wanted to pick the stuff up for Tara's shower. I assumed you'd be up. Was I right?"

"No problem. You've got your key, don't you?"

"As always. Go about your business. You left everything downstairs, right?"

"Uh-huh. Everything Lisbet has outgrown is in the living room. I had to put it in trash bags, since I didn't have any boxes."

"Not a problem. I'll have time to find some boxes at work to make it look a little festive. I'm in," she said, with Avery able to hear her moving around downstairs. "You don't have to come down."

"Okay. The baby's just waking up. I'll let her go at her own pace."

"Just make sure she's ready to party," Casey said, chuckling. "This will be her first baby shower."

"I'll make sure she's ready to rock and roll. See you later."

After hanging up, Avery sat in the rocker and slipped her hand between the crib rails, reaching in to gently pat Lisbet's back. While she was glad her mother and Casey were going so far out of their way to set Tara up with clothing, an infant seat, a floor chair, and even a stroller, she felt like the two of them talked about Tara nonstop. Given she'd never met the woman, that was beginning to get old.

She put her hand on Lisbet's head, smoothing down the few long strands of her mostly wispy hair. "Tell your mommy to stop being such a whiner, will you? Casey's helping out a young woman who has no idea what she's getting into, and a nice person would be touched by her generosity." She patted the baby again when she stretched and shivered. "That's my girl. Time to wake up, sleepy-head. You're going to go to your first big party today. Just please don't throw a fit when you realize I've given almost all of your toys away. We'll replace them, one at a time. Or maybe we'll do what Casey says to do and just give you boxes to play in. The world could use a lot less plastic, you know."

At dinner that night, Avery cooked while her mom and Casey sat at the kitchen table, regaling her with Baby Brewers gossip. It was hard to keep up, since Avery hadn't been able to attend a single meeting, so she didn't have faces to go with the names. But they seemed like a very tight-knit group. She wasn't sure how Tara would fit in, given that the others seemed to regard her as a child, but they'd probably start treating her differently once she gave birth.

"So? Was Tara thrilled by all of the presents you two brought?"

"We just gave her hand-me-downs," her mom said. "Well, Casey bought her something, but the rest of us just loaded her up with everything we weren't using any longer."

"What did you buy her, Casey?"

She slid off her chair to hold Lisbet's shape-sorting box. The baby loved to play with it very roughly, and it drove her crazy when she had to chase it around the room.

Casey shrugged, looking, to Avery's eye, a little embarrassed. "I spent some time looking on the internet, and I got a couple of things I thought she might not know about."

"Like...?"

"Um, I got her a nice nursing pillow, and three swaddling wraps. Thin ones for summer."

"Three?" Avery asked, turning to meet her gaze.

"One to use, one in the laundry, and one for emergencies. Lisbet was already six months old when I met her, but she was still spitting up a lot. I assume that's worse when they're right out of the oven." She smiled, looking up at Avery. "I can't wait to find out."

"Tara hit the lottery when she showed up at Baby Brewers," Avery said, unable to observe the goofy look on Casey's face for another second. Lisbet wasn't even able to speak yet, and Casey was throwing her over for the new kid in town.

⸺

Casey was goofing off on Saturday afternoon, trying to decide how to spend her evening. She had a couple of options, but the most attractive one was to go down to East Fishkill with some of her co-workers to check out a brewery that had just relocated to a former IBM factory. But even though she wanted to go, she didn't want to drive. Part of the fun of going to a brewery was hanging out in the tasting room, but drinking and driving didn't mix. She was tempted to ask Avery to go, and drive, but that hardly seemed fair. Avery really liked beer, and had a pretty well-developed appreciation of it. Visiting a tasting room would be a lot more fun when someone else drove, but she didn't know anyone who'd be up for it except Kathy, and the poor woman deserved a night off.

Her other option was to go to a birthday party for a woman she'd known in college. That had the potential of being fun, but she only knew the guest of honor. While she wasn't shy, she didn't always like being around a large group of strangers. So going to the brewery with her work friends might be more fun, even if she had to make a single pint last all night.

It was only four, so she had time to make up her mind. Heading back to bed, she found the audio book of short stories by Lorrie Moore that Avery had lent her. She was about halfway through one of her favorites when her phone rang. Not many people called, so she took a peek at the display, seeing it was Tara. She answered quickly. "Hi, there. You don't have a baby yet, do you?"

"God, no. Don't rush me. Even though I'm ready to not be pregnant, I'm not ready to have a baby in the house."

"I think they come when they come, but I'm sure you're up to the challenge."

"Maybe. But I'm not up to assembling the crib I bought."

"You're not?" Casey teased. "A lesbian who can't use a ratcheting screwdriver? Are you sure you're gay?"

"I'm as gay as they come. But the UPS guy was sweating when he got the thing into the apartment. It weighs a hundred and seven pounds, and he had to wrestle it up the stairs all alone. When he got to my apartment, he dropped it flat on the floor, and I can't even get it onto its side."

"I'll swing by and give you a hand. I don't have anything planned for tomorrow."

"Ahh...don't worry about it. If I still need help, I'll give you a call."

"Um, why wouldn't you need help?"

She laughed a little. "Because I'm going to do it myself. I might not be able to get up once I get down on the floor, but my apartment isn't very big, and it annoys me to have this huge thing taking up most of my living room."

Casey smiled, thinking that was exactly how she'd be if she were in the same situation. "What are you doing right now?"

"Now? I'm trying to convince myself to ignore this huge box. Why?"

"Because I can come over now, but I've got to be somewhere at seven. Text me your address. I'll be there in a half hour."

"Ooo, now I feel like I guilt-tripped you into helping."

"You did," Casey said, chuckling. "But I don't mind. Text me that address, and stay off the floor!"

Tara lived on the other side of the Hudson, so Casey had to cross the Rip Van Winkle to get to the west side of the river. But she didn't have to backtrack too much, and was at Tara's apartment complex by five. After buzzing at the entry gates, Tara's voice came over the intercom, then the gate opened slowly. The complex looked pretty nice, and was brand new. But Casey knew enough about construction to assume they'd slapped it together quickly and cheaply. If the walls were as poorly insulated as she guessed, the neighbors would go through the pain of the baby's infanthood with none of the pleasure.

She took the stairs up to the second floor, then turned left when Tara opened her door.

"Hi there," Casey said, starting to laugh when she had to jump over a huge box that lay on the floor. "Seriously? The guy just dropped it here and took off?"

"He didn't drop it, exactly. He pushed it. I don't think he could carry it another inch, so he shoved it over the threshold and ran away before I could say a word."

"I thought people went out of their way to be nice to pregnant women." She took a look at Tara's belly, which had turned ginormous in the last month. "Maybe he couldn't tell."

"Not funny! Didn't anyone ever tell you pregnant women were emotional messes? You don't want to make me cry."

"No, I really don't," Casey said, gentling her voice. "I want to give you a hand. I brought a few tools, so let me get right to it."

"Do you need help? I'm very good at reading instruction booklets."

Casey put her fingertips under the box and picked it up an inch. Then she slid her hands underneath and gave it a yank. "Whoa!" she said, nearly losing it. "Heavy!"

"I told you what it weighed." She pointed at the label on the side, colored a very bright safety orange. "What do you think 'exceeds one hundred pounds' means?"

"I think it means it's heavy," Casey admitted. "But the arrows clearly say to open it on the side, and I thought it would be easier to cut the box open when I had some leverage." She pulled out her utility knife and carefully cut along the seam. "Yes, I'm being careful," she said. "I can see the other sign saying not to use a knife. But I'm not going to pry those staples off. That'll take forever." She lowered the box back to the floor and slit it down both sides. "Wa la," she said as she pulled the top away.

"Ooo. You speak French," Tara teased.

Casey stared at her for a minute. "That's French?"

"Um, yeah. What did you think—"

"Huh." She put her hands on her hips, thinking. "I thought it was some kind of nonsense word. How do you spell it?"

"V-o-i-l-a."

Casey started to laugh. "Are you shitting me? There's a 'V'? I thought it was w-a-l-a. I'm glad I've never had to write that down at work. My crew doesn't need any more ammo to tease me with."

"Spelling's kind of hard," Tara said. "We've got too many other languages we borrowed from."

Laughing again, Casey said, "Avery says English is three languages stacked on top of each other, wearing a trench coat so they look like one." Still chuckling to herself, she took out the instructions, just one sheet, with no words, just basic diagrams with each part labeled by number. "If you can tell me which part goes where, we'll have this thing whipped into shape in no time."

"I think I can," Tara said. She stuck the tip of her tongue out, which made her look like a pre-schooler who was trying to teach herself to read.

Casey watched her for a minute, having never spent much time just checking her out. But it was impossible not to notice how cute Tara was. Not in a brainy, sexy, maternal way like Avery, of course. More of a sporty lesbian who'd pop out a kid, then get right back to softball practice. Tara's kind of androgyny had always been a turn-on for Casey, and she had to remind herself that gawping at an eight-months-pregnant woman was kind of pervy. She wasn't really sure why she thought that, though. Maybe nature gave you a built-in aversion to mixing sexy thoughts with pregnant women.

She watched Tara figuring out the diagram, and tried to imagine what she'd looked like pre-pregnancy. Casey noticed some framed photos on the wall, and moved over to check them out. *Yup.* There was a good shot of Tara whipping a ball across the infield. She didn't look like anyone's mama when she was hiking up a pretty impressive hill, wearing just a sports bra and really short shorts. But she was going to be someone's mom in just a couple of weeks, and that baby needed a bed, or he'd be sleeping in a cardboard box in the middle of the floor.

⌣

It took nearly an hour to get the right dowels into the right holes, tighten up fourteen screws, and check the whole thing for any rough spots or weaknesses. "Now all you need is a mattress. Sold separately, of course."

"It'll be here on Monday. And I'm going to try to talk the delivery guy into putting it into the crib. I'll work on looking helpless."

"He won't buy it," Casey said. "You look super confident."

"Depends on the day," she said, shrugging as she blushed slightly. "How about dinner? I was going to make myself some macaroni and cheese, and I'll have plenty to go around."

"Um..." Casey didn't really have a good reason to refuse, so she nodded. "Sure. That'll be nice. I'm going to check out a brewery later, but I don't have to be on time."

"Great!" Tara gave her such a big smile Casey felt bad for even thinking about refusing. "Come on into the kitchen."

"I think I'll move the crib into the bedroom first. Do you know where you want it?"

"There isn't a lot of room in my bedroom, so…wherever it fits. Need me to help push?"

"Nah. You'll be pushing soon enough. I can handle it."

Tara patted her on the back, then left to make dinner. The crib didn't fit easily into the room, since it was only about ten by twelve, but if Tara only used the left side of her bed, she'd be fine.

When Casey went into the kitchen, Tara was making a white sauce. There were two stools near a breakfast bar, and Casey pulled one out to sit. "Have you been cooking a lot?"

"Pretty much. It's a lot less expensive, and I can usually eat more balanced meals if I cook at home. Not that macaroni and cheese is very healthy, but I had nothing but vegetables for lunch."

"I think you're doing great. Not many people I know would take on this responsibility alone. I hope you're proud of yourself."

"Eh…" She shrugged. "To be honest, I should have worked harder on getting my parents to come around. They were just starting to get used to me being gay, then I did this." She turned and showed a sad smile. "My timing kind of sucked, but I'm not great at waiting."

"I'm the same way. That trait has come back to bite me in the butt a few times, but I can't say it's taught me patience."

"You know, I've got a friend who's my birth coach," she said, having turned around to stir the sauce again, "but the people at the hospital suggested I have a back-up. I was going to ask my mom, but I'm sure she'd refuse." She looked over her shoulder and briefly met Casey's eyes. "Any chance you'd…"

"Me? A birth coach?" Casey was staring at her, trying to figure out what signals she'd given off to make Tara think they were that close.

"Well, my friend Gretchen would be the one doing the job. You'd just be a backup if she was sick or something…" She took in a long breath. "Um, I know we're not that close, Casey, but I kind of thought we might get closer."

She was studiously stirring the sauce, and Casey could see that the back of her neck had gotten pink. *Shit!* She got up and walked over to stand next to the stove so Tara had to look at her. "Do you mean romantically?"

"Um...maybe? Bad idea?" She looked up at Casey, and for just a second she could imagine herself slipping right into Tara's life. She was kind of perfect in a lot of ways; attractive, independent, confident, and a jock. Casey had noticed she didn't have books lying around the house, having filled her bookcases with everything from roller blades to ski boots. Dating a fellow jock would be kind of awesome. Not to mention getting in on the ground floor of baby creation. She'd always been fascinated by the birth process, and getting to see it up close and personal was damned tempting.

But then she thought of Avery, who was unlike Tara in almost every way. But Casey couldn't even try to argue that she wasn't fascinated by her. Avery had cast her spell early on, and Casey hadn't been able to resist it, even though she hadn't had the nerve to put herself out there and ask for what she wanted.

It made no damn sense, but Avery was the one. Or the two, when you added Lisbet to the mix. And those two were so much better than one.

"Um..." Casey sucked in a breath and told the truth. "I'm really interested in Lisbet's mom. I kind of wish I wasn't, but I am. And until I know what's going on between us, I'm just not available."

CHAPTER TWENTY-SEVEN

ON THE LAST THURSDAY IN APRIL, Avery and Faith spent over six hours together at Faith's home, finalizing the editing on the stories for their first reading, scheduled for the first Wednesday in June. Avery was feeling pretty good about the first event, partially since it was going to be held in a big tent at Bard, her Alma Mater. She hadn't even had to call in any favors to secure the venue, which was a bonus. Bard was invested in the series because of the content, not merely to do a favor for a graduate.

Visions of happy listeners and happy writers communing under the tent on a warm June evening gave her a thrill, one even more satisfying than her original program in Brooklyn had provided. That was probably because she'd had remarkable freedom to do this one her way. Being over a hundred miles from the home office had been a very nice circumstance when you had a vision and needed no hand-holding.

It was well after three, and even though she had a million things to work on, she had an even greater desire to see what this Baby Brewers thing was all about. Both her mom and Casey acted like it was the highlight of their weeks, but Avery had never been able to get away to attend.

When she got into her car, she fought with her conscience for just a minute, quickly deciding she deserved a little playtime. So she plugged in her phone, cranked up the music, rolled the window down a little to smell the scent of spring, and started to head south.

By the time she arrived, it was almost four. The stated meeting time was from three to five, but for the last few weeks her mom hadn't gotten home until after six. Everyone was still getting used to the lengthening days, along with the warmer afternoons, and her mom reported it was almost impossible to pull Lisbet away from her little friends now that they were sometimes playing outside.

When Avery pulled up close to the Pub, she saw some toddlers stumbling around in the grass, but Lisbet wasn't in sight. She poked her head inside, and in a matter of seconds Lisbet saw her, began to giggle, and scrambled over so fast she almost made sparks. The baby was able to walk quite well now, but she was still unstable on uneven surfaces. She sometimes walked almost like an older kid, but it was just as common for her to walk on her toes, looking like she was at risk for falling over face-first with every step.

Avery's heart swelled as she squatted down and extended her arms, waiting for Lisbet. There were definitely highs to be found in many of life's experiences, but having your baby show how stunningly happy she was to unexpectedly see you had to be near the top of the list.

"Lisbet," she crooned. "I've missed you so much!"

For the last few feet of her journey, Lisbet stopped fighting gravity and flung her body into Avery's embrace.

"I think she likes you," Casey said, wandering over with a big smile on her face.

Avery looked up and nearly swallowed her tongue. Casey always looked pretty darned good, but every once in a while she pinged on Avery's attraction radar in a big, big way.

Most people wouldn't have noticed anything different from her regular look. Casey had been at work, so she was dressed very casually. But it was almost seventy degrees, and very warm in the Pub, given that the structure was, in fact, a repurposed greenhouse, made specifically to attract heat.

The interior of the plant was often hot when they were brewing, so Casey had obviously been expecting a warm day, wearing a chambray shirt whose sleeves had been cut off, along with khaki shorts. Her hair was back in a ponytail, and it poked through the hole in the back of her Kaaterskill Brewery baseball cap. She'd probably had on her usual steel-toed work-boots, but she'd obviously decided summer was here, since she'd removed them, along with her socks, now wandering around the straw-covered floor barefoot.

"I think you're the first person I've seen in shorts this year," Avery said, eyeing her long, lean legs from just inches away. "I approve."

"It was hotter than Hades in the brewery today. This shirt had sleeves until nine o'clock this morning, but they had to go."

Avery was tempted to tell her she heartily approved of her choice, but she tried not to flirt too blatantly. Casey's arms were simply things of beauty—lean and strong, with muscles hidden beneath soft skin that was already slightly tan. They hadn't had many warm days, but she'd obviously spent every possible weekend moment sitting out by that fantastic pool.

Lisbet had been patient long enough, and she tried to wriggle out of Avery's embrace, determined to get back to an area by the bar, where a couple of blankets lay on the floor, with toys scattered around them. The second Lisbet reached the toy she was looking for, she yanked it from a little boy's hand and shook it in the air, shrieking at her victory.

Avery could have set a timer, so confident she was that the little guy would cry before three seconds had elapsed. By the time she moved to settle the dispute, her mom slid off a bar stool to intervene. She looked over at Avery, cocked her head in surprise, then got down on the floor to take the toy from Lisbet and hand it back to its owner. Avery could hear her say, "You can play *with* Colvin, but you can't take his toys."

The baby looked up at her grandmother, clearly on the verge of crying, then she turned her head sharply and reached for another toy. In seconds, she was happily playing with it, acting like she didn't even know Colvin was in the building.

Avery and Casey walked over to the bar as a woman emerged from the back room. She was very cute, very pregnant, and a little unsteady on her feet. In a flash, Casey was next to her, holding her arm and guiding her to a stool.

"I can run into the brewery and find a real chair," she said. "It'll just take a second."

"I'm fine," the woman said, smiling warmly at her. "I can still get on a stool. Barely."

Casey put her hands next to her hips, ready for action if she needed steadying. It would have been funny if they didn't act so friggin' comfortable around each other, but if Avery hadn't known better she would have guessed they were an expectant couple. At least she thought she knew better, but Casey wasn't always very forthcoming. While she never lied, she also didn't reveal a lot, especially about her personal life. For all Avery knew, she and Tara had gotten closer. Maybe a whole lot closer.

Once the woman was settled, and Casey was able to stand down, she signaled for Avery. "Come meet Tara. Since you're the last person here to have given birth, you can reassure her that it's no big deal." Casey moved to stand behind Tara, and made a funny face. One that was silently entreating Avery to lie about the pains of childbirth. Actually, it would have been funny if Avery wasn't already struggling with her jealousy.

Avery put her hand out to shake, and now that they were just a foot from each other she could see how remarkably young Tara was. Her heart went out to her, with the thought of this child-like woman having a baby on her own seeming like a very big task to take on. "Avery Nichols," she said when they shook. "Lisbet's mine."

Her mom was behind her, and she put her arm around Avery's waist. "And Avery's mine," she said, leaning close to kiss her cheek.

"Tara Phillips," she said. Patting her belly, she added, "and this is Landry. The doctor says he's not due for another week, but I'm hoping for Sunday, since that's my birthday. I think it would be fun to celebrate together every year."

Casey went around behind the bar to pull a cider for Colvin's dad, and Avery chatted with Tara while keeping an eye on Lisbet. Another little girl had joined them, but she was walking steadily, obviously a bit older and taller, which required Avery to keep an eye on the group since no other parent seemed to be watching them.

"Pardon?" Avery said, turning to look at Tara when she felt a hand on her arm.

"I thanked you for the infant seat," Tara said. "And all of the clothes and toys. I can't wait to use everything." She laughed, showing a very fetching grin. "I just need this baby to come out and play."

"Oh, no need to thank me. Casey borrowed the infant seat from her friend here at work. To be honest, Casey's bought most of the toys. She's the middleman in this whole enterprise."

"Ahh. I should have known. She never wants any credit for the things she does."

"Oh, that's Casey," Avery's mom said. "Generous to a fault."

"She's done so much for me," Tara said. "I wouldn't have half of the things I need without her." She let her gaze travel across the bar and Avery was certain she could see sparks of desire in her pale eyes. "But the things she does don't come close to the way she's helped me..." She shrugged. "Emotionally, I guess." She made eye contact with Avery. "You know what I mean, right? She makes me feel like I'll be able to do this."

"You will," Avery said, grasping her arm and squeezing it. "Women have been giving birth for a very long time. We've all learned from each other."

"We're here for you, Tara," Avery's mom said. "Lisbet's old enough to be able to entertain herself more now, so I'm determined to give you a break at least once a week. We'll watch Landry for a few hours so you can get some things done."

"Oh, Kathy, you don't have to do that. I've got six weeks off, then I'll be working from home. I'll be able to work when Landry's sleeping, which they say will be up to eighteen hours a day."

Avery met her mom's gaze and they both bit their tongues. It was too late to tell the woman her plans were nuts. She'd figure that out all on her own on the first day she tried to work an eight-hour shift with a new baby in the house.

⌒

Avery got down on the blanket and played with Lisbet and Colvin for a while. Eventually, Colvin's dad joined them, and after a bit he commented that his wife worked in Manhattan. That gave them a conversational toe-hold, since they could chat about some of the things they both used to do when they lived in the city.

Lisbet seemed very taken with Tim, Colvin's dad, and she wound up on his lap, playing with a book she was very rough with. "Is today Thursday?" Tim asked.

"Uh-huh."

"I need to make a reminder to buy my lottery tickets," he said, taking his phone from his pocket to set an alarm.

"Is there a big jackpot?"

"I haven't checked," he said, typing a little more. "I buy ten tickets every week. If we won even a million…" He sighed. "Okay, two million, we'd be able to move back to the city." He lowered his voice slightly. "I know I'm not telling you anything new, but watching a kid all day can be so damn boring!"

Avery chuckled. "It certainly can be," she admitted. "A writer I love described parenthood as droplets of joy floating in an ocean of tedium."

"That's about right. I just didn't realize how tiny a droplet was," he said, with his laugh sounding a little bitter. "Don't you wish you could be sitting at some cool new restaurant with your friends right now?" He got a faraway look in his eye, and kept on going. "You'd go through a couple of bottles of wine, and talk about everything. Politics, culture, the latest books, movies. Damn, I miss movies," he added, sounding vaguely heartbroken.

"Netflix?"

He gave her a puzzled look. "No, no. Not the same at all. We used to go to Film Forum or the Angelika every week. Hell, I knew the ticket taker at the Walter Reade by *name*. But Colvin's ten months old now, and my wife and I haven't been to a movie together since he was born." He stared glumly at his son, who was oblivious to his dad's isolation. "I hired a babysitter a couple of weeks ago and spent the afternoon at Time and Space in Hudson, but it wasn't the same, since there were only about six people there. I'm used to fighting for a seat at the IFC to see some Romanian thriller that no one can understand. The more confused I am, the better I like it."

Avery wasn't sure what to say. The guy was clearly in a glum mood, but she didn't want to offer some vague platitudes. Instead, she tried for empathy. "I've had days, and weeks, for that matter, where I've wanted to hop on the train and run away from home. But then Lisbet does something adorable, and it hits me that my life has more meaning now. It's harder," she added. "No one can convince me that having a child is easy. But…" She made a gesture to show how helpless she was to resist her child's allure. "Having Lisbet and living close to my family was the right choice for me."

"But don't you miss the city?"

He looked like he was about to cry, and she definitely could share his longing. But it was a more distant longing now, kind of like dreaming about vacationing somewhere warm and sunny on a cold, grey day. More of a fleeting wish than a void. She found herself saying, "Not a lot, and not very often. Oh, I'll see that there's a concert or a play that I'd love to catch, then realize it would take a bigger effort than I'm willing to exert to see it, but that's about it. Now," she added, making it clear that hadn't always been the case. "I didn't think I'd get here, but I'm happy. This is my home."

"Mmm. We've got a great house that we spent two years renovating, and all of our friends from the city are jealous of our lives, but I'd trade in a minute."

"How about your wife? Is she happy here?"

"Blissfully," he said, looking even grumpier. "She gets to entertain clients one or two nights a week in the city. She enjoys all of the best restaurants and concerts, then comes home to her rural refuge."

"But not you, huh?"

"I'm supposed to be finishing a play I started before the baby was born, but the house feels like a prison. If we could just afford a three-bedroom two bath in a neighborhood with a good grade school, we could use our house on the weekends. Then we'd both be happy."

She patted him on the shoulder as she stood. "You'd better double-down on those lottery tickets, Tim. You're going to need a few million, after taxes, to realize that dream."

Avery went out of her way to talk to all of the other parents, really pleased to see that most of them seemed fond of her sweet pea. By five, almost everyone had taken off, and she watched Casey practically carry Tara out to her car. She was like a nervous father, helping her get the seat belt around herself, then walking alongside the car as it bumped down the rutted path, calling out instructions and tips until she couldn't keep up.

Avery went back into the Pub, and took Lisbet into the back room to give her a snack. She sat her on her lap and tried to get her to have a few of the pitted and quartered cherries she'd recently fallen in love with. But the baby was keyed up from all of the activity, and couldn't concentrate. She reached for everything that wasn't food, finally wrenching Avery's glasses right off her face to throw them across the room.

"Hey! I know I normally wear contacts, but those aren't a toy. Unless you've got some cash on you to replace them, knock it off."

Lisbet pulled away and craned her neck to look at her, giving her one of those brief moments of intense connection that she'd been talking about with Tim. Then the baby batted her big blue eyes and settled back against Avery's arm to put both hands on a breast and pull it close.

"You want to nurse, honey?"

She stared at Avery for a second, looking like she was thinking of something important. Then she spoke, as if forming a clear word was her norm. "Mama," she said, then smiled as she began to nuzzle again.

"You called me mama," Avery whispered, tears coming to her eyes. She wanted to call for her mom, but was afraid she'd yell out the call in a way that would alert everyone still in the building. Then, realizing she didn't want an audience, she pulled her shirt up, and unhooked her bra, then snuggled Lisbet tightly against her body, once again feeling that nearly indescribable connection that she'd never felt with another living soul. It was stunning, really, and she let her mind wander to all sorts of happy places.

One word would lead to many, and soon she and Lisbet would be able to converse. After that, it was just a short hop to reading aloud together.

She sighed with pleasure. Would anything beat the thrill of sharing the stories you'd loved with your baby?

She cried out sharply when it hit her. Lisbet wasn't going to be a baby for long. Technically, she'd already passed that point, but the fact she hadn't spoken yet had let Avery continue to believe she was just a tall, mobile infant. But she wasn't. She was a toddler, and in just a year and a half she'd be in pre-school, then kindergarten, then grade school, then college, then…

Grasping the baby tightly, she wanted nothing less than to keep her just as she was. That was a crazy, ridiculous wish, and she knew it, but she couldn't stop herself from feeling that way. She wanted her baby to stay a *baby*. Forever. Actually, she wanted time to stop right where it was. No matter what happened in the future, nothing could be better than having a healthy, happy, baby. She sniffed her hair, then kissed her again and again as she let the tears flow. None of this made sense, and she knew her feelings were ephemeral, but they were very real at that moment. Lisbet had taken a massive step today, but instead of celebrating, Avery was feeling the loss that came with her child's maturation. She was embarrassed by her feelings, since she knew they were so selfish. Every good mother should focus on the ultimate goal—of raising a kind, thoughtful, emotionally-connected adult. But she just wanted to mourn the loss of her infant, the sweetest little pea in the world.

⁓

Casey had been busy shutting down the bar, and when she'd finished carting everything back to the brewery she found only Kathy in the Pub, sitting on a stool looking at her phone, and Lisbet, spread out on the floor atop a blanket, sound asleep.

"Well, this is a nice picture of parental neglect," she teased. "Mother missing in action, grandmother's attention locked onto her phone, and a baby asleep on the dirty floor."

"Don't forget we're in a bar," Kathy said, smiling at her.

"We are, but Avery didn't have anything to drink, so I know she's not passed out somewhere."

"Actually, she went out for a walk ages ago," Kathy said, shutting her phone off and putting it away. "But I've got to get home and start dinner."

"Want me to go find her?"

"No need." She stood and pulled her purse close. "I'll take Lisbet home with me. Why don't you two go out for a meal? Avery never gets an uninterrupted dinner, and I think she could use one."

Casey stopped and gave her a curious look. "Um, okay. I guess we could. Is…everything okay?"

"I'm fine and Lisbet's fine, but something's up with my girl. She wouldn't say what, but she was upset when she left. If you two have a little time alone, she might open up."

"I'm guess I'm up to the challenge. Do you have milk at your house?" She wiggled her eyebrows. "I might have to pour a large quantity of liquor down Avery's throat to get her to talk."

"We have plenty. She can have a couple of cocktails if you drive."

"Oh, great," Casey said, trying to sound dramatic. "I have to pull a cranky woman out of a bad mood while staying sober as a judge?"

Kathy patted her on the back, then squatted down to pick up the completely limp baby. "Fraid so. Unless you're not in the mood, that is. If you'd rather, I can go find her and drag her home with me."

"I'm happy to spend the evening with Avery. Having a meal she can actually concentrate on, along with a glass of wine or two, might pull her out of whatever kind of bad mood she's in."

⌐

The fields were a beautiful shade of yellowish green, with short stalks of wheat and barley swaying softly in the breeze. As Avery walked, she approached the hops, which were vibrant and healthy and a much more vivid green than the other plants.

They grew on sturdy wires supported by telephone poles that kept the wires stretched taut. Now the plants were barely as tall as she was, but by the end of the summer they'd be two or three times as high.

It felt fantastic to walk among the plants, with their smell so herbal and fresh. But she couldn't shake the melancholy that had settled upon her shoulders. It was time to fetch Lisbet and head home, but she didn't want to talk yet, and knew her mother would never allow her to go home if she didn't. That was the only downside of having a very close relationship with your mom. Hiding your feelings wasn't easy.

She felt, then saw Casey striding down the row, hands shoved into her back pockets, elbows out. She'd put her boots on again, which only made her look cuter, damn it. When she got close, she said, "Lisbet was out cold, so your mom took her home. How about having dinner with me?" She revealed a sweet smile. "You don't get many weeknights off."

"I…um…" Avery couldn't think of a polite way to refuse, but she truly didn't feel like talking.

"No pressure. I just thought you might like to go out." She brushed the legs of her shorts, sending dust into the still air. "I'd run home and shower first. Promise."

"I do want to go out. I mean, I would, but I'm…" She shrugged, unable to put words to her state of mind. "I don't think I'd be very good company."

"All right." She pulled her hands from her back pockets, only to slip them into the ones in front. "I'm going to walk around and check on things. Come with me."

Now she was really stuck. Instead of trying to think of an excuse, Avery tagged along, hoping Casey wasn't feeling very chatty, either.

They'd walked about halfway down a row, with Casey leaning over to inspect the plants every few feet. Avery wasn't sure what she was looking for, but she seemed very focused. "We've had a good spring so far," she said quietly. "Now we just need some sun and a little warmth and we can let the irrigation take care of the rest. These are thirsty little devils, but they'd rather get their water from their feet, rather than their heads. They're fussier than I'd like."

"Mmm."

"Today was your first time at Baby Brewers, wasn't it?"

"Uh-huh. It was fun."

"Yeah," she said reflectively. "We have a good time. We need to keep recruiting, though. Especially if we're going to keep it for kids under three.

Landry will be a good edition. Get 'em while they're young," she said, chuckling. "Although in utero is pushing it."

Avery didn't comment, so Casey kept talking. "What did you think of Tara?"

"She seemed nice. And naïve. I'm afraid she's going to be in for a shock."

"Yeah. I think so too. We're going to have our hands full."

Avery desperately wanted to ignore the comment, but she simply couldn't. Not when she was already feeling so raw. "We?" she said, feeling the burn in the back of her throat as her eyes welled up. "You're already a 'we?'"

"I meant everybody in Baby Brew—"

"Oh, that's just great! I'm glad you're getting exactly what you've always wanted, Casey. You'll be there at the beginning this time." Casey's mouth had dropped open, giving Avery the opportunity to keep talking.

"It's working out in every way, isn't it. Tara's younger, and prettier, for that matter, than I am. And Langtree or Landon or whomever can pick up right where Lisbet left off. You'll have a tiny little infant to care for while Lisbet's trying to make the friggin' debate team."

"What in the hell are you—"

"I bought in!" she yelled, feeling like she was going to lose control and never get it back. "I love it here! I see my home in a whole new way now, and I see my place in the world with a different perspective."

"You do?" Casey looked like she was thoroughly puzzled, but she leaned in close and tilted her head slightly. "How do you see your place in the world?"

"Oh, God," she sighed, truly not wanting to get into this. But the words were already forming in her mouth, and she didn't know how to stop them.

"I used to think Lisbet would be an addition to my life. Like I'd be able to go along as I always had, and figure out work-arounds when I had to. I expected her to crawl into the space I'd carved out for her and learn to adjust."

"But you don't think that now?" She moved even closer, seeming like she was as interested in Avery's answer as Moses had been in reading the tablets.

"Of course not! You can't make a baby fit into your life. You've got to carve out a new life that puts the focus on her. Even if we lived in the same apartment in Carroll Gardens, with Freya right down the hall, it wouldn't be the life I lived before."

"It wouldn't?"

"No!" she yelled. "That life is *gone*. Having a baby makes you start over, with new priorities." She looked into Casey's dark, warm eyes, seeing the concern she was now going to lavish on Tara and Langtree. "What matters now is making sure Lisbet's surrounded by people who love her."

As she let that thought fill her mind, images of the last few months began to pummel her. There were dozens of them, most of them with Casey right in the bullseye. She'd been there for Lisbet's first…everything. Soothing her, encouraging her, making her feel that the world was not just her oyster, but a safe haven in which she could explore without fear. The emotion begin to bubble up before she knew what hit her, and Avery barely knew what was going to come out of her mouth when she started to talk. "And now…" She wiped the tears from her eyes, so full of fury that she was sick to her stomach. "Now that I finally feel like I'm home, you're going to kick me out of my house and fill it up with your new family. Lisbet and I will have to move to some cold-water flat in Brooklyn and subsist on ramen noodles." She sucked in a breath and spit it out in a rush. "Because there's no god damned way in hell I'm going to stay here and watch you fall for another woman." She slapped her hands onto Casey's shoulders and pulled her close, so close she could see flecks of green and amber in her dark brown eyes. "It would kill me to see that," she whispered, her voice having lost all of its power. She started to sob, then strong, warm arms engulfed her, holding on tightly.

Casey's mouth was close to her ear when she murmured, "What in the hell are you talking about, you silly thing? Even though you have degrees from some very fancy schools, sometimes you've got no sense at all."

Avery's whole body was shaking, but she pulled away while trying to suck in some air. "I have sense," she said, her voice quavering. "I have the sense to see you're attached to Tara now, and no one has time for two babies."

"Well, people with twins would disagree," she said with a silly grin, "but I don't plan on being attached to more than one baby." She put her hands on Avery's shoulders and gripped them firmly. "You know how I feel about Lisbet." She bit at her lip for a second, then spoke again, with her voice a little louder, and a little stronger. "And I want her to have a hugely important place in my life. But it's her mother I'm in love with."

"Love?" Avery blinked her eyes slowly, sure she was having some kind of auditory hallucination. "Did you say you love…me?"

"You," Casey said, closing her eyes for a second. "I love you, Avery, and if you're having a meltdown just because I'm worried about some pregnant kid, I think you might love me, too."

Avery grasped her hard, squeezing until Casey whimpered. "I do," she whispered. "I love you." She looked up, seeing tears in Casey's eyes. The words came tumbling out now, spilling from her quickly now that she was able to share them. "It finally dawned on me a while ago, but I didn't think it was fair to say anything until I knew whether Helena would keep funding the program up here. But I don't care!" She threw her head back and shouted the words to the sky. "I'll quit my job if I have to. I just can't quit you."

Casey ran her strong, callused hand across Avery's cheek, gazing into her eyes with such love she thought her heart might stop. "I'll admit I don't always move from A directly to B, but even I've never told a woman I loved her before we'd even kissed."

Avery dried her eyes with the backs of her hands, still looking up into the warmth of Casey's gaze. "We've done a few things that are kind of backwards. But I think we're in a pretty good spot to finally get things moving in the right direction."

Casey's gaze moved from left to right, making a show of it. "Out in a field of hops? This is where you want me to kiss you?"

"I'd take a field, a glade, a glen, a thicket, a copse, a dell—"

Casey bent slightly, tilted her head, then laughed softly. "Quit showing off that big vocabulary and let me kiss you." She gently pressed her lips to Avery's, whose eyes fluttered closed. Then she breathed in, trying to imprint the sensation deep into her memory. Every momentous event she'd experienced in her life had already been stored away, just waiting for this one to be added to the collection. This kiss, the first of what she hoped would be millions upon millions of them, would live in her heart for the rest of her life. She let her hands slide up Casey's back until she was pressing into her body, needing to have more of her, to let the sensation of those warm lips fill her heart to overflowing.

"Take me home," Avery murmured as she gently pulled away, with her lips tingling with sensation. Then her eyes opened wide. "Where's my baby?"

"Your mom took her," Casey said, smiling. "As I already mentioned. Do you think I left her on the floor of the Pub?"

"I have no idea what I thought. Other than having my heart break because Lisbet called me mama today." She threw her arms around Casey and held on tightly, unable to keep the tears away. "I'm so happy she said it, Casey. She looked me right in the eye and called me mama. Clear as day."

Casey pulled away and placed her hands on Avery's jawline, holding her head still. "That upset you?"

"Only because she's not a baby anymore. Once she can talk, she's almost out of the house."

"Ooo, you want to keep her little, too." They held each other for a long time, getting used to each other's bodies while they simultaneously soothed each other over the loss they both clearly felt. Avery hardly had words for it, but knowing that they shared that longing was one of the best feelings she'd had since the day she'd learned she was pregnant. As marvelous as it had been to have such a wonderful baby, she'd always felt the pressure of dealing with many of the bumps and bruises alone. But now...

Casey sighed, with the wistful sound caressing Avery's ear. "I always feel guilty when I have the instinct to keep her just like she is, but she's so perfect. What if she's a sucky toddler? Can we trade her in for another infant?"

"Absolutely not," Avery said, able to see the humor in what had felt so melodramatic moments earlier. "The three of us are an insoluble trio."

"Ha!" Casey said. "You think you can trick me with your big words, but I know that one. I had to take chemistry in college, you know."

"I don't ever want to trick you. I only want to love you."

"That's a big ditto from me." She gave Avery one of the prettiest, most guileless smiles she thought she'd ever seen. "If you don't mind, I'd love to kiss you again. I've never kissed a woman I love in a field of hops." Her grin turned slightly shy. "That might sound silly to you, but hops mean a lot to me, and to be surrounded by their scent while I kiss the woman I love—"

Avery put a hand behind her head and pulled her down so their lips were an inch apart. "I will always try to satisfy your desires. If you want to gather up a box of hops and cover our bed in them…"

"Right here's fine," Casey said, with a soft, warm laugh as she closed the distance to capture Avery's lips again. This time she was a little more bold, a little more determined as their mouths met.

In just a few seconds, Casey's tongue slid into Avery's mouth, and she felt herself begin to purr. She wasn't actually sure if the sound was even audible, but the kisses soothed her soul in a way she'd once known, but had nearly forgotten. She was deeply loved by some awesome people, but having this—this bone-deep desire for Casey's body and mind, nearly brought her to her knees.

Her hands couldn't stop moving, tickling from the back of Casey's neck all the way down to her ass, gripping her flesh as that slippery tongue explored her mouth so thoroughly she was shaking with desire. She was about to wrestle Casey to the ground when a cooler head prevailed. "Let's go home," Casey murmured, giving Avery another thrill. Her house would now be their home.

⌒

Before they could take off, Casey had to act like an adult and lock up. If she hadn't been certain that she'd lose her job if anyone broke in, she would have just run for her truck to get to the house as soon as humanly possible. But she just wasn't wired that way. Business before pleasure, even when she could taste the pleasure on her tongue.

It was a short walk back to the brewery, but she took Avery's hand, just because she could. Avery smiled up at her and that unguarded, open expression hit Casey right in the chest, making her heart skip a beat. "It's a little strange, isn't it?" she asked. "I mean, adding this." She held their linked hands up and gave them a glance.

"Little bit," Avery agreed, giving her a shy grin. "It's going to take some time to get used to this."

"Maybe." Casey let go of her hand and draped an arm across Avery's shoulders. "But the best way to get over feeling uncomfortable is to jump right in."

Avery seemed very willing to do just that, moving closer so their bodies touched all along their lengths as they walked. "It won't take long," she said, with a little confidence beginning to show. "I'm already comfortable with having your arm around me, and it's only been a few minutes." When she smiled this time, any trace of shyness had evaporated. "So? What do we do now? Our timeline's a little wonky, as usual. I've told you I love you before I've actually..." She waggled her fair eyebrows, which made her look really silly. "Loved you."

"We do everything a little backwards. I mean, I clearly fell for Lisbet long before I fell for you. I guess we should keep that a secret, huh?"

"I don't think we should," she said, with that terrifically cute frown she often wore when she was thinking hard about something. "If we don't tell her the whole truth, she'll wonder why you're not in her baby pictures until she's six months old." Avery put her arm around Casey's waist and squeezed her tightly. "She's going to start understanding stories soon, and I bet she's going to love hearing about how we fell for each other because of her."

"Should I tell her I used to see you at school and wish I could trade places with the guy who had his arm around you?"

Avery looked up at her, grinning broadly. "Really?"

Casey just nodded, so happy to see the delighted expression that covered Avery's face.

"You can tell, but you can't add that you thought I was a jerk."

"*That* can be our little secret. Kids don't have to know everything about their parents."

They'd reached the door of the brewery, and Casey keyed in the code to hear the lock switch off. Avery walked in front of her, and when Casey let the door close she paused to shut her eyes as they entered the production area. She often got more information from her nose than her eyes, and tonight the place smelled just right. Nothing sour, or moldy, or acrid. Just the right blend of hops, toasted barley, yeast, and water, all working together to produce something magical.

"Hey, I've been working on a limited edition, and I pulled off a growler of it earlier today. Want to taste?"

"Why not? We can toast our…discovery?"

"Sounds good."

"What kind of beer is it?"

She smiled at Avery's expectant expression. "Why don't you guess. You've got a good nose."

"Why, thanks. I bet it's going to get much better when you teach me a whole lot more."

Casey walked over to the two chillers near her office. She kept one at forty and one at sixty degrees, preferring some styles of beer colder, and some warmer. After snagging a couple of clean glasses, she poured a portion into each, making sure they developed the head she was looking for.

When she handed a glass over, they tapped the rims together. "To us," Avery said, smiling brightly. "Isn't that cool to say?"

"I think that's the coolest thing I've ever heard, and, believe me, I've heard a lot of toasts."

Avery held the glass up to the late afternoon light and observed it for a minute. "The color's interesting. Not quite gold and not quite orange." She looked up at Casey. "I like the pure white head. Very pretty."

"It is. It doesn't last long, though."

"Mmm. But as it dies away, the lacing on the glass is nice." She held it to her nose and took a big sniff. "Wow. There's some funk in that thing!"

"Uh-huh. It's definitely got a funk."

Avery looked up at her again, with a sly smile forming. "Want to hear a secret?"

Casey leaned close and tilted her head. "I love secrets."

"I like the way you smell after you've been at work all day."

Casey pulled back and stared at her. "You do?"

"Uh-huh." Her cheeks colored the slightest bit, like she was embarrassed, but not very embarrassed. "You smell a little like this beer, but I'm never sure if it's from the brewery or you." She shrugged. "Either way, I'm kind of addicted to it."

"Thank god!"

"Oh, yeah. Smell's important to me. We're good on that point." She stopped. "At least I'm good. I'm not sure if you like my scent."

"You don't have much, since all you do is sit at a desk and type. I don't think I've ever seen you break a sweat." She leaned close and sniffed all around her neck, making Avery giggle. "I smell soap and detergent and some baby stuff. We're going to have to investigate further, but I think we're good."

"Oh, we're going to investigate. As soon as we get a couple of things clear, we're going to do a lot of investigating."

Casey tapped at the glass in Avery's hand. "You know, I usually advise people to let the beer warm in their hands for a few seconds, but...are you going to try that today? I worked awfully hard on it."

"One more sniff."

They both breathed in through their mouths, with Avery nodding with pleasure. "Mmm. I still get the same notes. It's yeasty, and grassy, with a bright citrus."

"Exactly what I get," Casey said, really pleased with how serious Avery was taking this. "I get a some oak, too."

"Uh-huh. But yeast and that overall funk are stronger for me."

"Let's taste."

They lifted their glasses at the same time, and Avery smacked her lips with a smile on her face. "It's a funky champagne."

Casey laughed. "It kind of is. I made this with a wild yeast, which I'm really happy with. Do you get any green apple?"

"Maybe," she said, taking another sip. "But just a touch. It's pretty carbonated, but it still goes down easy."

"Right. I've been working on the balance, and I think it's pretty good."

"Oh, yeah. I could grow to love this. I hope it's not a limited edition."

Casey almost didn't reveal a detail she was a little embarrassed about, but she had to get over hiding things if she wanted to open her heart to Avery. "Um, I suggested naming it for Lisbet," she said, knowing her cheeks were coloring.

"Ooo!" Avery threw her arm around her and hugged her tightly. "That's so sweet of you."

"Yeah," she said, shrugging off the compliment. "But my bosses thought it made it sound too girly, which it kind of does. So I switched it to something else." She walked over to her desk and found the artwork their graphic designer had come up with. Holding it to her chest, she said, "I was thinking about us... Even though there wasn't an us yet."

"I think there's been an us for a long time," Avery said, smiling up at her. "We were both too shy, or tentative, or frightened to admit it."

"I'm not shy, but god knows I can let things ride when I should push ahead. Anyway, I was thinking of when we met, and how that was a launching pad for the surprising trip to where we are now." She turned the art around, smiling down at the image, liking it upside down as well as the proper way.

"Hudson High," Avery said, nearly squealing. "This is so cool!" She put her glass down, then wrapped her arms around Casey, who settled into the embrace feeling like they'd been touching each other that way for years. "But…" Avery murmured. "Your memories about high school are so…"

"They're not great. But the things that happened then gave me the motivation to stop listening to anyone who tried to cut me down, which was the best decision I've ever made. Well, maybe second best." She touched Avery's chin, tilting it up so their eyes met. "We wouldn't have talked at the Pub that night if your mom hadn't used her Hudson High connections to find me. And I promise you that all of the bullshit I had to work through then was well worth having you now."

"Oh, you smooth talker, you," Avery said, grinning up at her.

"You're the talker. I'm the doer." She reached out to set her glass on her desk, then held Avery close and kissed her again, really letting herself go this time. She'd never kissed a woman who'd just had a glass of a beer she'd labored over, and she had to admit it was a rush. Tasting the grassy, yeasty, citrusy flavors on Avery's lips took the beer from a ninety five to an even hundred. "I like doing that. A lot," she murmured, staying very close for another kiss. She nuzzled against Avery's neck, feeling blissfully warm and content. "We're going to have a wonderful time together. Are you ready to start?"

Avery pulled away to gaze into her eyes, searching them deeply. "I am," she said, looking a bit tentative. "Are you sure you're ready for this? It's not just me, Casey. Lisbet's involved, too."

"Um, I think I noticed," she said, trying to tease and lighten Avery's mood. "Short little thing. Very demanding. A real attention hog—"

Avery gripped her arms, holding on firmly. "I need to know where you see this going. Ideally, we'd co-parent. But if you'd rather be one step removed—"

"Removed? I'd push you out of the way to be number one if I could," Casey said, laughing at her own exaggeration. "Seriously, if you'd let me—"

"I want what's best for Lisbet," she said, her expression sill sober and thoughtful. "And having you be one of her two mommys is what's best. For both of us."

"For all three of us," Casey said, feeling her eyes fill with tears. "God damn," she said, sighing. "I had no idea this was going to be such a ridiculously awesome day, but if I have many more like this my circuits will fry."

"So you're all in? You're ready to take the leap?"

"I'm so in there's no more in to be."

"You'll live with us?"

"I can pack up on Saturday." She let out a laugh. "My parents are going to be a little surprised, but they'll adjust."

"Will you?" Avery asked, moving closer to press her body against Casey's. "Can you adjust to all of these changes? They're sure not minor ones."

"I'm very adaptable. Everyone at work already assumes we're... something...even though they can't figure out what. Once I move in, they'll be able to stop gossiping about us."

"I guess we should do one more thing. I mean...what if we don't have any chemistry?"

"Oh, right," Casey said, finding that just short of ridiculous. "Like that's going to be a problem."

"I didn't say it was," Avery insisted, giving her another sexy, sly look. "I just want to have my suspicions confirmed. My house? Like now?"

Casey checked the clock over the door. "It's seven," she said, sighing. "I didn't realize it was so late. Lisbet has to go to bed soon."

"My mom would be happy to keep her if I tell her I need a night off. And that will give us a whole day where only the two of us know about this. Once my mom knows..."

"What will happen then?"

"Once she knows, you won't be able to get away, even if you wanted to."

Casey laughed at that. "I don't think you'll turn into some kind of ogre who makes me want to run." She tightened her hold, smiling when Avery rested her cheek on her chest and let out a sigh. "But why risk starting off our lives together with an unhappy baby?"

"Why would she be unhappy?"

"Didn't you think she was acting a little weird today?"

"Maybe a little…"

"I don't know if it's teething pain or if she's catching a cold, but she was unusually grouchy this afternoon. I think she might need her mommy." She gave Avery a gentle kiss, saying, "You're going to have to put up with my cautious nature to live with me. Do you mind starting now?"

Avery's eyes scanned Casey's for a solid minute, probably trying to see how firm her resolve was. It must have been clear, since she sighed heavily and said, "I want to start off right, too. I'll go get her."

"Good choice. While I'll admit I'd rather be footloose and fancy free, that train has left the station."

"I know." She turned her head to see the big clock over the main door. "I'll be at home by eight. Meet me there?"

Casey delayed for just a moment, certain Avery wasn't going to like her next suggestion either. "I know Lisbet will mostly be a few feet away from us for the next couple of years. So wouldn't it be nice to have a whole day alone to start this relationship off right? Having uninterrupted time with you sounds awfully good to me. I think we need to be alone to start this off right."

Avery stared at her for a very long time. "Are you saying you want me to go home *alone*?"

"No, no, I don't *want* that." She took in a breath as some of the tension seemed to leave Avery's body, knowing she was about to put it right back in. "I want to be with you right now. But I don't want to have Lisbet be cranky or wake up while we're getting to know each other. I'd like a block of time when we're awake and alert and completely alone. I thought we could both take tomorrow off and spend it in bed."

Avery nodded, finally meeting Casey's gaze with a small smile. "I think that's a great idea." She slipped her arms around Casey's neck and pulled her down for a long, sensual kiss, the kind of kiss that took you to the verge of forgetting your own name. As she moved back a tiny amount she batted her eyes and said, "We'll have all day tomorrow to recover from tonight."

"But you're going home with Lisbet…"

"That's where you're wrong," Avery said, shaking her head a tiny bit. "You're right that we're going to spend the next few years with Lisbet right between us, and that's going to be a tough way to start a relationship. So…" She put her hands on Casey's shoulders and pulled her down so they were nose to nose. "We're going to have this night to ourselves."

"We are?"

"We're going to be selfish. Tonight, Lisbet doesn't come first."

"But—"

"Your forehead's all wrinkled up," she said, looking up at her with such affection that it made Casey slightly weak in the knees. "Come on now, stop worrying," she said, smoothing out the skin with her fingertips. "It's not like I'm proposing we tie her to a chair on the porch. Lisbet's an incredibly adaptable child. She can be with my mom for twenty-four hours."

"The whole day?"

"Uh-huh. We're going to have tonight and all day tomorrow to spend in bed. I'll admit that's not what Lisbet would vote for, but we have wants and desires, too."

"But—"

Firmly, Avery said, "The baby has to come first in terms of needs, since she can't provide for her own. But she doesn't have to come first in terms of wants. Tonight, I want you all to myself." She smiled as her fingers slipped down Casey's back, sending shivers everywhere they touched. Her smile was luminous, and so filled with sexual innuendo that Casey was hardly able to focus. "I think I can make a good case that I *need* to be with you tonight."

"Don't you want to run over to your parents' house and say goodnight?" she asked, still feeling edgy about leaving the baby for an overnight stay without any preparation.

"Let it go," Avery said. "You can start being the overprotective mommy tomorrow. Tonight, you're mine."

"All right," she said, trying to look like she'd given up after a long battle. "If you insist."

Avery stopped on a dime and put her hands flat up against Casey's chest. "If you're not a hundred percent—"

She let out a laugh as she put her arms around Avery's waist to lift her off her feet. "I'm on the verge of tossing you over my shoulder to carry you off to bed. If I was any more into this…"

Avery's face was just an inch in front of Casey's, and she was smiling like she'd won the lottery. "I think I'd like it if you threw me over your shoulder. I've never dated anyone bigger and stronger than I am…"

Casey lowered her to the floor, then wrapped her in a tender, but firm hug. "I assume I could do that, but I'm definitely not going to spend our first night together in the emergency room. Clearly, I'm going to have to be the practical one in this relationship."

"I'm pretty practical too," Avery said as she nuzzled her face against Casey's neck. "But you shake the foundations of my practicality." She backed away and took Casey's hand. "Ready?"

"I am."

"Then pull off a growler of our beer and let's hit the road."

"A growler? Seriously?"

"No baby. No nursing. No curfew. No alarm in the morning. Let's light it up!"

"Well, well, well," Casey said as she went to find a box of growlers with the Kaaterskill logo on them. "If I'd had a thousand years to dream when I was a kid, I don't think I would have ever gotten to the 'have hot sex with Avery Nichols while drinking a half gallon of beer I created' fantasy. But now that I'm here, I think it's a pretty darned good idea."

She'd only walked a few feet when Avery said, "Catch me!" and launched herself at Casey's back. She'd had time to brace herself, and had bent over slightly, standing her ground when Avery's arms whipped around her neck as her body draped along her back.

Casey reached back to grab her thighs. "Scoot up so you're helping, you goofball!"

"If we're going to be carefree for a whole day, I'm going all in. I haven't acted like a kid in years and years. I'm due."

"I like this," Casey said, reaching back to give her a swat on the seat. "I've never given an adult woman a piggy-back ride, but I think we should start doing this on a routine basis."

"I want to tell you a secret," Avery said, holding on a little tighter as she craned her head around to be able to speak right into Casey's ear. "Want to know about the first time I touched myself while fantasizing about you?"

"Definitely!"

"Senior year."

"Are you shitting me? I was going out of my way to avoid you in the hall while you were spanking it to me?"

"I wasn't spanking it," she said, laughing softly. "And if you think that's the right way to do it, we need to have another talk."

Casey had reached the storage area where they kept logoed material, and she found a box of the growlers. "I think I did all right the night we had, as you call it, pity sex."

"Point taken. So," she said, whispering again. "It was senior year, and it was cold out. Maybe it was November or even December. I had Ms. Valentine for P.E., and she had us outside running around the track. We were freezing our asses off, but no one minded since it was always better to be outside than in."

"I didn't have Ms. Valentine," Casey said.

"I know. So…I was running around and noticed someone way out in the area where the football team practiced, but it was too early for the team to be out there. This person was kicking footballs, really rocketing them toward the track."

"I bet I know who the person was, especially if this story ends with you spanking it when you thought of me."

"You're incredibly psychic," she said, laughing. "Anyway, you had a bunch of footballs, and when you'd kicked them all you ran close to the track to kick them back in the other direction."

"Sounds like me goofing off, which I was really good at."

"Right. But you were all alone. It's not like you were with a coach or anything. I couldn't figure out if you were cutting class, or if you had permission to be out there."

"Cutting class," Casey admitted. "I never went to English class, and Mr. Potter never gave me a hard time since he knew I was unreachable," she said, feeling a little sting at how certain she'd been that she was a dunce.

"You simply hadn't had your awakening yet," Avery said. "But even though you weren't confident of your academic skills, you were one cocky girl when it came to kicking those balls. One of them had rolled close to the fence, and I rounded the track right when you went to pick it up. You gave me a devastatingly sexy smile, winked at me, then grabbed the ball and kicked it for a mile!"

"I did? Jesus! I must have been flooded with some kind of confidence hormone from working out. I can't imagine doing that!"

"Well, you did," Avery said, clearly certain of herself. "I almost fell down as I tried to go around that turn, and when I got home, I imagined you doing all sorts of things to me. Sexy things," she added, "even though I had to guess at what those might be."

"Did I kick a football for you?" Casey asked, chuckling.

"No way. I imagined you coming over to my house for some unexplained reason, then taking me to bed. I'd never been to bed with anyone at that point, and I hadn't even looked at porn yet, but my imagination must have been good enough. It worked like a charm," she added. "My very first Casey Van Dyke-induced orgasm."

"Have you been keeping this little secret from me all this time? I mean, I can see why you would…"

"No, I haven't. This hit me about a month or two ago. It came from nowhere, but I'm certain it really happened."

"This was when you were happily straight, right? When all of the smart guys were chasing you around, and you kept letting yourself be caught?"

"Uh-huh," she said lightly, clearly unbothered by the contradiction. "I fantasized about all sorts of things, and all sorts of people. I thought I was just open-minded." She took a little nibble from Casey's ear. "I was, but a couple of years later I realized that most of my best fantasies were about girls. That's when it clicked."

"Fascinating," Casey said. "Well, that day might have give you your *first* Casey Van Dyke-induced orgasm, but it won't be the last, and that's a promise."

They were near the door then, and Casey gave Avery's butt a firm pat. "Mind if I put you down? I don't want to risk dropping the beer while I lock up."

"I appreciate that you're good at prioritizing," Avery said, sliding to the floor. "I've had a blast while we're still fully dressed. Kind of awesome."

"You're not going to be dressed for long. Let's go replay that old fantasy. But this time, we're playing for keeps."

⌒

Casey had insisted on going home to shower and change, so Avery used the time to go freshen up. She hadn't done anything vigorous, so she could have gotten by without a shower, but she hadn't shaved her legs in weeks, and she wanted every part of herself to be smooth for Casey's lips.

Once she was finished, she put on her sexiest bra, one she'd recently bought to reign in her breasts when she got dressed up to go into the city. It was one size smaller than the nursing bras she'd bought, which was a good sign that things were slowly going back to normal. She'd always been a little larger than she would have liked, but the girls had gotten out of control when Lisbet was nursing eight to ten times a day. If she dropped down one more size she'd be happy.

After putting on clean shorts and a blouse, she sat on the wide sill of her dormer window. It was a little strange sitting there waiting for Casey to come over and have sex with so little lead-up, and she was more nervous than she wanted to be. Even though Avery had been with a good number of women, and had experienced a wide variety of encounters, she'd never had a first like this.

Every other time had come about pretty organically, usually after meeting at a club or some other kind of social event, often after a drink or two. While she'd just put a growler of good beer in the fridge, she didn't need a drink to get over her nerves. She and Casey would figure out a way to get in sync, or they'd just have a fumbling, stiff first time. They'd just have to keep at it until they nailed it. When you were deeply attracted to each other, and determined to start off your lives with a bang, it was only a matter of time.

She smiled to herself, puzzled, yet relieved to feel so calm about the sexual part of their relationship. Letting out a laugh, she thought that maybe having had tearful, pity sex on the polyester pod had made it clear they could get the technical details figured out without a problem. And since she felt like she knew Casey's heart—there was literally nothing to worry about. But she was still annoyingly nervous, and couldn't wait for Casey to arrive.

She heard the truck when it turned onto her street, feeling like a dog who can detect the postal service truck a minute before anyone else.

Then the big vehicle rolled down her gravel drive, and she heard the engine cut. A minute later a sweet voice called out through the open front door. "I've got a delivery here for Avery...middle name unknown... Nichols."

"You've come to the right place," Avery said, walking over to the top of the staircase, sucking in a breath when she caught sight of Casey in a salmon-colored linen shirt. Avery had never guessed how fantastic she would look in that color, but it was perfect for her.

Casey acted like she was looking down at a delivery ticket. "Says here I'm supposed to deliver a fun-filled, yet emotion-packed twenty-four hours of lovemaking." She peered up the stairs with a sly grin. "Will I get overtime for this?"

"Come up here and get to work," Avery said, surprised to hear her voice already sounding smoky.

Casey walked in to close and lock both parts of the Dutch door. Then she took the stairs two at a time to stand in front of Avery. "Now I'm frozen," she said, looking surprised. "All of a sudden, this feels like a very big deal."

"Come on now. You're taking this too seriously." Avery approached her to rest her hands on Casey's hips as her head tilted down. "Where's my confident brewmaster, huh? I still remember how you sauntered up to our table at the Pub that first night we reconnected. You looked like you owned the place."

"That's my comfort zone. This…is a new one for me. " She gazed into Avery's eyes for a few moments. "I've grown to love women I've had sex with, but I've never had sex with a woman I already love. It feels…" Her forehead wrinkled slightly. "Like something we have to get right—like right now."

"Not true at all," Avery promised. "You're just nervous because making love means a lot to you. You're building this first time up in your mind a little too much."

Her eyes opened wide, then blinked slowly. "It doesn't mean a lot to you?"

"Of course it does. With you it means everything." She let out a sigh, and pulled Casey even closer. "We're going to get to show each other more of ourselves. That's pretty cool, isn't it?"

"Yeah," she said, nodding. "I like that."

"I do too. I haven't wanted to have casual sex ever since I had the baby." She laughed a little. "Not that I've had people knocking down my door to get at me, of course. But even if there had been a line stretching out to the street I wouldn't have wanted to. Now that I have Lisbet, I only want to do things that will make us a stronger family. And being your partner is definitely going to do that."

"I always said you need at least four people to raise a baby," she said, showing a lopsided grin.

"The two of us can handle it. I just want to make sure you understand I'm not choosing you mostly as a co-parent, Casey. You're the main event." She placed a tender kiss to her mouth. "I'm so lucky to be with someone I admire so much."

"Do you really admire me?" she asked, looking adorably shy.

"Oh, yeah," Avery said as she let her hands play along the muscles in her back. "I really do. There's so much about you that I admire. I've actually got a long list that I'm going to tell you all about whenever you're feeling down."

She smiled sweetly, nodding a little. "I haven't had someone to prop me up in a long time. I'm really looking forward to that."

"I am too. For now, let's just agree that you've got a pure soul, and if Lisbet can turn out anything like you, I'll be thrilled."

"Thanks." She looked mischievous when she said, "You're not so bad yourself, if we edit out your troubled teen years when you didn't look out for the underdog."

"I'm so glad you let yourself get to know me. I realize Lisbet was some great bait, but you still had to risk a little to get close." She slid a hand behind her head and urged her forward until their lips were just an inch apart. "I'm so thankful for that."

"I love you," Casey whispered. As their lips met, her normal personality began to emerge, and Avery could feel her begin to loosen up, with the muscles in her back getting pliable. She sighed when their lips parted for a moment. "I've been dreaming about doing this for months, and now we're here. Doing it," she said, letting out a short laugh.

"We've got some ways to go until we're actually doing it," Avery said, seeing that Casey was up for some teasing. "But we're getting there."

"We're definitely getting there." She entered the bedroom and put her arms around Avery, holding her in an embrace that soothed her soul. With her soft breasts and that delicious curve to her hips there was no mistaking it was a woman's body that held her tight, but those firm muscles added something—something fantastic.

Avery let out a soft moan, then Casey's embrace tightened even more, possessively enveloping her. Now that they were so close, she kept her eyes closed and breathed her in. Some of the aromas that Avery had assumed were from work were just her. A delicate herbal scent clung to her skin, making Avery's mouth water. There was something else, too, something that reminded her of spring, or maybe just the scent of the earth. It was real, and true, and natural. Just like Casey. No artifice. No posturing. She was the epitome of what you see is what you get, and Avery was so powerfully drawn to her it kept knocking her feet out from under her.

"Are you super tired?" Casey asked, chuckling softly. "Or do I make your knees weak?"

"Knees weak," Avery replied lazily. "We'd better find someplace to lie down, or you're going to have to carry me."

"I can lift a fifty pound sack of grain and carry it up a ladder, but I learned today that you weigh a little more than that." Casey leaned over and whispered into Avery's ear. "You're a lot sexier than a bag of grain, just in case you were wondering."

"I know there's a compliment in there…"

Casey put her hand on Avery's chin and lifted it so their gazes were locked together. "If I start listing every part of you that I'm attracted to, we'll still be right here at dawn." She moved in for a long, slow kiss, which once again made Avery think that her knees might not hold her up. Then Casey pulled back to say, "The quick version is that you're the prettiest woman I've ever seen, and everything inside here…" She patted over Avery's heart. "Is more attractive than all of the other parts put together." With a silly grin, she ran her hands over Avery's body, touching from her shoulders to her thighs and back up again. "But I think," she added, with her grin growing stronger. "I might have to double-check."

When Avery wrapped her arms around Casey's neck, she slowly backed up until she was perched on the edge of the desk. "I didn't want you to get a stiff neck from kissing me," she said, her easy smile slightly dichotomous to the sexy edge her voice had taken on.

"We could go to bed," Avery said, appreciating how much more intense Casey's eyes were from this angle.

"We haven't earned it yet," she said, not explaining herself more fully before she put her hands low on Avery's back and pulled her in close. "Show me how you feel," she murmured, having grasped Avery in a very firm hold.

Avery took in a deep breath, welcoming Casey's clean, herbal scent into her body before threading her fingers through her hair. Then she poured her heart into the kisses she was sure she'd never have enough of. Casey responded just like she'd dreamed she would, opening herself up without reservation, completely in the moment.

She simply couldn't get enough of the feel of her sturdy body, the silkiness of her mouth, or the tenderness of her touch. The hands that roamed over her body were as gentle as any Avery had ever experienced, but they were focused and determined as well.

Her own hands were just as active as her mouth. As the kisses grew hotter, her questing touch centered on Casey's back, probing the muscles that felt so firm, yet were covered by silky soft skin.

Avery's determined fingers sought out the hem of her shorts, then slid up and down her leg, barely resisting the powerful urge to travel all the way up. But playing at this bit by bit was kind of a charge, and creeping along at a snail's pace was making the whole experience hotter.

Casey seemed to have an insatiable appetite for kissing, and Avery happily let her take the lead. There was something so incredibly alluring about a woman who knew where she wanted to go, and could keep them right on track. But Avery couldn't go along without attending to her own agenda. She kept pulling away from the increasingly hot kisses to bury her face into the crook of Casey's neck to breathe in lustily. "God, I love the way you smell," she murmured, feeling slightly drunk from the sensation.

"We're getting so close to earning that bed," Casey whispered, with her words having lost their crispness, too.

Avery rested her forehead against Casey's, taking a second to catch her breath. Then she dove back in again, slipping her hands under her breasts to feel their weight, marveling that they felt like they'd been made expressly for her enjoyment.

She'd never been partial to any particular size of breast, but she was very, very fond of shape. The ones that always caught her attention were those exactly like Casey's—round and full. She hadn't intentionally started to purr, but she was certain the satisfied sound she heard was coming from her own chest.

Casey gripped her hands and pressed them into herself, sucking in a shuddering breath as she pressed firmly. "My nipples are so hard they ache," she murmured. "I can't wait until you kiss them—"

Before she could finish the sentence, Avery stood tall to get some leverage, wrapped her arms around Casey's waist, and pulled her along as she backed up to the bed. "I don't care if I've earned the right to be here or not," she said, laughing as she sank onto the mattress. "I can't stand up any longer, and you're coming with me."

Casey stood in front of her, gazing down with a sexy smile. The emotion of the moment hit Avery hard, and she pulled Casey close, grasping her thighs as she held her tightly. "I love getting to know your body," she said softly as she rested her head on her belly. "It feels as good as it looks, by the way. I still pull up that image of you in your swimsuit when I need help getting to sleep."

"You do? Really?"

"Uh-huh. Better than porn, which really isn't my thing."

"Mine either. My imagination lets me see exactly what I want... Which is you, if I haven't made that clear."

Their eyes met for another tender moment. While Avery couldn't know exactly what was in Casey's heart, the expression on her face revealed everything she needed to know. No one could summon up a look that conveyed so much love if she didn't feel it deep in her heart.

Closing her eyes, Avery unzipped Casey's shorts and let them drop to the floor. Then she leaned forward to kiss her belly, relishing the warmth as well as the flawless skin that her skimpy purple bikinis revealed. Her hands reached around to cup Casey's very firm ass as she let out a sigh. "If this is what climbing up and down ladders with sacks of grain does for a body..."

"I only carry grain on the climb up," she said, laughing a little. "The sack's empty when I come back down."

"Come back down here," Avery said. She lay back, waiting for Casey to lie on top of her. But she took a little detour, winding up next to her.

"I'm trying to be careful until I know how gentle I have to be," she said, as her hand hovered over Avery's breast. "The last time we talked about it, you said these beauties were off limits."

"No more. I wouldn't go wild, but they're only slightly more tender than they ever were." She took Casey's hand and settled it gently upon her breast. "One warning. Don't suck on them if you don't want a surprise."

"Um, that's not one of my turn-ons. I think I prefer breasts that are just ornamental." She moved her hand to the side, jiggling the flesh as her smile grew. "They feel fantastic," she murmured softly. "If I can forget they're functional, they're a huge turn-on."

"They won't need to function for much longer. Lisbet's losing interest, so it won't be long until my breasts can be all for you."

"They're cranking me up just fine right now, so there's no need to rush." She ran her hand down Avery's side as she kissed her again, keeping up the pressure until they were facing each other, tongues gently teasing. "Even though I'm crazy for breasts, every part of you is sexy."

Once again, Avery felt the brakes begin to take hold, and her annoyance with herself flared. Being fixated on the changes her body had gone through was so stupid, but she couldn't help herself. "Um, I'm not sure what I was doing agreeing to have our first time be in the light of day, but I guess you'd eventually see everything. Just believe me when I tell you this body's peak was only two years ago. I might be able to get close to that —"

"Shh," Casey said, pulling back to look at her soberly. "I know you're joking a little, but I'm not interested in you because of a flat belly or a rock-hard butt. I'm not here because of your body at all, Avery. I love you, and I'll continue to love you when you're thirty or forty or fifty years older."

"Are you sure?" she asked, hating to hear the neediness in her own voice.

"Positive. We all fall apart physically, so it's a damn good idea to love the whole person." She pulled back further and gave her a cute smile. "I know *you're* attracted to more than hard bodies, because I'm certain you would have made a play for Faith if she'd been a lesbian."

"She's very cute," Avery agreed, feeling some of her unease lessen. "Her age wouldn't have been a barrier, but her husband would have been. I don't shop when I can't buy."

"Well, if she ever gets single, and you convince me to have an open-relationship, and believe me, you'd need all of your salesmanship skills for that, Faith can be your third."

"Not yours?"

"One's plenty for me," she said, smiling again. "I'm confident you'll keep me busy."

"God, I hope so," Avery murmured. "I want to be enough for you. I promise I'll work hard to keep the spark alive."

"You don't need to work hard," Casey said, stroking her gentle hand across Avery's features. "Just be yourself, and let me get inside. Simple. Really simple."

"Kiss me again," Avery sighed. "When you kiss me, I believe every word."

"Then I'll just have to keep kissing you until you're a true believer," she said, with that slow, sexy smile covering her mouth again. Casey placed a few delicate kisses to her lips, then tilted her head slightly to trail gentle bites across her throat, winding up at her ear, Avery's most sensitive spot. She let out a gurgle as Casey's talented tongue artfully painted the skin all around it, nibbling on the flesh, but never getting too aggressive. *Perfection.*

Avery was just about to touch Casey again when determined hands started to unbutton her blouse. Then her jeans were open, with the cool spring air tickling her skin. Casey's hand teased her flesh as her tongue mirrored the touch across her neck and ears, making Avery float on a cloud of sensation, without a single worry about the health of her libido. She was *back*.

With a surge of energy, she shifted her body to lie upon Casey, loving the way their bodies compressed against one another. "I love you," she murmured. "I'm so happy you're mine."

"I'm all yours," Casey said, grinning sexily. "And I'm going to show you how much I want you the minute I wrestle your clothes off."

"I can help," Avery said, starting to roll off so she could sit up. But Casey gently pulled her back down and began to tug her shorts off her body. "I love to undress a sexy woman, so you can just forget how to do this for yourself. I'll take over."

"I've already forgotten how to work a zipper. You'll be my official dresser."

"Mmm," Casey murmured when she slipped Avery's undies off with just a little help as Avery lifted her hips. "I can't guess what you looked like two years ago, but if you don't think this body's awesome, your standards are messed up." She flipped her onto her back, then dipped her head and kissed all across Avery's belly, making her giggle. "Come on," Casey teased. "Admit your standards are messed up."

"Stop!" she begged, gripping her shoulders to push her away.

But Casey was relentless, and she came back for more, this time with soft, slow kisses. The instinct to push her away dissolved in an instant, and Avery just closed her eyes to let her meander, consciously letting go of her niggling insecurities about her body. If Casey found her sexy, it was crazy to try to convince her she was wrong.

That soft, silky mouth kept searching, covering every part of Avery's belly, then her thighs. Gentle hands bracketed her breasts, with Casey squeezing them slightly as she growled.

Then she put her hands on the bed and easily pushed herself up until she hovered over Avery's chest. "I'm going to wait to dive in until I don't have to share these, but I can't resist a little exploration."

"All yours. They don't feel like they're part of my sexual response right now, but they used to be a big factor. I'm confident we can reprogram them."

"Well, I was into them long before Lisbet was, so…"

"You were? Really? Back then?"

"Uh-huh. I thought about you a lot after we met that night at the brewery, wishing things had been different."

"They are now," Avery said, stroking her head gently. "Things are fantastic."

"And getting better by the minute." With a playful grin, she rested on her forearms and nuzzled against Avery's breasts, limiting herself to the flesh not covered by the bra. She moved around delicately, pressing her lips into the cleavage, then audibly sniffing her. Her appetite seemed limitless, and Avery simply watched her enjoy herself, occasionally stroking her hair.

Even though Casey was clearly trying to control herself, she started to get a little rambunctious, nuzzling until she was panting softly. Then she pushed herself up to rest on her fists, elbows locked, her gaze unfocused. "I'm not as disciplined as I thought I was. My brakes almost gave way."

Avery petted her tenderly. "Have I told you I love you in the last five minutes?"

"Nope. But you can catch up later. Right now, I've got work to do." With a hungry smile on her face, she slid back down the bed to sink to the floor. Then she gently but firmly burrowed between Avery's legs, finally placing them just where she wanted them—draped over her shoulders. "I'm going to be spending a lot of time down here," she said, her voice having taken on a sexy, rough purr. "I hope you like this half as much as I'm going to."

Avery was afraid to look, terrified that the reality wouldn't meet Casey's expectations. Her body had recovered, for the most part, but it didn't look or feel exactly the same, and she was still having trouble getting used to the new geography.

Casey's fingers slid down her inner thigh as she softly said, "We're having fun here, Avery. This isn't the baby exit any more, so you can relax. This is our playground now."

She said the words with a straight face, but they sounded so silly to Avery that she allowed herself to relax a little. "I'm trying," she said, hearing that her voice was still tight. "It just used to look different, and it feels slightly alien to me."

"Since this is the first time I get to take a good look, it seems like it always was—beautiful," Casey said, smiling up at her. "And since I can get a lot closer, shouldn't my vote count for more? I mean, you wouldn't judge art from across the room, would you? You'd get up right next to it." She pressed her mouth right into the center of Avery's sex, then gently moved her tongue, letting out such a satisfied purr that even Avery had to smile. Casey lifted her head, and with an expression on her face that made her seem drunk, asked, "Have I mentioned how turned on it makes me to go down on a woman? Especially a woman I love?"

"I love you too," Avery sighed, feeling tears sting her eyes again. "I'm sorry I'm so emotional and insecure. It's..."

"Don't apologize," Casey murmured. "Your body's been through an awful lot in the last two years." She smiled again, with their gazes locked together. "But look at what it's accomplished. This body created a human being. One little cell from you made that fantastic child we're going to raise. Think about that," she said, her voice growing stronger. "No. Really think about it." She grasped her thighs and held on tightly. "Your body did something awesome, and now it deserves lots of pleasure to reward it for the work it's done. It's payback time," she added, laughing a little.

"I understand that logically, but I'm having a hard time forgetting about the changes."

"Okay. You think your body has a few minor dings. Should a few dents or scapes stop me from wanting to jump into what looks to me like a brand new Lamborghini? None of the changes you see are going to affect *my* enjoyment, and I don't think you should let them change the way you think about your body, either. Concentrate on the miracle you've performed, Avery. Moms are superheroes," she said, with her grin making Avery's eyes fill with tears again.

Avery ran her hand over Casey's hair, letting her fingers trail down to rub along the nape of her neck, her favorite spot. "Will you always try so hard to make me feel pretty?"

"I will always try," she said, with her own eyes looking a little watery. "If you could see yourself like I do, you'd..." She let out a laugh. "You'd toss me aside so you could date yourself." Laughing again, she added, "That didn't wind up where I thought it would, but the meaning's perfect. I think you're fantastic in every way."

"How about coming up here to kiss me again? I've lost a little steam."

"You ask, you get," she said, climbing onto the bed again to lie next to Avery. "I'm being totally sincere," she said, her dark eyes filled with emotion. "I'm in awe of your body and its strength. But it's also super sexy, and that's the part that's on my mind right now. I can't wait to dive back in."

"Come here," Avery said, grasping her by the shoulders to pull her onto her body. "Crank me up again, you silver-tongued romantic."

"First time I've been called that," Casey said, smiling warmly. "But I like it." She placed her hands on Avery's arms and pushed her firmly against the bed, holding her tightly while she began to kiss her, the intensity climbing with every beat of her heart. They went back and forth for what seemed like a long time, with Avery finally squirming under the kisses that rained down on her, feeling in her soul just how much Casey wanted her. She wasn't sure if she pushed her down, or if Casey went on her own, but her legs were once again over Casey's shoulders, and that silky mouth was loving her full-tilt. It might have been seconds, and it might have been minutes, but Casey figured her out with little trouble. As the tip of her tongue hit the exact spot that Avery was thrilled to learn still sent her soaring, she closed her legs around Casey, trapping her as spasms unexpectedly began to wrack her body. She felt like she was tumbling over a cliff to explode with pleasure that thrummed within her for long seconds, pulsing through every muscle.

"Good god," she murmured, struggling to catch her breath. Then Casey gently nuzzled a little more, but Avery grasped her shoulders and squeezed. "Time out," she said, with her voice rising in pitch. "Need a second to catch my breath."

"You know what I've got?" Casey asked, looking up. Her hair was a tangled mess, and she appeared a little drunk, but her smile was full and rich.

"What do you have?"

"All day," she said as she rested her cheek against Avery's thigh, looking perfectly sated. "We're going to stay right here until we have to go pick up our baby." She lifted her head again, grinning. "See how easy I slid into parenthood? I didn't have to do a thing to get her, but I'm claiming Lisbet as my own."

"We're all claiming each other," Avery said, tears once against filling her eyes. "I'm yours. Lisbet's yours. And you're ours."

"I've never wanted to be a part of something more," she said. Gently, she climbed up to take Avery in her arms, holding on tight. "We're all over the place, aren't we? Laughing, crying… I've been all over the map."

"You haven't been everywhere," Avery said, tickling just under her ear. "The minute I can move again, I'm taking you to orgasm-town."

Casey laughed at that, continuing to chuckle for a few seconds. "I've been there before, but I'm always ready to go back. It's one of my favorite places."

"Get ready to rock," Avery said, nuzzling against Casey's chest as she felt her eyelids begin to get heavy. "Any minute now…"

⌒

Since Casey had worked a full day, had supervised Baby Brewers, then had been all over the emotional roller coaster with Avery, she should have been tired. But she wasn't. Not at all. In fact, she was buzzing with energy. She kissed Avery's temple and scooted over to share her pillow, needing to be as close as possible.

Smiling to herself, she had to admit that they were going to be quite a trio. Lisbet had an almost unquenchable desire to be held and cuddled, and Casey was afraid she was going to be just as thirsty for affection. It had been too long since she'd had a connection anywhere near this intense, and she realized it would take some time to adjust to it. But she knew they'd figure it all out. You couldn't have too much love.

Looking at Avery, so innocent-looking in sleep, made Casey's heart beat heavily in her chest. She was going to need every bit of her heart to love the Nichols girls like they deserved, and she pledged to never give less than that.

Avery stirred, then her eyes blinked open as a slow smile curled her lips. "I thought we were going to orgasm-town. Did the train derail?"

"It took a detour to sleepy-town," Casey said. She slipped an arm under Avery's head and tumbled her into an embrace. "Did you have a nice nap?"

"Uh-huh." She shivered as she stretched out. "I used to be the queen of the power-nap, but I've had to drop those from my schedule."

"Well, from now on we can tag-team Lisbet, at least on the weekends. Or we can nap when she does and work to catch up on things later. We have options," she insisted, cuddling Avery close.

"Options," she sighed. "I've missed options." She pulled away from Casey's hold and sat up a little to rest on a forearm. "Speaking of options, you're officially out of them. The train to orgasm-town's ready to leave the station."

Casey laughed. "I don't think I can concentrate on revving back up if I think of being on a train headed for orgasm-town." She stuck her hand out and waggled it. "Kind of not the sexiest image I've ever heard." Smiling at Avery, she added, "As a writer, I thought you'd be the silver-tongued one."

"I can get there," she said, acting much more confident than she did when she was on the receiving end. "Just put yourself in my hands."

Casey took Avery's free hand and slapped it onto her belly. "Done."

"I love playing with you," Avery sighed, settling down to rest her head on Casey's shoulder. "I just knew sex with you would be fun."

"Well, if it's drudgery, you're not doing it right."

Avery elbowed her gently. "You know what I mean. You're good at finding the fun parts of things. You're a serious adult, but you're also playful. That's a super nice pairing."

"I'm just being myself. It's not all that hard."

"I know," Avery said, scooting even closer. "I love the fact that you're just you. You aren't doing handstands to make sure people like you."

"I can't do a handstand." She thought for a moment. "At least, I don't think I can. But now I want to try." She started to get up, but Avery held her still.

"Not so fast. I've hardly had a taste of you. It's my turn to make you happy."

"Aww…" Casey looked at her shining blue eyes, seeing how perfectly content she looked. "I don't know if you can make me happier than you did when you told me you loved me." She chuckled softly. "After your dramatic threat to eat ramen noodles in a cold-water flat, that is." She cocked her head. "Is it just me, or was that a weird threat?"

"Don't make fun of me," Avery pouted. "I was heartsick." She moved her hand across Casey's stomach, inching up under her shirt to reach her bra and slide her finger under the band. "But I'm feeling much, much better now. Actually, I'm bursting with happiness."

"I am too. This is right where I've wanted to be for a very long time."

"It's after eight," Avery said, glancing at the clock on the bedside table. "We've only got…what? Twenty hours or so until we have to pick up the baby? Time to get busy." She laughed when she wrapped her arms around Casey and pulled her close. Their noses were almost touching when she said, "I love you so much."

"So much," Casey echoed.

"Kiss me," Avery whispered. "I need your lips." She shifted again to get into a better position, then lavished kisses upon Casey's lips, with each a little softer, a little sweeter. She was clearly starting off slowly and gently, making Casey feel her love as well as the depths of her caring.

They kissed for the longest time, still learning the intricacies of each other's response. Casey was sure she'd never tire of this, opening herself to the subtle variations in the way Avery teased her. She was gliding along on a river of sensation, deeply enjoying the ride, when Avery climbed on top of her. She looked down at Casey for a moment, eyes bright with desire. "I think some of my nerve endings are waking up," she said, smiling. "Mind if I check by rubbing myself all over you?"

"Give me a second to take my clothes off. If you're going to rub against anything, I want it to be skin."

They worked together, unbuttoning, then unfastening her shorts. They and her bikinis were tossed aside so Avery could sit on her lap. "I know just what I want to do to this temple of perfection," she said, sounding so sexy that Casey was covered in goosebumps in a matter of seconds.

"Whatever it is, you have my permission."

She pushed Casey to the bed, then sat back on her haunches to finally take off her shirt, leaving her with just a dark blue bra covering her luscious, ripe breasts. Casey was sure her mouth was open, but she was equally sure she wasn't able to speak. The thought of having the breasts of her dreams to play with for the rest of her life was making her feel a little dizzy.

Avery's mouth quirked into a smile as she stretched out along Casey's body, then lowered herself to move gently against her. "Leaving our bras on might work," she said. "I can ease into this."

"Perfect," Casey murmured as Avery's breasts brushed against her own. "You can do that for a very long time."

"I like it too," she said, with her eyes closing as she continued to move. Casey was glad she'd let her be in charge, since she wouldn't have moved as delicately as Avery did. But the sensation was kind of perfect, with the fabric from Avery's bra providing just enough friction to make her nipples as hard as rocks.

"This is going to be my favorite way to play with your breasts," Avery said, her voice barely a sigh. "Hands are nice, but breast on breast is much better."

As she continued to move, Casey's excitement grew to a fever pitch. It wasn't even the actual sensation, although that was fantastic. It was the sultry expression on Avery's face that made her clit throb, and *that* made her even more certain about how well they were matched. When your body reacted this strongly to another woman's face, you'd found the perfect partner.

Avery's arms were getting tired, given they'd started to shake, but she was clearly getting off on taking some pleasure for herself. While she was obviously trying to please Casey, she was sure she was focusing inward at the moment, trying to reclaim her breasts for adult pleasure.

Even though Casey was about to squirm off the bed, she put her hands on Avery's ass and started to knead the skin, speaking softly as her hands took over. "I'm so turned on I'm about to cry," she murmured. "But you look so damned sexy I don't want you to stop. Nothing turns me on as much as watching my partner get into a groove."

"Oh, I'm in a groove," Avery murmured, with her eyes closed tightly. "It's not exactly the same as it used to be... But it's damn good."

Casey couldn't resist the lure, and she slid her hand around to gently circle Avery's sex. "Can I...?" she asked, slipping her fingers inside, only to hear Avery let out a soft gasp.

"Ooo. I didn't know that was coming..."

Casey's eyes shot open. "You don't...?"

"I *used* to love it. But I've been worried about exploring down there." A determined expression covered her face, making her look very serious. "Let's see if I still like it."

"Are you sure? This isn't mandatory for me."

"No, I want to," Avery said. "I need to reclaim a lot of spots I've been ignoring. Letting you remind me of how much I used to like this is perfect."

"I'll go slow," Casey soothed. "I'll be so gentle you won't know I'm even moving..." She gazed into Avery's eyes, searching them for any signs of discomfort. "How's that?"

"You're in?"

Casey laughed. "If I were a guy, I'd lose my boner. I'm definitely in. Feels good?"

"It certainly doesn't hurt, which is what I've been worried about."

"I think our goal should be a little higher than not painful. How about this?" she asked, moving slowly and delicately, gently teasing around the opening.

"Ooo. That's better than good. If my arms don't fall off, I could get somewhere fast if you keep that up..."

Taking that as a challenge, Casey moved her other hand between their bodies. Her wrist was in a seriously uncomfortable position, but she barely noticed. Arousal must have been a great pain reliever, because the discomfort disappeared by the time her fingers slid across Avery's heated sex.

"Oh, Jesus," she groaned, sucking in a deep, ragged breath. "Keep that up. Perfect."

Casey watched her carefully, mesmerized by the expression on her face. It was a cross between intense concentration and pure bliss, and she tried hard to lock the image away in her memory bank.

"I'm so close."

"I'm right with you. Feel my fingers touching every part of you. Let the sensation take over."

Her flesh began to contract around Casey's hand, and as soon as she started to spasm Avery's arms gave way, dropping her flat onto Casey's body with a slap.

"Whoa!" Casey yelped, having to catch her breath. "We were on the verge of an injury timeout there."

Avery tilted her head to meet her eyes. Her hair was everywhere, gaze unfocused, but her smile was luminous. "God, I've missed having sex with someone who cares for me."

"You've never had sex with anyone who cares for you as much as I do," Casey said, rolling them onto their sides and dipping her head to kiss her with all of the emotion she could summon.

Avery stroked her cheek tenderly when they broke apart, their faces still so close she could see each individual eyelash. "I'm not normally so greedy," she said, with a bright smile lighting up her face. "But I'm feeling like I did when I was in puberty, and I can't wait to try everything." With a gleam in her eye, she pushed Casey onto her back, then lay on top of her. "My power nap must have been rejuvenating, because I can't wait to try something I'm very, very fond of."

"I'm the last person who's going to stop you."

Avery's expression was playful, almost giddy. "I'm just going to slow down and make sure I've tasted everything that's caught my eye over the last year." She reached behind and unhooked Casey bra, sliding it down her arms to gaze at her with rabid interest. Then their eyes met as she scooted down to devote some attention to a nipple now so hard it ached.

Casey put a hand to the back of her head, gently encouraging her. "I'm not overly sensitive," she murmured, tingling with sensation. "You can do whatever you want."

Avery looked up and smiled. "What I want is to have an extra mouth. I can't choose which one looks more enticing."

"Ooo, two mouths wouldn't be a good look for you," Casey said, urging her right back to work. "You don't have to be in a hurry. We've got hours."

"Hours. What a beautiful word," Avery sighed. "Once I've worked my way around this gorgeous body, I'm going to start at the top and take another lap." She let out a laugh. "Little play on words there."

"Lap away," Casey said. "Every part likes being licked."

"Kismet, since everything I've licked so far is delicious." She continued to kiss and lick Casey's breasts until the nipples grew so sensitive she was squirming under the interest Avery lavished upon her. With a grin, Avery started to slide down the bed, her gaze locked on Casey's. "There's one part that I haven't tried yet, but I have a really good feeling about it."

"Don't let yourself be talked out of sampling the merchandise. I'm confident you're going to love it." She let out a soft laugh. "I'm a little full of myself sometimes."

"Your confidence is a huge turn-on," Avery said, now centered between Casey's legs. "Let's get this party started."

Casey laughed at that, but the sound caught in her throat when the sensation hit her a second later. There was simply nothing better than having a lover bathe your most sensitive skin with her tongue. "Wonderful," she sighed.

Avery placed a gentle kiss to her flesh, looking up briefly. "Don't be afraid to direct me. I'm happy to have feedback."

"You're doing great," Casey said, with their gazes meeting again, their growing bond making her heart race.

"I just want to please you. Every day."

"You're pleasing me an awful lot right now," Casey murmured, sinking into the pillow to open up her senses to Avery's determined tongue. She let her mind drift a little, unable to process so much sensation at once. But she never let herself get too far adrift. Knowing Avery was focused on her pleasure kept her on track, just having to tilt her head to see her, eyes closed, clearly enjoying herself.

A dextrous hand crept up her thigh, then it slipped between her legs as Avery's talented fingers entered her.

"So nice," Casey sighed. "Your touch is so gentle."

Avery didn't reply in words, but she made some cute moan-like sounds to highlight her own pleasure. They were so connected, body and soul, that Casey felt herself getting emotional again. But she didn't want to spend these precious moments on the verge of tears. This was a joyful celebration, and she tried harder to stay in the moment to experience all of the pleasure Avery could offer.

Just that slight change of focus had her racing along, and she felt Avery increasing the pressure from both her hand and her tongue. "Close," Casey croaked out, unable to utter another word before her climax started deep in her body to radiate out, pulsing hard as she struggled to catch a breath. She lay there, spent, taking in deep breaths to recover. Avery was still nuzzling against her, licking her thighs as her hands climbed up to delicately tickle across Casey's ribs. "You remembered my less obvious erogenous zones," she said, smiling as their eyes met.

"I'm going to get around to the backs of your knees before the night's out. Then I'm going to find a few new ones. I'm on a quest."

"Come up here so I can kiss you again," Casey said. "But stop on the way and get my phone out of my shorts."

"Your phone? You want to check your mail *now?*"

"I've forgotten what mail is," she said, laughing a little. "But I'm kind of fixated on having a memory of this afternoon. Just before I climaxed I looked out the window, and almost cried."

"Cried?"

"Uh-huh. It was the combination of being in this room, seeing the trees bursting with new life, and realizing our new family is being made—right here. I want to take a photo to keep that image in my head."

"Sounds perfect." Avery found the phone and handed it over as she stretched out next to Casey. She tossed her head, with the fine, blonde strands sliding across her shoulder, reminding Casey of one of those paintings of the voluptuous nudes by the French artist whose name Avery would surely know.

Casey got up and stood behind the bed, spending some time composing the image she wanted to recall. "I'm going to frame this and put it on the mantel."

"We don't have a mantel," Avery said, smiling up at her.

"Only because the fireplace is behind a wall. It might take years, but I'm going to figure out how to get this house looking a little more like it did a hundred years ago."

"Just a hundred?"

She nodded. "We'll start at a hundred, and keep going back in the time machine if we've got money to burn."

Turning the phone around for Avery to take a look, Casey said, "This is how I want to remember today."

"Oh, my god!" she squealed. "How'd you do that? I didn't even know I was going to be in the picture."

"You were looking at me, not posing. I like it better that way." She held the camera in front of herself and gazed at it for the long time. "I've caught your beautiful face, your messy hair, the satisfied smile on your lips, and the trees through the window. Perfect," she decided, dropping the phone onto the bed.

"That might be the best I've ever looked," Avery said. "But by the time Lisbet's eleven or so she'll realize that was taken right before or after lovemaking. Kids are surprisingly good at figuring that out."

Casey smiled at her, then gently touched her face. "Are you saying you don't want her to know we make love?"

Avery stopped and stared at her for a second. "I'm not saying that at all. We're her role models for how fulfilling it is to have a loving, sexual relationship with someone you truly care for." She took her finger and slowly trailed it down between Casey's breasts, then brought it back up to touch her lips. "And that's going to be the easiest, most enjoyable lesson we'll ever impart."

The End

EPILOGUE

ON SATURDAY MORNING, AVERY blinked her eyes open slowly, with the bat-like hearing motherhood had created informing her that Lisbet was awake, and happy. She could stand down for a little while.

A second later she jerked upright, with her head turning sharply to the right, looking for Casey. They'd slept together for just the past two nights, and she still wasn't used to having a bed partner. Obviously, she wasn't used to that bed partner slipping away from her, either. The bathroom door was open, but the door to the bedroom was shut securely. It didn't take a genius to figure out where she was, and when Avery heard her soft, warm voice on the baby monitor, she lay back and luxuriated in the feel of her bed. Few things felt better than lazing about on a Saturday morning, and squeezing another fifteen minutes of sleep in was awfully compelling. Knowing Casey, she wouldn't complain if she was on sole baby-duty for an hour or two. But now that Avery had a partner to share the load, she found she didn't want to avail herself of that option. She wanted to jump into the first day of their new family dynamic.

It was a warm morning, and she tossed off the sheet that had covered them. But just as her feet hit the floor, she heard Casey's voice, louder now.

"Here's the deal," she said. "Your mom and I have changed things up a little."

Charmed, Avery lay back down, scooting over to be able to hear the monitor even better.

"You're probably kind of confused about who I am, and why I'm over here so much. But we've finally got an answer for all of that."

Avery's heart skipped a beat when she heard the emotion that now colored Casey's voice. "Your mom and I love each other very much, Lisbet, and I'm going to live here from now on so I can be with her—and you—every day."

Avery had only seen her cry once or twice, but there was no doubt in her mind that tears were rolling down Casey's cheeks at that very moment. She had to bite her lip to distract herself enough to not join in, but she was hanging onto every word, and didn't want her emotions to get in the way.

"The cool part, the part I didn't think I'd ever get to experience, is that I'm going to be...well, you'll decide what you want to call me, but your mom and I are going to be your parents. Isn't that fantastic?" Her voice had risen, and sounded very playful. Lisbet reacted as she always did when someone was playing with her, by babbling along, trying to mimic them. She could get a few understandable syllables out in order, and one or two of them now sounded clear as day to Avery.

"Yeah, you think it's fantastic too, don't you?" Casey asked. "You'll have a mama and me."

"Mama!"

"Mama's still asleep, sweetheart," she soothed. Lisbet must have made it clear she was addressing Casey as well, because she said, "You've only got one mama, baby girl. I'm going to be...something else."

"Mama!" Lisbet insisted, with Avery thrilled to hear her child give voice to the truth. No matter what they called themselves, Lisbet had three women who loved her with every fibre of their beings. It made perfect sense that she would want to use the same term for them.

Finding the T-shirt she'd put on when they'd rocked Lisbet to sleep the night before, Avery put it on, then padded into the baby's room, finding her and Casey in a very amusing stand-off. She was in Casey's arms, hair askew, leaning back to stare at her. "Mama!" she shrieked, the tone of voice she used when the adults in her life didn't quite understand the point she was trying to make.

"I think Lisbet has two mommies," Avery said, laughing at the befuddled expression on Casey's face.

"But...!" She was so flustered she didn't seem able to finish her thought.

Lisbet stuck her arms out and tried to lean over, with Avery catching her and lifting her into the air. "You know the truth, don't you, precious. You've had two mommies for a long time now. We've just been too... whatever to admit to ourselves that we're a family."

She stopped at the changing table, but Casey put a hand on her back. "I took care of that already. I couldn't handle breakfast, though," she said, smiling. "She kept asking." Her T-shirt was askew, and she pulled it into position, then gave Lisbet's cheek a pinch. "She thinks everyone can feed her if she just gets their shirt off."

Avery met her eyes. "Not true. She's never done that to my dad, and she hasn't tried it with my mom for months now." She put the baby on her hip and wrapped her other arm around Casey. "Lisbet knows you're in a different category." Their eyes met, and she could see that Casey was still feeling emotional. "She knows you and I are in this together."

"But you're her *mom*," Casey stressed. "You've done all of the hard work."

Avery shrugged. "None of that's important to her. At least at this point in her life. She knows there's something special between us, and she clearly loves you. That's all that matters to her. We're her people."

"But *you're* her mom," Casey insisted.

"I was there on her birth day," Avery said, laughing a little. "You don't have to remind me." She gave Casey a hug, with Lisbet shifting her weight to be able to lean against her as well. "One day she'll want to know who carried her, but for now I want to stress that we're her parents. I assume she'll eventually use different names for us, but if she wants to have two mamas, that's fine with me."

Casey now looked more confused than ever. "You're serious. You don't mind if she calls me mama."

"I'd love it." She moved so they were facing each other, then gave Casey a full body hug, with Lisbet cuddled up between them. "I want Lisbet to be one hundred percent secure in the knowledge that she has two parents. So while she's getting used to that we'll downplay my role a little."

"But why?"

Avery looked up into her warm brown eyes, seeing how utterly confused she was. "I think it's best for Lisbet. Get used to that answer," she added, smiling at Casey's sweet, puzzled expression. "Whenever something comes up, that should be our number one goal. If it's best for her, it's best."

"I just think she'll be confused…"

Avery let go and walked over to sit on the rocker, with Lisbet settling against her, already licking her lips when Avery tugged her shirt up. "Let's face facts. Even though she's weaning herself, she'll remember that I fed her like this. She won't be confused that my role has been different from yours. I promise you that."

Casey stood there like she'd been hit on the head, kind of dopey looking. "I've never watched you feed her," she said, with a touch of embarrassment tinting her voice. "Do you mind?"

"Mind?" She looked up at her and smiled. "I was just going to tell you to go get your phone." Casey didn't move, so she added, "I've always wanted a photo of her nursing, but I felt weird asking my mom to take one."

"Be right back," she said, making sparks as she raced out of the room.

"Your mama's silly," Avery said, stroking Lisbet's flyaway hair into place as she latched on properly and started smacking away. The baby was almost always *very* enthusiastic when she started to eat, then she settled down once a couple of ounces of food hit her stomach and eased her hunger.

Casey was back well before that happened, with Lisbet eating like she'd never had anything better, or more necessary. Avery watched Casey try to get into position, looking as focused and determined as Lisbet did at the moment.

"The light's perfect," she said quietly, sounding reverential. "The wall behind you is getting the sun, and it's reflecting off both of you."

"Take a lot," Avery said. "I'm going to start distracting her in the morning so we can skip this feeding, so we have a short time-window for breakfast photos."

Casey got down on her knees, quietly snapping away, with Avery able to see she was about to lose it again.

"I don't think I've ever seen anything more beautiful," she said, reaching up to wipe her eyes. "I can't cry like this every morning, you two. You've got to give me a break!"

"I'm falling in love with you just a little bit more this morning," Avery said, meeting her gaze. "When a woman cries at seeing a baby nurse, you're with a real sweetheart. Not that I had any doubt," she added.

"Can I get a few shots from behind? I think I can fit."

"Sure. We can scoot forward—"

"I'm thinner than I look." She slipped between the chair and the wall, then scooted down so she was directly over Avery's right shoulder. "Ooo. This is good," she said, her voice as soft as a sigh. "My two favorite people, showing how crazy they are about each other."

Avery turned her head slightly. "We're both crazy about you, too. And you're not a milk dispenser, so her love for you is purer."

"Not buying it," Casey said, with her voice breaking slightly. "You two are so close it's... I don't have a good word for it." She gently touched Avery's head. "But I bet you do."

"I've got a few words that get close to how I feel about Lisbet. But having a baby kind of goes beyond words." Casey grasped the rocker and moved it forward a few inches so she could slip out. Avery met her gaze, adding, "Do you know what I mean?"

"I do." She folded her legs under herself, then leaned forward, resting her head upon Avery's thigh. Lisbet purposefully shifted so her foot reached Casey's shoulder, and she started to rhythmically push against her. Casey removed the little sock that covered Lisbet's foot and kissed the flawless pink skin that covered it. "Now's a great time for not having words."

"A perfect time," Avery said, closing her eyes to preserve this moment in her mind. Their first full day as a family. If a word had been created to encompass all of the love she had for these two people, Avery was entirely sure she'd never learned it. And equally sure she didn't need it. The feeling was everything.

By Susan X Meagher

Novels

Arbor Vitae
All That Matters
Cherry Grove
Girl Meets Girl
The Lies That Bind
The Legacy
Doublecrossed
Smooth Sailing
How To Wrangle a Woman
Almost Heaven
The Crush
The Reunion
Inside Out
Out of Whack
Homecoming
The Right Time
Summer of Love
Chef's Special
Fame
Vacationland
Wait For Me
The Keeper's Daughter
Friday Night Flights

Short Story Collection

Girl Meets Girl

Serial Novel

I Found My Heart In San Francisco

Awakenings: Book One
Beginnings: Book Two
Coalescence: Book Three
Disclosures: Book Four
Entwined: Book Five
Fidelity: Book Six
Getaway: Book Seven
Honesty: Book Eight
Intentions: Book Nine
Journeys: Book Ten
Karma: Book Eleven
Lifeline: Book Twelve
Monogamy: Book Thirteen
Nurture: Book Fourteen
Osmosis: Book Fifteen
Paradigm: Book Sixteen
Quandary: Book Seventeen
Renewal: Book Eighteen
Synchronicity: Book Nineteen
Trust: Book Twenty
United: Book Twenty-One
Vengeance: Book Twenty-Two

Anthologies

Undercover Tales
Outsiders

You can contact Susan at Susan@briskpress.com

Information about all of Susan's books can be found at
www.susanxmeagher.com or www.briskpress.com

To receive notification of new titles, send an email to newsletters@briskpress.com

facebook.com/susanxmeagher

twitter.com/susanx